The Shadow of the East

The Shadow of the East

E.M. Hull

MINT EDITIONS

The Shadow of the East was first published in 1921.

This edition published by Mint Editions 2021.

ISBN 9781513277455 | E-ISBN 9781513277868

Published by Mint Editions®

 MINT
EDITIONS

minteditionbooks.com

Publishing Director: Jennifer Newens
Design & Production: Rachel Lopez Metzger
Project Manager: Micaela Clark
Typesetting: Westchester Publishing Services

Contents

I

The American yacht lying off the harbour at Yokohama was brilliantly lit from stem to stern. Between it and the shore the reflection of the full moon glittered on the water up to the steps of the big black landing-stage. The glamour of the eastern night and the moonlight combined to lend enchantment to a scene that by day is blatant and tawdry, and the countless coloured lamps twinkling along the sea wall and dotted over the Bluff transformed the Japanese town into fairyland.

The night was warm and still, and there was barely a ripple on the water. The Bay was full of craft—liners, tramps, and yachts swinging slowly with the tide, and hurrying to and fro sampans and electric launches jostled indiscriminately.

On board the yacht three men were lying in long chairs on the deck. Jermyn Atherton, the millionaire owner, a tall thin American whose keen, clever face looked singularly youthful under a thick crop of iron-grey hair, sat forward in his chair to light a fresh cigar, and then turned to the man on his right. "I guess I've had every official in Japan hunting for you these last two days, Barry. If I hadn't had your wire from Tokio this morning I should have gone to our Consul and churned up the whole Japanese Secret Service and made an international affair of it," he laughed. "Where in all creation were you? I should hardly have thought it possible to get out of touch in this little old island. The authorities, too, knew all about you, and reckoned they could lay their hands on you in twelve hours. I rattled them up some," he added, with evident satisfaction.

The Englishman smiled.

"You seem to have done," he said dryly. "When I got into Tokio this morning I was fallen on by a hysterical inspector of police who implored me with tears to communicate immediately with an infuriated American who was raising Cain in Yokohama over my disappearance. As a matter of fact I was in a little village twenty miles inland from Tokio—quite off the beaten track. There's an old Shinto temple there that I have been wanting to sketch for a long time."

"Atherton's luck!" commented the American complacently. "It generally holds good. I couldn't leave Japan without seeing you, and I must sail tonight."

"What's your hurry—Wall Street going to the dogs without you?"

"No. I've cut out from Wall Street. I've made all the money I want, and I'm only concerned with spending it now. No, the fact is I—er—I left home rather suddenly."

A soft chuckle came from the recumbent occupant of the third chair, but Atherton ignored it and hurried on, twirling rapidly, as he spoke, a single eyeglass attached to a thin black cord.

"Ever since Nina and I were married last year we've been going the devil of a pace. We had to entertain every one who had entertained us—and a few more folk besides. There was something doing all day and every day until at last it seemed to me that I never saw my wife except at the other end of a dining table with a crowd of silly fools in between us. I reckoned I'd just about had enough of it. Came on me just like a flash sitting in my office down town one morning, so I buzzed home right away in the auto and told her I was sick of the whole thing and that I wanted her to come away with me and see what real life was like—out West or anywhere else on earth away from that durned society crowd. I'll admit I lost my temper and did some shouting. Nina couldn't see it from my point of view.

"My God, Jermyn! I should think not," drawled a sleepy voice from the third chair, and a short, immensely stout man struggled up into a sitting position, mopping his forehead vigorously. "You've the instincts of a Turk rather than of an enlightened American citizen. You've not seen my sister-in-law yet, Mr. Craven," he turned to the Englishman. "She's a peach! Smartest little girl in N'York. Leader of society—dollars no object—small wonder she didn't fall in with Jermyn's prehistoric notions. You're a cave man, elder brother—I put my money on Nina every time. Hell! isn't it hot?" He sank down again full length, flapping his handkerchief feebly at a persistent mosquito.

"We argued for a week," resumed Jermyn Atherton when his brother's sleepy drawl subsided, "and didn't seem to get any further on. At last I lost my temper completely and decided to clear out alone if Nina wouldn't come with me. Leslie was not doing anything at the time, so I persuaded him to come along too."

Leslie Atherton sat up again with a jerk.

"*Persuaded*!" he exploded, "A dam' queer notion of persuasion. Shanghaied, I call it. Ran me to earth at the club at five o'clock, and we sailed at eight. If my man hadn't been fond of the sea and keen on the trip himself, I should have left America for a cruise round the world in the clothes I stood up in—and Jermyn's duds would be about as useful to me as a suit of reach-me-downs off the line. Persuasion? Shucks! Jermyn thought it was kind of funny to start right off on an ocean trip at a moment's notice and show Nina he didn't care a durn. Crazy notion of humour." He lay back languidly and covered his face with a large silk handkerchief.

Barry Craven turned toward his host with amused curiosity in his grey eyes.

"Well?" He asked at length.

Atherton returned his look with a slightly embarrassed smile.

"It hasn't been so blamed funny after all," he said quietly. "A Chinese coffin-ship from 'Frisco would be hilarious compared with this trip," rapped a sarcastic voice from behind the silk handkerchief.

"I've felt a brute ever since we lost sight of Sandy Hook," continued Atherton, looking away toward the twinkling lights on shore, "and as soon as we put in here I couldn't stand it any longer, so I cabled to Nina that I was returning at once. I'm quite prepared to eat humble pie and all the rest of it—in fact I shall relish it," with a sudden shy laugh.

His brother heaved his vast bulk clear of the deck chair with a mighty effort.

"Humble pie! Huh!" he snorted contemptuously. "She'll kill the fatted calf and put a halo of glory round your head and invite in all the neighbours 'for this my prodigal husband has returned to me!'" He ducked with surprising swiftness to avoid a book that Atherton hurled at his head and shook a chubby forefinger at him reprovingly.

"Don't assault the only guide, philosopher and friend you've got who has the courage to tell you a few home truths. Say, Jermyn, d'y'know why I finally consented to come on this crazy cruise, anyway? Because Nina got me on the phone while you were hammering away at me at the club and ordered me to go right along with you and see you didn't do any dam foolishness. Oh, she's got me to heel right enough. Well! I guess I'll turn in and get to sleep before those fool engines start chump-chumping under my pillow. You boys will want a pow-wow to your two selves; there are times when three is a crowd. Good-bye, Mr. Craven, pleased to have met you. Hope to see you in the Adirondacks next summer—a bit more crowded than the Rockies, which are Jermyn's Mecca, but more home comforts—appeal to a man of my build." He slipped away with the noiseless tread that is habitual to heavy men.

Jermyn Atherton looked after his retreating figure and laughed uproariously.

"Isn't he the darndest? A clam is communicative compared with Leslie. Fancy him having that card up his sleeve all the while. Nina's had the bulge on me right straight along."

He pushed a cigar-box across the wicker table between them.

"No, thanks," said Craven, taking a case from his pocket. "I'll have a cigarette, if you don't mind."

The American settled himself in his chair, his hands clasped behind his head, staring at the harbour lights, his thoughts very obviously some thousands of miles away. Craven watched him speculatively. Atherton the big game-hunter, Atherton the mine-owner, he knew perfectly—but Atherton the New York broker, Atherton married, he was unacquainted with and he was trying to adjust and consolidate the two personalities.

It was the same Atherton—but more human, more humble, if such a word could be applied to an American millionaire. He felt a sudden curiosity to see the woman who had brought that new look into his old friend's keen blue eyes. He was conscious of an odd feeling of envy. Atherton became aware at last of his attentive gaze and grinned sheepishly.

"Must seem a bit of a fool to you, old man, but I feel like a boy going home for the holidays and that's the truth. But I've been yapping about my own affair all evening. What about you—staying on in Japan? Been here quite a while now, haven't you?"

"Just over a year."

"Like it?"

"Yes, Japan has got into my bones."

"Lazy kind of life, isn't it?"

There was no apparent change in Atherton's drawl, but Craven turned his head quickly and looked at him before answering.

"I'm a lazy kind of fellow," he replied quietly.

"You weren't lazy in the Rockies," said Atherton sharply.

"Oh, yes I was. There are grades of laziness."

Atherton flung the stub of his cigar overboard and selecting a fresh one, cut the end off carefully.

"Still got that Jap boy who was with you in America?"

"Yoshio? Yes. I picked him up in San Francisco ten years ago. He'll never leave me now."

"Saved his life, didn't you? He spun me a great yarn one day in camp."

Craven laughed and shrugged. "Yoshio has an Oriental imagination and quite a flair for romance. I did pull him out of a hole in 'Frisco but he was putting up a very tidy little show on his own account. He's the toughest little beggar I've ever come across and doesn't know the meaning of fear. If I'm ever in a big scrap I hope I shall have Yoshio behind me."

"You seem to be pretty well known over yonder," said Atherton with a vague movement of his head toward the shore.

"It is not a big town and the foreign population is not vast. Besides, there are traditions. I am the second Barry Craven to live in Yokohama—my father lived several years and finally died here. He was obsessed with Japan."

"And with the Japanese?"

"And with the Japanese."

Atherton frowned at the glowing end of his cigar.

"Nina and I ran down to see Craven Towers when we were on our wedding trip in England last year," he said at length with seeming irrelevance. "Your agent, Mr. Peters, ran us round."

"Good old Peters," murmured Craven lazily. "The place would have gone to the bow-wows long ago if it hadn't been for him. He adored my mother and has the worst possible opinion of me. But he's a loyal old bird, he probably endowed me with all the virtues for your benefit."

But Atherton ignored the comment. He polished his eyeglass vigorously and screwed it firmly into position.

"If I was an Englishman with a place like Craven Towers that had been in my family for generations," he said soberly, "I should go home and marry a nice girl and settle down on my estate."

"That's precisely Peters' opinion," replied Craven promptly with a good-tempered laugh. "I get reams from him to that effect nearly every mail—with detailed descriptions of all the eligible debutantes whom he thinks suitable. I often wonder whether he runs the estate on the same lines and keeps a matrimonial agency for the tenants."

Atherton laughed with him but persisted.

"If your own countrywomen don't appeal to you, take a run out to the States and see what we can do for you."

The laugh died out of Craven's eyes and he moved restlessly in his chair.

"It's no good, Jermyn. I'm not a marrying man," he said shortly.

Atherton smiled grimly at the recollection of a similar remark emphatically uttered by himself at their last meeting.

For a time neither spoke. Each was conscious of a vague difference in the other, developed during the years that had elapsed since their last meeting—an intangible barrier checking the open confidence of earlier days.

It was growing late. The sampans had nearly all disappeared and only an occasional launch skimmed across the harbour.

A neighbouring yacht's band that had been silent for the last hour began to play again—appropriately to the vicinity—Puccini's well-known opera. The strains came subdued but clear across the water on the scent-laden air. Craven sat forward in his chair, his heels on the ground, his hands loosely clasped between his knees, whistling softly the Consul's solo in the first act. From behind a cloud of cigar smoke Atherton watched him keenly, and as he watched he was thinking rapidly. He was used to making decisions quickly—he was accustomed to accepting risks at which others shied, but the risk he was now contemplating meant the taking of an unwarranted liberty that might be resented and might result in the loss of a friendship that he valued. But he was going to take the risk—as he had taken many another—he had known that from the first. He screwed his eyeglass firmer into his eye, a characteristic gesture well-known on the New York stock market.

"Ever see *Madame Butterfly*? he asked abruptly.

"Yes."

Atherton blew another big cloud of smoke.

"Damn fool, Pinkerton," he said gruffly, "Never could see the attraction myself—dancing girls—almond eyes—and all that sort of thing."

Craven made no answer but his whistling stopped suddenly and the knuckles of his clasped hands whitened. Atherton looked away quickly and his eyeglass fell with a little tinkle against a waistcoat button. There was another long pause. Finally the music died away and the stillness was broken only by the soft slap-slap of the water against the ship's side.

Atherton scowled at his immaculate deck shoes and then seized his eyeglass again decisively.

"Say, Barry, you saved my life in the Rockies that trip and I guess a fellow whose life you've saved has a pull on you no one else has. Anyhow I'll chance it, and if I'm a damned interfering meddler it's up to you to say so and I'll apologise—handsomely. Are you in a hole?"

Craven got up, walked away to the side of the yacht and leaning on the rail stared down into the water. A solitary sampan was passing the broad streak of moonlight and he watched it intently until it passed and merged into the shadows beyond.

"I've been the usual fool," he said at last quietly.

"Oh, hell!" came softly from behind him. "Chuck it, Barry. Clear out right now—with us. I'll put off sailing until tomorrow."

"I—can't."

Atherton rose and joined him, and for a moment his hand rested on the younger man's shoulder.

"I'm sorry—dashed sorry," he murmured. "Gee!" he added with a half shy, half humorous glance, wiping his forehead frankly, "I'd rather face a grizzly than do that again. Leslie keeps telling me that my habit of butting in will land me in the family vault before my time."

Craven smiled wryly.

"It's all right. I'm grateful—really. But I must hoe my own row."

The American swung irresolutely on his heels.

"That's so, that's so," he agreed reluctantly. "Oh damn it all," he burst out, "have a drink!" and going back to the table he pounded in the stopper of a soda-water-bottle savagely.

Craven laughed constrainedly as he tilted the whisky into a glass.

"Universal panacea," he said a little bitterly, "but it's not my method of oblivion."

He put the peg tumbler down with a smothered sigh.

"I must be off, Jermyn. It's time you were getting under way. It's been like the old days to have had a yarn with you again. Good luck and a quick run home—you lucky devil."

Atherton walked with him to the head of the gangway and watched him into the launch.

"We shall count on you for the Adirondacks in the summer," he called out cheerily, leaning far over the rail.

Craven looked up with a smile and waved his hand, but did not answer and the motor boat shot away toward the shore.

He landed on the big pier and lingered for a moment to watch the launch speeding back to the yacht. Then he walked slowly down the length of the stage and at the entrance found his rickshaw waiting. The two men who were squatting on the ground leaped up at his approach and one hurriedly lit a great dragon-painted paper lantern while the other held out a light dustcoat. Craven tossed it into the rickshaw and silently pointing toward the north, climbed in. He leaned back and lit a cigarette. The men sprang away in a quick dog-trot along the Bund, and then started to climb the hillside at the back of the town. They wound slowly up the narrow tortuous roads, past numberless villas, hung with lights, from which voices floated out into the quiet air.

The moon was brilliant and the night wonderfully light, but Craven paid no attention to the beauty of the scene or to the gaily lit villas. Atherton's invitation had been curiously hard to decline and even now an almost overpowering desire came over him to bid his men retrace their steps to the harbour. Then hard on the heels of that desire came thoughts that softened the hard lines that had gathered about his mouth. He pitched his cigarette away as if with it he threw from him an actual temptation, and resolutely put out of his mind Atherton and the suggestion of flight.

Still climbing upward the rickshaw passed the last of the outlying European villas and turned down a side road where there were no houses. For a couple of miles the men raced along a level track cut on the side of a hill that rose steeply on the one hand and on the other fell away precipitously down to the sea until they halted with a sudden jerk beside a wooden gateway with a creeper-covered roof on either side of which two matsu trees stood like tall sentinels.

Waiting by the open gate was a short, powerful looking Japanese dressed in European clothes. He came forward as Craven alighted and gathering up the coat and hat from the floor of the rickshaw, dismissed the Japanese who vanished further along the road into the shadows. Then he turned and waited for his master to precede him through the gateway, but Craven signed to him to go on, and as the man disappeared up the garden path he crossed the road and standing on the edge of the cliff looked down across the harbour. The American yacht was the biggest craft of her kind in the roads and easily discernible in the moonlight. The brilliant deck illumination had been shut off and only a few lights showed. He gave a quick sigh. Atherton's coming had been like a bar drawn suddenly across the stream down which he was drifting. If Jermyn had only come last year! The envy he had felt earlier in the evening increased. He thought of the look he had seen in Atherton's eyes and the intonation of his voice when the American spoke of the wife to whom he was returning. What did love like that mean to a man? What factor in Atherton's strenuous and adventurous life had affected him as this had done? What were the ethics of a love that rose purely above physical attraction—environment—temperament; a love that grew and strengthened and absorbed until it ceased to be a part of life and became life itself—the main issue, the fundamental essence?

And as Craven watched he saw the yacht steam slowly down the bay. He drew a deep breath.

"You lucky, lucky devil," he whispered again and swung on his heel. He paused for a moment just within the gateway where on the only level part of the garden lay a miniature lake, hedged round with bamboo, clumps of oleander, fed by a little twisting stream that came tumbling and splashing down the hillside in a series of tiny waterfalls, its banks fringed with azalea bushes and slender cherry trees. Then he walked slowly along the path that led upward, winding to and fro through clusters of pines and cedars and over mossy slopes to the little house which stood in a clearing at the top of the garden surrounded by fir trees and backed by a high creeper-clad palisade.

From the wide verandah, built out on piles over the terrace, there was an uninterrupted view of the harbour. He climbed the four wooden stairs and on the top step turned and looked again down on to the bay. The yacht was now invisible, but in his mind he followed her slipping down toward the open sea. And Atherton—what were his thoughts while pacing the broad deck or lying in his cabin listening to the screw whose every revolution was taking him nearer the centre of his earthly happiness? Were they anything like his own, he wondered, as he stood there bareheaded in the moonlight, looking strangely big and incongruous on the balcony of the little fairylike doll's house?

He shrugged impatiently. The comparison was an insult, he thought bitterly. Again he stared out to sea, straining his eyes; trying vainly to pick up the yacht's lights far down the bay. It was very still, a tiny breeze whispered in the pines and drifted across his face the sweet perfume of a flowering shrub. A cicada chirped in the grass at his feet.

Then behind him came a faint rustle of silk. He heard the soft sibilant sound of a breath drawn quickly in.

"Will my lord honourably be pleased to enter?" the voice was very low and sweet and the English very slow and careful.

Craven did not move.

"Try again, O Hara San."

A low bubble of girlish laughter rippled out.

"Please to come in, Bar-ree."

He turned slowly, looking bigger than ever by contrast with the slender little Japanese girl who faced him. She was barely seventeen, dainty and fragile as a porcelain figure, wholly in keeping with her exquisite setting and yet the flush on her cheeks—free from the thick disfiguring white paste used by the women of her country—and the vivid animation of her face were oddly occidental, and the eyes raised so eagerly to Craven's were as grey as his own.

He held out his arms and she fluttered into them with a little breathless murmur, clinging to him passionately.

"Little O Hara San," he said gently as she pressed closer to him. He tilted her head, stooping to kiss the tiny mouth that trembled at the touch of his lips. She closed her eyes and he felt an almost convulsive shudder shake her.

"Have you missed me, O Hara San?"

"It is a thousand moons since you are gone," she whispered unsteadily.

"Are you glad to see me?"

Her grey eyes opened suddenly with a look of utter content and happiness.

"You know, Bar-ree. Oh, Bar-ree!"

His face clouded, the teasing word that rose to his lips died away unspoken and he pressed her head against him almost roughly to hide the look of trusting devotion that suddenly hurt him. For a few moments she lay still, then slipped free of his arms and stood before him, swaying slightly from side to side, her hands busily patting her hair into order and smiling up at him happily.

"Being very rude. Forgetting honourable hospitality. You please forgive?"

She backed a few steps toward the doorway and her pliant figure bent for an instant in the prescribed form of Japanese courtesy and salutation. Then she clasped both hands together with a little cry of dismay. "Oh, so sorree," she murmured in contrition, "forgot honourable lord forbidding that."

"Your honourable lord will beat you with a very big stick if you forget again," said Craven laughing as he followed her into the little room. O Hara San pouted her scarlet lips at him and laughed softly as she subsided on to a mat on the floor and clapped her hands. Craven sat down opposite her more slowly. In spite of the months he had spent in Japan he still found it difficult to adapt his long legs to the national attitude.

In answer to the summons an old armah brought tea and little rice cakes which O Hara San dispensed with great dignity and seriousness. She drank innumerable cupfuls while Craven took three or four to please her and then lit a cigarette. He smoked in silence watching the dainty little kneeling figure, following the quick movements of her hands as she manipulated the fragile china on the low stool before her, the restraint she imposed upon herself as she struggled with the excited happiness that manifested itself in the rapid heaving of her bosom, and the transient smile on her lips, and a heavy frown gathered on his face. She looked up suddenly, the tiny cup poised in her hand midway to her mouth.

"You happy in Tokio?"

"Yes."

It was not the answer for which she had hoped and her eyes dropped at the curt monosyllable. She put the cup back on the tray and folded her hands in her lap with a faint little sigh of disappointment, her head drooping pensively. Craven knew instinctively that he had hurt her and hated himself. It was like striking a child. But presently she looked up again and gazed at him soberly, wrinkling her forehead in unconscious imitation of his.

"O Hara San very bad selfish girl. Hoping you very *un*happy in Tokio," she said contritely.

He laughed at the naive confession and the gloom vanished from his face as he stood up, his long limbs cramped with the uncongenial attitude.

"What have you been doing while I was away?" he asked, crossing the room to look at a new kakemono on the wall.

She flitted away silently and returned in a few moments carrying a small panel. She put it into his hands, drawing near to him within the arm he slipped round her and slanted her head against him, waiting for his criticism with the innate patience of her race.

Craven looked long at the painting. It was a study of a solitary fir tree, growing at the edge of a cliff—wind-swept, rugged. The high precipice on which it stood was only suggested and far below there was a hint of boundless ocean—foam-crested.

It was the tree that gripped attention—a lonely outpost, clinging doggedly to its jutting headland, rearing its head proudly in its isolation; the wind seemed to rustle through its branches, its gnarled trunk showed rough and weather-beaten. It was a poem of loneliness and strength.

At last Craven laid it down carefully, and gathering up the slender clasped hands, kissed them silently. The mute homage was more to her than words. The colour rushed to her cheeks and her eyes devoured his face almost hungrily.

"You like it?" she whispered wistfully.

"Like it?" he echoed, "Gad! little girl, it's wonderful. It's more than a fir tree—it's power, tenacity, independence. I know that all your work is symbolical to you. What does the tree mean—Japan?"

She turned her head away, the flush deepening in her cheeks, her fingers gripping his.

"It means—more to me than Japan," she murmured. "More to me than life—it means—you," she added almost inaudibly.

He swept her up into his arms and carrying her out on to the verandah, dropped into a big cane chair that was a concession to his western limbs.

"You make a god of me, O Hara San," he said huskily.

"You are my god," she answered simply, and as he expostulated she laid her soft palm over his mouth and nestled closer into his arms.

"I talk now," she said quaintly. "I have much to tell."

But the promised news did not seem forthcoming for she grew silent again, lying quietly content, rubbing her head caressingly from time to time against his arm and twisting his watch-chain round her tiny fingers.

The night was very quiet. No sound came from within the house, and without only the soft wind murmuring in the trees, cicadas chirping unceasingly and the little river dashing down the hillside, splashing noisily, broke the stillness. Nature, the sleepless, was awake making her influence felt with the kindly natural sounds that mitigate the awe of absolute silence—sounds that harmonized with the peacefulness of the little garden. Tonight the contrast between Yokohama, with its pitiful western vulgarity obtruding at every turn, and the quiet beauty of his surroundings struck Craven even more sharply than usual. It seemed impossible that only two miles away was Theatre Street blazing and rioting with all its tinsel tawdriness, flaring lights and whining gramophones. Here was another world—and here he had found more continuous contentment than he had known in the last ten years. The garden was an old one, planned by a master hand. By day it was lovely, but by night it took on a weird beauty that was almost unreal. The light of the moon cast strong black shadows, deep and impenetrable, that hovered among the trees like sinister spirits lurking in the darkness.

The trees themselves, contorted in the moonlight, assumed strange forms—vague shapes played in and out among them—the sombre bushes seemed alive with peeping faces. It was the Garden of Enchantment, peopled with a thousand djinns and demons of Old Japan. The atmosphere was mysterious, the air was saturated with sweet heavy scents.

Craven was a passionate lover of the night. The darkness, the silence, the mystery of it appealed to him. He was familiar with its every phase in many climates. It enticed him for long solitary rambles in all the countries he had visited during the ten years of his wanderings. Nature, always fascinating, was then to him doubly attractive, doubly alluring. To the night he went for sympathy. To the night he went for inspiration. It was during his midnight wanderings that he seemed to get nearer the fundamental root of things. It was to the night he turned for consolation in times of need. It was then that he exorcised the demon of unrest that entered into him periodically. All his life the charm of the night had called to him and all his life he had responded obediently. As a tiny boy one of his earliest recollections was of slipping out of bed and, evading nurses and servants, stealing out into the park at Craven Towers to seek the healing of the night for some childish heartache. He had crept down the long avenue and climbing the iron fence had perched on the rail and watched the deer feeding by the light of the moon until all the sorrow had been chased away and his baby heart was singing with a kind of delirious happiness that he did not understand and that gave way in its turn to a natural childish enjoyment of an adventure that was palpably forbidden. He had slid down from the fence and retraced his steps up the avenue until he came to the path that led to the rose garden and eventually to the terrace near the house. He had trotted along on his little bare feet, shivering now and then, but more from excitement than from cold, until he had come to the long flight of stone steps that led to the terrace. He had laboriously climbed them one foot at a time, his toes curling at the contact with the chill stone, and at the top he had halted suddenly, holding his breath. Close to him was a tall indistinct figure wrapped in dark draperies. For a moment fear gripped him and then an immense curiosity swamped every other feeling and he moved forward cautiously. The tall figure had turned suddenly and it was his mother's sad girlish face that looked down at him. She had lifted him up into her arms, wrapping her warm cloak round his slightly clad little body—she had asked no questions and she had not scolded. She had seemed to understand, even though he gave no explanation, and it was the beginning of a sympathy between them that had developed to an unusual degree and lasted until her death, ten years ago. She had hugged him tightly and he had always remembered, without fully understanding in his childhood, the half incredulous, half regretful whisper in his ear, "Has it come to you so soon, little son?"

The hereditary instinct, born thus, had grown with his own growth from boyhood to manhood until it was an integral part of himself.

And the lure of the eastern nights—more marvellous and compelling even than in colder climates—had become almost an obsession.

Little O Hara San, firm believer in all devils, djinns and midnight workers of mischief, had grown accustomed to the eccentricities of the man who was her whole world. If it pleased him to spend long hours of the night sitting on the verandah when ordinary folk were sensibly shut up in their houses she did not care so long as she might be with him. No demon in Japan could harm her while she lay securely in his strong arms. And if unpleasant shadows crept uncomfortably near the little house she resolutely turned her head and hiding her face against him shut out all disagreeable sights and slept peacefully, confident in his ability to keep far from her all danger. Her love was boundless and her trust absolute. But tonight there was no thought of sleep. For three long weeks she had not seen him and during that time for her the sun had ceased to shine. She had counted each hour until his return and she could not waste the precious moments now that he had really come. The djinns and devils in the garden might present themselves in all their hideousness if it so pleased them but tonight she was heedless of them. She had eyes for nothing but the man she worshipped. Even in his silent moods she was content. It was enough to feel his arms about her, to hear his heart beating rhythmically beneath her head and, lying so, to look up and see the firm curve of his chin and the slight moustache golden brown against his tanned cheek.

She stirred slightly in his arms with a little sigh of happiness, and the faint movement woke him from his abstraction.

"Sleepy?" he asked gently.

She laughed gaily at the suggestion and sat up to show how wide awake she was. The light from a lantern fell full on her face and Craven studied it with an intensity of which he was hardly aware. She bore his scrutiny in silence for a few moments and then looked away with a little grimace.

"Thinking me very ugly?" she hazarded tentatively.

"No. Very pretty," he replied truthfully. She leaned forward and laid her cheek for a second against his, then cuddled down into his arms again with a happy laugh. He lit a cigarette and tossed the match over the verandah rail.

"What is your news, O Hara San?"

She did not speak for a moment, and when she did it was no answer to his question. She reached up her hands and drawing his head down toward her, looked earnestly into his eyes.

"You loving me?" she asked a little tremulously.

"You know I love you," he answered quietly.

"Very much?"

"Very much."

Her eyes flickered and her hands released their hold.

"Men not loving like women," she murmured at length wistfully. And then suddenly, with her face hidden against him, she told him—of the fulfilling of all her hope, the supreme desire of eastern women, pouring out her happiness in quick passionate sentences, her body shaking with emotion, her fingers gripping his convulsively.

Craven sat aghast. It was a possibility of which he had always been aware but which with other unpleasant contingencies he had relegated to the background of his mind. He had put it from him and had drifted, careless and indifferent. And now the shadowy possibility had become a definite reality and he was faced with a problem that horrified him. His cigarette, neglected, burnt down until it reached his fingers and he flung it away with a sharp exclamation. He did not speak and the girl lay motionless, chilled with his silence, her happiness slowly dying within her, vaguely conscious of a dim fear that terrified her. Was the link that she had craved to bind them closer together to be useless after all? Was this happiness that he had given her, the culminating joy of all the goodness and kindness that he had lavished on her, no happiness to him? The thought stabbed poignantly. She choked back a sob and raised her head, but at the sight of his face the question she would have asked froze on her lips.

"Bar-ree! you are not angry with me?" she whispered desperately.

"How could I be angry with you?" he replied evasively. She shivered and clenched her teeth, but the question she feared must be asked.

"Are you not glad?" it was a cry of entreaty. He did not speak and with a low moan she tried to free herself from him but she was powerless in his hold, and soon she ceased to struggle and lay still, sobbing bitterly. He drew her closer into his arms and laid his cheek on her dark hair, seeking for words of comfort, and finding none. She had read the dismay in his face, had in vain waited for him to speak and no tardy lie would convince her now. He had wounded her cruelly and he could make no amends. He had failed her at the one moment when she had most need of him. He cursed himself bitterly. Gradually her sobs subsided and her hand slipped into his clutching it tightly. She sat up at last with a little sigh, pushing the heavy hair off her forehead wearily, and forcing herself to meet his eyes—looked at him sorrowfully, with quivering lips.

"Please forgive, Bar-ree," she whispered humbly and her humility hurt him more even than her distress.

"There is nothing to forgive, O Hara San," he said awkwardly, and as she sought to go this time he did not keep her. She walked to the edge of the verandah and stared down into the garden. Problematical ghosts and demons paled to insignificance before this real trouble. She fought with herself gallantly, crushing down her sorrow and disappointment and striving to regain the control she had let slip. Her feminine code Was simple—complete abnegation and self-restraint. And she had broken down under the first trial! He would despise her, the daughter of a race trained from childhood to conceal suffering and to suppress all signs of emotion. He would never understand that it was the alien blood that ran in her veins and the contact with himself that had caused her to abandon the stoicism of her people, that had made her reveal her sorrow. He had laughed at her undemonstrativeness, demanding expressions and proofs of her affection that were wholly foreign to her upbringing until her Oriental reserve had slipped from her whose only wish was to please him. She had adopted his manners, she had made his ways her ways, forgetting the bar that separated them. But tonight the racial difference of temperament had risen up vividly between them. Her joy was not his joy. If he had been a Japanese he would have understood. But he did not understand and she must hide both joy and sorrow. It was his contentment not hers that mattered. All through these last months of wonderful happiness there had lurked deep down in her heart a fear that it would not last, and she had dreaded lest any unwitting act of hers might hasten the catastrophe.

E.M. HULL

She glanced back furtively over her shoulder. Craven was leaning forward in the cane chair with his head in his hands and she looked away hastily, blinded with tears. She had troubled him—distressed him. She had "made a scene"—the phrase, read in some English book, flashed through her mind. Englishmen hated scenes. She gripped herself resolutely and when he left his chair and joined her she smiled at him bravely.

"See, all the djinns are gone, Bar-ree," she said with a little nervous laugh.

He guessed the struggle she was making and chimed in with her mood.

"Sensible fellows," he said lightly, tapping a cigarette on the verandah rail. "Gone home to bed I expect. Time you went to bed too. I'll just smoke this cigarette." But as she turned away obediently, he caught her back, with a sudden exclamation:

"By Jove! I nearly forgot."

He took a tiny package from his pocket and gave it to her. Girlishly eager her fingers shook with excitement as she ripped the covering from a small gold case attached to a slender chain. She pressed the spring and uttered a little cry of delight. The miniature of Craven had been painted by a French artist visiting Yokohama and was a faithful portrait.

"Oh, Bar-ree," she gasped with shining eyes, lifting her face like a child for his kiss. She leaned against him studying the painting earnestly, appreciating the mastery of a fellow craftsman, ecstatically happy—then she slipped the chain over her head and closing the case tucked it away inside her kimono.

"Now I have two," she murmured softly.

"Two?" said Craven pausing as he lighted his cigarette. "What do you mean?"

"Wait, I show," she replied and vanished into the house. She was back in a moment holding in her hand another locket. He took it from her and moved closer under the lantern to look at it. It hung from a thick twisted cable of gold, and set round with pearls it was bigger and heavier than the dainty case O Hara San had hidden against her heart. For a moment he hesitated, overcoming an inexplicable reluctance to open it—then he snapped the spring sharply.

"Good God!" he whispered slowly through dry lips. And yet he had known, known intuitively before the lid flew back, for it was the second time that he had handled such a locket—the first he had seen and left lying on his dead mother's breast.

He stood as if turned to stone, staring with horror at the replica of his own face lying in the hollow of his hand. The thick dark hair, the golden brown moustache, the deep grey eyes—all were the same. Only the chin in the picture was different for it was hidden by a short pointed beard; so was it in the miniature that was buried with his mother, so was it in the big portrait that hung in the dining-room at Craven Towers.

"Who gave you this?" he asked thickly, and O Hara San stared at him in bewilderment, frightened at the strangeness of his voice.

"My mother," she said wonderingly. "He was Bar-ree, too. See," she added pointing with a slender forefinger to the name engraved inside the case.

A nightbird shrieked weirdly close to the house and a sudden gust of wind moaned through the pine trees. The sweat stood out on Craven's forehead in great drops and the cigarette, fallen from his hand, lay smouldering on the matting at his feet.

He pulled the girl to him and turning her face up stared down into the great grey eyes, piteous now with unknown fear, and cursed his blindness. Often the unrecognised likeness had puzzled him. He dropped the miniature and ground it savagely to powder with his heel, heedless of O Hara San's sharp cry of distress, and turned to the railing gripping it with shaking hands.

"Damn him, damn him!"

Why had instinct never warned him? Why had he, knowing the girl's mixed parentage and knowing his own family history, made no inquiries? A wave of sick loathing swept over him. His head reeled. He turned to O Hara San crouched sobbing on the matting over the little heap of crushed gold and pearls. Was there still a loop-hole?

"What was he to you?" he said hoarsely, and he did not recognise his own voice.

She looked up fearfully, then shrank back with a cry—hiding her eyes to shut out the distorted face that bent over her.

"He was my father," she whispered almost inaudibly. But it sounded to Craven as if she had shouted it from the housetop. Without a word he turned from her and stumbled toward the verandah steps. He must get away, he must be alone—alone with the night to wrestle with this ghastly tangle.

O Hara San sprang to her feet in terror. She did not understand what had happened. Her mother had rarely spoken of the man who had first betrayed and then deserted her—she had loved him too faithfully; with the girl's limited experience all western faces seemed curiously alike and the similarity of an uncommon name conveyed nothing to her for she did not realize that it was uncommon. She could not comprehend this terrible change in the man who had never been anything but gentle with her. She only knew that he was going, that something inexplicable was taking him from her. A wild scream burst from her lips and she sprang across the verandah, clinging to him frantically, her upturned face beseeching, striving to hold him.

"Bar-ree, Bar-ree! you must not go. I die without you. Bar-ree! my love—" Her voice broke in a frightened whisper as he caught her head in his hands and stared down at her with eyes that terrified her.

"Your—love?" he repeated with a strange ring in his voice, and then he laughed—a terrible laugh that echoed horribly in the silent night and seemed to snap some tension in his brain. He tore away her hands and fled down the steps into the garden. He ran blindly, instinctively turning to the hillside track that led further into the country, climbing steadily upward, seeking the solitary woods. He did not hear the girl's shriek of despair, did not see her fall unconscious on the matting, he did not see a lithe figure that bounded from the back of the house nor hear the feet that tracked him. He heard and saw nothing. His brain was dulled. His only impulse was that of the wounded animal—to hide himself alone with nature and the night. He plunged on up the hillside climbing fiercely, tirelessly, wading mountain streams and forcing his way through thick brushwood. He had taken off his coat earlier in the evening and his silk shirt was ripped to ribbons. His hair lay wet against his forehead and his cheek dripped blood where a splintered bamboo had torn it, but he did not feel it. He came at last to a tiny clearing in the forest where the moon shone through a break in the trees. There he halted, rocking unsteadily on his feet, passing his hand across his face to clear the blood and perspiration from his eyes, and then dropped like a log. The next moment the bushes parted and his Japanese servant crept noiselessly to his side. He bent down over him for an instant. Craven lay motionless with his face hidden in his arms, but as the Jap watched a shudder shook him from head to foot and the man backed cautiously, disappearing among the bushes as silently as he had come.

The breeze died away and it was quite still within the moonlit clearing. A broad shaft of cold white light fell directly on the prone figure. He was morally stunned and for a long time the agony of his mind was blunted. But gradually the first shock passed and full realization rushed over him. His hands dug convulsively into the soft earth and he writhed at his helplessness. What he had done was irremediable. It was a sudden thunderbolt that had flashed across his clear sky. This morning the sun had shone as usual and everything had seemed serene to him whose life had always been easy—tonight he was wrestling in a hell of his own making. Why had it come to him? He knew that his life had been comparatively blameless. Why should this one sin, so common throughout the world, recoil on him so terribly? Why should he, among all the thousands of men who had sinned similarly, be reserved for such a nemesis? Why of him alone should such a reckoning be demanded? Surely the fault was not his. Surely it lay with the man who had wrecked his mother's life and broken her heart, the man who had neglected his duties and repudiated his responsibilities and who had been faithful to neither wife nor mistress. He was to blame. At the thought of his father an access of rage passed over Craven and he cursed him in a kind of dull fury. His fingers gripped the ground as if they were about the throat of the man whom he hated with all the strength of his being. The mystery of his father had always lain like a shadow across his life. It was a subject that his mother had refused to discuss. He shivered now when he realized the agony his perpetual boyish questions must have caused her. His petulance because "other fellows' fathers" could be produced when necessary and were not shrouded away in unexplained obscurity. He remembered her unfailing patience with him, the consistent loyalty she had shown toward the husband who had failed her so utterly, the courage with which she had taken the absent father's place with the son whom she idolized. He understood now her intolerant hatred of Japan and the Japanese, an intolerance for which—in his ignorance—he had often teased her. One memory came to him with striking vividness—a winter evening, in the dawn of his early manhood, when they had been sitting after dinner in the library at Craven Towers—his mother lying on the sofa that had been rolled up before the fire, and himself sprawled on the hearthrug at her feet. Already tall and strong beyond his years and confident in the full flush of his adolescence he had launched into a glowing anticipation of the life that lay before him. He had noticed that his mother's answers were monosyllabic and vague, and then when he had broken off, hurt at her seeming lack of interest, she had suddenly spoken—telling him what she had all the evening nerved herself to say. Her voice had faltered once or twice but she had steadied it bravely and gone on to the end, shirking nothing, evading nothing, dealing faithfully with the whole sex problem as far as she was able—outraging her own reserve that her son might learn the pitfalls and temptations that would assuredly lie in wait for him, sacrificing her own modesty that he might remain chaste. He remembered the vivid flush that had risen to his face and the growing sense of hot discomfort with which he had listened to her low voice; his half grateful, half shocked feeling. But it was not until he had glanced furtively at her through his thick lashes and seen her shamed scarlet cheeks and quivering downcast eyes that he had realized what it cost her and the courage that had made it possible for her to speak. He had mumbled incoherently, his face hidden against her knee, and with innate chivalry had kissed the little white hand he held between his own great brown ones—"Keep clean, Barry," she had whispered tremulously, her hand on his ruffled hair—"only keep clean."

And later on in the same evening she had spoken to him of the woman who would one day inevitably enter his life. "Be gentle to her, Barry-boy, you are such a great strong fellow, and women, even the strongest women, are weak compared with men. We are poor creatures, the best of us, we *bruise* so easily," she had said with a laugh that was more than half a sob. And for his mother's sake he had vowed to be gentle to all women who might cross his path. And how had he kept his vow? Tonight his egoism had swallowed his oath and he had fled like a coward to be alone with his misery. A great sob rose in his throat. Craven by name and craven by nature he thought bitterly and he cursed again the father who had bequeathed him such an inheritance, but as he did so he stopped suddenly for a soft clear voice sounded close to his ear. "No man need be fettered for life by an inherited weakness. Every man who is worthy of the name can rise above hereditary deficiencies." He lay tense and his heart gave a great throb and then he remembered. The voice was inward—it was only another memory, an echo of the young mother who had died, ten years before. Overwhelming shame filled him. "Mother, Mother!" he whispered chokingly, and deep tearing sobs shook his broad shoulders. The moon had passed beyond the break in the trees and it was dark now in the little clearing and to the man who lay stripped of all his illusions the blackness was merciful. He saw himself as he was clearly—his selfishness, his arrogance, his pride, and a nausea of self-hatred filled him. The eagerness with which he had sought to lay on his father the blame of his own sin now seemed to him despicable. He would always hate the memory of the man whose neglect had killed his mother, but the responsibility for this horror rested on himself. He

II

Craven woke abruptly a few hours later with a spasmodic muscular contraction that jerked him into a sitting position. Half dazed as yet with sleep he swung his heels to the floor and sat on the edge of the bed looking stupidly at his dusty boots and earth-stained fingers. Then remembrance came and he clenched his hands with a stifled groan. He drank thirstily the tea that was on a table beside him and went to the open window. As he crossed the room the reflection of his blood-stained haggard face, seen in a mirror, startled him. A bath and clean clothes were indispensable before he went back to the lonely little house on the hillside. He lingered for a few minutes by the window, glad of the cool morning breeze blowing against his face, trying to pull himself together, trying to brace himself to meet the consequences of his folly, trying to drag his disordered thoughts into something approaching coherence. He stared down over the bay and the sunlit waters mocked him with their dancing ripples sliding lightheartedly one after the other toward the shore. The view that he looked upon had been until this morning a never-failing source of pleasure, now it moved him to nothing but the recollection of the hackneyed line in the old hymn—"where only man is vile," and he was vile—with all power of compensation taken from him. To some was given the chance of making reparation. For him there was no chance. He could do nothing to mitigate the injury he had done. She whom he had wronged must suffer for him and he was powerless to avert that suffering. His helplessness overwhelmed him. O Hara San, little O Hara San, who had given unstintingly, with eager generous hands. His face was set as he turned from the window and, starting to pull off his torn shirt, called for Yoshio. But no Yoshio was forthcoming and at his second impatient shout another Japanese servant bowed himself in, and, kowtowing, intimated that Yoshio had already gone on the honourable lord's errand and would there await him, and that in the meantime his honourable bath was prepared and his honourable breakfast would be ready in ten minutes.

Craven paused with his shirt half off.

"What errand?" he said, perplexed, unaware that he was asking the question audibly.

The man bowed again, with hands outspread, and gravely shook his head conveying his total ignorance of a matter that was beyond his province, but the pantomime was lost on Craven who was wrestling with his shirt and not even aware that he had spoken aloud. It was the first time in ten years' service that Yoshio had failed to answer a call and Craven wondered irritably what could have taken him away at that time in the morning, and concluded that it was some order given by himself the day before, now forgotten, so dismissing Yoshio and his affairs from his mind he signed to the still gently explaining servant to go.

His brain felt dull and tired, his thoughts were chaotic. He saw before him no clear course. Whichever way he looked at it the horrible tangle grew more horrible. There was a recurring sense of unreality, a visionary feeling of detachment which enabled him to view the situation from an impersonal standpoint, as one criticises a nightmare, confident in the knowledge that it is only a dream. But in this case the confidence was based on nothing tangible and the illusion faded as quickly as it rose and left him confronted with the brutal truth from which there was no escape.

In the dressing room everything that he needed had been laid out in readiness for him, and he dressed mechanically with a feverish haste that struggled ineffectually with a refractory collar stud, and caused him to execrate heartily the absent valet and his enigmatical errand. Another ten minutes was lost while he hunted for his watch and cigarette case which he suddenly remembered were in the coat that he had left at the little house. Or had he searched genuinely? Had he not rather been—perhaps unconsciously—procrastinating, shrinking from the task he had in hand, putting off the evil moment? He swung on his heel violently and passed out on to the verandah. But at the head of the steps a vigilant figure rose up, bowing obsequiously, announcing blandly that breakfast was waiting.

Craven frowned at him a moment until the meaning of the words filtered through to his tired brain, then he pushed him aside roughly.

"Oh, damn breakfast!" he cried savagely, and cramming his sun helmet on his head ran down the garden path to the waiting rickshaw. It never occurred to him to wonder how it came to be there at an unusual hour. He huddled in the back of the rickshaw, his helmet over his eyes. His nerves were raw, his mind running in uncontrollable riot. The way had never seemed so long. He looked up impatiently. The rickshaw was crawling. The slow progress and the forced inaction galled him and a dozen times he was on the point of calling to the men to stop and jumping out, but he forced himself to sit quietly, watching the play of their abnormally developed muscles showing plainly through the thin cotton garments that clung to their sweat-drenched bodies, while they toiled up the steep roads. And today the sight of the men's straining limbs and heaving chests moved him more than usual. He used a rickshaw of necessity, and had never overcome his distaste for them.

Emerging from a grove of pines they neared the little gateway and as the men flung themselves backward with a deep grunt at the physical exertion of stopping, Craven leaped out and dashed up the path, panic-driven. He took the verandah steps in two strides and then stopped abruptly, his face whitening under the deep tan.

Yoshio stood in the doorway of the outer room, his arms outstretched, barring the entrance. His face had gone the grey leaden hue of the frightened Oriental and his eyes held a curious look of pity. His attitude put the crowning touch to Craven's anxiety. He went a step forward.

"Stand aside," he said hoarsely.

But Yoshio did not move.

"Master not going in," he said softly.

Craven jerked his head.

"Stand aside," he repeated monotonously.

For a moment longer the Jap stood obstinately, then his eyes fell under Craven's stare and he moved reluctantly, with a gesture of mingled acquiescence and regret. Craven passed through into the room. It was empty. He stood a moment hesitating—indefinite anxiety giving place to definite fear.

"O Hara San," he whispered, and the whisper seemed to echo mockingly from the empty room. He listened with straining ears for her answer, for her footstep—and he heard nothing but the heavy beating of his own heart. Then a moan came from the inner room and he followed the sound swiftly. The room was darkened and for a moment he halted in the doorway, seeing nothing in the half light. The moaning grew louder and as he became accustomed to the darkness he saw the old armah crouching beside a pile of cushions.

In a second he was beside her and at his coming she scrambled to her feet with a sharp cry, staring at him wildly, then fled from the room.

He stood alone looking down on the cushions. His heart seemed to stop beating and for a moment he reeled, then he gripped himself and knelt down slowly.

"O Hara San—" he whispered again, with shaking lips, "little O Hara San—little—" the whisper died away in a terrible gasping sob.

She lay as if asleep—one arm stretched out along her side, the other lying across her breast with her small hand clenched and tucked under her chin, her head bent slightly and nestled naturally into the cushion. The attitude was habitual. A hundred times Craven had seen her so—asleep. It was impossible that she could be dead.

He spoke to her again—crying aloud in agony—but the heavily fringed eyelids did not open, no glad cry of welcome broke from the parted lips, the little rounded bosom that had always heaved tumultuously at his coming was still under the silken kimono. He bent over her with ashen face and laid his hand gently on her breast, but the icy coldness struck into his own heart and his touch seemed a profanation. He drew back with a terrible shudder.

How dared he touch her? Murderer! For it was murder. His work as surely as if he had himself driven a knife into that girlish breast or squeezed the breath from that slender throat. He was under no delusion. He understood the Japanese character too well and he knew O Hara San too thoroughly to deceive himself. He knew the passionate love that she had given him, a love that had often troubled him with its intensity. He had been her god, her everything. She had worshipped him blindly. And he had left her—left her alone with the memory of his strangeness and his harshness, alone with her heart breaking, alone with her fear. And she had been so curiously alone. She had had nobody but him. She had trusted him—and he had left her. She had trusted him. Oh, God, she had trusted him!

His quick imagination visualised what must have happened. Frantic with despair and desperate at the seeming fulfilment of her fears she had not stopped to reason nor waited for calmer reflection but with the curious Oriental blending of impetuosity and stolid deliberation she had killed herself, seeking release from her misery with the aid of the subtle poison known to every Japanese woman. He flung his arm across the little still body and his head fell on the cushion beside hers as his soul went down into the depths.

An hour of unspeakable bitterness passed before he regained his lost control.

Then he forced himself to look at her again. The poison had been swift and merciful. There was no distortion of the little oval face, no discoloration on the fair skin. She was as beautiful as she had always been. And with death the likeness had become intensified until it seemed to him that he must have been blind beyond belief to have failed to detect it earlier.

He looked for the last time through a blur of tears. It seemed horrible to leave her to the ministrations of others, he longed to gather up the slender body in his arms and with his own hands lay her in the loveliest corner of the garden she had loved so much. He tried to stammer a prayer but the words stuck in his throat. No intercession from him was possible, nor did she need it. She had passed into the realm of Infinite Understanding.

He rose to his feet slowly and lingered for a moment looking his last round the little room that was so familiar. Here were a few of her most treasured possessions, some that had come to her from her mother, some that he had given her. He knew them all so well, had handled them so often. A spasm crossed his face. It had been the home of the enchanted princess, shut off from all the world—until he had come. And his coming had brought desolation. Near him a valuable vase, that she had prized, lay smashed on the floor, overturned by the old armah in the first frenzy of her grief. It was symbolical and Craven turned from it with quivering lips and went out heavily.

He winced at the strong light and shaded his eyes for a moment with his hand.

Yoshio was waiting where he had left him. Craven walked to the edge of the verandah and stood for a few moments in silence, steadying himself.

"Where were you last night, Yoshio?" he asked at length, in a flat and tired voice.

The Jap shrugged.

"In town," he said, with American brevity learned in California.

"Why did you come here this morning?"

Yoshio raised eyes of childlike surprise.

"Master's watch. Came here to find it," he said nonchalantly, with an air that expressed pride at his own astuteness. But it did not impress Craven. He looked at him keenly, knowing that he was lying but not understanding the motive and too tired to try and understand. He felt giddy and his head was aching violently—for a moment everything seemed to swim before his eyes and he caught blindly at the verandah rail. But the sensation passed quickly and he pulled himself together, to find Yoshio beside him thrusting his helmet into his hands.

"Better Master going back to bungalow. I make all arrangements, understanding Japanese ways," he said calmly.

His words, matter-of-fact, almost brutal, brought Craven abruptly to actualities. There was necessity for immediate action. This was the East, where the grim finalities must unavoidably be hastened. But he resented the man's suggestion. To go back to the bungalow seemed a shirking of the responsibility that was his, the last insult he could offer her. But Yoshio argued vehemently, blunt to a degree, and Craven winced once or twice at the irrefutable reasons he put forward. It was true that he could do no real good by staying. It was true that he was of no use in the present emergency, that his absence would make things easier. But that it was the truth made it no less hard to hear. He gave in at last and agreed to all Yoshio's proposals—a curious compound of devotion to his master, shrewd commonsense and knowledge of the laws of the country. He went quickly down the winding path to the gate. The garden hurt him. The careless splashing of the tiny waterfall jarred poignantly—laughing water caring nothing that the hand that had planted much of the beauty of its banks was stilled for ever. It had always seemed a living being tumbling joyously down the hillside, it seemed alive now—callous, self-absorbed.

Craven had no clear impression of the run back into Yokohama and he looked up with surprise when the men stopped. He stood outside the gate for a moment looking over the harbour. He stared at the place in the roadstead where the American yacht had been anchored. Only last night had he laughed and chatted with the Athertons? It was a lifetime ago! In one night his youth had gone from him. In one night he had piled up a debt that was beyond payment. He gave a quick glance up at the brilliant sky and then went into the house. In the sitting-room he started slowly to pace the floor, his hands clasped behind him, an unlit cigarette clenched between his teeth. The mechanical action steadied him and enabled him to concentrate his thoughts. Monotonously he tramped up and down the long narrow room, unconscious of time, until at last he dropped on to a chair beside the writing table and laid his head down on his arms with a weary sigh. The little still body seemed present with him. O Hara San's face continually before him—piteous as he had seen it last, joyous as she had greeted him and thoughtful as when he had first seen it.

That first time—the memory of it rose vividly before him. He had been in Yokohama about a month and was settled in his bungalow. He had gone to the woods to sketch and had found her huddled at the foot of a steep rock from which she had slipped. Her ankle was twisted and she could not move. He had offered his assistance and she had gazed at him, without speaking, for a few moments, with serious grey eyes that looked oddly out of place in her little oval face. Then she had answered him in slow carefully pronounced English. He had laughingly insisted on carrying her home and had just gathered her up into his arms when the old armah arrived, voluble with excitement and alarm for her charge. But the girl had explained to her in rapid Japanese and the woman had hurried on to the house to prepare for them, leaving Craven to follow more slowly with his light burden. He had stayed only a few minutes, drinking the ceremonial tea that was offered so shyly.

The next day he had convinced himself that it was only polite for him to enquire about the injured foot. Then he had gone again, hoping to relieve the tedium of her forced inactivity, until the going had become a habit. The acquaintance had ripened quickly. From the first she had trusted him, quickly losing her awe of him and accepting his coming with the simplicity of a child. She had early confided to him the story of her short life—of her solitude and friendlessness; of the mother who had died five years before, bequeathing to her the little house which had been the last gift of the Englishman who had been O Hara San's father and who had tired of her mother and left her two years after her own birth; of the poverty against which they had struggled—for the Englishman had left no provision for them; of the faithful old servant, who had been her mother's nurse; of O Hara San's discovery of her own artistic talent which had enabled her to provide for the simple wants of the little household. She had grown up alone—apart from the world, watched over by the old woman, her mind a tangle of fairy-tales and romance—living for her art, content with her solitude. And into her secluded life had come Barry Craven and swept her off her feet. Child of nature that she was she had been unable to hide from him the love that quickly overwhelmed her. And to Craven the incident of O Hara San had come merely as a relief to the monotony of lotus-eating, he had drifted into the connection from sheer ennui. And then had come interest. No woman had ever before interested him. He had never been able to define the attraction she had had for him, the odd tenderness he had felt for her. He had treated her as a plaything, a fragile toy to be teased and petted. And in his hands she had developed from an innocent child into a woman—with a woman's capacity for devotion and self-sacrifice.

She had given everything, with trust and gladness. And he had taken all she gave, with colossal egoism, as his right—accepting lightly all she surrendered with no thought for the innocence he contaminated, the purity he soiled. He had stained her soul before he had killed her body. His hands clenched and unclenched convulsively with the agony of remorse. Recollection was torture. Repentance came too late. *Too late! Too late!* he words kept singing in his head as if a demon from hell was howling them in his ear. Nothing on earth could undo what he had done. No power could animate that little dead body. And if she had lived! He shuddered. But she had not lived, she had died—because of him. Because of him, Merciful God, because of him! And he could make no restitution. What was there left for him to do? A life of expiation was not atonement enough. There seemed only one solution—a life for a life. And that was no reparation, only justice. He put no value on his own life—he wished vaguely that the worth of it were greater—he had merely wasted it and now he had forfeited it. Remained only to end it—now. There was no reason for delay. He had no preparations to make. His affairs were all in order. His heir was his aunt, his father's only sister, who would be a better guardian of the Craven estates and interests than he had ever been. Peters was independent and Yoshio provided for. There was nothing to be done. He rose and opening a drawer in the table took out a revolver and held it a moment in his hand, looking at it dispassionately. It was not the ultimate purpose for which it had been intended. He had never imagined a time when he might end his own life. He had always vaguely connected suicide with cowardice. Was it the coward's way? Perhaps! Who can say what cowardice or courage is required to take the blind leap into the Great Unknown? That did not trouble him. It was no question of courage or cowardice but he felt convinced that his death was the only payment possible.

But as his finger pressed the trigger there was a slight sound beside him, his wrist and arm were caught in a vice-like grip and the weapon exploded harmlessly in the air as he staggered back, his arm almost broken with the jiu-jitsu hold against which even his great strength could do nothing. He struggled fruitlessly until he was released, then reeled against the table, with teeth set, clasping his wrenched wrist— the sudden frustration of his purpose leaving him, shaking. He turned stiffly. Yoshio was standing by him, phlegmatic as usual, showing no signs of exertion or emotion as he proffered a lacquer tray, with the usual formula: "Master's mail."

Craven's eyes changed slowly from dull suffering to blazing wrath. Uncontrolled rage filled him. How dared Yoshio interfere? How dared he drag him back into the hell from which he had so nearly escaped? He caught the man's shoulder savagely.

"Damn you!" he cried chokingly. "What the devil do you mean—" But the Jap's very impassiveness checked him and with an immense effort he regained command of himself. And imperturbably Yoshio advanced the tray again.

"Master's mail," he repeated, in precisely the same voice as before, but this time he raised his veiled glance to Craven's face. For a moment the two men stared at each other, the grey eyes tortured and drawn, the brown ones lit for an instant with deep devotion. Then Craven took the letters mechanically and dropped heavily into a chair. The Jap picked up the revolver and, quietly replacing it in the drawer from which it had been taken, left the room, noiseless as he had entered it. He seemed to know intuitively that it would be left where he put it.

Alone, Craven leaned forward with a groan, burying his face in his hands.

At last he sat up wearily and his eyes fell on the letters lying unopened on the table beside him. He fingered them listlessly and then threw them down again while he searched his pockets absently for the missing cigarette case. Remembering, he jerked himself to his feet with an exclamation of pain. Was all life henceforward to be a series of torturing recollections? He swore, and flung his head up angrily. Coward! whining already like a kicked cur!

He got a cigarette from a near table and picking up the letters carried them out on to the verandah to read. There were two, both registered. The handwriting on one envelope was familiar and his eyes widened as he looked at it. He opened it first. It was written from Florence and dated three months earlier. With no formal beginning it straggled up and down the sides of various sheets of cheap foreign paper, the inferior violet ink almost indecipherable in places.

"I wonder in what part of the globe this letter will find you? I have been trying to write to you for a long time—and always putting it off—but they tell me now that if I am to write at all there must be no more *mañana*. They have cried 'wolf' so often in the last few months that I had grown sceptical, but even I realise now that there must be no delay. I have delayed because I have procrastinated all my life and because I am ashamed—ashamed for the first time in all my shameless career. But there is no need to tell you what I am—you told me candidly enough yourself in the old days—it is sufficient to say that it is the same John Locke as then—drunkard and gambler, spendthrift and waster! And I don't think that my worst enemy would have much to add to this record, but then my worst enemy has always been myself. Looking back now over my life—queer what a stimulating effect the certainty of death has to the desire to find even one good action wherewith to appease one's conscience—it is a marvel to me that Providence has allowed me to cumber the earth so long. However, it's all over now—they give me a few days at the outside—so I must write at once or never. Barry, I'm in trouble, the bitterest trouble I have ever experienced—not for myself, God knows I wouldn't ask even your help, but for another who is dearer to me than all the world and for whose future I can do nothing. You never knew that I married. I committed that indiscretion in Rome with a little Spanish dancer who ought to have known better than to be attracted by my *beaux yeux*—for I had nothing else to offer her. We existed in misery for a couple of years and then she left me, for a more gilded position. But I had the child, which was all I cared about. Thank God, for her sake, that I was legally married to poor little Lola, she has at least no stain on her birth with which to reproach me. The officious individual who is personally conducting me to the Valley of the Shadow warns me that I must be brief—I kept the child with me as long as I could, people were wonderfully kind, but it was no life for her. I've come down in the social scale even since you knew me, Barry, and at last I sent her away, though it broke my heart. Still even that was better than seeing her day by day lose all respect for me. My miserable pittance dies with me and she is absolutely unprovided for. My family cast off me and all my works many years ago, but I put my pride in my pocket and appealed for help for Gillian and they suggested—a damned charitable institution! I was pretty nearly desperate until I thought of you. I know no one else. For God's sake, Barry, don't fail me. I can and I do trust Gillian to you. I have made you her guardian, it is all legally arranged and my lawyer in London has the papers. He is a well-known man and emanates respectability—my last claim to decency! Gillian is at the Convent of the Sacred Heart in Paris. My only consolation is that you are so rich that financially she will be no embarrassment to you. I realize what I am asking and the enormity of it, but I am a dying man and my excuse is—Gillian. Oh, man, be good to my little girl. I always hoped that something would turn up, but it didn't! Perhaps I never went to look for it, *quien sabe?* I shall never have the chance again. . ."

The signature was barely recognisable, the final letter terminating in a wandering line as if the pen had dropped from nerveless fingers.

Craven stared at the loose sheets in his hands for some time in horrified dismay, at first hardly comprehending, then as the full significance of John Locke's dying bequest dawned on him he flung them down and, walking to the edge of the verandah, looked over the harbour, tugging his moustache and scowling in utter perplexity. A child—a girl child! How could he with his soiled hands assume the guardianship of a child? He smiled bitterly at the irony of it. Providence was dealing hard with the child in the Paris convent, from dissolute father to criminal guardian. And yet Providence had already that morning intervened on her behalf—two minutes later and there would have been no guardian to take the trust. Providence clearly held the same views as John Locke on charitable institutions.

He thought of Locke as he had known him years ago, in Paris, a man twenty years his senior—penniless and intemperate but with an irresistible charm, rolling stone and waster but proud as a Spaniard; a man of the world with the heart of a boy, the enemy of nobody but himself, weak but lovable; a ragged coat and the manners of a prince; idealist and failure.

Craven read the letter through again. Locke had forced his hand—he had no option but to take up the charge entrusted to him. What a legacy! Surely if John Locke had known he would have rather committed his daughter to the tender mercies even of the "institution." But he had not known and he had trusted him. The thought was a sudden spur, urging him as nothing else could have done, bringing out all that was best and strongest in his nature. In a few hours he had crashed from the pinnacle on which he had soared in the blindness of egoism down into depths of self-realisation that seemed bottomless, and at the darkest moment when his world was lying in pieces under his feet—this had come. Another chance had been given to him. Craven's jaw set squarely as he thrust Locke's dying appeal into his pocket.

He ripped open the second letter. It was, as he guessed, from the lawyer and merely confirmed Locke's letter, with the additional information that his client had died a few hours after writing the said letter and that he had forwarded the news to the Mother Superior of the Convent School in Paris.

Craven went back into the sitting-room to write cables.

III

Owing to a breakdown on the line the boat-train from Marseilles crawled into the Gare du Lyon a couple of hours late. Craven had not slept. He had given his berth in the waggon-lit to an invalid fellow passenger and had sat up all night in an overcrowded, overheated carriage, choked with the stifling atmosphere, his long legs cramped for lack of space.

It was early March, and the difference between the temperature of the train and the raw air of the station struck him unpleasantly as he climbed down on to the platform.

Leaving Yoshio, equally at home in Paris as in Yokohama, to collect luggage, he signalled to a waiting taxi. He had the hood opened and, pushing back his hat, let the keen wind blow about his face. The cab jerked over the rough streets, at this early hour crowded with people— working Paris going to its daily toil—and he watched them hurrying by with the indifference of familiarity. Gradually he ceased even to look at the varied types, the jostling traffic, the bizarre posters and the busy newspaper kiosks. His thoughts were back in Yokohama. It had been six weeks before he could get away, six interminable weeks of misery and self-loathing. He had shirked nothing and evaded nothing. Much had been saved him by the discreet courtesy of the Japanese officials, but the ordeal had left him with jangling nerves. Fortunately the ship was nearly empty and the solitude he sought obtainable. He felt an outcast. To have joined as he had always previously done in the light-hearted routine of a crowded ship bent on amusements and gaiety would have been impossible.

He sought mental relief in action and hours spent tramping the lonely decks brought, if not relief, endurance.

And, always in the background, Yoshio, capable and devoted, stood between him and the petty annoyances that inevitably occur in travelling—annoyances that in his overwrought state would have been doubly annoying—with a thoughtfulness that was silently expressed in a dozen different devices for his comfort. That the Jap knew a great deal more than he himself did of the tragedy that had happened in the little house on the hill Craven felt sure, but no information had been volunteered and he had asked for none. He could not speak of it. And Yoshio, the inscrutable, would continue to be silent. The perpetual reminder of all that he could wish to forget Yoshio became, illogically, more than ever indispensable to him. At first, in his stunned condition, he had scarcely been sensible of the man's tact and care, but gradually he had come to realize how much he owed to his Japanese servant. And yet that was the least of his obligation. There was a greater—the matter of a life; whatever it might mean to Craven, to Yoshio the simple payment of a debt contracted years ago in California. That more than this had underlain the Japanese mind when it made its quick decision Craven could not determine; the code of the Oriental is not that of the Occidental, the demands of honour are interpreted and satisfied differently. Life in itself is nothing to the Japanese, the disposal of it merely the exigency of a moment and withal a personal prerogative. By all the accepted canons of his own national ideals Yoshio should have stood on one side—but he had chosen to interfere. Whatever the motive, Yoshio had paid his debt in full.

The weeks at sea braced Craven as nothing else could have done. As the ship neared France the perplexities of the charge he was preparing to undertake increased. His utter unfitness filled him with dismay. On receipt of John Locke's amazing letter he had both cabled and written to his aunt in London explaining his dilemma, giving suitable extracts from Locke's appeal, and imploring her help. And yet the thought of his aunt in connection with the upbringing of a child brought a smile to his lips. She was about as unsuited, in her own way, as he. Caro Craven was a bachelor lady of fifty—spinster was a term wholly inapplicable to the strong-minded little woman who had been an art student in Paris in the days when insular hands were lifted in horror at the mere idea, and was a designation, moreover, deprecated strongly by herself as an insult to one who stood—at least in her own sphere—on an equality with the lords of creation. She was a sculptor, whose work was known on both sides of the channel. When at home she lived in a big house in London, but she travelled much, accompanied by an elderly maid who had been with her for thirty years. And it was of the maid as much as of the mistress that Craven thought as the taxi bumped over the cobbled streets.

"If we can only interest Mary." There was a gleam of hope in the thought. "She will be the saving of the situation. She spoiled me thoroughly when I was a nipper." And buoyed with the recollection of grim-visaged angular Mary, who hid a very tender heart beneath a somewhat forbidding exterior, he overpaid the chauffeur cheerfully.

There was an accumulation of letters waiting for him at the hotel, but he shuffled them all into his overcoat pocket, with the exception of one from Peters which he tore open and read immediately, still standing in the lounge.

An hour later he set out on foot for the quiet hotel which had been his aunt's resort since her student days, and where she was waiting for him now, according to a telegram that he had received on his arrival at Marseilles. The hall door of her private suite was opened by the elderly maid, whose face lit up as she greeted him.

"Miss Craven is waiting in the salon, sir. She has been tramping the floor this hour or more, expecting you," she confided as she preceded him down the corridor.

Miss Craven was standing in a characteristic attitude before an open fireplace, her feet planted firmly on the hearthrug, her short plump figure clothed in a grey coat and skirt of severe masculine cut, her hands plunged deep into her jacket pockets, her short curly grey hair considerably ruffled. She bore down on her nephew with out-stretched hands.

"My dear boy, there you are at last! I have been waiting *hours* for you. Your train must have been very late—abominable railway service! Have you had any breakfast? Yes? Good. Then take a cigarette—they are in that box at your elbow—and tell me about this amazing thunderbolt that you have hurled at me. What a preposterous proposition for two bachelors like you and me! To be sure your extraordinary friend did not include me in his wild scheme—though no doubt he would have, had he known of my existence. Was the man mad? Who was he, anyhow? John Locke of where? There are dozens of Lockes. And why did he select you of all people? What fools men are!" She subsided suddenly into an easy chair and crossed one neat pump over the other. "All of 'em!" she added emphatically, flicking cigarette ash into the fire with a vigorous sidelong jerk. Her eyes were studying his face attentively, seeking for themselves the answer to the more personal inquiries that would have seemed necessary to a less original woman meeting a much-loved nephew after a lapse of years. Craven smiled at the characteristically peculiar greeting and the well remembered formula. He settled his long limbs comfortably into an opposite chair.

"Even Peter?" he asked, lighting a cigarette.

Miss Craven laughed good temperedly.

"Peter," she rejoined succinctly, "is the one brilliant exception that proves the rule. I have an immense respect for Peter." He looked at her

E.M. HULL

curiously. "And—me, Aunt Caro?" he asked with an odd note in his voice. Miss Craven glanced for a moment at the big figure sprawled in the chair near her, then looked back at the fire with pursed lips and wrinkled forehead, and rumpled her hair more thoroughly than before.

"My dear boy," she said at last soberly, "you resemble my unhappy brother altogether too much for my peace of mind."

He winced. Her words probed the still raw wound. But unaware of the appositeness of her remark Miss Craven continued thoughtfully, still staring into the fire:

"The Supreme Sculptor, when He made me, denied me the good looks that are proverbial in our family—but in compensation he endowed me with a solid mind to match my solid body. The Family means a great deal to me, Barry—more than anybody has ever realised—and there are times when I wonder why the solidity of mind was given to the one member of the race who could not perpetuate it in the direct line." She sighed, and then as if ashamed of unwonted emotion, jerked her dishevelled grey head with a movement that was singularly reminiscent of her nephew. Craven flushed.

"You're the best man of the family, Aunt Caro."

"So your mother used to say—poor child." Her voice softened suddenly. She got up restlessly and resumed her former position before the fire, her hands back in the pockets of her mannish coat.

"What about your plans, Barry? What are you going to do?" she said briskly, with an evident desire to avoid further moralising. He joined her on the hearthrug, leaning against the mantelpiece.

"I propose to settle down—at any rate for a time, at the Towers," he replied. "I intend to interest myself in the estates. Peter insists that I am wanted, and though that is nonsense and he is infinitely more necessary than I am, still I am willing to make the trial. I owe him more than I can even repay—we all do—and if my presence is really any help to him—he's welcome to it. I shall be about as much real use as the fifth wheel of a coach—a damned rotten wheel at that," he added bitterly. And for some minutes he seemed to forget that there was more to say, staring silently into the fire and from time to time putting together the blazing logs with his foot.

Miss Craven was possessed of the unfeminine attribute of holding her tongue and reserving her comments. She refrained from comment now, rocking gently backward and forward on her heels—a habit associated with mental concentration.

"I shall take the child to the Towers," he continued at length, "and there I shall want your help, Aunt Caro." He paused stammering awkwardly—"It's an infernal impertinence asking you to—to—"

"To turn nursemaid at my time of life," she interrupted. "It is certainly a career I never anticipated. And, candidly, I have doubts about its success," she laughed and shrugged, with a comical grimace. Then she patted his arm affectionately—"You had much better take Peter's advice and marry a nice girl who would mother the child and give her some brothers and sisters to play with."

He stiffened perceptibly.

"I shall never marry," he said shortly. Her eyebrows rose the fraction of an inch but she bit back the answer that rose to her lips.

"Never—is a long day," she said lightly. "The Cravens are an old family, Barry. One has one's obligations."

He did not reply and she changed the conversation hastily. She had a horror of forcing a confidence.

"Remains—Mary," she said, with the air of proposing a final expedient. Craven's tense face relaxed.

"Mary had also occurred to me," he admitted with an eagerness that was almost pathetic.

Miss Craven grunted and clutched at her hair.

"Mary!" she repeated with a chuckle, "Mary, who has gone through life with Wesley's sermons under her arm—and a child out of a Paris convent! There are certainly elements of humour in the idea. But I must have some details. Who was this Locke person?"

When Craven had told her all he knew she stood quite still for a long while, rolling a cigarette tube between her firm hands.

"Dissolute English father—and Spanish mother of doubtful morals. My poor Barry, your hands will be full."

"Our hands," he corrected.

"Our hands! Good heavens, the bare idea terrifies me!" She shrugged tragically and was dumb until Mary came to announce lunch.

Across the table she studied her nephew with an attention that she was careful to conceal. She was used to his frequent coming and going. Since the death of his mother he had travelled continually and she was accustomed to his appearing more or less unexpectedly, at longer or shorter intervals. They had always been great friends, and it was to her house in London that he invariably went first on returning to England— sure of his welcome, sure of himself, gay, easy-going and debonair. She was deeply attached to him. But, with something akin to terror, she had watched the likeness to the older Barry Craven growing from year to year, fearful lest the moral downfall of the father might repeat itself in the son. The temptation to speak frankly, to warn, had been great. Natural dislike of interference, and a promise given reluctantly to her dying sister-in-law, had kept her silent. She had loved the tall beautiful woman who had been her brother's wife and a promise made to her was sacred—though she had often doubted the wisdom of a silence that might prove an incalculable danger. She respected the fine loyalty that demanded such a promise, but her own views were more comprehensive. She was strong enough to hold opinions that were contrary to accepted traditions. She admitted a loyalty due to the dead, she was also acutely conscious of a loyalty due to the living. A few minutes before when Miss Craven had, somewhat shamefacedly, owned to a love of the family to which they belonged she had but faintly expressed her passionate attachment thereto. Pride of race was hers to an unusual degree. All that was best and noblest she craved for the clan. And Barry was the last of the Cravens. Her brother had failed her and dragged her high ideals in the dust. Her courage had restored them to endeavour a second time. If Barry failed her too! Hitherto her fears had had no definite basis. There had been no real ground for anxiety, only a developing similarity of characteristics that was vaguely disquieting. But now, as she looked at him, she realised that the man from whom she had parted nearly two years before was not the man who now faced her across the table. Something had happened—something that had changed him utterly. This man was older by far more than the actual two years. This was a man whom she hardly recognised; hard, stern, with a curiously bitter ring at times in his voice, and the shadow of a tragedy lying in the dark grey eyes that had changed so incredibly for lack of their habitual ready smile. There were lines about his mouth and a glint of grey in his hair that she was quick to observe. Whatever had happened—he had suffered. That was written plainly on his face. And unless he chose to speak she was powerless to help him. She refused to intrude, unbidden, into another's private concerns. That he was an adored nephew, that the intimacy between them was great made no difference, the restriction remained the same. But she was woman enough to be fiercely jealous for him. She resented the change she saw—it was not the change she had desired but something far beyond her understanding that left her with the feeling that she was confronting a total stranger. But she was careful to hide her scrutiny, and though her mind speculated widely she continued to chatter, supplementing the home news her scanty letters had afforded and retailing art gossip of the moment. One question only she allowed herself. There had come a silence. She broke it abruptly, leaning forward in her chair, watching him keen-eyed.

"Have you been ill—out there?"—her hand fluttered vaguely in an easterly direction. Craven looked up in surprise.

"No," he said shortly, "I never am ill."

Miss Craven's nod as she rose from the table might have been taken for assent. It was in reality satisfaction at her own perspicacity. She had not supposed for one moment that he had been ill but in no other way could she express what she wanted to know. It was in itself an innocuous and natural remark, but the sudden gloom that fell on him warned her that her ingenuity was, perhaps, not so great as she imagined.

"Triple idiot!" she reflected wrathfully, as she poured out coffee, "you had better have held your tongue," and she set herself to charm away the shadow from his face and dispel any suspicion he might have formed of her desire to probe into his affairs. She had an uncommon personality and could talk cleverly and well when she chose. And today she did choose, exerting all her wit to combat the taciturn fit that emphasized so forcibly the change in him. But though he listened with apparent attention his mind was very obviously elsewhere, and he sat staring into the fire, mechanically flicking ash from his cigarette. Conversation languished and at length Miss Craven gave it up, with a wry face, and sat also silent, drumming with her fingers on the arm of the chair. Her thoughts, in quest of his, wandered far away until the sudden ringing of the telephone beside her made her jump violently.

She answered the call, then handed the receiver to Craven.

"Your heathen," she remarked dryly.

Though the least insular of women she had never grown accustomed to the Japanese valet. He turned from the telephone with a look of mingled embarrassment and relief.

"I sent a message to the convent this morning. Yoshio has just given me the answer. The Mother Superior will see me this afternoon." He endeavoured to make his voice indifferent, pulling down his waistcoat and picking a minute thread from off his coat sleeve. Miss Craven's mouth twitched at the evident signs of nervousness while she glanced at him narrowly. Prompt action in the matter of an uncongenial duty had not hitherto been a conspicuous trait in his character.

"You are certainly not letting the grass grow under your feet."

He jerked his head impatiently.

"Waiting will not make the job more pleasant," he shrugged. "I will see the child at once and arrange for her removal as soon as possible."

Miss Craven eyed him from head to foot with a grim smile that changed to a whole-hearted laugh of amusement.

"It's a pity you have so much money, Barry, you would make your fortune as a model. You are too criminally good looking to go fluttering into convents."

A ghost of the old smile flickered in his eyes.

"Come and chaperon me, Aunt Caro."

She shook her head laughingly.

"Thank you—no. There are limits. I draw the line at convents. Go and get it over, and if the child is presentable you can bring her back to tea. I gather that Mary is anticipating a complete failure on our part to sustain the situation and is prepared to deputise. She has already ransacked *Au Paradis Des Enfants* for suitable bribes wherewith to beguile her infantile affection. I understand that there was a lively scene over the purchase of a doll, the cost of which—clad only in its birthday dress—was reported to me as 'a fair affront.' Even after all these years Mary jibs at Continental prices. It is her way of keeping up the prestige of the British Empire, bless her. An overcharge, in her opinion, is a deliberate twist of the lion's tail."

In the taxi he looked through the correspondence he had received that morning for the lawyer's letter that would establish his claim to John Locke's child. Then he leaned back and lit a cigarette. He had an absurd feeling of nervousness and cursed Locke a dozen times before he reached the convent. He was embarrassed with the awkward situation in which he found himself—just how awkward he seemed only now fully to appreciate. The more he thought of it, the less he liked it. The coming interview with the Mother Superior was not the least of his troubles. The promise of the morning had not been maintained, overhead the sky was leaden, and a high wind drove rain in sharp splashes against the glass of the cab. The pavements were running with water and the leafless trees in the avenues swayed and creaked dismally. The appearance of the streets was chill and depressing. Craven shivered. He thought of the warmth and sunshine that he had left in Japan. The dreariness of the present outlook contrasted sufficiently with the gay smiling landscape, the riotous wealth of colour, and the scent-laden air of the land of his recollections. A feeling almost of nostalgia came to him. But with the thought came also a vision—a little still body lying on silken cushions; a small pale face with fast shut eyes, the long lashes a dusky fringe against the ice-cold cheek. The vision was terribly distinct, horribly real—not a recollection only, as on the morning that he had found her dead—and he waited, with the sweat pouring down his face, for the closed eyes to open and reveal the agony he had read in them that night, when he had torn her clinging hands away and left her. The faint aroma of the perfume she had used was in his nostrils, choking him. The slender limbs seemed to pulsate into life, the little breasts to stir perceptibly, the parted lips to tremble. He could not define the actual moment of the change but, as he bent forward, with hands close gripped, all at once he found himself looking straight into the tortured grey eyes—for a second only. Then the vision faded, and he was leaning back in the cab wiping the moisture from his forehead. God, would it never leave him! It haunted him. In the big bungalow on the Bluff; rising from the sea as he leaned on the steamer rail; during the long nights on the ship as he lay sleepless in the narrow brass cot; last night in the crowded railway carriage—then it had been so vivid that he had held his breath and glanced around stealthily with hunted eyes at his fellow passengers looking for the horrified faces that would tell him that they also saw what he could see. He never knew how long it lasted, minutes or seconds, holding him rigid until it passed to leave him bathed in perspiration. Environment seemed to make no difference. It came as readily in a crowd as when he was alone. He lived in perpetual dread of betraying his obsession. Once only it had happened—in the bungalow, the night before he left Japan, and his involuntary cry had brought the watchful valet. And as he crossed the room Craven had distinctly seen him pass through the little recumbent figure and, with blazing eyes, had dragged him roughly to one side, pointing and muttering incoherently. And Yoshio had seemed to understand. Sceptical as he was about the supernatural, at first Craven's doubt had been rudely shaken; but with the steadying of his nerves had come the conviction that the vision was inward, though at the moment so real that often his confidence momentarily wavered, as last night in the train. It came with no kind of regularity, no warning that might prepare him. And recurrence brought no mitigation, no familiarising that could temper the acute horror it inspired. To what pitch of actuality might it attain? To what lengths might it drive him? He dragged his thoughts up sharply. To dwell on it was fatal, that way lay insanity. He set his teeth and forced himself to think of other things. There was ample material. There was primarily the salvage of a wasted life. During the last few weeks he had been forced to a self-examination that had been drastically thorough. The verdict had been an adverse one. Personal criticism, once aroused, went far. The purposeless life that he had led seemed now an insult to his manhood. It had been in his power to do so much—he had actually done disastrously little. He had loafed through life without a thought beyond the passing interest of the moment. And even in the greater interests of his life, travel and big game, he had failed to exert himself beyond a mediocre level. He had travelled far and shot a rare beast or two, but so had many another—and with greater difficulties to contend with than he who had never wrestled with the disadvantages of inferior equipment and inadequate attendance. Muscularly and constitutionally stronger than the average, physically he could have done anything. And he had done nothing—nothing that others had not done as well or even better. It was sufficiently humiliating. And the outcome of his reflections had been a keen desire for work, hard absorbing work, with the hope that bodily fatigue might in some measure afford mental alleviation. It did not even need finding. With a certain shame he admitted the fact. It had waited for him any time these last ten years in his own home. The responsibility of great possessions was his. And he had shirked. He had evaded the duty he owed to a trust he had inherited. It was a new view of his position that recent thought had awakened. It was still not too late. He would go back like the prodigal—not to eat the fatted calf, but to sit at the feet of Peters and learn from him the secret of successful estate management.

For thirty years Peter Peters had ruled the Craven properties, and they were all his life. For the last ten years he had never ceased urging his employer to assume the reins of government himself. His entreaties, protestations and threats of resignation had been unheeded. Craven felt sure that he would never relinquish his post, he had grown into the soil and was as firmly fixed as the Towers itself. He was an institution in the county, a personality on the bench. He ruled his own domains with a kindly but absolute autocracy which succeeded perfectly on the Craven estates and was the envy of other agents, who had not his ability to do likewise. Well born, original and fearless he was popular in castle and in cottage, and his advice was respected by all. He neither sought nor abused a confidence, and in consequence was the depository of most of the secrets of the countryside. To his sympathetic ears came both grave offences and minor indiscretions, as to a kindly safety-valve who advised and helped—and was subsequently silent. His exoneration was considered final. "I confessed to Peter" became a recognised formula, instituted by a giddy young Marchioness at the north end of the county, whose cousin he was. And there, invariably, the matter ended. And for Craven it was the one bright spot in the darkness before him. Life was going to be hell—but there would always be Peter.

At the Convent gates the taxi skidded badly at the suddenly applied brakes, and then backed jerkily into position. Craven felt an overwhelming inclination to take to his heels. The portress who admitted him had evidently received orders, for she silently conducted him to a waiting room and left him alone. It was sparsely furnished but had on the walls some fine old rosewood panelling. The narrow heavily leaded windows overlooked a paved quadrangle, glistening with moisture. For a few moments the rain had ceased but drops still pattered sharply on to the flagstones from the branches of two large chestnut trees. The outlook was melancholy and he turned from the window, shivering. But the chill austere room was hardly more inspiring. The atmosphere was strange to him. It was a world apart from anything that had ever touched him. He marvelled suddenly at the countless lives living out their allotted span in the confined area of these and similar walls. Surely all could not submit willingly to such a crushing captivity? Some must agonize and spend their strength unavailingly, like birds beating their wings against the bars of a cage for freedom. To the man who had roamed through all the continents of the world this forced inactivity seemed appalling—stultifying. The hampering of personal freedom, the forcing of independent minds into one narrow prescribed channel that admitted of no individual expansion, the waste of material and the fettering of intellects, that were heaven-sent gifts to be put out to usury and not shrouded away in a napkin, revolted him. The conventual system was to him a survival of medievalism, a relic of the dark ages; the last refuge of the shirkers of the world. The communities themselves, if he had thought of them at all, had been regarded as a whole. He had never troubled to consider them as composed of single individuals. Today he thought of them as separate human beings and his intolerance increased. An indefinite distaste never seriously considered seemed, during the few moments in the bare waiting room, to have grown suddenly into active dislike. He was wholly out of sympathy with his surroundings, impatient of the necessity that brought him into contact with what he would have chosen to avoid. He looked about with eyes grown hard and contemptuous. The very building seemed to be the embodiment of retrogression and blind superstition. He was filled with antagonism. His face was grim and his figure drawn up stiffly to its full height when the door opened to admit the Mother Superior. For a moment she hesitated, a faint look of surprise coming into her face. And no antagonism, however intolerant, could have braved her gentle dignity. "It is—*Monsieur* Craven?" she asked, a perceptible interrogation in her soft voice.

She took the letters he gave her and read them carefully—pausing once or twice as if searching for the correct translation of a word—then handed them back to him in silence. She looked at him again, frankly, with no attempt to disguise her scrutiny, and the perplexity in her eyes grew greater. One small white hand slid to the crucifix hanging on her breast, as if seeking aid from the familiar symbol, and Craven saw that her fingers were trembling. A faint flush rose in her face.

"*Monsieur* is perhaps married, or—happily—he has a mother?" she asked at last, and the flush deepened as she looked up at the big man standing before her. She made a little gesture of embarrassment but her eyes did not waver. They would not, he thought with sudden intuition. For he realised that it was one of his own order who confronted him. It was not what he had anticipated. The Mother Superior's low voice continuing in gentle explanation broke into his thoughts.

"*Monsieur* will forgive that I catechise him thus but I had expected one—much older." Her distress was obvious. And Craven divined that as a prospective guardian he fell short of expectation. And yet, his lack of years was apparently to her the only drawback. His lack of years—Good God, and he felt so old! His youth was a disadvantage that counted for nothing in the present instance. If she could know the truth, if the anxious gaze that was fixed so intently on him could look into his heart with understanding, he knew that she would shrink from him as from a vile contamination.

He conceived the horror dawning in her eyes, the loathing in her attitude, and seemed to hear her passionate protest against his claim to the child who had been sheltered in the safety of the community that he had despised. The safety of the community—that had not before occurred to him. For the first time he considered it a refuge to those who there sought sanctuary and who were safeguarded from such as—

he. He winced, but did not spare himself. The sin had been only his. The child who had died for love of him had been as innocent of sin as the birds who loved and mated among the pine trees in her Garden of Enchantment. She had had no will but his. Arrogantly he had taken her and she had submitted—was he not her lord? Before his shadow fell across her path no blameless soul within these old convent walls had been more pure and stainless than the soul of O Hara San. It was the sins of such as he that drove women to this shelter that offered refuge and consolation, to escape from such as he they voluntarily immured themselves; surrendering the purpose of their being, seeking in bodily denial the salvation of their souls.

The room had grown very dark. A sudden glare of light made Craven realise that a question asked was still unanswered. He had not, in his abstraction, been aware of any movement. Now he saw the Mother Superior walking leisurely back from the electric switch by the door, and guessed from her placid face that the interval had been momentary and had passed unnoticed. Some answer was required now. He pulled himself together.

"I am not married," his voice was strained, "and I have no mother. But my aunt—Miss Craven—the sculptor—" he paused enquiringly and she smiled reassurance.

"Miss Craven's beautiful work is known to me," she said with ready tact that put him more at ease.

"My aunt has, most kindly, promised to—to co-operate," he finished lamely.

The anxiety faded from the Mother Superior's face and she sat down with an air of relief, motioning Craven to a chair. But with a curt bow he remained standing. He had no wish to prolong the interview beyond what courtesy and business demanded. He listened with a variety of feelings while the Nun spoke. Her earnestness he could not fail to perceive, but it required a decided effort to concentrate, and follow her soft well modulated voice.

She spoke slowly, with feeling that broke at times the tone she strove to make dispassionate.

"I am glad for Gillian's sake that at last, after all these years, there has come one who will be concerned with her future. She has no vocation for the conventual life and—I was beginning to become anxious. For ourselves, we shall miss her more than it is possible to say. She had been with us so long, she has become very dear to us. I have dreaded that her father would one day claim her. She has been spared that contamination—God forgive me that I should speak so." For a moment she was silent, her eyes bent on her hands lying loosely clasped in her lap.

"Gillian is not altogether friendless," she resumed, "she will go to you with a little more knowledge of the world than can be gained within these old walls." She glanced round the panelled room with half-sad affection. "She is popular and has spent vacations in the homes of some of her fellow pupils. She has a very decided personality, and a facility for attracting affection. She is sensitive and proud—passionate even at times. She can be led but not driven. I tell you all this, *Monsieur*, not censoriously but that it may help you in dealing with a character that is extraordinarily complex, with a nature that both demands and repels affection, that longs for and yet scorns sympathy." She looked at Craven anxiously. His complete attention was claimed at last. A new conception of his unknown ward was forcing itself upon him, so that any humour there might have been in the situation died suddenly and the difficulties of the undertaking soared. The Mother Superior smothered a sigh. His attitude was baffling, his expression inscrutable. Had her words touched him, had she said what was best for the welfare of the girl who was so dear to her, and whose departure she felt so keenly? How would she fare at this man's hands? What lay behind his stern face and sombre tragic eyes? Her lips moved in silent prayer, but when she spoke her voice was serene as before.

"There is yet another thing that I must speak of. Gillian has an unusual gift." A sentence in Locke's letter flashed into Craven's mind.

"She doesn't *dance*?" he asked, in some dismay.

"Dance, *Monsieur*—in a convent?" Then she pitied his hot confusion and smiled faintly.

"Is dancing so unusual—in the world? No, Gillian sketches—portraits. Her talent is real. She does not merely draw a faithful likeness, her studies are revelations of soul. I do not think she knows herself how her effects are obtained, they grow almost unconsciously, but they result always in the same strange delineation of character. It was so impossible to ignore this exceptional gift that we procured for her the best teacher in Paris, and continued her lessons even after—" She stopped abruptly and Craven finished the broken sentence.

"Even after the fees ceased," he said dryly. "For how many years has my ward lived on your charity, Reverend Mother?"

She raised a protesting hand.

"Ah—charity. It is hardly the word—" she fenced.

He took out a cheque book.

"How much is owing, for everything?" he said bluntly.

She sought for a book in a bureau standing against the rosewood panelling and, scanning it, gave a sum with evident reluctance.

"Gillian has never been told, but it is ten years since *Monsieur* Locke paid anything." There was diffidence in her voice. "In an institution of this kind we are compelled to be businesslike. It is rare that we can afford to make an exception, though the temptation is often great. The head and the heart—*voyez, vous, Monsieur*—they pull in contrary directions." And she slipped the book back into a pigeon-hole as if the touch of it was distasteful. She glanced perfunctorily at the cheque he handed to her, then closer, and the colour rose again to her sensitive face.

"But *Monsieur* has written treble the amount," she murmured.

"Will you accept the balance," he said hurriedly, "in the name of my ward, for any purpose that you may think fit? There is one stipulation only—I do not wish her to know that there has been any monetary transaction between us." His voice was almost curt, and the Nun found herself unable to question a condition which, though manifestly generous, she deemed quixotic. She could only bend to his decision with mingled thankfulness and apprehension. Despite the problem of the girl's future she had it in her heart to wish that this singular claimant had never presented himself. His liberality was obvious but—. She locked the slip of paper away in the bureau with a feeling of vague uneasiness. But for good or ill the matter was out of her hands. She had said all that she could say. The rest lay with God.

"I do accept it," she said, "with all gratitude. It will enable us to carry out a scheme that has long been our hope. Your generosity will more than pave the way. I will send Gillian to you now."

She left him, more embarrassed than he had been at first, more than ever dreading the task before him. He waited with a nervous impatience that irritated himself.

Turning to the window he looked out into the dusk. The old trees in the courtyard were almost indistinguishable. The rain dripped again steadily, splashing the creeper that framed the casement. A few lights showing dimly in the windows on the opposite side of the quadrangle served only to intensify the gloom. The time dragged. Fretfully he drummed with his fingers on the leaded panes, his ears alert for any sound beyond the closed door. The echo of a distant organ stole into the room and the soft solemn notes harmonised with the melancholy pattering of the raindrops and the gusts of wind that moaned fitfully around the house.

In a sudden revulsion of feeling the life he had mapped out for himself seemed horrible beyond thought. He could not bear it. It would be tying his hands and burdening himself with a responsibility that would curtail his freedom and hamper him beyond endurance. A great restlessness, a longing to escape from the irksome tie, came to him. Solitude and open spaces; unpeopled nature; wild desert wastes—he craved for them. The want was like a physical ache. The desert—he drew his breath in sharply—the hot shifting sand whispering under foot, the fierce noontide sun blazing out of a brilliant sky, the charm of it! The fascination of its false smiling surface, its treacherous beauty luring to hidden perils called to him imperatively. The curse of Ishmael that was his heritage was driving him as it had driven him many times before. He was in the grip of one of the revolts against restraint and civilisation that periodically attacked him. The wander-hunger was in his blood—for generations it had sent numberless ancestors into the lonely places of the world, and against it ties of home were powerless. In early days to the romantic glamour of the newly discovered Americas, later to the silence of the frozen seas and to the mysterious depth of unexplored lands the Cravens had paid a heavy toll. A Craven had penetrated into the tangled gloom of the Amazon forests, and had never returned. In the previous century two Cravens had succumbed to the fascination of the North West Passage, another had vanished in Central Asia. Barry's grandfather had perished in a dust storm in the Sahara. And it was to the North African desert that his own thoughts turned most longingly. Japan had satisfied him for a time—but only for a time. Western civilisation had there obtruded too glaringly, and he had admitted frankly to himself that it was not Japan but O Hara San that kept him in Yokohama. The dark courtyard and the faintly lighted windows faded. He saw instead a tiny well-remembered oasis in Southern Algeria, heard the ceaseless chatter of Arabs, the shrill squeal of a stallion, the peevish grunt of a camel, and, rising above all other sounds, the whine of the tackling above the well. And the smell—the cloying smell that goes with camel caravans, it was pungent! He flung up his head inhaling deeply, then realised that the scent that filled the room was not the acrid smell of the desert but the penetrating odour of incense filtering in through the opened door. It shut and he turned reluctantly.

He saw at first only a pair of great brown eyes, staring almost defiantly, set in a small pale face, that looked paler by contrast with the frame of dark brown hair. Then his gaze travelled slowly over the slender black-clad figure silhouetted against the polished panels. His fear was substantiated. Not a child who could be relegated to nurses and governesses, but a girl in the dawn of womanhood. Passionately he cursed John Locke.

He felt a fool, idiotically tongue-tied. He had been prepared to adopt a suitably paternal attitude towards the small child he had expected. A paternal attitude in connection with this self-possessed young woman was impossible, in fact ludicrous. For the moment he seemed unable to cope with the situation. It was the girl who spoke first. She came forward slowly, across the long narrow room.

"I am Gillian Locke, *Monsieur*."

IV

O n the cushioned window seat in her bedroom at Craven Towers Gillian Locke sat with her arms wrapped round her knees waiting for the summons to dinner. With Miss Craven and her guardian she had left London that morning, arriving at the Towers in the afternoon, and she was tired and excited with the events of the day. She leant back against the panelled embrasure, her mind dwelling on the last three crowded months they had spent in Paris and London waiting until the house was redecorated and ready to receive them. It had been for her a wonderful experience. The novelty, the strangeness of it, left her breathless with the feeling that years, not weeks, had rushed by. Already in the realisation of the new life the convent days seemed long ago, the convent itself to have receded into a far off past. And yet there were times when she wondered whether she was dreaming, whether waking would be inevitable and she would find herself once more in the old dormitory to pray passionately that she might dream again. And until tonight there had scarcely been time even to think, her days had been full, at night she had gone to bed to sleep in happy dreamlessness. The hotel bedrooms with their litter of trunks suggesting imminent flight had held no restfulness. To Gillian the transitory sensation had strained already over-excited nerves and heightened the dreamlike feeling that made everything seem unreal. But here, the visible evidences of travel removed, the deep silence of a large country house penetrating her mind and conducing to peace, she could think at last. The surroundings were helpful. There was about the room an air of permanence which the hotel bedrooms had never given, an atmosphere of abiding quiet that soothed her. She was sensitive of an influence that was wholly new to her and very sweet, that brought with it a feeling of laughter and tears strangely mingled, that made the room appear as no other room had ever done. It Was her room, and it had welcomed her. It was like a big friendly silent person offering mute reception, radiating repose. In a few hours the room had become intimate, dear to her. She laughed happily—then checked at a guilty feeling of treason against the grey old walls in Paris that had so long sheltered her. She was not ungrateful, all her life she would remember with gratitude the love and care she had received. But the convent had been prison. Since her father had left her there, a tiny child, she had inwardly rebelled; the life was abhorrent to her, the restraint unbearable. With childish pride she had hidden her feelings, living through a period of acute misery with no hint to those about her of what she suffered. And the habit of suppression acquired in childhood had grown with her own development. As the years passed the limitations of the convent became more perceptible. She felt its cramping influence to the full, as if the walls were closing in to suffocate her, to bury her alive before she had ever known a fuller freer life. She had longed for expansion—ideas she could not formulate, desires she could not express, crowded, jostled in her brain. She wanted a wider outlook on life than the narrow convent windows offered. Brief excursions into the world to the homes of her friends had filled her with a yearning for freedom and for independence, for a greater range of thought and action. Her artistic studies had served to foster an unrest she struggled against bravely and to conceal which she became daily more self-contained. Her reserve was like a barrier about her. She was sweet and gentle to all around her, but a little aloof and very silent. To the other girls she had been a heroine of romance, puzzling mystery surrounded her; to the Nuns an enigma. The Mother Superior, alone, had arrived at a partial understanding, more than that even she could not accomplish. Gillian loved her, but her reserve was stronger than her love. Sitting now in the dainty English bedroom, revelling in the warm beauty of the exquisite landscape that, mellowed in the evening light, lay spread out beneath her eyes, Gillian thought a little sadly of her parting with the Reverend Mother. She had tried to hide the happiness that the strange feeling of freedom gave her, to smother any look or word that might wound the gentle sensibility of the frail robed woman whose eyes were sad at the approaching separation. Her conscience smote her that her own heart held no sadness. She had said very little, nothing of the new life that lay ahead of her. She hid her hopes of the future as jealously as she had hidden her longings in the past, and she had left the convent as silently as she had lived in it. She had driven back to the hotel with a sense of relief predominating that it was all over, breathing deeply with a sigh of relaxed tension. It seemed to her then as if she had learned to breathe only within the last few days, as if the air itself was lighter, more exhilarating.

From the convent her mind went back to earlier days. She thought of her father, the handsome dissolute man, whose image had grown dim with years. As a tiny child she had loved him passionately, the central figure of her chequered and wandering little life—father and mother in one, playmate and hero. Her recollection seemed to be of constant travelling; of long hours spent in railway trains; of arrivals at strange places in the dark night; of departures in the early dawn, half awake—but always happy so long as the familiar arms held her weary little body and there was the shabby old coat on which to pillow her brown curls. A jumbled remembrance of towns and country villages; of kind unknown women who looked compassionate and murmured over her in a dozen different languages. It had all been a medley of impressions and experiences—everything transient, nothing lasting, but the big untidy man who was her all. And then the convent. For a few years John Locke had reappeared at irregular intervals, and on the memory of those brief visits she had lived until he came again. Then he had ceased to come and his letters, grown short and few, full of vague promises—unsatisfying—meagre, had stopped abruptly. At first she had refused to admit to herself that he had forgotten, that she could mean so little to him, that he would deliberately put her out of his life. She had waited, excusing, trusting, until, heart-sick with deferred hope, she had come to think of him as dead. She was old enough then to realise her position and in spite of the love and consideration surrounding her she had learned misery. Her popularity even was a source of torment, for in the happy homes of her friends she had felt more cruelly her own destitute loneliness.

When the lawyer's letter had come enclosing a few scrawled lines written by her dying father she had felt that life could hold no more bitterness. She had worshipped him—and he had abandoned her callously. She was bone of his bone and he had made no effort even for his own flesh. He had thrown her a burden on the convent that sheltered her so willingly only for want of will power to conquer the weakness that had devitalised brain and body. The thought crushed her. As she read his confession, full of tardy remorse, her proud heart had been sick with humiliation. She groped blindly through a sea of despair, her faith broken, her trust gone. She hid her sorrow and her shame, fulfilling her usual tasks, following the ordinary routine—a little more silent, a little more reserved—her eyes alone betraying the storm that was overwhelming her. She had loved him so dearly—that was the sting. She had guarded her memory of him so tenderly, weaving a thousand extravagant tales about him, pinnacling him above all men, her hero, her knight, her *preux chevalier*. And now she realised that her memory was no memory, that she had built up a fantastic figure of romance whose origin rested on nothing tangible, whose elevation had been so lofty that his overthrow was demolition. Her god had feet of clay. Her superman was nothing. All that she had ever had, memory that was delusion, was taken from her. Woken abruptly to the brutal truth she felt that she had nothing left to cling to—a loneliness far greater than she had known before. Then gradually her own honesty compelled her to admit her fantasy. The dream man she had evolved had been of her own making, the virtues with which she had endowed him bred of her own imagination. Of the real man she knew nothing, and for the real man there dawned slowly—though love for him had died—pity. It came to her, passionately endeavouring to understand, that in the sheltered life she led she had no knowledge of the temptations that beset a man outside in the great world. Dimly she realised that some win out—and some go under. He had failed. And it seemed to her that on her had fallen his debt. She must take the place he had forfeited in the universe, she must succeed where he had failed. Her strength must rise out of his weakness. His honour was hers to re-establish, given the opportunity. And the opportunity had been given. She had waited for the coming of her unknown guardian with a feeling of dull revolt against the degradation of being handed over inexorably to the disposal and charity of a stranger. Though she had not been told she had guessed, years ago, that money for her maintenance was wanting. The kindly deception of the Mother Superior had been ineffectual. Gillian knew she was a pauper. The charity of the convent school had been hard to bear. The charity of a stranger would be harder. She writhed with the humiliation of it. She was nineteen—for two years she must go and be and endure at the whim of an unknown. And what would he be like, this man into whose hands her father had thrust her! What choice would John Locke be capable of making—what love had he shown during these last years that he should choose carefully and well? From among what class of man, of the society into which he had sunk, would he select one to give his daughter? He had written of "my old friend, Barry Craven." The name conveyed nothing—the adjective admitted of two interpretations. Which? Day and night she was haunted with visions of old men—recollections of faces seen when driving with her friends or visiting their homes; old men who had interested her, old men from whom she had instinctively shrunk. What type of man was it that was coming for her? There were times when her courage deserted her and the constantly recurring question made her nearly mad with fear. She was like a wild creature caught in a trap, listening to the feet of the keeper nearing—nearing. She had longed for the time when she could leave the Convent, she clung to it now with dread at the thought of the future. The London lawyer had written that Mr. Craven was returning from Japan to assume his guardianship, and she had traced his route with growing fear as the days slipped by—the keeper's tread coming closer and closer. She had masked the terror the thought of him inspired, preserving an outward apathy that seemed to imply complete indifference. And in the end he had come sooner than she expected, for they thought he would go first to London. One morning she had learned he was in Paris, that very afternoon she would know her fate. The day had been interminable. During his interview with the Mother Superior she had paced the room where she was waiting as it seemed for hours, her nerves at breaking point. When the Reverend Mother came back she could have shrieked aloud and her desperate eyes failed to interpret the expression on the Nun's face; she tried to speak, a husky whisper that died away inarticulately. Faintly she heard the gentle words of encouragement and with an effort of pride she walked quickly to the door of the visitors' room. There she paused, irresolute, and the low peaceful roll of the organ echoing from the distant chapel seemed to mock her. So often it had comforted, giving courage to go forward— today its very peacefulness jarred; nerve-racked she was out of tune with the atmosphere of calm tranquillity about her. She felt alien— that more than ever she stood alone. Then pride flamed afresh. With head held high and lips compressed she went in. As he turned from the window it was his great height and broad shoulders that struck her first—men of his physique were rare in France—and, in the thought of a moment, the well cut conventional morning coat had seemed absurd, and mentally she had clothed his long limbs in damascened steel. Then she had seen that he was young, how young she could not guess, but younger far than she had imagined. As their eyes met the sombre tragedy in his had hurt her. She divined a sorrow before which her own paled to nothingness and quick pity killed fear. The sadness of his face lifted her suddenly into full realisation of her womanhood. Compassion rose above self. Instinctively she knew that the interview that was to her so momentous was to him only an embarrassing interlude. Shyness remained but the terror she had felt gave place to a feeling she had not then understood. As quickly as possible he had taken her to the hotel, leaving to his aunt all explanations that seemed necessary. And since then he had remained consistently in the background, delegating his authority to Miss Craven. But from the first his proximity had troubled her—she was always conscious of his presence. Hypersensitive from her convent upbringing she knew intuitively when he entered a room or left it. Men were to her an unknown quantity; the few she had met—brothers and cousins of school friends—had been viewed from a different standpoint. Hedged about with rigid French convention there had been no chance of acquaintance ripening into friendship— she had been merely a schoolgirl among other girls, touching only the fringe of the most youthful of the masculine element in the houses where she had stayed. She had been unprepared for the change to the daily contact with a man like Barry Craven. It would take time to accustom herself, to become used to the continual masculine presence.

Miss Craven, to her nephew's relief, had taken the shy pale-faced girl to her eccentric heart with a suddenness and enthusiasm that had surprised herself.

And Gillian's reserve and pride had been unable to withstand the whirlwind little lady. Miss Craven's personality took a strong hold on her; she loved the woman, she admired the artist, and she was quick to recognise the real feeling and deep kindness that lay under brusque manner and quizzical speeches. She had good reason. She glanced now round the big room. Everywhere were evidences of lavish generosity, showered on her regardless of protest. Gillian's eyes filled slowly with tears. It was all a fairy story, too wonderful almost to be true. Why were they so good to her—how would she ever be able to repay the kindness lavished on her? Her thoughts were interrupted by the latest gift that rose out of his basket with a sleepy yawn and stretching luxuriously came and laid his head on her knee, looking up at her with sad brown eyes. She had always loved animals, the possession of some dog had been an ardent desire, and she hugged the big black poodle now with a little sob.

"Mouston, you pampered person, have you ever been lonely? Can you imagine what it is like to be made to feel that you *belong* to somebody again?" She rubbed her cheek against his satiny head, crooning over him, the dog thrilling to her touch with jerking limbs and sharp half-stifled whines. It was her first experience of ownership, of responsibility for a living creature that was dependent on her and for which she was answerable. And it was likely to prove an arduous responsibility. He was single-minded and jealous in his allegiance; Miss Craven he tolerated indifferently, of Craven he was openly suspicious. He followed Gillian like a shadow and moped in her absence, yielding to Yoshio, who had charge of him on such occasions, a resigned obedience he gave to no other member of the household. Through Mouston Gillian and Yoshio had become acquainted.

Mouston's affection this evening became over-enthusiastic and threatening to fragile silks and laces. Gillian kissed the top of his head, shook solemnly an insistent paw, and put him on one side. She moved to the dressing table and inspected herself critically in the big mirror. She looked with grave amusement. Was that Gillian Locke? She wondered did a butterfly feel more incongruous when it shed its dull grub skin. For so many years she had worn the sombre garb of the convent schoolgirl, the change was still new enough to delight and the natural woman within her responded to the fascination of pretty clothing. The dark draperies of the convent had palled, she had craved colour with an almost starved longing.

The general reflection in the long glass satisfied, a more detailed personal survey raised serious doubts. She had never recognised the grace of her slender figure, the uncommon beauty of her pale oval face—other types had appealed more, other colouring attracted. She had studied her face often, disapprovingly. Once or twice, lacking a model, she had essayed to reproduce her own features. She had failed utterly. The faithful portraiture she achieved for others was wanting. She was unable to express in her own likeness the almost startling exposition of character that distinguished her ordinary work. She had been her own limitation. Her failure had puzzled her, causing a searching mental inquiry. She had no knowledge herself of how her special gift took form, the work grew involuntarily under her hand. She was aware of no definite impression received, no attempt at soul analysis. Vaguely she supposed that in some subtle mysterious way the character of her sitter communicated itself, influencing her; in fact her best work had often had the least care bestowed upon it. Did her inability to transfer to canvas a living copy of her own face argue that she herself was without character—had she failed because there was in truth nothing to delineate? Or was it because she sought to see something unreal—sought to control a purely inherent impulse? It was a problem she had never solved.

She looked now at the mirrored figure with her usual disapproval, great brown eyes scowling back at her from the glass, then made a little obliterating movement with her hand and shook her head. Appearance had never mattered before, but now she wanted so much to please—to be a credit to the interest shown, to repay the time and money spent upon her. Her eyes grew wistful as she leant nearer to see if there were any tell-tale traces of tears, then danced with sudden amusement as she picked up a powder puff and dabbed tentatively.

"Oh, Gillian Locke, what would the Reverend Mother say!" she murmured, and laughed.

The poodle, jealous for attention, leaped on to a chair beside her, his paws on the plate glass slab scattering brushes and bottles, and still laughing she smothered his damp eager nose with powder until he sneezed disgusted protest.

With a conciliatory caress she left him to disarrange the dressing table further, and went back to the window. Beneath her lawns extended to a wide terrace, stone balustraded, from the centre of which a long flight of steps led down to a formal rose garden sheltered by a high yew hedge and backed by a little copse beyond which the heavily timbered park stretched indefinitely in the evening light. The sense of space fascinated her. She had always longed for unimpeded views, for the stillness of the country. On the smooth shaven lawns great trees were set like sentinels about the house; fancifully she thought of them as living vigilant keepers maintaining for centuries a perpetual guard—and smiled at her childish imagination. Her pleasure in the prospect deepened. Already the charm of the Towers had taken hold of her, from the first moment she had loved it. Throughout the long railway journey and during the five mile drive from the station, she had anticipated, and the actuality had outstripped her anticipation. The beauty of the park, the herds of grazing deer, had delighted her; the old grey house itself had stayed her spellbound. She had not imagined anything half so lovely, so impressively enduring. She had seen nothing to compare with its fine proportions, with the luxury of its setting. It differed utterly from the French Chateaux where she had visited; there toil obtruded, vineyards and rich fields of crops clustered close to the very walls of the seigneur's dwellings, a source of wealth simply displayed; here similar activities were banished to unseen regions, and scrupulously kept avenues, close cut lawns and immaculate flower-beds formed evidence of constant labour whose results charmed the eye but were materially profitless. The formal grandeur appealed to her. She was not altogether alien, she reflected, with a curious smile—

despite his subsequent downfall John Locke had sprung from just such stock as the owner of this wonderful house. A sudden panic of lateness interrupted her pleasure and she turned from the window, calling to the dog. Her suite opened on to a circular gallery—from which bedrooms opened—running round the central portion of the house and overlooking the big square hall which was lit from above by a lofty glazed dome; eastward and westward stretched long rambling wings, a story higher than the main block, crowned with the turrets that gave the house its name.

A low murmur of men's voices came from below, and leaning over the balustrade she saw Craven and his agent standing talking before the empty fireplace. Sudden shyness overcame her; her guardian was still formidable, Peters she had seen for the first time only a few hours ago when he had met them at the station—a short broad-shouldered man inclining to stoutness, with thick grey hair and close-pointed beard. To go down deliberately to them seemed impossible. But while she hesitated in an agony of self-consciousness Mouston precipitated the inevitable by dashing on ahead down, the stairs and plunging into the bearskin hearthrug, ploughing the thick fur with his muzzle and sneezing wildly. The sense of responsibility outweighed shyness and she hurried after him, but Peters anticipated her and already had the dog's unwilling head firmly between his hands.

"What on earth has he got on his nose, Miss Locke?" he asked, in a tone of wonder, but the keen blue eyes looking at her from under bushy grey eyebrows were twinkling and her shyness was not proof against his friendliness.

She dropped to her knees and flicked the offended organ with a scrap of lace and lawn.

"Powder," she said gravely.

"You can have no idea," she added, looking up suddenly, "how delightful it is to powder your nose when you have been brought up in a convent. The Nuns consider it the height of depravity," and she laughed, a ringing girlish outburst of amusement that Craven had never yet heard. He looked at her as she knelt on the rug soothing the poodle's outraged feelings and smiling at Peters who was offering his own more adequate handkerchief. That laugh was a revelation—in spite of her self-possession, of her reserve, she was in reality only a girl, hardly more than a child, but influenced by her quiet gravity he had forgotten the fact.

As he watched her a slight frown gathered on his face. It seemed that Peters, in a few hours, had penetrated the barrier outside which he, after months, still remained. With him she was always shyly silent. On the few rare occasions in Paris and in London when he had found himself alone with her she had shrunk into herself and avoided addressing him; and he had wondered, irritably, how much was natural diffidence and how much due to convent training. But he had made no effort at further understanding, for the past was always present dominating inclinations and impulses—perpetual memory, jogging at his elbow. There were days when the only relief was physical exhaustion and he disappeared for hours to fight his devils in solitude. And in any case he was not wanted, it was better in every way for him to efface himself. There was nothing for him to do—thanks to the improvidence of John Locke no business connected with the trust. Miss Craven had taken complete possession of Gillian and he held aloof, not attempting to establish more intimate relations with his ward. But tonight, with a fine inconsistency, it piqued him that she should respond so readily to Peters. He knew he was a fool—it mattered not one particle to him— Peters' magnetism was proverbial—but, illogically, the frown persisted.

As if conscious of his scrutiny Gillian turned and met his searching gaze. The colour flooded her face and she pushed the dog aside and rose hastily to her feet. Shyness supervened again and she was thankful for the arrival of Miss Craven, who was breathless and apologetic.

"Late as usual! I shall be late when the last trump sounds. But this time it was really not my fault. Mrs. Appleyard descended upon me!— our old housekeeper, Gillian—and her tongue has wagged for a solid hour by the clock. I am now *au fait* with everything that has happened at the Towers since I was here last—do your ears burn, Peter?— metaphorically she has dragged me at her heels from garrets to cellars and back to the garrets again. She is pathetically pleased to have the house open once more."

Still talking she led the way to the dining room. It was an immense room, panelled like most of the house, the table an oasis on a desert of Persian carpet, a huge fireplace predominating, and some of the more valuable family portraits on the walls.

As Miss Craven entered she looked instinctively for the portrait of her brother, which since his death had hung—following a family custom—in a panel over the high carved mantelpiece. But it had been removed and for it had been substituted a beautiful painting of

Barry's mother. She stopped abruptly in the middle of a sentence. "An innovation?" she murmured to her nephew, with her shrewd eyes on his face.

"A reparation," he answered shortly, as he moved to his chair. And his tone made any further comment impossible. She sat down thoughtfully and began her soup in silence, vaguely disturbed at the departure from a precedent that had held for generations. Unconventional and ultra-modern as she was she still clung to the traditions of her family, and from time immemorial the portrait of the last reigning Craven had hung over the fireplace in the big dining room waiting to give place to its successor. It all seemed bound up somehow with the terrible change that had taken place in him since his return from Japan—a change she was beginning more and more to connect with the man whose portrait had been banished, as though unworthy, from its prominence. Unworthy indeed—but how did Barry know? What had he learned in the country that had had such a fatal attraction for his father? The old shameful story she had thought buried for ever seemed rising like a horrible phantom from the grave where it had lain so long hidden.

With a little shudder she turned resolutely from the painful thoughts that came crowding in upon her and entered into animated conversation with Peters.

Gillian, content to be unnoticed, looked about her with appreciative interest; the big room, its sombre, rather formal furniture and fine pictures, appealed to her. The arrangements were in perfect harmony, nothing clashed or jarred, electric lighting was carefully hidden and only wax candles burnt in heavy silver candlesticks on the table.

The fascination of the old house was growing every moment more insistent, like a spell laid on her. She gave herself up to it, to the odd happiness it inspired. She felt it curiously familiar. A strange feeling came to her—it was as if from childhood she had been journeying and now come home. An absurd thought, but she loved it. She had never had a home, but for the next two years she could pretend. To pretend was easy. All her life she had lived in a land of dreams, tenanted with shadowy inhabitants of her own imagining—puppets who moved obedient to her will through all the devious paths of make-believe; a spirit world where she ranged free of the narrow walls that restricted her liberty. It had been easy to pretend in the convent—how much easier here in the solid embodiment of a dream castle and stimulated by the real human affection for which her heart had starved. The love she had hitherto known had been unsatisfying, too impersonal, too restrained, too interwoven with mystical devotion. Mass Craven's affection was of a hardier, more practical nature. Blunt candour and sincerity personified, she did not attempt to disguise her attachment. She had been attracted, had approved, and had finally co-opted Gillian into the family. She had, moreover, great faith in her own judgment. And to justify that faith Gillian would have gone through fire and water.

She looked gratefully at the solid little figure sitting at the foot of the table and a gleam of amusement chased the seriousness from her eyes. Miss Craven was in the throes of a heated discussion with Peters which involved elaborate diagrams traced on the smooth cloth with a salt spoon, and as Gillian watched she completed her design with a fine flourish and leant back triumphant in her chair, rumpling her hair fantastically. But the agent, unconvinced, fell upon her mercilessly and in a moment she was bent forward again in vigorous protest, drumming impatiently on the table with her fingers as he laughingly altered her drawing. They were the best of friends and wrangled continually. To Gillian it was all so fresh, so novel. Then her attention veered. Throughout dinner Craven had been silent. When once started on a discussion his aunt and Peters tore the controversy amicably to tatters in complete absorption. He had not joined in the argument. As always Gillian was too shy to address him of her own accord, but she was acutely conscious of his nearness. She deprecated her own attitude, yet silence was better than the banal platitudes which were all she had to offer. Her range was so restricted, his—who had travelled the world over—must be so great. With the exception of one subject her knowledge was negligible. But he too was an artist—hopeless to attempt that topic, she concluded with swift contempt for her own limitations; to offer the opinions of a convent-bred amateur to one who had studied in famous Paris ateliers and was acquainted with the art of many countries would be an impertinence. But yet she knew that sometime she must break through the wall that her own diffidence had built up; in the intimacy of country house life the continuance of such an attitude would be both impossible and ridiculous. Contritely she acknowledged that the tension between them was largely her own fault, a disability due to training. But she could not go through life sheltering behind that wholly inadequate plea. If there was anything in her at all she must rise above the conventions in which she had been reared; she had done with the narrowness of the past, now she must think broadly, expansively, in all things—even in the trivial matter of social intercourse. A saving sense of humour sent a laugh bubbling into her throat which nearly escaped. It was such a little thing, but she had magnified it so greatly. What, after all, did it amount to—the awkwardness of a schoolgirl very properly ignored by a guardian who could not be other than bored with her society. *Tant pis!* She could at least try to be polite. She turned with the heroic intention of breaking the ice and plunging into conversation, banal though it might be. But her eyes did not arrive at his face, they were caught and held by his hand, lying on the white cloth, turning and twisting an empty wineglass between long strong fingers. Hands fascinated her. They were indicative of character, testimonies of individual peculiarities. She was sensitive to the impression they conveyed. With the limited material available she had studied them—nuns' hands, priests' hands, hands of the various inmates of the houses where she had stayed, and the hands of the man who had taught her. From him she had learned more than the mere rudiments of her art; under his tuition a crude interest had developed into a definite study, and as she sat looking at Barry Craven's hand a sentence from one of his lectures recurred to her—"there are in some hands, particularly in the case of men, characteristics denoting certain passions and attributes that jump to the eye as forcibly as if they were expressions of face."

Engaged in present study she forgot her original purpose, noting the salient points of a fresh type, enumerating details that formed the composite whole. A strong hand that could in its strength be merciless—could it equally in its strength be merciful? The strange thought came unexpectedly as she watched the thin stem of the wineglass turning rapidly and then more slowly until, with a little tinkle, it snapped as the hand clenched suddenly, the knuckles showing white through the tanned skin. Gillian drew a quick breath. Had she been the cause of the mishap—had she stared noticeably, and he been angry at an impertinence? Her cheeks burned and in a misery of shyness she forced her eyes to his face. Her contrition was needless. Heedless of her he was looking at the splintered glass between his fingers with a faint expression of surprise, as if his wandering thoughts were but half recalled by the accident. For a moment he stared at the shattered pieces—then laid them down indifferently.

Gillian smothered an hysterical inclination to laugh. He was so totally negligent of her presence that even this little incident had failed to make him sensible of her scrutiny. Immersed in his thoughts he was very obviously miles away from Craven Towers and the vicinity of a troublesome ward. And suddenly it hurt. She was nothing to him but a shy *gauche* girl whose very existence was an embarrassment. The determination so bravely formed died before his cold detachment. More than ever was speech impossible.

She shrugged faintly with a little pout. So, confident of his preoccupation, she continued to study him. Had the homecoming intensified the sadness of his eyes and deepened the lines about his mouth?—were memories of the mother he had adored sharpening tonight the look of suffering on his face? Or was her imagination, over-excited, exaggerating what she saw and fancying a great sorrow where there was only boredom? She pondered, and had almost concluded that the latter was the saner explanation when—watching—she saw a sudden spasm cross his face of such agony that she caught her lip fiercely between her teeth to stifle an exclamation. In the fleeting expression of a moment she had seen the revelation of a soul in torment. She looked away hastily, feeling dismayed at having trespassed. She had discovered a secret wound. She sat tense, and a quick fear came lest the others might have also seen. She glanced at them furtively. But the argument was still unsettled, the tablecloth between them scored and creased with conflicting sketches. She drew a sharp little sigh of relief. Only she had noticed, and she did not matter. For a few moments her thoughts ran riot until she pulled them up frowningly. It was no business of hers—she had no right even to speculate on his affairs. Angry with herself she turned for distraction to the portraits on the walls—they at least would offer no disturbing problem. But her determination to keep her thoughts from her guardian met with a check at the outset for she found herself staring at Barry Craven as she had visualised him in that first moment of meeting—steel-clad. It was the picture of a young man, dressed in the style of the Elizabethan period, wearing a light inlaid cuirass and leaning negligently against a stone balustrade, a hooded falcon on his wrist. The resemblance to the owner of Craven Towers was remarkable—the same build, the same haughty carriage of the head, the same features and colouring; the mouth only of the painted gallant differed, for the lips were not set sternly but curved in a singularly winning smile. The portrait had recently been cleaned and the colours stood out freshly. The pose of the figure was curiously unrestrained for the period, a suggestion of energy—barely concealed by the indolent attitude—broke through the conventional treatment of the time, as if the painter had responded to an influence that had overcome tradition. The whole body seemed to pulsate with life. Gillian looked at it entranced; instinctively her eyes sought the pictured hands. The one that held the falcon was covered with an embroidered leather glove, but the other was bare, holding a set of jesses. And even the hands were similar, the characteristics faithfully transmitted. Peters' voice startled her. "You are looking at the first Barry Craven, Miss Locke. It is a wonderful picture. The resemblance is extraordinary, is it not?"

She looked up and met the agent's magnetic smile across the table.

"It is—extraordinary," she said slowly; "it might be a costume portrait of Mr. Craven, except that in treatment the picture is so different from a modern painting."

Peters laughed.

"The professional eye, Miss Locke! But I am glad that you admit the likeness. I should have quarrelled horribly with you if you had failed to see it. The young man in the picture," he went on, warming to the subject as he saw the girl's interest, "was one of the most romantic personages of his time. He lived in the reign of Elizabeth and was poet, sculptor, and musician—there are two volumes of his verse in the library and the marble Hermes in the hall is his work. When he was seventeen he left the Towers to go to court. He seems to have been universally beloved, judging from various letters that have come down to us. He was a close friend of Sir Philip Sidney and one of Spenser's numerous patrons. A special favourite with Elizabeth—in fact her partiality seems to have been a source of some embarrassment, according to entries in his private journal. She knighted him for no particular reason that has ever transpired, indeed it seems to have been a matter of surprise to himself, for he records it in his journal thus:

"'—dubbed knight this day by Gloriana. God He knoweth why, but not I.' He was an idealist and visionary, with the power of putting his thoughts into words—his love poems are the most beautiful I have ever read, but they are quite impersonal. There is no evidence that his love was ever given to any 'faire ladye.' No woman's name was ever connected with his, and from his detached attitude towards the tender passion he earned, in a fantastical court, the euphuistic appellation of *L'amant d' Amour.* Quite suddenly, after ten years in the queen's household, he fitted out an expedition to America. He gave no reason. Distaste for the artificial existence prevailing at Court, sorrow at the death of his friend Sidney, or a wander-hunger fed on the tales brought home by the numerous merchant adventurers may have been the cause of this surprising step. His decision provoked dismay among his friends and brought a furious tirade from Elizabeth who commanded him to remain near her. But in spite of royal oaths and entreaties—more of the former than the latter—he sailed to Virginia on a land expedition. Two letters came from him during the next few years, but after that—silence. His fate is not known. He was the first of many Cravens to vanish into oblivion searching for new lands." The pleasant voice hesitated and dropped to a lower, more serious note. And Gillian was puzzled at the sudden anxiety that clouded the agent's smiling blue eyes. She had listened with eager interest. It was history brought close and made alive in its intimate connection with the house. The dream castle was more wonderful even than she had thought. She smiled her thanks at Peters, and drew a long breath.

"I like that," and looking at the picture again, "the Lover of Love!" she repeated softly; "it's a very beautiful idea."

"A very unsatisfactory one for any poor soul who may have been fool enough to lose her heart to him." Miss Craven's voice was caustic.

"I have often wondered if any demoiselle 'pined in a green and yellow melancholy for his sake,' she added, rising from the table.

"Reason enough, if he knew of it, for going to Virginia," said Craven, with a hard laugh. "The family traditions have never tended to undue consideration of the weaker sex."

"Barry, you are horrible!"

"Possibly, my dear aunt, but correct," he replied coolly, crossing the room to open the door. "Even Peter, who has the family history at his fingers' ends, cannot deny it." His voice was provocative but Peters, beyond a mildly sarcastic "—thank you for the 'even,' Barry—" refused to be drawn.

Her nephew's words would formerly have aroused a storm of indignant protest from Miss Craven, touched in a tender spot. But now some intuition warned her to silence. She put her arm through Gillian's and left the room without attempting to expostulate.

In the drawing room she sat down to a patience table, lit a cigarette, rumpled her hair, and laid out the cards frowningly. More than ever was she convinced that in the two years he had been away some serious disaster had occurred. His whole character appeared to have undergone a change. He was totally different. The old Barry had been neither hard nor cynical, the new Barry was both. In the last few weeks she had

had ample opportunity for judging. She perceived that a heavy shadow lay upon him darkening his home-coming—she had pictured it so very differently, and she sighed over the futility of anticipation. His happiness meant to her so much that she raged at her inability to help him. Until he spoke she could do nothing. And she knew that he would never speak. The nightly occupation lost its usual zest, so she shuffled the cards absently and began a fresh game.

Gillian was on the hearthrug, Houston's head in her lap. She leant against Miss Craven's chair, dreaming as she had dreamt in the old convent until the sudden lifting of the dog's head under her hands made her aware of Peters standing beside her. He looked down silently on the card table for a few moments, pointed with a nicotine-stained finger to a move Miss Craven had missed and then wandered across the room and sat down at the piano. For a while his hands moved silently over the keys, then he began to play, and his playing was exquisite. Gillian sat and marvelled. Peters and music had seemed widely apart. He had appeared so essentially a sportsman; in spite of the literary tendency that his sympathetic account of the Elizabethan Barry Craven had suggested she had associated him with rougher, more physical pursuits. He was obviously an out-door man; a gun seemed a more natural complement to his hands than the sensitive keys of a piano, his thick rather clumsy fingers manifestly incompatible with the delicate touch that was filling the room with wonderful harmony. It was a check to her cherished theory which she acknowledged reluctantly. But she forgot to theorise in the sheer joy of listening.

"Why did he not make music a career?" she whispered, under cover of some crashing chords. Miss Craven smiled at her eager face.

"Can you see Peter kow-towing to concert directors, and grimacing at an audience?" she replied, rescuing a king from her rubbish heap.

With an answering smile Gillian subsided into her former position. Music moved her deeply and her highly strung artistic temperament was responding to the beauty of Peters' playing. It was a Russian folk song, plaintive and simple, with a curious minor refrain like the sigh of an aching heart—wild sad harmony with pain in it that gripped the throat. Swayed by the sorrow-haunted music a wave of foreboding came over her, a strange indefinite fear that was formless but that weighed on her like a crushing burden. The happiness of the last few weeks seemed suddenly swamped in the recollection of the misery rampant in the world. Who, if their inmost hearts were known, were truly happy? And her thoughts, becoming more personal, flitted back over the desolate days of her own sad girlhood and then drifted to the tragedy of her father. Then, with a forward leap that brought her suddenly to the present, she thought of the sorrow she had seen on Craven's face in that breathless moment at dinner time. Was there only sadness in the world? The brooding brown eyes grew misty. A passionate prayer welled up in her heart that complete happiness might touch her once, if only for a moment.

Then the music changed and with it the girl's mood. She gave her head a little backward jerk and blinked the moisture from her eyes angrily. What was the matter with her? Surely she was the most ungrateful girl in the universe. If there was sorrow in the world for her then it must be of her own making. She had been shown almost unbelievable kindness, nothing had been omitted to make her happy. The contrast of her life only a few weeks ago and now was immeasurable. What more did she want? Was she so selfish that she could even think of the unhappiness that was over? Shame filled her, and she raised her eyes to the woman beside her with a sudden rush of gratitude and love. But Miss Craven, interested at last in her game, was blind to her surroundings, and with a little smile Gillian turned her attention to the silent occupant of the chair near her. Craven had come into the room a few minutes before. He was leaning back listlessly, one hand shading his face, a neglected cigarette dangling from the other. She looked at him long and earnestly, wondering, as she always wondered, what association there had been between him and such a man as her father—what had induced him to take upon himself the burden that had been laid upon him. And her cheeks grew hot again at the thought of the encumbrance she was to him. It was preposterous that he should be so saddled!

She stifled a sigh and her eyes grew dreamy as she fell to thinking of the future that lay before her. And as she planned with eager confidence her hand moved soothingly over the dog's head in measure to the languorous waltz that Peters was playing.

After a sudden unexpected chord the player rose from the piano and joined the circle at the other end of the room. Miss Craven was shuffling vigorously. "Thank you, Peter," she said, with a smiling nod, "it's like old times to hear you play again. Gillian thinks you have missed your vocation, she would like to see you at the Queen's Hall."

Peters laughed at the girl's blushing protest and sat down near the card table. Miss Craven paused in a deal to light a fresh cigarette.

"What's the news in the county?" she asked, adding for Gillian's benefit: "He's a walking chronicle, my dear."

Peters laughed. "Nothing startling, dear lady. We have been a singularly well-behaved community of late. Old Lacy of Holmwood is dead, Bill Lacy reigns in his stead and is busy cutting down oaks to pay for youthful indiscretions—none of 'em very fierce when all's said and done. The Hamer-Banisters have gone under at last—more's the pity—and Hamer is let to some wealthy Australians who are possessed apparently of unlimited cash, a most curious phraseology, and an assurance which is beautiful to behold. They had good introductions and Alex has taken them up enthusiastically—there are kindred tastes."

"Horses, I presume. How are the Horringfords?"

"Much as usual," replied Peters. "Horringford is absorbed in things Egyptian, and Alex is on the warpath again," he added darkly.

Miss Craven grinned.

"What is it this time?"

Peters' eyebrows twitched quaintly.

"Socialism!" he chuckled, "a brand new, highly original conception of that very elastic term. I asked Alex to explain the principles of this particular organization and she was very voluble and rather cryptic. It appears to embrace the rights of man, the elevation of the masses, the relations between landlord and tenant, the psychological deterioration of the idle rich—"

"Alex and psychology—good heavens!" interposed Miss Craven, her hands at her hair, "and the amelioration of the downtrodden poor," continued Peters. "It doesn't sound very original, but I'm told that the propaganda is novel in the extreme. Alex is hard at work among their own people," he concluded, leaning back in his chair with a laugh.

"But—the downtrodden poor! I thought Horringford was a model landlord and his estates an example to the kingdom."

"Precisely. That's the humour of it. But a little detail like that wouldn't deter Alex. It will be an interest for the summer, she's always rather at a loose end when there's no hunting. She had taken up this socialistic business very thoroughly, organizing meetings and lectures. A completely new scheme for the upbringing of children seems to be a special sideline of the campaign. I'm rather vague there—I know I made Alex very angry by telling her that it reminded me of intensive market gardening. That Alex has no children of her own presents no difficulty to her—she is full of the most beautiful theories. But theories don't seem to go down very well with the village women. She was routed the other day by the mother of a family who told her bluntly to her face she didn't know what she was talking about—which was doubtless perfectly true. But the manner of telling seems to have been disagreeable and Alex was very annoyed and complained to Thomson, the new agent. He, poor chap, was between the devil and the deep sea, for the tenants had also been complaining that they were being interfered with. So he had to go to Horringford and there was a royal row. The upshot of it was that Alex rang me up on the 'phone this morning to tell me that Horringford was behaving like a bear, that he was so wrapped up in his musty mummies that he hadn't a spark of philanthropy in him, and that she was coming over to lunch tomorrow to tell me all about it—she's delighted to hear that the house is open again, and will come on to you for tea, when you will doubtless get a second edition of her woes. Half-an-hour later Horringford rang me up to say that Alex had been particularly tiresome over some new crank which had set everybody by the ears, that Thomson was sending in a resignation daily, altogether there was the deuce to pay, and would I use my influence and talk sense to her. It appears he is working at high pressure to finish a monograph on one of the Pharaohs and was considerably ruffled at being interrupted."

"If he cared a little less for the Pharaohs and a little more for Alex—" suggested Miss Craven, blowing smoke rings thoughtfully. Peters shook his head.

"He did care—that's the pity of it," he said slowly, "but what can you expect?—you know how it was. Alex was a child married when she should have been in the schoolroom, without a voice in the matter. Horringford was nearly twenty years her senior, always reserved and absorbed in his Egyptian researches. Alex hadn't an idea in the world outside the stables. Horringford bored her infinitely, and with Alex-like honesty she did not hesitate to tell him so. They hadn't a thought in common. She couldn't see the sterling worth of the man, so they drifted apart and Horringford retired more than ever into his shell."

"And what do you propose to do, Peter?" Craven's sudden question was startling, for he had not appeared to be listening to the conversation.

Peters lit a cigarette and smoked for a few moments before answering. "I shall listen to all Alex has to say," he said at last, "then I shall tell her a few things I think she ought to know, and I shall persuade her to ask Horringford to take her with him to Egypt next winter."

E.M. HULL

"Why?"

"Because Horringford in Egypt and Horringford in England are two very different people. I know—because I have seen. It's an idea, it may work. Anyhow it's worth trying."

"But suppose her ladyship does not succumb to your persuasive tongue?"

"She will—before I've done with her," replied Peters grimly, and then he laughed. "I guessed from what she said this morning that she was a little frightened at the hornet's nest she had raised. I imagine she won't be sorry to run away for a while and let things settle down. She can ease off gently in the meantime and give Egypt as an excuse for finally withdrawing."

"You think Alex is more to blame than Horringford?" said Miss Craven, with a note of challenge in her voice.

Peters shrugged. "I blame them both. But above all I blame the system that has been responsible for the trouble."

"You mean that Alex should have been allowed to choose her own husband? She was such a child—"

"And Horringford was such a devil of a good match," interposed Craven cynically, moving from his chair to the padded fireguard. Gillian was sitting on the arm of Miss Craven's chair, sorting the patience cards into a leather case. She looked up quickly. "I thought that in England all girls choose their own husbands, that they marry to please themselves, I mean," she said in a puzzled voice.

"Theoretically they do, my dear," replied Miss Craven, "in practice numbers do not. The generality of girls settle their own futures and choose their own husbands. But there are still many old-fashioned people who arrogate to themselves the right of settling their daughters' lives, who have so trained them that resistance to family wishes becomes almost an impossibility. A good suitor presents himself, parental pressure is brought to bear—and the deed is done. Witness the case of Alex. In a few years she probably would have chosen for herself, wisely. As it was, marriage had never entered her head."

"She couldn't have chosen a better man," said Peters warmly, "if he had only been content to wait a year or two—"

"Alex would probably have eloped with a groom or a circus rider before she reached years of discretion!" laughed Miss Craven. "But it's a difficult question, the problem of husband choosing," she went on thoughtfully. "Being a bachelor I can discuss it with perfect equanimity.

But if in a moment of madness I had married and acquired a houseful of daughters, I should have nervous prostration every time a strange man showed his nose inside the door."

"You don't set us on a very high plane, dear lady," said Peters reproachfully.

"My good soul, I set you on no plane at all—know too much about you!" she smiled. Peters laughed. "What's your opinion, Barry?"

Since his one interruption Craven had been silent, as if the discussion had ceased to interest him. He did not answer Peters' question for some time and when at last he spoke his voice was curiously strained. "I don't think my opinion counts for very much, but it seems to me that the woman takes a big risk either way. A man never knows what kind of a blackguard he may prove in circumstances that may arise."

An awkward pause followed. Miss Craven kept her eyes fixed on the card table with a feeling of nervous apprehension that was new to her. Her nephew's words and the bitterness of his tone seemed fraught with hidden meaning, and she racked her brains to find a topic that would lessen the tension that seemed to have fallen on the room. But Peters broke the silence before it became noticeable. "The one person present whom it most nearly concerns has not given us her view. What do you say, Miss Locke?"

Gillian flushed faintly. It was still difficult to join in a general conversation, to remember that she might at any moment be called upon to put forward ideas of her own.

"I am afraid I am prejudiced. I was brought up in a convent—in France," she said hesitatingly. "Then you hold with the French custom of arranged marriages?" suggested Peters. Her dark eyes looked seriously into his. "I think it is—safer," she said slowly.

"And consequently, happier?" The colour deepened in her face. "Oh, I don't know. I do not understand English ways. I can speak only of France. We talked of it in the convent—naturally, since it was forbidden, *que voulez vous?*" she smiled. "Some of my friends were married. Their parents arranged the marriages. It seems that—" she stammered and went on hurriedly—"that there is much to be considered in choosing a husband, much that—girls do not understand, that only older people know. So it is perhaps better that they should arrange a matter which is so serious and so—so lasting. They must know more than we do," she added quietly.

"And are your friends happy?" asked Miss Craven bluntly.

"They are content."

Miss Craven snorted. "Content!" she said scornfully. "Marriage should bring more than contentment. It's a meagre basis on which to found a life partnership."

A shadow flitted across the girl's face.

"I had a friend who married for love," she said slowly. "She belonged to the old noblesse, and her family wished her to make a great marriage. But she loved an artist and married him in spite of all opposition. For six months she was the happiest girl in France—then she found out that her husband was unfaithful. Does it shock you that I speak of it—we all knew in the convent. She went to Capri soon afterwards, to a villa her father had given her, and one morning she went out to swim—it was a daily habit, she could do anything in the water. But that morning she swam out to sea—and she did not come back." The low voice sank almost to a whisper. Miss Craven looked up incredulously. "Do you mean she deliberately drowned herself?" Gillian made a little gesture of evasion. "She was very unhappy," she said softly. And in the silence that followed her troubled gaze turned almost unconsciously to her guardian. He had risen and was standing with his hands in his pockets staring straight in front of him, rigidly still. His attitude suggested complete detachment from those about him, as if his spirit was ranging far afield leaving the big frame empty, impenetrable as a figure of stone. She was sensitive to his lack of interest. She regretted having expressed opinions that she feared were immature and valueless. A quick sigh escaped her, and Miss Craven, misunderstanding, patted her shoulder gently. "It's a very sad little story, my dear."

"And one that serves to confirm your opinion that a girl does well to accept the husband who is chosen for her, Miss Locke?" asked Peters abruptly, as he glanced at his watch and rose to his feet.

Gillian joined in the general move.

"I think it is—safer," she said, as she had said before, and stooped to rouse the sleeping poodle.

V

Miss Craven was sitting alone in the library at the Towers. She had been reading, but the book had failed to hold her attention and lay unheeded on her lap while she was plunged in a profound reverie.

She sat very still, her usually serene face clouded, and once or twice a heavy sigh escaped her.

The short November day was drawing in and though still early afternoon it was already growing dark. The declining light was more noticeable in the library than elsewhere in the house—a sombre room once the morning sun had passed; long and narrow and panelled in oak to a height of about twelve feet, above which ran a gallery reached by a hammered iron stairway, it housed a collection of calf and vellum bound books which clothed the walls from the floor of the gallery to within a few feet of the lofty ceiling. On the fourth side of the room, whither the gallery did not extend, three tall narrow windows overlooked the drive. The furniture was scanty and severely Jacobean, having for more than two hundred years remained practically intact; a ponderous writing table, a couple of long low cabinets, and half a dozen cavernous armchairs recushioned to suit modern requirements of ease. Some fine old bronzes stood against the panelled walls. There was about the room a settled peacefulness. The old furniture had a stately air of permanence. The polished panels, and, above, the orderly ranks of ancient books suggested durability; they remained—while generations of men came and passed, transient figures reflected in the shining oak, handling for a few brief years the printed treasures that would still be read centuries after they had returned to their dust.

The spirit of the house seemed embodied in this big silent room that was spacious and yet intimate, formal and yet friendly.

It was Miss Craven's favourite retreat. The atmosphere was sympathetic. Here she seemed more particularly in touch with the subtle influence of family that seemed to pervade the whole house. In most of the rooms it was perceptible, but in the library it was forceful.

The house and the family—they were bound up inseparably.

For hundreds of years, in an unbroken line, from father to son. . . from father to son. . . Miss Craven sat bolt upright to the sound of an unmistakable sob. She looked with amazement at two tears blistering the page of the open book on her knee. She had not knowingly cried since childhood. It was a good thing that she was alone she thought, with a startled glance round the empty room. She would have to keep a firmer hold over herself than that. She laughed a little shakily, choked, blew her nose vigorously, and walked to the middle window. Outside was stark November. The wind swept round the house in fierce gusts before which the big bare-branched trees in the park swayed and bowed, and trains of late fallen leaves caught in a whirlwind eddied skyward to scatter widely down again.

Rain lashed the window panes. Yet even when storm-tossed the scene had its own peculiar charm. At all seasons it was lovely.

Miss Craven looked at the massive trees, beautiful in their clean nakedness, and wondered how often she would see them bud again. Frowning, she smothered a rising sigh and pressing closer to the window peered out more attentively. Eastward and westward stretched long avenues that curved and receded soon from sight. The gravelled space before the house was wide; from it two shorter avenues encircling a large oval paddock led to the stables, built at some distance facing the house, but hidden by a belt of firs.

For some time Miss Craven watched, but only a game-keeper passed, a drenched setter at his heels, and with a little shiver she turned back to the room. She moved about restlessly, lifting books to lay them down immediately, ransacking the cabinets for prints that at a second glance failed to interest, and examining the bronzes that she had known from childhood with lengthy intentness as if she saw them now for the first time.

A footman came and silently replenished the fire. Her thoughts, interrupted, swung into a new channel. She sat down at the writing table and drawing toward her a sheet of paper slowly wrote the date. Beyond that she did not get. The ink dried on the pen as she stared at the blank sheet, unable to express as she wished the letter she had intended to write.

She laid the silver holder down at last with a hopeless gesture and her eyes turned to a bronze figure that served as a paper weight. It was a piece of her own work and she handled it lovingly with a curiously sad smile until a second hard sob broke from her and pushing it away she covered her face with her hands.

"Not for myself, God knows it's not for myself," she whispered, as if in extenuation. And mastering herself with an effort she made a second attempt to write but at the end of half a dozen words rose impatiently, crumpled the paper in her hand and walking to the fireplace threw it among the blazing logs.

She watched it curl and discolour, the writing blackly distinct, and crumble into ashes. Then from force of habit she searched for a cigarette in a box on the mantelpiece, but as she lit it a sudden thought arrested her and after a moment's hesitation the cigarette followed the half—written letter into the fire.

With an impatient shrug she went back to an arm chair and again tried to read, but though her eyes mechanically followed the words on the printed page she did not notice what she was reading and laying the book down she gave up all further endeavour to distract her wandering thoughts. They were not pleasant and when, a little later, the door opened she turned her head expectantly with a sigh of relief. Peters came in briskly.

"I've come to inquire," he said laughing, "the family pew held me in solitary state this morning. Time was when I never minded, but this last year has spoiled me. I was booked for lunch but I came as soon as I could. Nobody ill, I hope?"

Miss Craven looked at him for a moment before answering as he stood with his back to the fire, his hands clasped behind him, his face ruddy with the wind and rain, his keen blue eyes on hers, reliable, unchanging. It was a curious chance that had brought him—just at that moment. The temptation to make an unusual confidence rose strongly. She had known him and trusted him for more years than she cared to remember. How much to say? Indecision held her.

"You are always thoughtful, Peter," she temporised. "I am afraid there is no excuse," with a little smile; "Barry rode off somewhere quite early this morning and Gillian went yesterday to the Horringfords. I expect her back to-day in time for tea. For myself, I had gout or rheumatism or the black dog on my back, I forget which! Anyhow, I stayed at home." She laughed and pointed to the cigarettes. He took one, tapping it on his thumbnail.

"You were alone. Why didn't you 'phone? I should have been glad to escape the Australians. They are enormously kind, but somewhat—er—overwhelming," he added with a quick laugh.

"My dear man, be thankful I never thought of it. I've been like a bear with a sore head all day." She looked past him into the fire, and struck by a new note in her voice he refrained from comment, smoking slowly and luxuriating in the warmth after a cold wet drive in an open motor.

E.M. HULL

He never used a closed car. But some words she had used struck him. "Barry is riding—?" with a glance at the storm raging outside.

"Yes. He had breakfast at an unearthly hour and went off early. Weather seems to make no difference to him, but he will be soaked to the skin."

"He's tough," replied Peters shortly. "I thought he must be out. As I came in just now Yoshio was hanging about the hall, watching the drive. Waiting for him, I suppose," he added, flicking a curl of ash into the fire. "He's a treasure of a valet," he supplemented conversationally. But Miss Craven let the observation pass. She was still staring into the leaping flames, drumming with her fingers on the arms of the chair. Once she tried to speak but no words came. Peters waited. He felt unaccountably but definitely that she wished him to wait, that what was evidently on her mind would come with no prompting from him. He felt in her attitude a tension that was unusual—to-day she was totally unlike herself. Once or twice only in the course of a lifelong friendship she had shown him her serious side. She had turned to him for help then—he seemed presciently aware that she was turning to him for help now. He prided himself that he knew her as well as she knew herself and he understood the effort it would cost her to speak. That he guessed the cause of her trouble was no short cut to getting that trouble uttered. She would take her own time, he could not go half-way to meet her. He must stand by and wait. When had he ever done anything else at Craven Towers? His eyes glistened curiously in the firelight, and he rammed his hands down into his jacket pockets with abrupt jerkiness. Suddenly Miss Craven broke the silence.

"Peter—I'm horribly worried about Barry," the words came with a rush. He understood her too well to cavil.

"Dear lady, so am I," he replied with a promptness that did not console.

"Peter, what is it?" she went on breathlessly. "Barry is utterly changed. You see it as well as I. I don't understand—I'm all at sea—I want your help. I couldn't discuss him with anybody else, but you—you are one of us, you've always been one of us. Fair weather or foul, you've stood by us. What we should have done without you God only knows. You care for Barry, he's as dear to you as he is to me, can't you do something? The suffering in his face—the tragedy in his eyes—I wake up in the night seeing them! Peter, can't you *do* something?" She was beside him, clutching at the mantel-shelf, shaking with emotion. The sight of her unnerved, almost incoherent, shocked him. He realised the depth of the impression that had been made upon her—deep indeed to produce such a result. But what she asked was impossible. He made a little negative gesture and shook his head.

"Dear lady, I can't do anything. And I wonder whether you know how it hurts to have to say so? No son could be dearer to me than Barry—for the sake of his mother—" his voice faltered momentarily, "but the fact remains—he is not my son. I am only his agent. There are certain things I cannot do and say, no matter how great the wish," he added with a twisted smile.

Miss Craven seemed scarcely to be listening. "It happened in Japan," she asserted in fierce low tones. "Japan! Japan!" she continued vehemently, "how much more sorrow is that country to bring to our family! It happened in Japan and whatever it was—Yoshio knows! You spoke of him just now. You said he was hanging about—waiting—watching. Peter, he's doing it all the time! He watches continually. Barry never has to send for him—he's always there, waiting to be called. When Barry goes out the man is restless until he comes in again—haunting the hall—it gets on my nerves. Yet there is nothing I can actually complain of. He doesn't intrude, he is as noiseless as a cat and vanishes if he sees you, but you know that just out of sight he's still there—waiting—listening. Peter, what is he waiting for? I don't think that it is apparent to the rest of the household, I didn't notice it myself at first. But a few months ago something happened and since then I don't seem able to get away from it. It was in the night, about two o'clock; I was wakeful and couldn't sleep. I thought if I read I might read myself sleepy. I hadn't a book in my room that pleased me and I remembered a half-finished novel I had left in the library. I didn't take a light—I know every turn in the Towers blindfold. As you know, to reach the staircase from my room I have to pass Barry's door, and at Barry's door I fell over something in the darkness—something with hands of steel that saved me from an awkward tumble and hurried me down the passage and into the moonlit gallery before I could find a word of expostulation. Yoshio of course. I was naturally startled and angry in consequence. I demanded an explanation and after a great deal of hesitation he muttered something about Barry wanting him—which is ridiculous on the face of it. If Barry had really wanted him he would have been inside the room, not crouched outside on the door mat. He seemed very upset and kept begging me to say nothing about it. I don't remember how he put it but he certainly conveyed the impression that it would not be good for Barry to know. I don't understand it—Barry trusts him implicitly—and yet this. . . I'm afraid, and I've never been afraid in my life before." The little break in her voice hurt him. He felt curiously unable to cope with the situation. Her story disturbed him more than he cared to let her see in her present condition of unwonted agitation. Twice in the past they had stood shoulder to shoulder through a crisis of sufficient magnitude and she had showed then a cautious judgment, a reliability of purpose that had been purely masculine in its strength and sanity. She had been wholly matter-of-fact and unimaginative, unswayed by petty trivialities and broad in her decision. She had displayed a levelness of mind which had almost excluded feeling and which had enabled him to deal with her as with another man, confident of her understanding and the unlikelihood of her succumbing unexpectedly to ordinary womanly weaknesses. He had thought that he knew her thoroughly, that no circumstance that might arise could alter characteristics so set and inherent. But to-day her present emotion which had come perilously near hysteria, showed her in a new light that made her almost a stranger. He was a little bewildered with the discovery. It was incredible after all these years, just as if an edifice that he had thought strongly built of stone had tumbled about his ears like a pack of cards. He could hardly grasp it. He felt that there was something behind it all—something more than she admitted. He was tempted to ask definitely but second reflection brought the conviction that it would be a mistake, that it would be taking an unfair advantage. Sufficient unto the day—his present concern was to help her regain a normal mental poise. And to do that he must ignore half of what her suggestions seemed to imply. He felt her breakdown acutely, he must say nothing that would add to her distress of mind. It was better to appear obtuse than to concur too heartily in fears, a recollection of which in a saner moment he knew would be distasteful to her. She would never forgive herself—the less she had to forget the better. She trusted him or she would never have spoken at all. That he knew and he was honoured by her confidence. They had always been friends, but in her weakness he felt nearer to her than ever before. She was waiting for him to speak. He chose the line that seemed the least open to argument. He spoke at last, evenly, unwilling alike to seem incredulous or overanxious, his big steady hand closing warmly over her twitching fingers.

"I don't think there is any cause—any reason to doubt Yoshio's fidelity. The man is devoted to Barry. His behaviour certainly sounds—curious, but can be attributed I am convinced to over-zealousness. He is an alien in a strange land, cut off from his own natural distractions and amusements, and with time on his hands his devotion to his master takes a more noticeable form than is usual with an ordinary English man-servant. That he designs any harm I cannot believe. He has been with Barry a long time—on the several occasions when he stayed with him at your house in London did you notice anything in his behaviour then similar to the attitude you have observed recently? No? Then I take it that it is due to the same anxiety that we ourselves have felt since Barry's return. Only in Yoshio's case it is probably based on definite knowledge, whereas ours is pure conjecture. Barry has undoubtedly been up against something—momentous. Between ourselves we can admit the fact frankly. It is a different man who has come back to us—and we can only carry on and notice nothing. He is trying to forget something. He has worked like a nigger since he came home, slogging away down at the estate office as if he had his bread to earn. He does the work of two men—and he hates it. I see him sometimes, forgetful of his surroundings, staring out of the window, and the look on his face brings a confounded lump into my throat. Thank God he's young—perhaps in time—" he shrugged and broke off inconclusively, conscious of the futility of platitudes. And they were all he had to offer. There was no suggestion he could make, nothing he could do. It was repetition of history, again he had to stand by and watch suffering he was powerless to aid, powerless to relieve. The mother first and now the son—it would seem almost as if he had failed both. The sense of helplessness was bitter and his face was drawn with pain as he stared dumbly at the window against which the storm was beating with renewed violence. The sight of the angry elements brought almost a feeling of relief; it would be something that he could contend with and overcome, something that would go towards mitigating the galling sense of impotence that chafed him. He felt the room suddenly stifling, he wanted the cold sting of the rain against his face, the roar of the wind in the trees above his head. Abruptly he buttoned his jacket in preparation for departure. Miss Craven pulled herself together. She laid a detaining hand on his arm. "Peter," she said slowly, "do you think that Barry's trouble has any connection with—my brother? The change of pictures in the dining-room—it was so strange.

He said it was a reparation. Do you think Barry—found out something in Japan?"

Peter shook his head. "God knows," he said gruffly. For a moment there was silence, then with a sigh Miss Craven moved towards a bell.

"You'll stay for tea?"

"Thanks, no. I've got a man coming over, I'll have to go. Give my love to Gillian and tell her I shall not, forgive her soon for deserting me this morning. Has she lost that nasty cough yet?"

"Almost. I didn't want her to go to the Horringfords, but she promised to be careful." Miss Craven paused, then:

"What did we do without Gillian, Peter?" she said with an odd little laugh.

"'You've got me guessing,' as Atherton says. She's a witch, bless her!" he replied, holding out his hands. Miss Craven took them and held them for a moment.

"You're the best pal I ever had, Peter," she said unsteadily, "and you've given all your life to us Cravens."

The sudden gripping of his hands was painful, then he bent his head and unexpectedly put his lips to the fingers he held so closely.

"I'm always here—when you want me," he said huskily, and was gone.

Miss Craven stood still looking after him with a curious smile.

"Thank God for Peter," she said fervently, and went back to her station by the window. It was considerably darker than before, but for some distance the double avenue leading to the stables was visible. As she watched, playing absently with the blind-cord, her mind dwelt on the long connection between Peter Peters and her family. Thirty years—the best of his life. And in exchange sorrow and an undying memory. The woman he loved had chosen not him but handsome inconsequent Barry Craven and, for her choice, had reaped misery and loneliness. And because he had known that inevitably a day would come when she would need assistance and support he had sunk his own feelings and retained his post. Her brief happiness had been hard to watch—the subsequent long years of her desertion a protracted torture. He had raged at his own helplessness. And ignorant of his love and the motive that kept him at Craven Towers she had come to lean on him and refer all to him. But for his care the Craven properties would have been ruined, and the Craven interests neglected beyond repair.

For some time before her sister-in-law's death Miss Craven had known, as only a woman can know, but now for the first time she had heard from his lips a half-confession of the love that he had guarded jealously for thirty years.

The unusual tears that to-day seemed so curiously near the surface rose despite her and she blinked the moisture from her eyes with a feeling of irritated shame.

Then a figure, almost indistinguishable in the gloom, coming from the stables, caught her eye and she gave a sharp sigh of relief.

He was walking slowly, his hands deep in his pockets, his shoulders hunched against the storm of wind and rain that beat on his broad back. His movements suggested intense weariness, yet nearing the house his step lagged even more as if, despite physical fatigue and the inclement weather, he was rather forcing himself to return than showing a natural desire for shelter.

There was in his tread a heaviness that contrasted forcibly with the elasticity that had formerly been characteristic. As he passed close by the window where Miss Craven was standing she saw that he was splashed from head to foot. She thought with sudden compassion of the horse that he had ridden. She had been in the stables only a few weeks before when he had handed over another jaded mud-caked brute trembling in every limb and showing signs of merciless riding to the old head groom who had maintained a stony silence as was his duty but whose grim face was eloquent of all he might not say. It was so unlike Barry to be inconsiderate, toward animals he had been always peculiarly tender-hearted.

She hurried out to the hall, almost cannoning with a little dark-clad figure who gave way with a deep Oriental reverence. "Master very wet," he murmured, and vanished.

"There's some sense in him," she muttered grudgingly. And quite suddenly a wholly unexpected sympathy dawned for the inscrutable Japanese whom she had hitherto disliked. But she had no time to dwell on her unaccountable change of feeling for through the glass of the inner door she saw Craven in the vestibule struggling stiffly to rid himself of a dripping mackintosh. It had been no protection for the driving rain had penetrated freely, and as he fumbled at the buttons with slow cold fingers the water ran off him in little trickling streams on to the mat.

She had no wish to convey the impression that she had been waiting for him. She met him as if by accident, hailing him with surprise that rang genuine.

"Hallo, Barry, just in time for tea! I know you don't usually indulge, but you can do an act of grace on this one occasion by cheering my solitude. Peter looked in for ten minutes but had to hurry away for an engagement, and Gillian is not yet back."

His face was haggard but he smiled in reply, "All right. In the library? Then in five minutes—I'm a little wet."

In an incredibly short time he joined her, changed and immaculate. She looked up from the tea urn she was manipulating, her eyes resting on him with the pleasure his physical appearance always gave her. "You've been quick!"

"Yoshio," he replied laconically, handing her buttered toast.

He ate little himself but drank two cups of tea, smoking the while innumerable cigarettes. Miss Craven chatted easily until the tea table was taken away and Craven had withdrawn to his usual position on the hearthrug, lounging against the mantelshelf.

Then she fell silent, looking at him furtively from time to time, her hands restless in her lap, nerving herself to speak. What she had to say was even more difficult to formulate than her confidence to Peters. But it had to be spoken and she might never find a more favourable moment. She took her courage in both hands.

"I want to speak to you of Gillian," she said hesitatingly.

He looked up sharply. "What of Gillian?" The question was abrupt, an accent almost of suspicion in his voice and she moved uneasily.

"Bless the boy, don't jump down my throat," she parried, with a nervous little laugh; "nothing of Gillian but what is sweet and good and dear. . . and yet that's not all the truth—it's more than that. I find it hard to say. It's something serious, Barry, about Gillian's future," she paused, hoping that he would volunteer some remark that would make her task easier. But he volunteered nothing and, stealing a glance at him she saw on his face an expression of peculiar stoniness to which she had lately become accustomed. The new taciturnity, which she still found so strange, seemed to have fallen on him suddenly. She stifled a sigh and hurried on:

"I wonder if the matter of Gillian's future has ever occurred to you? It has been in my mind often and lately I have had to give it more serious attention. Time has run away so quickly. It is incredible that nearly two years have passed since she became your ward. She will be twenty-one in March—of age, and her own mistress. The question is—what is she to do?"

"Do? There is no question of her *doing* anything," he replied shortly. "You mean that her coming of age will make no difference—that things will go on as they are?" Miss Craven eyed him curiously.

"Yes. Why not?"

"You know less of Gillian than I thought you did." The old caustic tone was sharp in her voice.

He looked surprised. "Isn't she happy here?"

"Happy!" Miss Craven laughed oddly. "It's a little word to mean so much. Yes, she is happy—happy as the day is long—but that won't keep her. She loves the Towers, she is adored on the estate, she has a corner in that great heart of hers for all who live here—but still that won't keep her. In her way of thinking she has a debt to pay, and all these months, studying, working, hoping, she has been striving to that end. She is determined to make her own way in the world, to repay what has been expended on her—"

"That's dam' nonsense," he interrupted hotly.

"It's not nonsense from Gillian's point of view," Miss Craven answered quickly, "it's just common honesty. We have argued the matter, she and I, scores of times. I have told her repeatedly that in view of your guardianship you stand *in loco parentis* and, therefore, as long as she is your ward her maintenance and artistic education are merely her just due, that there can be no question of repayment. She does not see it in that light. Personally—though I would not for the world have her know it—I understand and sympathize with her entirely. Her independence, her pride, are out of all proportion to her strength. I cannot condemn, I can only admire—though I take good care to hide my admiration. . . and if you could persuade her to let the past rest, there is still the question of her future."

"That I can provide for."

Miss Craven shook her head.

"That you can not provide for," she said gravely.

The flat contradiction stirred him. He jerked upright from his former lounging attitude and stood erect, scowling down at her from his great height. "Why not?" he demanded haughtily.

Miss Craven shrugged. "What would you propose to do?" He caught the challenge in her tone and for a moment was disconcerted. "There would be ways—" he said, rather vaguely. "Something could be arranged—"

"You would offer her—charity?" suggested Miss Craven, wilfully dense.

"Charity be damned."

"Charity generally is damnable to those who have to suffer it. No, Barry, that won't do."

He jingled the keys in his pocket and the scowl on his face deepened.

"I could settle something on her, something that would be adequate, and it could be represented that some old investment of her father's had turned up trumps unexpectedly."

But Miss Craven shook her head again. "Clever, Barry, but not clever enough. Gillian is no fool. She knows her father had no money, that he existed on a pittance doled out to him by exasperated relatives which ceased with his death. He told her plainly in his last letter that there was nothing in the world for her—except your charity. Think of what Gillian is, Barry, and think what she must have suffered—waiting for your coming from Japan, and, to a less extent, in the dependence of these last years."

He moved uncomfortably, as if he resented the plainness of his aunt's words, and having found a cigarette lit it slowly. Then he walked to the window, which was still unshuttered, and looked out into the darkness, his back turned uncompromisingly to the room. His inattentive attitude seemed almost to suggest that the matter was not of vital interest to him.

Miss Craven's face grew graver and she waited long before she spoke again. "There is also another reason why I have strenuously opposed Gillian's desire to make her own way in the world, a reason of which she is ignorant. She is not physically strong enough to attempt to earn her own living, to endure the hard work, the privations it would entail. You remember how bronchitis pulled her down last year; I am anxious about her this winter. She is constitutionally delicate, she may grow out of it—or she may not. Heaven knows what seeds of mischief she has inherited from such parents as hers. She needs the greatest care, everything in the way of comfort—she is not fitted for a rough and tumble life. And, Barry, I can't tell her. It would break her heart."

Her eyes were fixed on him intently and she waited with eager breathlessness for him to speak. But when at length he answered his words brought a look of swift disappointment and she relaxed in her chair with an air of weary despondency. He replied without moving.

"Can't you arrange something, Aunt Caro? You are very fond of Gillian, you would miss her society terribly; cannot you persuade her that she is necessary to you—that it would be possible for her to work and still remain with you? I know that some day you will want to go back to your own house in London, to take up your own interests again, and to travel. I can't expect you to take pity much longer on a lonely bachelor. You have given up much to help me—it cannot go on for ever. For what you have done I can never thank you, it is beyond thanks, but I must not trade on your generosity. If you put it to Gillian that you, personally, do not want to part with her—that she is dear to you—it's true, isn't it?" he added with sudden eagerness. And in surprise at her silence he swung on his heel and faced her. She was leaning back in the big armchair in a listless manner that was not usual to her.

"I am afraid you cannot count on me, Barry," she said slowly. He stared in sheer amazement.

"What do you mean, Aunt Caro?—you do care for her, don't you?"

"Care for her?" echoed Miss Craven, with a laugh that was curiously like a sob, "yes, I do care for her. I care so much that I am going to venture a great deal—for her sake. But I cannot propose that she should live permanently with me because all future permanencies have been taken out of my hands. I hate talking about myself, but you had to know some day, this only accelerates it. I have not been feeling myself for some time—a little while ago I went to London for definite information. The man had the grace to be honest with me—he bade me put my house in order." Her tone left no possibility of misunderstanding. He was across the room in a couple of hasty strides, on his knees beside her, his hands clasped over hers.

"Aunt Caro!" The genuine and deep concern in his voice almost broke her self-control. She turned her head, catching her lip between her teeth, then with a little shrug she recovered herself and smiled at him.

"Dear boy, it must come some day—it has come a little sooner than I expected, that is all. I'm not grumbling, I've had a wonderful life—I've been able to do something with it. I have not sat altogether idle in the market-place."

"But are you sure? Doctors are not infallible."

"Quite sure," she answered steadily; "the man I went to was very kind, very thorough. He insisted I should have other opinions. There was a council of big-wigs and they all arrived at the same conclusion, which was at least consoling. A diversity of opinion would have torn my nerves to tatters. I couldn't tell you before, it would have worried me. I hate a fuss. I don't want it mentioned again. You know—and there's an end of it." She squeezed his hands tightly for a moment, then got up abruptly and went to the fireplace.

"I have only one regret—Gillian," she said as he followed her. "You see now that it is impossible for me to make a definite home for her, even supposing that she were to agree to such a proposal. They gave me two or three years at the longest—it might be any time."

Craven stood beside her miserable and tongue-tied. Her news affected him deeply, he was stunned with the suddenness of it and amazed at the courage she displayed. She might almost have been discoursing on the probable death of a stranger. And yet, he reflected, it was only in keeping with her general character. She had been fearless all through life, and for her death held no terrors.

He tried to speak but words failed him. And presently she spoke again, hurriedly, disjointedly.

"I am helpless. I can do nothing for Gillian. I could have left her money in my will, despite her pride she would have had to accept it. I can't even do that. At my death all I have, as you know, goes back into the estate. I have never saved anything—there never seemed any reason. And what I made with my work I gave away. There is only you—only one way—Barry, won't you—Barry!" She was crying undisguisedly, unconscious even of the unaccustomed tears. "You know what I mean—you must know," she whispered entreatingly, struggling with emotion.

He was standing rigid, to her strained fancy he seemed almost to have stopped breathing and there was in his attitude something that frightened her. It came to her suddenly that, after all, he was to all intents and purposes a stranger to her. Even the intimacy of these last months, living in close contiguity to him in his own house had not broken down the barrier that his sojourn in Japan had raised. She understood him no better than on the day of his arrival in Paris. He had been uniformly thoughtful and affectionate but had never reverted to the old Barry whom she had known so well. He had, as it were, retired within himself. He lived his life apart, with them but not of them, daily carrying through the arduous work he set himself with a dogged determination in which there was no pleasure. Yet, beyond a certain gravity, to the casual observer there was in him no great change. He entertained frequently and was a popular host, interesting and appearing interested. Only Miss Craven and Peters, more intimate, saw the effort that he made. To Miss Craven it seemed sometimes as if he were deliberately living through a self-appointed period— she had found herself wondering what cataclysm would end it. She was conscious of the impression, which she tried vainly to dismiss as absurd, of living over an active volcano. What would be the result of the upheaval when it came? She had prayed earnestly for some counter-distraction that might become powerful enough to surmount the tragic memory with which he lived—a memory she was convinced and the tragedy was present in his face. She had cherished a hope, born in the early days of their return to Craven Towers and maintained in the face of seeming improbability of fulfilment, that had grown to be an ardent desire. In the realization of that hope she thought she saw his salvation. With the knowledge of her own precarious hold on life she clung even more closely to what had become the strongest wish she had ever known. She had never deluded herself into imagining the consummation of her wish imminent, she had frankly acknowledged to herself that his inscrutability was impenetrable, and now hope seemed almost extinguished. She realized it with a feeling of helplessness. And yet she had a curious impulse, an inner conviction that urged with a peremptoriness that over-rode subterfuge. She would speak plainly, be the consequences what they were. It was for the ultimate happiness of the two beings whom she loved best on earth—for that surely she might venture something. She had never been afraid of plain speaking, it would be strange if she let convention deter her now. Convention! it had wrecked many a life—so had interference, she thought with sudden racking indecision. What if by interference she hindered now, rather than helped? What if speech did more mischief than silence? Irresolutely she wavered, and to her indecision there came suddenly the further disturbing thought—if Barry acceded to her earnest wish what ground had she for pre-supposing that it would result in his happiness? She had no definite knowledge, no positive assurance wherewith to press her request. The inmost feelings of both were hidden from her. Her meddling might only bring more sorrow to him who seemed already weighed down under a crushing burden of grief. Gratitude and an intense admiration she knew existed. But between admiration and any deeper feeling there was a wide gulf. And yet what might not be hidden behind the grave seriousness of those great dark eyes that looked with apparently equal frankness at every member of the household? Months spent in the proximity of an unusually handsome man, the romance of the tie between them—it was an experience that any woman, least of all an unsophisticated convent-bred girl, could hardly pass through unscathed. It was surely enough to gamble on, she reflected with grim humour that did not amuse. It was a great hazzard, the highest stakes she had ever played for who had never been afraid of losing. The thought spurred her. If it was to be the last throw then let there be no hesitation. A reputation for courage and coolness had gone with her through life.

She turned to him abruptly, all indecision gone, complete mistress of herself again.

"Barry, don't you understand?" she said with slow distinctness. "I want you to ask Gillian to marry you."

He started as if she had stabbed him.

"Good God," he cried violently, "you don't know what you are saying!" And from his tortured face she averted her eyes hastily, sick at heart. But she held her ground, aware that retreat was not now possible.

She answered gently, steadying her voice with difficulty.

"Is it so extraordinary that I should wish it, should hope for it? I care for you both so deeply. To know that your mother's place would be filled by one who is worthy to follow her—how worthy only I, who have been admitted to her high ideals, appreciate; to know that there would be the happiness of home ties here for you, to know that I leave Gillian safe in your hands—it would make my going very easy, Barry."

His head was down on his arms on the mantelshelf, his face hidden from her. "Gillian—safe—in my hands—*my God*!" he groaned, and shuddered like a man in mortal agony.

All the deep love she had for him, all the fears she entertained for him leaped up in her with sudden strength, forcing utterance and breaking down the reticence she had imposed upon herself. She caught his arm.

"Barry, what is it—for heaven's sake speak! Do you think I have been blind all these months, that I have seen nothing? Can't you tell me—anything?" her voice, quivering with emotion, was strange to him, strange enough to recall him to himself. He straightened slowly and drew away from her with a little shiver. "There is nothing I can tell you," he replied dully, "nothing that I can explain, only this—I went through hell in Japan. I don't want any sympathy—it was my own fault, my own doing. . . Just now I made a fool of myself, I was off my guard, your words startled me. Forget it, you can do me no good by remembering."

He made an abrupt movement as if to leave the room but Miss Craven stood squarely in front of him, her chin raised stubbornly. She knew now that she was face to face with something even more terrible than she had imagined. He had avoided a definite answer. By all reasoning she should have accepted his rebuff but intuition, stronger than reason, impelled her. If he went now it would be the end. She knew that positively. The question could never be opened up again. She could not let it pass without a final effort. It was inconceivable that this shadow could always lie across his life. Whatever tragical event had occurred belonged to the past—surely the future might hold some alleviation, some happiness that might compensate for the sorrow that had lined his face and brought the silver threads that gleamed in his thick dark hair. Surely in the care for another life memory might be dulled and there might dawn for him a new hope, a new peace. Despite his broken suggestive words her trust in him was still maintained; she had no fear for Gillian—with him her future would be assured. And there seemed no other alternative. Her confidence in herself furthermore was not shaken, she had a deep unalterable conviction that the wish for the union she so desired was based upon something deeper than mere fancy. It was not anything that she could put into words or even into concrete thought, but the belief was strong. It was a vivid assurance that went beyond reasoning, that made it possible for her to speak again.

"Are you going to let the past dominate the rest of your life," she asked slowly, "is the future to count for nothing? There are, in all probability, many years ahead of you—cannot you, in them, obliterate what has gone before?"

He turned from her with a hopeless gesture and a muttered word she could not catch. But he did not go as she feared he would. He lingered in the room, staring into the heart of the glowing fire and Miss Craven played her last card.

"And—Gillian?" she said firmly, all the Craven obstinacy in her voice, and waited long for his answer. When it came it was flat, monotonous.

"I cannot marry her. I cannot marry—anybody."

"Are you married already?" The question escaped before she could bite it back. With a quickening heartbeat she awaited an outburst, a retort that would end everything. But he answered quietly, in the same toneless voice: "No, I am not married."

She caught at the loop-hole it seemed to offer. "If there is no bar—" she began eagerly, but he cut her short. "I have done with all that sort of thing," he said harshly.

"Why?" she persisted, with a doggedness that matched his own. "If you have known sorrow, does that necessarily mean that you can never again know happiness? Must you for a—a memory, turn your

E.M. HULL

back irrevocably on any chance that may restore your peace of mind? I believe that such a chance is waiting for you."

He looked at her with strange intentness. "For me. . ." he smiled bitterly. "If you only knew!"

"I only know that you are hesitating at what most men would jump at," she retorted, suddenly conscious of strained nerves and feeling as if she were battering impotently against a granite rock-face. His hands clenched but he did not reply and swift contrition fell on her. She turned to him impulsively. "Forgive me, Barry. I shouldn't have said that, but I want this thing so desperately. I am convinced that it would mean happiness for you, for you both. And when I think of Gillian— alone—fighting against the world—" She broke down completely and he gripped her hands with a strength that made her wince.

"She'll never do that if I can help it," he said swiftly.

Miss Craven looked up with sudden hope. "You will ask her?" she whispered expectantly. He put her from him gently. "I can promise nothing. I must think," he said deliberately, and there was in his face a look that held her silent.

With uncertain feelings she watched him leave the room. . . Inevitable re-action set in, doubts overwhelmed her. Had she done what was best or had she blundered irretrievably? She went unsteadily to a chair, extraordinarily tired, exhausted in her new weakness by the emotional strain through which she had passed. She was beginning to be a little aghast at what she had done, at the force that she had set moving. And yet she had been actuated by the highest motives. She believed implicitly that the joining of the two lives whose future was all her care would result in the ultimate happiness of both. They had grown used to each other. A closer relationship than that of guardian and ward seemed, in view of the comparatively slight difference in age, a natural outcome of the intimacy into which they had been thrown. It was not without precedent; similar events had happened before and would doubtless happen again, she argued, striving to stifle the still lingering doubt that whispered that she had gone beyond her prerogative. And what she had done was in a way inexplicable even to herself. All through she had felt that involuntary forceful impulse that had been almost fatalistic, she had urged through the prompting of an inward conviction. She had perhaps attached too much importance to it, her own wish had been magnified until it assumed the appearance of fate.

Her closed eyes quivered as she leaned back in the chair.

She had done it for the best, she kept repeating mechanically to herself, to try and bring happiness into his life; to insure the safety of the girl who had become so dear to her. Had it been his thought too, even before she spoke? His manner had been so strange. He had recoiled from her suggestion but she had been left with the impression that it was no new one to him. She had caught a fleeting look, before his face had taken on that impenetrable mask, that had given the lie to his emphatic words. He had seemed to be wrestling with himself, she had seen the moisture thick on his forehead, his set face had looked as if it could never soften again. When he had gone he had given her no definite promise and she had no possibility of guessing what his decision would be. But on reflection she found hope in his deferring reply. It was all that was left to her. She had done her utmost, the rest lay with him. She sighed deeply, she had never felt such weariness of mind and body. As she gave way to a feeling of growing lassitude drowsiness came over her which she was too tired to combat and for some time she slept heavily. She awoke with a start to find Gillian, wide-eyed with concern, kneeling beside her, the girl's slim warm fingers clasped closely round her sleep-numbed hands. Dazed with sudden waking she looked up without speaking at the fresh young face that bent over her. Gillian rubbed the cold hands gently. "Aunt Caro, you were asleep! I've never caught you napping before," she laughed, but a hint of anxiety mingled with the wonder in her voice. Miss Craven slowly smiled reassurance. Her weakness seemed to have vanished with sleep, she felt herself once more strong enough to hide from the searching affectionate eyes anything that might give pain or cause uneasiness. She sat up straighter.

"Laziness, my dear, sheer laziness," she said sturdily. Gillian looked at her gravely. "Sure?" she asked, "you are sure that you are quite well? You looked so tired—your face was quite white."

"Quite sure—unbeliever! And you—did you have a good time; did you remember to take your tonic, and did you keep warm?"

Gillian laughed softly and stood up, ticking off the items on her fingers. "I did have a good time, I did remember to take my tonic, and this heavenly coat has kept me as warm as pie—Nina Atherton taught me that. That nice family considerably enlarged my vocabulary," she added with enjoyment, slipping out of a heavy fur coat and coming back to perch on the arm of Miss Craven's chair.

"Not yours only," was the answer, "Peter was quoting the husband this afternoon."

They were both silent for a moment thinking of the three charming Americans who had spent a couple of months at the Towers the previous summer, bringing with them an adored scrap of humanity and a host of nurses, valets and maids.

Then Gillian drew her arm closer around Miss Craven.

"Alex pressed me to stay until to-morrow, I had the greatest trouble to get away. But I promised to come back this afternoon, and, do you know, Aunt Caro, I had the queerest feeling this morning. I thought you *wanted* me, wanted me urgently. As if you could ever want anybody urgently, you self-reliant wonder." She gave the shoulder she was caressing an affectionate hug. "But it was odd, wasn't it? I nearly telephoned, and then I concluded you would think I had taken leave of my senses."

Miss Craven sat very still.

"I should have," she replied, and hoped that her voice appeared more natural than it sounded to herself. Gillian laughed.

"Anyhow, I'm glad you had Mr. Peters to cheer your solitary tea. I hated to think of you being alone."

"He didn't. He left early. But Barry condescended to take pity on me."

"Mr. Craven!" There was the slightest pause before she added: "I thought he scorned *le five o'clock*. He's not nearly so domesticated as David."

"As who, my dear?" asked Miss Craven, staring. Gillian gave another little laugh.

"Oh, that's my private name for Mr. Peters—he doesn't mind—he spoils me dreadfully—'the sweet singer in Israel'—you know. He has got the most beautiful tenor voice I have ever listened to."

"Peter—sing! I've never heard him sing," said Miss Craven in wonder, and she looked up with a new curiosity. "I've known him for thirty years, and in less than that number of months you discover an accomplishment of which everybody else is ignorant. How did you manage it, child?"

"By accident, one evening in the summer. You were dining out, and Mouston and I had gone for a ramble in the park—it's gorgeous there in the *crepuscule*—and we were quite close to the Hermitage. I heard him and I eaves-dropped—is there such a word? It was so lovely that I had to clap and he came out and found an unexpected audience on the windowsill. Wasn't it dreadful? He was so dear about it and explained that it was a very private form of amusement, but since the cat was out of the bag there was an end of the matter, only he positively declined to perform in public. I bullied him into singing some more, and then he walked home with me."

"You twist Peter round your little finger and trade on his good nature shamelessly," said Miss Craven severely, but her teasing held no terrors.

"He's such a dear," the girl repeated softly, and slipping off the arm of the chair she went to the fire and knelt down to put back a log that had fallen on to the hearth and was smouldering uselessly. Miss Craven looked at her as, the log replaced, she still knelt on the rug and held her hands mechanically to the blaze. She had an intense and wholly futile longing to speak what was in her mind and, demanding confidence for confidence, penetrate the secret of the heart that had confided to her all but this one thing. Little by little through no pressure but by mere telepathic sympathy, reserve had melted away and hopes and aspirations had been submitted and discussed. But of this one thing there could be no discussion. Miss Craven realised it and stifled a regretful sigh. Even she, dear as she knew herself to be, might not intrude so intimately. For by such an intrusion she might lose all that she had gained. She could not forfeit the confidence that had grown to mean so much to her, it was too high a price to pay even for the knowledge she sought. She must have patience, she thought, as she ran her fingers with the old gesture through her grey curls. But it was hard to be patient when any moment might bring the summons that would put her beyond the ken of earthly events. To go, leaving this problem still unsolved! She set her teeth and sat rigid, gripping the oak rails of the chair until her fingers ached, battling with herself. She looked again at the slim kneeling figure, the pale oval face half turned to her, the thick dark hair piled high on the small proud head glistening in the firelight. A thing of grace and beauty—in mind and body desirable. How could he hesitate. . .

"Barry was riding—all day—in this atrocious weather. He came in soaked," she said abruptly, almost querulously, unlike her usual tolerant intonation. There was no immediate answer and for a moment she thought she had not been heard. The girl had moved slightly, turning her face away, and with a steady hand was building the dying fire into a pyramid. She completed the operation carefully and sat back on her heels flourishing the tiny brass tongs.

"He's tough," she said lightly, unconsciously echoing Peters' words and apparently heedless of the interval between Miss Craven's remark and her own reply. She seemed more interested in the fire than in her guardian. Laying the tongs away leisurely she came back to Miss Craven's chair and settled down on the floor beside her, her arms crossed on the elder woman's knee. She looked up frankly, a faint smile lightening her serious brown eyes.

"I don't think Mr. Craven wants any sympathy, *cherie*," she said slowly, "I reserve all mine for Yoshio, he fusses so dreadfully when the 'honourable master' goes for those tremendous long rides or is out hunting. Have you noticed that he always waits in the hall, to be ready at the first moment to rush away and get dry clothes and a hot bath and all the other Oriental paraphernalia for checking chills and driving the ache out of sore bones? I don't suppose Mr. Craven has ever had sore bones—he is so splendidly strong—and Yoshio certainly seems determined he never shall. Mary thoroughly approves of him, she's a fusser by nature too; she deplores his heathenism but says he has more sense than many a Christian. Soon after we came here I found him in the hall one day staring through the window, looking the picture of misery, his funny little yellow face all puckered up. He saw me out of the back of his head, truly he did, for he never turned, and tried to slip away. But I made him stay and talk to me. I sat on the stairs and he folded himself up on the mat—I can't describe it any other way—and told me all about Japan, and California and Algeria and all the other queer places he has been to with Mr. Craven. He has such a quaint dramatic way of speaking and lapses into unintelligible Japanese just at the exciting moments—so tantalising! They seem to have been in some very—what do you say?—tight corners. We got quite sociable. I was so interested in listening to his description of the wonderful gardens they make in Japan that I never heard Mr. Craven come in and did not realise that he was standing near us until Yoshio suddenly shot up and fled, literally vanished, and left me *planteel*! I felt so idiotic sitting on the stairs hugging my knees and Mr. Craven, all splashed and muddy, waiting for me to let him pass—I was dreadfully frightened of him in those days," the faintest colour tinged her cheeks. "I longed for an earthquake to swallow me up," she laughed and scrambled to her feet, gathering the heap of furs into her arms and holding them dark and silky against her face. "You shouldn't have encouraged in me a love of beautiful furs, Aunt Caro," she said inconsequently, with sudden seriousness. "I've sense enough left to know that I shouldn't indulge it—and I'm human enough to adore them."

"Rubbish! furs suit you—please my sense of the artistic. I would not encourage you if you had a face like a harvest moon and no carriage—I can't bear sloppiness in anything," snapped Miss Craven in quite her old style. "When do the Horringfords start for Egypt?" she added by way of definitely changing the subject.

Gillian rubbed her cheek against the soft sealskin with an understanding smile. It was hopeless to try and curb Miss Craven's generosity, hopeless to attempt to argue against it. "Next week," she answered the inquiry. "Tuesday, probably. They stay in Paris for a month *en route;* Lord Horringford wants some data from the Louvre and also to arrange some preliminaries with the French Egyptologist who is joining their party."

"Hum! And Alex—still interested in mummies?"

"More than ever, she is full of enthusiasm. She talks of dynasties and tribal deities, of kings and *Kas* and symbols until my head spins. Lord Horringford teases her but it is easy to see that her interest pleases him. He says she is the mascot of the expedition, that she brought luck to the digging last year."

"Alex has had many hobbies but never one that ran for two seasons," said Miss Craven thoughtfully; "I am glad she has found an interest at last that promises to be permanent."

Gillian gathered the furs closer in her arms and made a few steps toward the door. "She has found more than that," she said softly, and the colour flamed in her sensitive face. Miss Craven nodded. "You mean that in unearthing the buried treasure of a dead past she has found the living treasure of a man's love? Yes, and not any too soon, poor silly child. Men like Horringford don't bear playing with. I wonder whether she knows how near she has been to making shipwreck of her life."

"I think she knows—now," said Gillian, with a little wise smile as she left the room.

The sound of her soft contralto singing an old French nursery rhyme echoed faintly back to the library:

> "*Mon père m'a donné un petit mari,*
> *Mon Dieu, quel homme!*"

And, listening, Miss Craven smiled half-sadly, for the quaint words carried her back to the days of her own childhood. But the exigencies of the present thrust aside past memories. She sat on, wrapped in her thoughts until the dropping temperature of the room sent through her a sudden chill, so she rose with a shiver and a startled glance at her watch.

"Dry bones and love," she said musingly, "it's a curious combination! Peter, my man, you gave wise advice there. . . But not all your wisdom can help *my* trouble."

VI

December had brought a complete change of weather. It was within a few days of Christmas, a typical old-fashioned Yuletide with a firm white mantle of snow lying thick over the country.

Underneath the ground was iron and for two weeks all hunting had been stopped.

Craven was returning to the Towers after an absence of ten days. The motor crawled through the park for in places the frozen road was slippery as glass and the chauffeur was a cautious North-countryman whose faith in the chains locked round the wheels was not unlimited; he was driving carefully, with a wary eye for the worst patches noted on the outward run, and, beside him, equally alert, sat Yoshio muffled to the ears in an immense overcoat, a shapeless bundle.

It was early afternoon, calm and clear, and in the air the intense stillness that succeeds a heavy snowfall. The pale sun, that earlier in the day had iridised the snow, was now too low to affect the dead whiteness of the scene against which the trees showed magnified and sharply black. Here and there across the smooth surface stretching on either side of the road lay the curiously differing tracks of animals. From the back seat of the car where he sat alone Craven marked them mechanically. He knew every separate spoor and could have named the owner of each; ordinarily they would have claimed from him a certain interest but today he passed them without a second thought. He did not resent the slow progress of the car, he was in no hurry to reach the Towers. He had come to a momentous decision but shrank from the action that must necessarily follow; once at the house he knew that he would permit himself no further delay, he would put his purpose into effect at the earliest opportunity—today if possible; here there was still time— vaguely he wondered for what? Not for reflection, that was done with. He had striven with all his strength to arrive at a right determination; he had thought until reasoning became a mere repetition of fixed ideas moving in a circle and arriving always at an unvaried starting point. There seemed no consequence that he had not weighed in his mind, no issue that he had not considered. To ponder afresh would be to cover again uselessly ground that he had gone over a hundred times. Three days ago he had made his choice, he had no intention of departing from it. For good or ill the thing must go forward now. And, after all, the ultimate decision did not lie with him. Admitting it his thoughts became introspective. Throughout his deliberations he had put self on one side, there had been no question of his own wishes; now for the first time he allowed personal considerations to rise unchecked. For what did he hope? He knew the reason of his reluctance to reach the house—he desired success and yet he feared it, feared the consequences that might result, feared the strength of his own will to persevere in the course he had chosen. For him there was no other way but, merciful God, it would be hard! He set his teeth and stared at the frozen landscape with unseeing eyes. Since her outburst four weeks ago Miss Craven had not spoken again of the wish that was nearest her heart, but he knew that she was waiting for an answer, knew that that answer must be given. One way or the other. Day had succeeded day in torturing indecision. He had lived, slept with the problem, at no time was it out of his mind. In the course of the long rides that had become more frequent, obtruding during the monotonous hours spent in the estate office, the problem persisted. In the sleepless hours of the night he wrestled with it. If it had been a matter of personal inclination, if the past had not risen between them there would have been no hesitation. He would have gone to her months ago, would have begged the priceless gift that she alone could give. He wanted her, almost above the hope of salvation, and the inducement to ignore the past had been all but overpowering. He loved and desired with all the strength of the passionate nature he had inherited. He craved for her with an intensity that was anguish, that set him wondering how far the power of endurance reached, how much a man could bear. He was torn with the fierce promptings of primeval forces. To take her, willing or unwilling, despite honour, despite all that stood between them, to make her his and hold her in the face of all the world—at times the temptation had been maddening. There had been days when he had not dared to look on her, when he had drawn himself more than ever apart from the common life, fearful of himself, fearful of circumstances that seemed beyond his ordering. And the thought that another could take what he might not had engendered an insensate jealousy that was beyond reason. He did not recognise himself, he had not known the depths of his own nature. If there had been no bar, if she could have come to him willingly, if there could indeed have been for him the full ties of home—the thought was agony. Miss Craven's words had been a sword turning in an open wound. To the burden he already carried had been added this.

The future of his ward had been his problem as well as Miss Craven's. Only a little while ago a way had seemed clear, not a way to his own happiness—by his own act he had put himself beyond all possibility of that—but a way that would mean security and happiness for her who had come to mean more than life to him. For her safety he would have given his soul. The term of his guardianship was drawing to an end, in a few months his legal control over her terminated. Miss Craven who had surrendered her independence for two years would be returning to her own home, to her old life; it had seemed a foregone conclusion that Gillian would accompany her.

But the double shock in the revelation of Miss Craven's precarious state and Gillian's delicacy had been staggering. He had not been prepared for a contingency that seemed to cut the ground from under his feet. With all the will in the world his aunt was powerless to further the plan he proposed, any day might bring the Great Summons. And Gillian! The little persistent cough rang in his ears always. Gillian and poverty—by day it haunted him, he woke in the night sweating at the very thought. It was intolerable. And yet there appeared no means of escaping it—save one. For a moment, with a fierce joy, he saw fate aiding him, forcing into his hands what he yearned to gather to himself, then he recoiled from even the thought of her purity linked with the stain of his past. He had racked his brain to discover an alternative. To force upon her an adequate income that would put her beyond want and the necessity of work would be easy. To induce her to use the money thus provided he divined would be impossible, he seemed to know intuitively that her will would not give way to his. During these last weeks he had looked at her with new understanding, it seemed incredible that he had never before recognised the determination that underlay her shy gentleness. Character shone in the frank brown eyes, there was a firmness that was unmistakable in the arched lips that were the only patch of colour in her delicate face. From his wealth she would accept nothing. Would she accept him—all that he dared offer? It was no new idea, the thought had been in his mind often but always he resolutely put it from him with a feeling of abhorrence. It was an insult to her womanhood, an expedient that nothing could justify. And yet step by step he was forced back upon it—there seemed no other way to save her from herself. Days of harrassing indecision, his only thought she, brought him no nearer to a conclusion. And time was passing. He had reached a point when further deliberation was beyond his power;

E.M. HULL

when all his strength seemed to turn into hopeless longing that, to the exclusion of all else, craved even the mockery of possession; when days were torment and nights a sleepless horror. Then change of scene had aided final determination. The factor of the Scotch estate had written of a sudden and unexpected difficulty for which he asked personal advice. A telegram had stopped his proposed visit to the Towers and Craven had himself gone instead to Scotland. And in the solitude of his northern home he had decided on the only course that seemed open to him. He would go to her with his poor offer, the poorest surely that ever a man made to a woman, and the rest would lie with her. But how would she receive it? He had a vision of the soft brown eyes blazing with scorn, of the slender figure he ached to hold in his arms turning from him in cold disgust, and he clenched his hands until the nails bit deep into his wet palms.

A bad skid that slewed the car half round broke his thoughts and in a few minutes they were at the house.

Forbes, the elderly butler who had been an under footman when Peters first came to the Towers, was waiting for him in the hall, informative with the garrulousness of an old and privileged servant. A late luncheon was waiting—he sighed patiently on hearing that it was not required—Miss Craven had gone to the Vicarage for tea; Mr. Peters was expected to dinner that night and he had telephoned in the morning to tell Mr. Craven—Craven cut him short. Peter's message could wait, only one thing seemed to matter just now.

"Where is Miss Locke?" he asked curtly. "In the studio, sir," replied Forbes with resignation. If Mr. Barry didn't want to hear what Mr. Peters had got to say he, for one, was not going to press the matter. Mr. Barry had had his own way of doing things since the days when he sat on the pantry table kicking his heels and flourishing stolen jam under Forbes' very nose—a masterful one always, he was. And if it was a case of Miss Gillian—Forbes retired with an armful of ulster and rugs into the cloakroom to hide a sympathetic grin.

Craven crossed the hall and went into the study. He looked without interest through an accumulation of letters lying on the writing table, then threw them down indifferently. Walking to the fireplace he lit a cigarette and stood staring at the cheerful blaze. At last he raised his head and gazed with deliberation at himself in the glass over the mantle. He scowled at the stern worn face reflected in the mirror, looking curiously at its deep cut lines, at the silver patches in the thick brown hair. Then with a violent exclamation he swung abruptly on his heel, flung the cigarette into the fire and left the room. He went upstairs slowly, surprised at the feeling of apathy that had come over him. In the face of direct action the high tension of the last few weeks had snapped, leaving him dull, almost inert, and reluctance to go forward grew with every step. But at the head of the stairs his mood changed suddenly. All that the coming interview meant to him revealed itself with startling clearness. With a deep breath he caught at the rail, for he was shaking uncontrollably, and covered his face with his hand.

"God!" he whispered, and again: "God!"

Then he gripped himself and went quickly across the gallery, turning down the corridor that led to the west wing. He followed the oddly twisting passage, contorted at the whim of succeeding generations where rooms had been enlarged or abolished, passing rows of closed doors and another staircase. The corridor terminated in the room he was seeking. It had been the old playroom; at the extreme end of the wing it faced northward and westward and was well suited for the studio into which it had been converted. It was Gillian's own domain and he had never asked to visit it. As he reached the door he heard from within the shrill treble of a boy's mirth and then a low soft laugh that made his heart beat quicker. He tapped and went in and for a moment stared in amazement. He did not recognise the room, it was a totally unexpected French *atelier* tucked away in the corner of a typically English house.

The polished rug-laid floor, the fluted folds of *toile-de-genes* clothing the walls, the litter of sketches and pictures, casts and easels, the familiar lay-figure grotesquely attitudinising in a corner, above all the atmosphere carried him straight to Paris. It was the room of an artist, and a French artist. His eyes leaped to her. She was standing before a big easel looking wonderingly over her shoulder at the opening door, the brush she was using poised in her hand, her eyes wide with astonishment, a faint flush creeping into her cheeks.

In the picturesque painter's blouse, her brown hair loosely framing her face, she seemed altogether different. He could not define wherein lay the change, he had no time to discriminate, he only knew that seen thus she was a thousand times more desirable than she had ever been and that his heart cried out for her more fiercely than before. He looked at her with hungry longing, then quickly—lest his eyes should betray him—from her to her model. A boy of ten with an intelligent small brown face, a mop of black curls, and red lips parted in a mischievous

E.M. HULL

smile, he stood on the raised platform with the easy assurance of a professional.

Craven shut the door behind him and came forward. She turned to meet him and the colour rushed in a crimson wave to the roots of her hair. "*Monsieur. . . vous etes de retour. . . mais, soyez le bienvenu!*" she stammered, with surprise unconsciously lapsing into the language of childhood. Then she caught herself up with a little laugh of confusion and hurried on in English: "I am so sorry. . . there is nobody in but me. Will you have some tea? It is only three o'clock," with a glance at her wrist, "but I expect you lunched early."

"I don't want any tea," he said bluntly. "I came to see you." He spoke in French, mindful of two sharp ears on the platform. The colour in her face deepened painfully and her eyes fell under his steady gaze. She moved slowly back to the easel.

"If you could wait a few moments—" she murmured.

"I don't want to interrupt," he said hastily. "Please finish your work. You don't mind if I stay? I haven't been here since I was a boy; you have changed the room incredibly. May I look round?"

She nodded assent over a tube of colour, and returned to her study.

Left to himself he wandered leisurely round the room, examining the pictures and sketches that were heaped indiscriminately. He had never before displayed any interest in her work, and was now amazed at what he saw. There was power in it that surprised him, that made him wonder what intuition had given the convent-bred girl the knowledge she exhibited. The tardy recognition of her talent strengthened his stranger feeling toward her. He went thoughtfully to the fireplace, and, from the rug, surveyed the room and its occupants. The atmosphere recalled old memories—he had studied in Paris after leaving Oxford—only one thing seemed lacking.

"May I smoke?" he asked abruptly.

Gillian turned with a quick smile.

"But, of course. What need to ask? After Aunt Caro has been here for an hour the room is blue."

For another ten minutes he watched her in silence, free to look as he would, for her back was toward him and in his position before the fire he was beyond the range of the little model's inquisitive black eyes.

Then she laid palette and brushes on a near table and stepped back, frowning at what she had done until a smile came slowly to chase the creases from her forehead. She spoke without moving, still looking at the canvas: "That is all for to-day, Danny. The light has gone."

The small boy stretched himself luxuriously, and descending from the platform, joined her and gazed with evident interest at his portrait. He peered in unconscious but faithful imitation of her own critical attitude, his head slanted at the same angle as hers. "It's coming on," he announced solemnly, and Craven guessed from the girl's laugh that it was a repetition of some remark heard and stored up for future use. The boy grinned in response, and slipping behind her went to the table where she had laid her tools. "Can I clean palut?" he asked hopefully, his hand already half-way to the coveted mass of colour.

"Not to-day, thanks, Danny."

"Shall I fetch th' dog, Miss?" more hopefully. Gillian turned to him quickly.

"He bit you last time."

Danny wriggled his feet and his small white teeth flashed in a wide smile. "He won't bite I again," he said confidently. "Mammy said 'twas 'cos he loved you and hated to have folks near you. She said I was to whisper in his ear I loved you too, 'cos then he wouldn't touch me. Dad he says 'tis a damned black devil," he added with candid relish and a sidelong glance of mischief at his employer.

Gillian laughed and gave his shoulder a little pat.

"I'm afraid he is," she admitted ruefully. The boy threw his head back. "I ain't afeard o' he," he said stoutly. "*Shall* I fetch 'im?"

"I think we'll leave him where he is, Danny," she said gravely, as if in confidence. "He's probably very happy. Now run away and come again on Saturday." She waved a paint-stained rag at him and turned again to the picture. Obediently he started towards the door, then hesitated, glancing irresolutely at Craven, and tip-toed back to the easel.

"Them things in the drawer," he muttered sepulchrally, in a voice not intended to reach the ears of the rather awe-inspiring personage on the hearthrug. Gillian whipped round contritely. "Danny, I forgot them!" she apologised, and tweaking a black curl went to a bureau and produced a square cardboard box. Danny tucked it under his arm with murmured thanks and a duck of the head, and crossing the room noiselessly went out, closing the door behind him softly. Craven came slowly to her. She moved to give him place before the easel. Craven looked at the small alert brown face, the odd black eyes dancing with almost unearthly merriment, the red lips curving upward to an enigmatical smile, and his wonder and admiration grew.

"Who is he?" he asked curiously, puzzled by a likeness he seemed to recognise dimly and yet was unable to place.

"Danny Major—the son of one of your gamekeepers," said Gillian; "his mother has gipsy blood in her."

Craven whistled. "I remember," he said, interested. "Old Major was head-keeper. Young Major lost his heart to a gipsy lass and his father kicked him out of doors. Peters, as usual, smoothed things over and kept the fellow on at his job, in spite of a great deal of opposition—he had seen the girl and formed his own opinion. I asked once or twice and he said that it had turned out satisfactorily. So this is the son—he's a rum-looking little beggar."

Gillian was cleaning brushes at the side table. "He's the terror of the neighbourhood," she said smiling, "but for some reason he is a perfect angel when he comes here. It isn't the chocolates," she added hastily as she saw a fleeting smile on his face, "he just likes coming. And he tells me the most wonderful things about the woods and the wood beasties."

"He would," said Craven significantly, "it's in the blood. What's this?" he asked, pointing to a smaller board propped face inward against the big canvas. For a moment she did not answer and the colour flamed into her face again. She put the brushes away, and wiping her fingers on a cloth, lifted the board and gave it into his hands.

"It's Danny as I see him," she said in an odd voice. And, looking at it, Craven realised that the cleverness of the painted head on the large canvas paled to mediocrity beside the brilliance of the sepia sketch he held. It was the same head—but marvellously different—set on the body of a faun. The dancing limbs were pulsing with life, the tiny hoofs stamping the flower-strewn earth in an ecstasy of movement; the head was thrown forward, bent as though to catch a distant echo, and among the tossing curls showed two small curving horns; to the enigmatical smile of the original had been added a subtle touch of mockery, and the wide eyes held a look of mystical knowledge that was uncanny. Craven held it silently, it seemed an incredible piece of work for the girl to have conceived. And, beside him, she waited nervously for his verdict, with close-locked twitching fingers. He had never come before, had never shown any interest in the work that meant so much to her. She was hungry for his praise, fearful of his censure. If he saw nothing in it now but the immature efforts of an amateur! Her heart tightened. She drew a little nearer to him, her eyes fixed apprehensively on his intent face, her breath coming quickly. At length he replaced the sketch carefully. "You have a wonderful talent," he said slowly. A little gasp of relief escaped her and her lips trembled in spite of all efforts to keep them steady. "You like it?" she whispered eagerly, and was terrified at the awful pallor that overspread his face. For a moment he could not speak. The words, the intonation! He was back again in Japan, looking at the painting of a lonely fir tree clinging to a jutting sea-washed cliff—the faintest scent of oriental perfume seemed stealing through the air. He drew his hand across his eyes. "Merciful God. . . not here. . . not now!" he prayed in silent agony. Then with a desperate effort he mastered himself and turned to the frightened girl with a forced smile. "Forgive me—I've a beastly headache—the room went spinning round for a minute," he said jerkily, wiping the moisture from his forehead. She looked at him gravely. "I think you are very tired, and I don't believe you had any lunch," she said with quiet decision. "I'm going to make some coffee. Aunt Caro says my coffee drinking is more vicious than her smoking," she went on, purposely giving him time to recover himself, and crossing the room she collected little cups and a small brass pot. "Any how it's the real article, and in spite of what she says Aunt Caro doesn't scorn it. She comes regularly to drink my *cafe noir* with her after-lunch cigarette."

Craven dropped down heavily on the broad cushioned window seat, his hands clasped over his throbbing temples, fighting to regain his shaken nerve. And yet there was a great hope dawning. For the first time the threatening vision had failed to materialise, and the fact gave him courage. If a time should come when it would definitely cease to haunt him! He could never forget, never cease to regret, but he would feel that in the Land of Understanding the hapless victim of his crime had forgiven the sin that had robbed her of her young life.

And as he grew calmer he began to be conscious that in the room where he sat there was a restfulness that he had not felt in any other part of the house since his return to Craven Towers. It was acting on him curiously and he wondered what it portended. And as he pondered it Gillian came to him with a cup of coffee in either hand.

"Monsieur est servi," she said with a little laugh. She seemed to have suddenly overcome shyness as if, in her own domain, the first surprise of his visit over, her surroundings gave her confidence. Or, perhaps, the womanliness that had been called out to meet his passing weakness had set her on another plane. All signs of giddiness had left him and, with

her usual intuition, she did not trouble him with questions. For the first time she found it easy to speak to him, and talked as she would have done to Peters. She spoke of his northern visit and, following his lead, of her work, freely and without embarrassment. Every moment the restraint that had been between them seemed growing less. She marvelled that she had ever found him unapproachable and wondered, contritely, if her shyness had been alone to blame. She had been always constrained and silent with him—small wonder that he had avoided her, she thought humbly. Yet how could it have been otherwise? The tie between them, the wonderful generosity he had shown, the aloofness he had maintained, had made it impossible for her to view him as an ordinary human being. She owed him everything and passionate recognition and a sense of her indebtedness had grown with equal fervour. She had almost worshipped him. He had taken her from a life that had grown unbearable, he had given her the opportunity to follow the career for which she longed. She could never repay him, she found it difficult to put into words even to herself just what she felt towards him. From the first she had raised him to the empty pedestal vacated by that fallen idol, her father. And out of hero-worship had grown love, at first the exalted devotion of an immature girl, adoration that was purely sexless and selfless—a mystical love without passion, spiritual. He had appeared to her as a being of another sphere and, mentally, she had knelt at his feet as to a patron saint. But with her own development love had expanded. She realised that what she felt for him was no longer childish adoration, but a greater, more wonderful emotion. She had grown to a full understanding of her own heart, the divinity had become a man for whose love she yearned. But she loved hopelessly as she loved deeply, she had no thought that her love could be returned. His proximity had always troubled her, and to-day as she sat on the window seat beside him she was conscious of a greater unrest than she had ever before felt, and her heart throbbed painfully with the vague formless longings, inexplicable and frightening, that stirred within her until it seemed impossible that her agitation could pass unnoticed. Shyness fell on her again, the ready words faltered, and gradually she became silent. Craven took the empty coffee cups and replaced them on the table by the fire. Going back to the window he found her kneeling up on the cushioned seat, her hands clasped before her, looking out at the white world. The childish attitude that seemed in keeping with the artist's blouse and tumbled hair made her look singularly young. He stood beside her, so close that he almost touched her shoulder, and his eyes ranged hungrily over the whole slim beauty of her, lingering on the little bent brown head, the soft curve of her girlish bosom, until the yearning for her grew intolerable and the restraint he put upon himself took all his resolution. The temptation to gather her into his arms was almost more than he could resist, he folded them tightly across his chest—he could not trust them. He could barely trust himself. The unwonted intimacy, the subtle torture of her nearness set his pulses leaping madly. The blood beat in his head, his body quivered with the passionate longing, the fierce desire that rushed over him. In the agony of the moment only the elemental man existed, and he was sensible alone of the burning physical need that rose above all higher purer sentiment. To hold her crushed against his throbbing heart, to bury his face in the fragrance of her soft hair, to kiss her lips till she should beg his mercy—there seemed no greater joy on earth. He wanted her as he had wanted nothing in his life before. And yet, if he gained what he had come to ask he knew that what he suffered now would be as nothing to what he would have to endure. To know her his wife, bound in every sense to him—and to turn his face from the happiness that by all laws was his! Had he the strength? Almost it seemed that he had not. He was only human—and there was a limit to human endurance. If circumstances proved too hard. . . The sound of a little smothered cough checked his thoughts abruptly. He realised that in self-commiseration he had lost sight of the purpose of his visit. It was only she who mattered; her health, her happiness that must be considered. He cursed himself and searched vainly for words to express what he must say. And the more he thought the more utterly speech evaded him. Then chance aided. She coughed again and with a little impatient gesture rose to her feet.

"Aunt Caro has decided to go to Cimiez for the rest of the winter—because of my cough. She settled it while you were away. I don't want to go, my cough is nothing. I wouldn't exchange this"—pointing to the snow-clad park—"for all the warmth and sunshine of the Riviera. I want to store up all the memories I can. You don't know how I have learned to love the Towers." It was as if the last words had escaped unintentionally for she flushed and turned again abruptly to the darkening window. His heart gave a sudden leap but he did not move.

"Then why leave it?" he asked brusquely.

She leaned her forehead on the frosting glass and her eyes grew misty.

"You *know*," she said softly, and her voice trembled. "In all the world I have only my—my talent and my self-respect. If I were to do what you and Aunt Caro, in your wonderful generosity, propose—oh, don't stop me, you *must* listen—I should only have my talent left. Can't you see, can't you understand that I must work, that I must prove my self-respect? For all that you have done, for all that you have given me I have tried to thank you—often. Always you have stopped me. Do you grudge me the only way in which I can show my gratitude, the only way in which I can prove myself worthy of your esteem?" Her voice broke in a little sob. Then she turned to him quickly, her hands out-stretched and quivering. "If I could only do something to repay—" she cried, with a passionate earnestness he had never heard in her before. He caught at the opening that offered. "You can," he said quietly, "but it is so big a thing—it would more than swamp the debt you think you owe me."

"Tell me," she whispered urgently as he paused.

He turned from her eager questioning face with acute embarrassment. He hated himself, he hated his task, only the darkness of the room seemed to make it possible.

"Gillian," he said, with constrained gravity. "I came to you to-day deliberately to ask you what I believe no man has any right to ask a woman. I have tried all the afternoon to tell you. Something you said just now makes it easier. You say you love the Towers—do you love it well enough to stay here as its mistress, on the only terms that I can offer?"

The look of incredulous horror that leaped into her startled eyes made him realise suddenly the interpretation that might be put upon his words. He caught her hands almost roughly. "Good heavens, child, not that!" he cried aghast. "What do you take me for? I am asking you to marry me—but not the kind of marriage that every woman has the right to expect. If I could offer you that, God knows how willingly I would. But there has been that in my life which comes between me and the happiness that other men can look forward to. For me that part of life is over. I have only friendship to offer. I know I am asking more than it seems possible for you to grant, more, a thousand times more than I ought to ask you—but I do ask it, most earnestly. If you can bring yourself to make so great a sacrifice, if you can accept a marriage that will be a marriage only in name—"

She shuddered from him with a bitter cry. "You are offering me *charity*!" she wailed, struggling to free her hands. But he held them firmer. "I am asking you to take pity on a very lonely man," he said gently. "I am asking you to care for a very lonely house. You have brought sunshine into the Towers, you have brought sunshine into the lives of many people living on the estate. I am asking you to stay where you are so much wanted—so much—loved."

Then he let her go and she walked unsteadily to the fireplace. She stood for a moment, her fingers working convulsively, staring into the smouldering embers, and then sank into a chair, for her limbs were shaking under her. He followed slowly and stooped to stir the fire to a blaze. Covertly she looked at him as the red light illuminated his face and scalding tears gathered in her eyes. And, curiously, it was not wholly of herself that she was thinking. She was envying, with a feeling of hopeless intolerable pain, that other woman whom he had loved. For his words could only have meant one thing, and the great sorrow she had imagined seemed all at once explained. She wondered what manner of woman she had been, if she had died—or if she had proved unworthy. And the last thought roused a sudden fierce resentment—how could a woman who had won his love throw it back at his feet, unwanted! The envious tears welled over and she brushed them furtively away. Then her thoughts turned in compassion to him. Through death or faithlessness love had brought no joy to him—he suffered as she was suffering now. She looked at the silver threads gleaming in his hair, at the deep lines in his face and the pain in her eyes gave place to a wonderful tenderness. She had prayed for a chance to show her gratitude; if what he asked could bring any alleviation to his life, if her presence could bring any sort of comfort to his loneliness, was not even that more than she had ever dared to hope? That he should turn to her was understandable. He had men friends in plenty, but women he openly and undisguisedly avoided. He had grown used to her presence at the Towers, a marriage such as he proposed would call for no great alteration in the daily routine to which he had become accustomed. If by doing this she could in any way repay. . .

The replenished fire was filling the room with soft flickering light, it cast strange shadows on the curtained walls and revealed the girl's strained white face pitilessly. Craven had risen and was standing looking down on her. She grew aware of his scrutiny and flinched, the hot blood rolling slowly, painfully over her face and neck. He spoke abruptly, as if the words were forced from him:

"But I want you to realise fully what this marriage with me would mean, for it is a very big sacrifice I am asking of you. Whatever happened, you would be bound to me. If"—his voice faltered momentarily—"if you were sometime to meet a man—and love him—you would be my wife, you would not be free to follow your heart."

She stared straight before her, her hands clasped tight around her knees, shivering slightly. "I shall never—want to marry—in that way," she said in a strangled voice. He smiled sadly. "You think that now— you are very young," he argued, "but we have the future to think of."

She did not answer and in the silence that ensued he wondered what had induced him to put forward an argument that might defeat his purpose. In any other case it would have been only the honourable thing to do, but in this it was a risk he should not have taken. He moved impatiently. Then suddenly he leaned forward and laid his hands on her shoulders, drawing her gently to her feet.

"Gillian!"

Slowly she raised her head. The touch of his hands was almost more than she could bear, but she steadied her trembling lips and met his gaze bravely as he spoke again.

"If you will agree to this—this *mariage de convenance*, I will do all that lies in my power to make your life happy. You will be free in everything. I ask nothing but that you will look on me as a friend to whom you can always come in any difficulty or any trouble. You will be complete mistress of yourself, your time, your inclinations. I will not interfere with you in any way."

She searched his face, trying to read what lay behind his inscrutable expression. His eyes were kind, but there was in them a curious underlying gleam that she could not understand. And his voice puzzled her. She was bewildered, torn with conflicting doubts. Sensitively she shrank from his inexplicable suggestion, she could see no reason for his amazing proposal save an extraordinary generosity that filled her with gratitude and yet against which she revolted.

"You are doing this in pity!" she cried miserably.

"Before God I swear that I am not," he said, with unexpected fierceness that startled her, and the sudden painful gripping of the strong hands on her shoulders made her for the first time aware of his strength. She thought of it wonderingly. If it had been otherwise, if he had loved her, how gladly she would have surrendered to it. It would have stood between her and the unknown world that loomed sometimes in spite of her confidence with a sinister horror on which she dared not dwell. In the safety of his arms she would never have known fear, his strength would have shielded her through life. And, in a lesser degree, his strength might still be hers to turn to, if she would. A new conception of the future she had planned rushed over her, the confidence she had felt fell suddenly away, leaving fear and dread and a terror of loneliness. His touch had destroyed her faith in herself. It had done more. In some subtle way it seemed to her he had by his touch claimed her. And with his hands still pressing her shoulders she felt a strange inability to oppose him. He had sworn that it was not pity that dictated his offer. He had said that love did not exist for him. What then could be his motive? She could find none.

"You wouldn't lie to me?" she whispered, tormented with doubt, "you wish this—this marriage—truly?"

He looked at her steadily.

"I wish it, truly," he said firmly.

"You would let me go on with my work?" she faltered, fighting for time.

"I have said that I would not interfere with you in any way, that you would be free in everything," he answered, and as if in earnest of the freedom promised his hands slipped from her.

The fire had died down again, and the room was almost dark, he could hardly see her where she stood. He waited, hoping she would speak, then abruptly: "Can you give me an answer, Gillian?"

He heard the quick intake of her breath, felt her trembling beside him.

"Oh, if you would give me time," she murmured entreatingly. "I want to think. It means so much."

"Take all the time you wish," he said, and went quietly away. And his going brought a sudden desolation. She longed to call him back, to promise what he asked, to yield without further struggle. But uncertainty held her. Motionless she stood staring through the darkness at the dim outline of the door that had closed behind him, her breast heaving tumultuously, until tears blinded her and with a gasping sob she slipped to the floor. She had never dared to hope that he could love her, but the truth from his own lips was bitter. And for a time the realisation of that bitterness deadened all other feeling. Overwrought with the emotion of the last few hours, her nerves strained to breaking point, she was unable to check the tide of grief that shook her to the very depths of her being. With her face hidden in the soft rug, her outflung hands clenching convulsively, she wept in an abandonment of sorrow.

E.M. HULL

If he had never spoken, if he had never made this strange proposal but had maintained until the end the detached reserve that had seemed to set so wide a gulf between them, it would have been easier to bear. He would have passed out of her life, inscrutable as he had always been. But with his change of attitude, in the intimacy of the few hours they had spent alone, she had seen him with new eyes. The mysterious unapproachable guardian had gone for ever, and in his place was a very human man revealing characteristics she had never imagined to exist, showing an interest and a gentleness she had never suspected. He had exhibited a similarity of tastes and ideas that agreed extraordinarily with her own, he had talked as to a comrade. The companionship had been very sweet—very sorrowful. She could never think of him again as he had been, and the new conception of him gave a poignant stab to her grief. In the brief happiness of the afternoon she had had a fleeting vision of what might have been "if he had loved me," she moaned, and it seemed to her that she had never known until now the real depth of her own love. What she had felt before was not comparable with the overwhelming passion that the touch of his hands had quickened. It swept her like a raging torrent, carrying her beyond the limit of her understanding, bringing with it strange yearnings that, half-understood, she shuddered from, ashamed.

Torn with emotion she wept until she had no tears left, until the hard racking sobs died away and her tired sorrow-shaken body lay still. For the moment, exhausted, her agony of mind was dulled and time was non-existent. She did not move or lift her head from the tear-wet rug. A great weariness seemed to deaden all faculty. The minutes passed unnoticed. Then some latent consciousness stirred in her brain and she looked up startled.

It was quite dark and she realised, shivering, that the room had grown very cold. The calm afternoon had given place to a stormy night and heavy gusts of wind were sweeping round the angle of the house, shrieking and whistling eerily; from the window came the soft *swish swish* of dry hard snow beating against the panes. She started to her feet. She had no idea of the hour but she knew it must be late. Perhaps the dinner gong had already sounded and, missed, somebody might come in search of her. She shrank from being found thus. Feeling her way to a lamp she turned the switch and the soft light flooding the room made her wince. A glance at her watch showed that she had still a few moments in which to gain her room unobserved.

She felt oddly lightheaded and her feet dragged wearily. The tortuous passage had never seemed so interminable, the succession of closed doors appeared unending. Reaching her own room she collapsed on to a sofa that was drawn up before the fire, her head aching, her limbs shivering uncontrollably, worn out with emotion. Exhausted in mind and body she seemed unable even to frame a thought logically or coherently—only an interrupted medley of unconnected ideas chased through her tired brain until her temples throbbed agonisingly. She knew that sometime she would have to rouse herself, that sometime a decision would have to be made, but not now. Now she could only lie still and make no effort. She was angry with herself, contemptuous of her weakness. She had disdained nerves, she was humiliated now by her present lack of control. But even self-scorn was a passing thought from which she turned wearily.

One fact only remained, clear and distinct from the confusion in her mind—he did not love her. He did not love her. It hurt so. She hid her face in the pillows, writhing with the shame the knowledge of her own love brought her. The deep booming of the dinner gong awoke her to the necessity of some kind of action. She rang the bell that hung within reach of her hand and, by the maid who answered her summons, sent her excuses to Miss Craven, pleading a headache for remaining upstairs.

A few minutes later Mary, grim-visaged and big-hearted, appeared with a tray, headache remedies and multifarious messages from the dining room. She bathed the girl's aching head, brushing the tumbled brown hair and piling it afresh into a soft loose knot. Grumbling gently at the long hours of work to which she attributed the unusual indisposition, she took full advantage of the rare opportunity of rendering personal attention and fussed to her heart's content, stripping off the stained overall and substituting a loose velvet wrapper; and then stood over her, a kindly martinet, until the light dinner she had brought was eaten. Afterwards she packed pillows, made up the fire, and administered a particularly nauseous specific emanating from a homeopathic medicine chest that was her greatest pride, and then took herself away, still mildly admonishing.

Gillian leaned back against the cushions with a feeling of greater ease and restfulness. Food had given her strength and under Mary's ministrations her mental poise had steadied. She would not let herself dwell on the question that must before long be settled, Miss Craven would be coming soon, and until she had been and gone no definite settlement could be attempted.

She lay looking at the fire, endeavouring to keep her mind a blank. It was odd to be alone, she missed the familiar black form lying on the hearth-rug, but tonight she could not bear even Mouston's presence, and Mary had taken a request to Yoshio, to whose room the dog had been banished from the studio, that he would keep him until the morning.

A tap at the door and Miss Craven appeared, anxious and questioning.

"Only a headache?—my dear, I don't believe it!" she protested, plumping down on the side of the sofa and clutching at her hair, that sure sign of perturbation. "You've never had a headache like this before. You've been working too hard. You were painting all the morning and they tell me you worked throughout the afternoon and had no tea. Gillian, dear, when will you learn sense? I don't at all approve of you having tea sent to the studio *only* when you ring for it. Young people require regular meals and as often as not neglect 'em; young artists are the worst offenders—you needn't contradict me, I know all about it. I did it myself." She patted the clasped hands lying near her and scrutinised the girl more closely. "You're as pale as a ghost and your eyes are too bright. Did Mary take your temperature? No?—the woman must have lost her senses. I'll telephone to Doctor Harris to come and see you in the morning. If you looked a fraction more feverish I'd send for you to-night, storm or no storm. Peter braved it, open car as usual. He sent his love. Barry turned up from Scotland this afternoon. He looks very tired—says he had a bothering time and a wretched journey—Gillian!" she cried sharply as the girl slid from the sofa on to her knees beside her and raised a quivering piteous face.

"Aunt Caro, I'm not ill," the words came in tumbling haste, "there's nothing bodily the matter with me—I'm only dreadfully unhappy. I know Mr. Craven is back—he came to me in the studio this afternoon. He asked me to marry him," the troubled voice sank to a whisper, "and I—I don't know what to do."

"My dear." The tenderness of Miss Craven's tone sent a strangling wave of emotion into Gillian's throat. "Aunt Caro, did you know? Do you wish it too?" she murmured wistfully.

Unwilling to admit a previous knowledge which would be difficult to explain, Miss Craven temporised. "I very greatly hoped for it," she said guardedly; "you and Barry are all I have to care for, and you are both so—alone. I know you think of a very different life, I know you have dreams of making a career for yourself. But a career is not all that a woman wants in her life; it can perhaps mean independence and fame, it can also mean great loneliness and the loss of the full and perfect happiness that should be every woman's. You mustn't judge all cases by me. I have been happy in my own way but I want a greater, richer happiness for you, dear. I want for you the best that the world can give, and that best I believe to be the shelter and the safety of a man's love."

The brown head dropped on her knee. "You are thinking of me—I am thinking of him," came a stifled whisper.

Miss Craven stroked the soft hair tenderly. "Then why not give him what he asks, my dear," she said gently. "He has known sorrow and suffering. If through you, he can forget the past in a new happiness, will you not grant it him? Oh, Gillian, I have so hoped that you might care for each other; that, together, you might make the Towers the perfect home it should be, a home of mutual trust and love. You and Barry and, please God, after you—your children." She choked with unexpected emotion and brushed the mist from her eyes impatiently.

And at her knee Gillian knelt motionless, her lip held fast between her teeth to stop the bitter cry that nearly escaped her, her heart almost bursting. The picture Miss Craven's words called up was an ideal of happiness that might have been. The suffering that reality promised seemed more than she could contemplate. What happiness could come from such a travesty? The strange yearnings she had experienced seemed suddenly crystallised into form, and the knowledge was a greater pain than she had known. What she would have gone down to the gates of death to give him he did not require—the unutterable joy that Miss Craven suggested would never be hers. She searched for words, for an explanation of her silence that must seem strange to the elder woman. Miss Craven obviously knew nothing of the unusual conditions attached to his proposal, her words proved it, and Gillian could not tell her. She could not betray his confidence even if she had so wished. If she could but speak frankly and show all her difficulty to the friend who had never yet failed in love and sympathy—She sought refuge in prevarication. "How can I marry him?" she cried miserably. "You don't know anything about me. I'm not a fit person to be his wife— my antecedents—"

"Bother your antecedents!" interrupted Miss Craven, with a somewhat shaky laugh. "My dearest girl, Barry isn't going to marry them, he's going to marry you. They can have been anything you like or imagine but it does not alter the fact that their daughter is the one woman on earth I want for Barry's wife." She stooped and gathered the girl into her arms.

"Gillian, can you give us, Barry and me, this great happiness?"

Gently Gillian disengaged herself and rose slowly to her feet. She made a little helpless gesture, swaying as she stood. "What can I say?" she said brokenly. "Do you think it means nothing to me! Don't you know that what I already owe you and Mr. Craven is almost more than I can bear, that I would give my life for either of you? But this—oh, you don't understand—I can't tell you—I can't explain—" She dropped back on the sofa and her voice came muffled and entreatingly from among the silken cushions, "If you knew how I long to repay you for your wonderful goodness, if you knew what your love has meant to me! Oh, dearest, I'd give the world to please you! But I don't know what to do, I don't know what is honest—and you can't help me, nobody can help me. I've got to settle it myself. I've got to think—"

Miss Craven guessed the crying need for solitude conveyed in the last faltering words and rose in obedience to the unspoken request. She stood for a moment, looking tenderly down on the slim prostrate figure, and a fear that grew momentarily stronger came to her that in her endeavour to bring happiness to these two lives she had blundered fatally. She had been a fool, rushing in. And with almost a feeling of dismay she realised it was beyond her ability now to stay what she had put in motion. She was as one who, having wantonly released some complex mechanism, stands aghast and powerless at the consequence of his rashness. And yet, despite the seeming setback to her hopes, the conviction that had urged her to this step was still strong in her; she still had faith in its ultimate achievement. She touched the girl's shoulder in a quick caress. "You are worn out, child. Go to bed and rest now, and think to-morrow," she said soothingly.

For long after she left the room Gillian lay without moving. Then with a long shuddering sigh she sat up. She tried to concentrate on the decision she must make but her thoughts, ungovernable, dwelt persistently on the unknown woman whom she had convinced herself he must have loved, and the passionate envy she had felt before swept her again until the pain of it sent a whispered prayer to her lips for strength to put it from her. Huddled on the side of the sofa, her head supported on her hands, she stared fixedly into the fire as if seeking in the leaping flames the answer to the problem that confronted her. Then in her agony of mind inaction became impossible and she rose and paced the room with hurried nervous tread.

To do what was right—to do what was honourable; to conquer the clamorous self that cried out for acceptance of this semblance of happiness that was offered. To bear his name, to have the right to be near him, to care for him and for his interests as far as she might. To be his wife—even if only in name. Dear God, did he know how he had tempted her? But she had no right. The crushing burden of debt she owed rose like an unsurpassable mountain between her and what she longed for. Only by repayment could she keep her self-respect. The dreams of independence, the place she had thought to make for herself in the world, the re-establishing of her father's name—could she forego what she had planned? Was it not a nobler aim than the gratification of self that urged the easier way? Yet would it be the easier way? Was she not really in her heart shrinking from the difficulty and sadness that this loveless marriage would bring? Was it not cowardice that prompted a supposed nobility of thought that now appeared ignoble? She wrung her hands in desperation. Had she no courage or steadfastness at all? Was the weakness of purpose that had ruined her father's life to be her curse as it had been his?

She felt suddenly very young, very inexperienced. Her early training that had denied the exercise of individual responsibility and had inculcated a passivity of mind that precluded self-determination had bitten deeper than she knew. Her life since leaving the convent had been smooth and uneventful, there had been no occasion to practise the new liberty of thought and action that was hers. And now before a decision that would be so irrevocable, that would involve her whole life—and not hers alone—she felt to the full the disability of her upbringing. Alone she must make her choice and she shrank from the burden of responsibility that fell upon her. She had nobody to turn to for counsel or advice. In her loneliness she longed for the solace of a mother's tenderness, the shelter of a mother's arms, and bitterness came to her as she thought of the parents who had each in their turn abandoned her so callously. She had been robbed of her birthright of love and care. She was alone in the world, alone to fight her own battles, alone in the moment of her direst need.

Then all at once she seemed to see in the trend of her thoughts only a supreme selfishness that had lost sight of all but personal consideration. Was her love of so little worth that in thought for herself she had forgotten him? He had asked her to pity his loneliness—and she had had only pity for herself. Her lips quivered as she whispered his name in an agony of self-condemnation.

Coming back slowly to the fireside she slipped to the floor and leaned her head against the sofa listening to the storm that beat with increasing violence against the house, and the roar of the tempest without seemed in strange agreement with the tumult that was raging in her heart. The words he had used came back to her. Did it really lie in her power to lessen the loneliness of his life? To give him what he asked—was not that, after all, the true way to pay her debt? With a little sob she bowed her head on her hands. . . An hour later she rose stiffly, cramped with long sitting, and moving nearer to the fire chafed her cold hands mechanically. Her face was very sad and her wide eyes heavy with unshed tears. She drew a long sobbing breath. "Because I love him," she murmured. "If I didn't love him I couldn't do it." A thought that brought new hope came to her. She loved him so deeply, might not her love, she wondered wistfully, perhaps some day be strong enough to heal the wound he had sustained—strong enough even to compel his love? Then doubt seized hold on her again. Would she, in the limited scope that she would have, find opportunity— would he ever allow her to get near enough to him? . . . She flung her hands out in passionate appeal.

"Oh, God! if this thing that I am doing is wrong, if it brings sorrow and unhappiness, let me be the only one to pay!"

A sudden longing to make retraction impossible came over her. She looked anxiously at her watch. Was it too late to go to him to-night? Only when she had told him would she be sure of herself. Her word once given there could be no withdrawal.

It was nearly midnight but she knew he rarely left his study until later. Peters would be gone, he was methodical in his habits and retired punctually at eleven o'clock with a regularity that was unvarying. She was sure of finding him alone. She dared not wait until the morning, she must go now while she had the courage. Delay might bring new doubts, new uncertainty. Impulsively she started towards the door, then paused on a sudden thought that sent the warm blood in a painful wave to her face. Would he misunderstand, think her unwomanly, attribute her hasty decision to a sordid desire for material gain, for the ease that would be hers, for the position that his name would give? It was the natural thought for him who offered so much to one who would give nothing in return. And not for him alone—in the eyes of the world she would be only a little adventuress who had skilfully seized the opportunity that circumstance had given to advantage herself. But the world did not matter, she thought with scornful curling lip, it was only in his eyes that she desired to stand well. Then with quick shame she knew that the sentiments she had ascribed to him were unworthy, the outcome only of her own strained imagination, and she put them from her. She went quickly to the gallery, dimly lit from a single lamp left alight in the hall below—left for Craven as she knew. Silence brooded over the great house. The storm that earlier had beat tempestuously against the dome as if striving to shatter the massive glass plates that opposed its fury had blown itself out and glancing upward Gillian saw the huge cupola shrouded with snow that gleamed palely in the soft light. The stillness oppressed her and odd thoughts chased through her mind. She looked to right and left nervously and in a sudden inexplicable panic sped down the wide staircase and across the shadowy hall until she reached the study door. There she halted with wildly beating heart, panting and breathless. It was a room which she had never before entered, and an almost paralysing shyness made her shake from head to foot. Nerving herself with a strong effort she tapped with trembling fingers and, at the sound of an answering voice, went in.

Strength seemed all at once to leave her. Physically and mentally exhausted, a feeling of unreality supervened. The strange room swam before her eyes. As in a dream she saw him start to his feet and come swiftly to her across a seemingly unending length of carpet that billowed and wavered curiously, his big frame oddly magnified until he appeared a very giant towering above her; as in a dream she felt him take her ice-cold hands in his. But the warm strong grasp, the grave eyes bent compellingly on her, dragged her back from the shuddering abyss into which she was sinking. Far away, as though coming from a great distance, she heard him speaking. And his voice, gentler than she had ever known it, gave her courage to whisper, so low that he had to bend his tall head to catch the fluttering words, the promise she had come to give.

VII

O n an afternoon in early September eighteen months after her marriage Gillian was driving across the park toward the little village of Craven that, old world and quite unspoiled, clustered round a tiny Norman church two miles distant from the Towers. She leaned back in the victoria, her hands clasped in her lap, preoccupied and thoughtful. A scented heap of deep crimson roses and carnations lay at her feet; beside her, in contrast to her listless attitude, Mouston sat up tense and watchful, his sharp muzzle thrust forward, his black nose twitching eagerly at the distracting agitating smells borne on the warm air tempting him from monotonous inactivity to a soul satisfying scamper over the short cropped grass but, conscious of the dignity of his position, ignoring them with a gravity of demeanour that was almost comical. Once or twice when his wrinkling nostrils caught some particularly attractive odour his pads kneaded the cushions vigorously and a snarly gurgle rose in his throat. But no other sign of restlessness escaped him—it was patience bred of experience. For miles around he was a well-known figure, sitting grave and motionless on his accustomed side of the victoria as it rolled through the country lanes. To the villagers of Craven, all directly or indirectly dependent on the estate, he was welcome in that he was inseparable from the gentle tender-hearted girl whom they worshipped, but their welcome was a qualified one that never descended to the familiar; his strange appearance and disdainful aloofness made him an object of curiosity to be viewed with most safety from a respectful distance; time had not accustomed them to him and tales of his uncanny understanding filtering through, richly embroidered, to the village from the house, did not tend to lessen the awe with which he was regarded. They marvelled, without comprehension, at the partiality of his mistress; he was the "black French devil" to more households than that of Major, the gamekeeper, an "unorranary brute" to those of less gifted imagination.

To Mouston Gillian's periodical visits to the village were a tedium endured for the sake of the coveted seat beside her.

The passing of a herd of deer, feeding intently and—save for one or two more timid hinds who started nervously—too used to the carriage to heed its approach, roused the poodle, as always, to a high pitch of excitement; they were old enemies and his annoyance gave vent to a sharp yelp as he sidled close to Gillian and endeavoured to attract her attention with an insistent paw. But for once she was heedless of the hints of her dumb companion, and, whining, he slunk back into his own corner, curling up on the seat with his forepaws brushing the mass of scented blossom. And ignorant of the pleading brown eyes fixed pathetically on her, Gillian followed the train of her own troubled thoughts. For eighteen months she had been Barry Craven's wife, for eighteen months she had endeavoured to fulfill her share of the contract they had made—and to herself she admitted failure.

The strain was becoming unendurable.

In the eyes of the world an ideal couple, in reality—she wondered if in the whole universe there were two more lonely souls than they. She knew now that the task she had set herself that stormy December night was beyond her power, that it had been the unattainable dream of an immature love-sick girl. She had fought to retain her high ideals, to believe that love—as great, as unselfish as hers—must beget love, but she had come to realise the utter futility of her dream and to wonder at the childish ignorance that had inspired it. The sustaining hope that she might indeed be a comfort to his loneliness had died hard, but surely. For he gave her no opportunity. Despite unfailing kindness and overwhelming generosity he maintained always a baffling reserve she found impossible to penetrate. Of his inner self she knew no more than she had ever done, she could get no nearer to him. But in all matters that dealt with their common life he was scrupulously frank and out-spoken; he had insisted on her acquiring a knowledge of his interests and a working idea of his affairs, from which she had shrunk sensitively, but he had persisted, arguing that in the event of his death—Peters not being immortal—it was necessary that she should be able to administer possessions that would be hers—and the thought of those possessions crushed her. It was only after a long struggle, in distress that horrified him, that she persuaded him to forego the big settlement he proposed making. If she had not loved him his liberality would have hurt her less, but because of her love his money was a scourge. She hated the wealth to which she felt she had no right, to herself she seemed an impostor, a cheat. She felt degraded. She would rather he had bought her, as women have from time immemorial been bought, that she might have paid the price, as they pay, and so retained the self-respect that now seemed for ever lost. It would have been a means of re-establishing herself in her own eyes, of easing the burden of his bounty that grew daily heavier and from which she could never escape. It was evident in all about her; in the greater state and ceremony observed at the Towers since their marriage, which, while it pleased the household, who rejoiced in the restoration of the old régime, oppressed her unspeakably; in the charities she dispensed—his charities that brought her no sense of sacrifice, no joy of self-denial; in the social duties that poured in upon her.

His wealth served only to strengthen the barrier between them, but for that she might have been to him what she longed to be. If the talent that now seemed so useless could have been used for him she would have found a measure of happiness even if love had never come to crown her service. In poverty she would have worked for him, slaved for him, with the strength and tirelessness that only love can give. But here the gladness of giving, of serving, was denied, here there was nothing she might do and the futility of her life choked her. She had conscientiously endeavoured to assume the responsibilities and duties of her new position, but there seemed little for her to do, for the big household ran smoothly on oiled wheels under the capable administration of Forbes and Mrs. Appleyard, with whom, both honest and devoted to the interests of the family they had served so long and faithfully, she knew it was unnecessary and unwise to interfere. In any unusual circumstance they would refer to her with tactful deference but for the rest she knew that, perforce, she must be content to remain a figure-head. Even her work—interrupted constantly by the social duties incumbent on her and performed from a sense of obligation—failed to comfort and distract. It was all so utterly useless and purposeless. The gift with which she had thought to do so much was wasted. She could do nothing with it. She was no longer Gillian Locke who had dreamed of independence, who had hoped by toil and endeavour to clear the stain from her father's name. She was the rich Mrs. Craven—who must smile to hide a breaking heart, who must play the part expected of her, who must appear always care-free and happy. And the constant effort was almost more than she could achieve. In the ceaseless watch she set upon herself, in the rigid self-suppression she exercised, it seemed to her as if her true self had died, and her entity faded into an automaton that moved in mechanical obedience to the driving of her will. Only during the long night hours or in the safe seclusion of the studio could she relax, could she be natural for a little while. That Craven might never learn the misery of her life, that she might not fail him as she had failed herself, was her one prayer. She welcomed eagerly the advent of guests, of foreign guests—more exigent in their demands upon her society—particularly; with the house filled the time of host and hostess was fully occupied and the difficult days passed more easily, more quickly. The weeks they spent alone she dreaded; from the morning greeting in the breakfast room to the moment when he gave her the quiet "Good-night" that might have come from an undemonstrative brother, she was in terror lest an unguarded word, a chance expression, might tell him what she sought to keep from him. But so insensible did his own constant pre-occupation of mind make him appear of much that passed, that she feared his intuition less than that of Peters who she was convinced had a very shrewd idea of the state of affairs existing between them. It was manifested in diverse ways; not by any spoken word direct or indirect, but by additional fatherly tenderness of manner, by unfailing tactfulness, by quick intervention that had saved many awkward situations. It was practically impossible in view of his almost daily association with the house and its inmates that he could be unaware of certain facts. But the wise kindly eyes that she had feared most were closed for ever.

The Great Summons for which Miss Craven had been so calmly prepared had come more suddenly, more tragically even than she had anticipated. She had passed over as she would have wished, had she been given the choice, not in the awful loneliness of death but one of a company of heroic souls who had voluntarily and willingly stood aside that others might have the chance to live.

A few months after the marriage on which she had set her heart the family curse had seized her as suddenly and as imperatively as it had ever done her nephew. An exhibition of statuary in America had served as an adequate excuse and she had started at comparatively short notice, accompanied by the faithful Mary, after a stormy interview with her doctor, whose gloomy warnings she refuted with the undeniable truism that one land was as good as another to die in. Within a few hours of the American coast the tragedy, short and overwhelming, had occurred. From the parent ice a thousand miles away in the north the stupendous white destruction had moved majestically down its appointed course to loom out of the pitch-black night with appalling consequence. A sudden crash, slight enough to be unnoticed by hundreds, a convulsive shudder of the great ship like the death struggle of a Titan, had been followed by unquellable panic, confusion of darkness, inadequate boats and jamming bulkheads. Miss Craven and Mary were among the first

E. M. HULL

on deck and for the short space of time that remained they worked side by side among the terror-stricken women and children, their own life-belts early transferred to dazed mothers who clutched wild-eyed at wailing babes. Together they had stood back from the overcrowded boats, smiling and unafraid; together they had gone down into the mystery of the deep, two gallant women, no longer mistress and maid but sisters in sacrifice and in the knowledge of that greater love for which they cheerfully laid down their lives.

And while Gillian mourned her bitterly she was yet glad that Miss Craven was spared the sadness of witnessing the complete failure of her cherished dream.

In the little Norman church toward which Gillian was driving there had been added yet another memorial to a Craven who had died tragically and far from home; a record of disastrous calamity that, beginning four hundred years before with the Elizabethan gallant, had relentlessly pursued an ill-starred family. The church lay on the outskirts of the village and close to the south entrance of the park.

Gillian stopped the carriage for a few moments to speak to the anxious-looking woman who had hurried out from the creeper-covered lodge to open the gates. Behind one of the casements of the cottage a child was fighting for life, a cripple, with an exquisite face, whom Gillian had painted. To the sorrowful mother the eager tender words, the soft impulsive hand that clasped her own work-roughened palm, the wide dark eyes, misty with sympathy were worth infinitely more than the material aid, so carefully packed by Mrs. Appleyard, that the footman carried up the narrow nagged path to the cottage door.

And as the impatient horses drew the carriage swiftly on again Gillian leaned back in her seat with a quivering sigh. The woman at the lodge, despite her burden of sorrow, despite her humbleness, was yet richer than she and, with intolerable pain, she envied her the crowning joy of womanhood that would never be her own. The child she longed for would never by the touch baby hands bring consolation to her starved and lonely heart. Her thoughts turned to her husband in a sudden passion of hopeless love and longing. To bear him a child—to hold in her arms a tiny replica of the beloved figure that was so dear to her, to watch and rejoice in the dawning resemblance that the ardour of her love would make inevitable. . . Hastily she brushed away the gathering tears as the carriage stopped abruptly with a jingle of harness at the lichgate.

Coaxing the reluctant Mouston from the seat where he still sulked she tied him to the gate, took the armful of flowers from the grave-faced footman, and dismissing the carriage walked slowly up the lime-bordered avenue. The orderliness and beauty of the churchyard struck her as it always did—a veritable garden of sleep, with level close-shorn turf set thick with standard rose trees, that even the clustering headstones could not make chill and sombre.

From the radiant sunshine without she passed into the cool dimness of the little building. With its tiny proportions, ornate and numerous Craven memorials and—for its size—curiously large chancel, it seemed less the parish church it had become than the private chapel for which it had been built. Then the house had been close by, but during the troublous years of Mary Tudor was pulled down and rebuilt on the present site.

Through the quiet silence Gillian made her way up the short central aisle until she reached the chancel steps. For a few minutes she knelt, her face crushed against the flowers she held, in silent passionate prayer that knew neither form nor words—a soundless supplication that was an inchoate appeal to a God of infinite understanding. Then rising slowly she pushed back the iron gate and went into the chancel. Directly to the left the new monument gleamed cleanly white against the old dark wall. Simple and bold, as she would herself have designed it, the sculptor's memorial was the work of the greatest genius of the day who had willingly come from France at Craven's invitation to perpetuate the memory of a sister artist who had also been a lifelong friend.

A rugged pedestal of green bronze—with an inset panel representing the tragedy—rose upward in the shape of billowing curling waves supporting a marble Christ standing erect with outstretched pitying hand, majestic and yet wholly human.

Gillian gazed upward with quivering lips at the Saviour's inclined tender face, and opening her arms let the scented mass of crimson blossom fall slowly to the slab at her feet that bore Miss Craven's name and Mary's cut side by side.

> "Greater love hath no man than this, that
> a man lay down his life for his friends."

She read the words aloud, and with a stifled sob slipped down among the roses and carnations that Caro Craven had loved, and leaned her aching head against the cool hard bronze. "Dearest," she whispered, in an agony of tears, "I wonder can you hear? I wonder are you allowed, where you are, to know what happens here on earth? Oh, Aunt Caro, *cherie*, do you know that I have failed—failed to bring him the peace and consolation I thought my love was strong enough to give, I have tried so hard to understand, to help. . . I have prayed so earnestly that he might turn to me, that I might be to him what you would have me be. . . but I have not been able. . . I have failed him. . . failed you. . . myself. Oh, dearest, do you know?"

Prone among the roses, at the feet of the pitying Christ, she cried aloud in her desperate loneliness to the dead woman who had given her the tenderest love she had ever known. The shadows lengthened widely before she rose and drew the scattered flowers into a fragrant heap. She stood for a while studying intently the relief of the wreck; it suggested a train of thought, and with a sudden impulse she traversed the chancel and sought among the memorials of dead Cravens for the tablets commemorating those who had disappeared or died tragically. By chance at first and later by design these had all been placed within the confines of the chancel that formed so large a part of the tiny church. Before the florid Italian monument that recorded all that was known of the short life of the Elizabethan adventurer she paused long, looking with quickening heart-beat at the graceful kneeling figure whose face and form were those of the man she loved.

Barry Craven. . . he set his eyes unto the west. . . Amongst the calamitous record there were four more of the name—their bodies scattered widely in distant unknown graves, victims of the spirit of adventure and unrest. She moved slowly from one to the other, reading again the tragical inscriptions she knew by heart, cut as deeply in her memory as on the marble slabs before her.

Barry Craven—Lost in the Amazon Forest.
Barry Craven—In the silence of the frozen seas.
Barry Craven—Perished in a sandstorm in the Sahara.
Barry Craven—In Japan.
Barry Craven—Barry Craven.

The name leaped at her from all sides until, with a shudder, she buried her face in her hands to shut out the staring capitals that flamed in black and gold before her eyes. The dread that was with her always seemed suddenly closer than it had ever been, menacing, inevitable. Would the fear that haunted her day and night become at some not far distant time an actual fact? Would the curse that had already led to ten years' perpetual wandering lay hold of him again—would he, too, in quest of the peace he had never found, disappear as they had done? Was it for this that he had insisted on her acquiring a knowledge of his affairs? With the quick intuition of love she had come to understand the deep unrest that beset him periodically, an unrest she recognised as wholly apart and separate from the other shadow that lay across his life. With unfailing patience she had learned to discriminate. Covertly she had watched him, striving to fathom the varying moods that swayed him, endeavouring to anticipate the alternating frames of mind that made any definite comprehension of his character so difficult. The charm of manner and apparent serenity that led others to think of him as one endowed beyond further desire with all that life could give did not deceive her. He played a part, as she did, a part that was contrary to his nature, contrary to his whole inclination. She guessed at the strain on him, a strain it seemed impossible for him to endure, which some day she felt must inevitably break. His habitual self-control was extraordinary—once only during their married life had he lost it when some event, jarring on his overstrung nerves, had evoked a blaze of anger that seemed totally out of proportion to the circumstance, that would have given her proof, had she needed one, of his state of mind.

His outburst had been a perfectly natural reaction, but while she admitted the fact she felt a nervous dread of its recurrence.

She feared anything that might precipitate the upheaval that loomed always before her like a threatening cloud. For sooner or later the unrest that filled him would have to be satisfied. The curse of Craven would claim him again and he would leave her. And she would have to watch him go and wait in agony for his return as other women of the race had watched and agonised. And if he went would he ever return? or would she too know the anguish of suspense, the long drawn horror of uncertainty, the fading hope that year by year would become slighter until at last it would vanish altogether and the bitter waters of despair close over her head? A moan, like the cry of a wounded animal, broke from her. In vivid self-torturing imagination she saw among the sinister record around her another tablet—that would mean finality. He was the last of the Cravens. Did it mean nothing to him—had the sorrow of that past that was unknown to her but which had become woven into her own life so inextricably, so terribly, killed in him even the pride of race? Had he, deep down in the heart that was hidden from her, no thought of parenthood, no desire to perpetuate the family name, the family traditions? It would seem that he had not—and yet she wondered. The woman he had loved—of whose existence she had convinced herself—if she had lived, or proved faithful, would he still have desired no son? She shrank from the stabbing thought with a very bitter sob.

A sudden horror of her environment came over her. Around her were suggestions from which she shuddered, evidences that raised the haunting dread with which she lived to a culmination of fear. It had never seemed so near, so strong. It was stronger than her will to put it from her and in it, with inherent superstition, she saw a premonition. The little peaceful church became all at once a place of terror, a grisly charnel house of vanished hopes and lives. The spirits of countless Cravens seemed all about her, hostile, malign, triumphing in her weakness, rejoicing in her fear—spectral figures of the dead crowding, hurrying, threatening. She seemed to see them, a dense and awful concourse, closing round her, to hear them whispering, muttering, jibing—at her, a thing apart, an alien soul whose presence they resented. The clamorous voices rang in her ears; vague shapes, illusive and shadowy, appeared to float before her eyes. She shrank from what seemed the contact of actual bodily forms. Unnerved and overwrought she yielded to the horror of her own imagination. With a stifled cry she turned and fled, her arms outstretched to fend from her the invisible host that seemed so real, not daring even to look again at the pitying Christ whose calm serenity formed such a striking contrast to her storm-tossed heart.

Blindly she sped down the chancel steps, along the short central aisle, out into the timbered porch, where she blundered sharply into somebody who was on the point of entering. Who, it did not at the moment seem to matter—enough that it was a human creature, real and tangible, to whom she clung trembling and incoherent. A strong arm held her, and against its strength she leaned for a few moments in the weakness of reaction from the nervous strain through which she had passed. Then as she slowly regained control of herself she realised the awkwardness of her position, and her cheeks burned hotly. She drew back, her fingers uncurling from the tweed coat they clutched so tightly, and, trying to slip clear of the arm that still lay about her shoulders, looked up shyly with murmured thanks.

Then: "David," she cried. "Oh, David—" and burst into tears. Guiding her to the bench that rested against the side of the porch Peters drew her down beside him. "Just David," he said, with rather a sad little smile, "I was passing and Mouston told me you were here." He spoke slowly, giving her time to recover herself, thanking fate that she had collapsed into his arms rather than into those of some chattering village busybody. He had caught a glimpse of her face as she came through the church door and knew that her agitation was caused by something more than sorrow for Miss Craven, great as that sorrow was. He had seen fear in the hunted eyes that looked unrecognisingly into his—a fear that he somehow resented with a feeling of helpless anger.

The affection he had for her was such as he would have given the daughter that might have been his had providence been kinder. And with the insight that affection gave he had seen, with acute uneasiness, a steadily increasing change in her during the last eighteen months. The marriage from which he, as well as Miss Craven, had hoped so much seemed after all to have brought no joy to either husband or wife. With his intimate knowledge and close association he saw deeper than the casual visitor to whom the family life at the Towers appeared an ideal of domestic happiness and concord. There was nothing he could actually take hold of, Craven was at all times considerate and thoughtful, Gillian a model of wifely attention. But there was an atmosphere that, super-sensitive, he discerned, a vague underlying feeling of tension that he tried to persuade himself was mere imagination but which at the bottom of his heart he knew existed. There had been times when he had seen them both, as it were, off their guard, had read in the face of each the same bitter pain, the same look of unsatisfied longing. Possessing in so high a degree everything that life could give they appeared to have yet missed the happiness that should by all reasoning have been theirs. Whose was the fault? Caring for them both it was a question that he turned from in aversion, he had no wish to judge between them, no desire to probe their hidden affairs. Thrown constantly into their society while guessing much he shut his eyes to more. But anxiety remained, fostered by the memory of the tragedy of Barry's father and mother. Was he fated to see just such another tragedy played out before him with no power to avert the ruin of two more lives? The pity of it! He could do nothing and his helplessness galled him.

To-day as he sat in the little porch with Gillian's hand clasped in his he felt more than ever the extreme delicacy of his position. Intuitively he guessed that he was nearer than he had ever been to penetrating the cloud that shadowed her life and Barry's but with equal intuition he knew he must convey no hint of his understanding. He gauged her shy sensitive mind too accurately and his own loyalty debarred him from forcing such a confidence. Instead he spoke as though the visit to Miss Craven's memorial must naturally be the cause of her agitation.

"Why come, my dear, if it distresses you?" he said, in quiet remonstrance; "she would not misunderstand. She had the sanest, the healthiest conception of death. She died nobly—willingly. It would sadden her immeasurably if she knew how you grieved." Her fingers worked convulsively in his. "I know—I know," she whispered, "but, oh, David, I miss her so—so inexpressibly."

"We all do," he answered; "one cannot lose a friend like Caro Craven lightly. But while we mourn the dead we have the living to consider—and you have Barry," he added, with almost cruel deliberation. She faced him with steady eyes from which she had brushed all trace of tears.

"Barry understands," she said with quick loyalty; "he mourns her too—but he doesn't *need* her as I do." It was an undeniable truth that reduced Peters to silence and for a while Gillian also was silent. Then she turned to him again with a little tremulous smile, the colour flooding her delicate face.

"I'm glad it was only you, David, just now. Please forget it. I don't know what's the matter with me to-day, I let my nerves get the upper hand—I'm tired—the sun was hot—"

"So of course you sent the carriage away and proposed walking two miles home by way of a rest cure!" he interrupted, jumping up with alacrity, and taking advantage of the turn in the conversation. "Luckily I've got the car. Plenty of room for you and the pampered one." And waving aside her protests he tucked her into the little two-seater, bundling Mouston unceremoniously in after her.

The village school was near the church, and while Peters steered the car carefully through groups of children who were loitering in the road she sat silent beside him, wondering, in miserable self-condemnation, how much she had betrayed during those few moments of hysterical outburst. Resolutely she determined that she would be strong, strong enough to put away the dread that haunted her, strong enough to meet trouble only when it came.

Clear of the children and running smoothly through the park Peters condescended to break the silence.

"How went Scotland?" he asked, slowing down behind a frightened fawn who was straying on the carriage road and cantering ahead of the car in panicky haste. "Your letters were not satisfactory."

"I wasn't taught to write letters. I never had any to write," she said with a smile that made the sensitive man beside her wince. "I did my best, David, dear. And there wasn't much to tell. There were only men— Barry said he couldn't stand women with the guns again after the bother they were last year. They were nice men, shy silent creatures, big game hunters mostly, and two doctors who have been doing research work in Central Africa. When any of them could be induced to talk of their experiences it was a revelation to me of what men will endure and yet consider enjoyment. You would have liked them, David. Why didn't you come? It would have done you more good than that horrid little yacht. And we were alone the last two weeks—we missed you," she added reproachfully.

Peters had had his own reasons for absenting himself from the Scotch lodge, reasons that, connected as they were with Craven and his wife, he could not enlarge upon. He turned the question with a laugh.

"The yacht was better suited to a crusty old bachelor, my dear," he smiled. Then he gave her a searching glance. "And what did you do all day long by yourself while the men were on the hills?"

She gave a little shrug.

"I sketched—and—oh, lots of things," she answered, rather vaguely. "There's always plenty to do wherever you are if you take the trouble to look for it."

"Which most people don't," he replied, bringing the car to a standstill before the front door.

"Is Barry back from London?"

"Coming this afternoon. Thanks for the lift, David, you've been a Good Samaritan this afternoon. I don't think I could have walked. Goodbye—and please forget," she whispered.

He smile reassuringly and waved his hand as he restarted the car.

Calling to Mouston, who was rolling happily on the cool grass, she went slowly into the house. With the poodle rushing round her she mounted thoughtfully the wide stairs and turned down the corridor leading to the studio. It seemed of all rooms the one best suited to her mood. She wanted to be alone, beyond the reach of any chance caller, beyond the possibility of interruption, and it was understood by all that in the studio she must not be disturbed.

E.M. HULL

In the passage she met her maid and, giving her her hat and gloves, ordered tea to be sent to her.

Mouston trotted on ahead into the room with the confident air of a proprietor, fussily inspecting the contents with the usual canine interest as if suspicious that some familiar article of furniture had been removed during his absence and anxious to reassure himself that all things were as he had left them. Then he curled up with a satisfied grunt on the chesterfield beside which he knew tea would be placed. Gillian looked about her with a sigh. The room, much as she loved it, had never been the same to her since that December afternoon that seemed so much longer than a bare eighteen months ago. The peace it had given formerly was gone. Now there was associated with it always the memory of bitter pain. She had never been able to recapture the old feeling of freedom and happiness it had inspired. It was her refuge still, where she came to wrestle with herself in solitude, where she sought forgetfulness in long hours of work but it was no longer the antechamber to a castle of dreams. There were no dreams left, only a crushing numbling reality. She thought of her husband, and the question that was always in her mind seemed to-day more than ever insistent. Why had he married her? The reason he had given had been disproved by his subsequent attitude. He had asked her to take pity on a lonely man—and he had given her no opportunity. She had tried by every means in her power to get nearer to him, to be to him what she thought he meant her to be and all her endeavour had come to nothing. Had she tried enough, done enough? Miserably she wondered would another have succeeded where she had failed? And had she failed because, after all, the reason he had given was no true reason? And suddenly, for the first time, in a vivid flash of illuminating comprehension she seemed to realise the true reason and the quixotic generosity that had prompted it. It was as if a veil had been rudely torn from before her eyes. It explained much, letting in an entirely new light upon many things that had puzzled her. It placed her in a new position, changing her whole mental standpoint. How could she have been so stupidly blind, so dense—how could she have misunderstood? He had lied to her, a kindly noble lie, but a lie notwithstanding—he had married her out of pity, to provide for her in the lack of faith he had in her power to provide for herself. To him, then, her dreams of independence had been only a childish ambition that he judged unsubstantial, and in his dilemma he had conceived it his duty to do what seemed to her now a thing intolerable. A burning wave of shame went through her. She was humiliated to the very dust, crushed with the sense of obligation. She was only another burden thrust upon him by a man who had had no claim to his liberality. Her father— the superman of her childish dreams! How had he dared? If love for him had not died years before it would have died at that moment in the fierce resentment that burned in her. But to the man who had so willingly accepted such an imposition her heart went out in greater love and deeper gratitude than she had yet known.

Yet, how, with this new knowledge searing her soul, could she ever face him again? She longed to creep away and hide like a stricken animal—and he was coming home to-day. Within a few hours she would have to meet him, conscious at last of the full extent of her indebtedness and conscious also of the impossibility of communicating her discovery. For she knew that she could never bring herself to refer to it, and she knew him well enough to be aware that any such reference was out of the question. The gulf between them was too wide. The two days she had spent alone at the Towers had seemed interminable, but with a revulsion of feeling she wished now that his coming could be delayed. She shrank from even the thought of seeing him. Though she called herself coward she determined to postpone the meeting she dreaded until dinner, when the presence of Forbes and a couple of footmen would brace her to meet the situation and give her time to prepare for the later more difficult hours when she would be alone with him. For he made a practice, rigidly adhered to, of sitting with her in the evenings during the short time she remained downstairs. He was punctilious in that courtesy as in all other acts of consideration. His own bed-hour was very much later and she often wondered what he did, what were his thoughts, alone in the solitary study that was his refuge as the studio was hers.

But she had come almost to fear the evening hours they spent together, the feeling of constraint was becoming more and more an embarrassment. The last two weeks in Scotland had been more difficult than any preceding them. Craven's restlessness had been more apparent, more pronounced. And looking back on it now she wondered whether it was association with the men with whom he had travelled and shot in distant countries that was stirring in him more acutely the wander-hunger that was in his blood. During the after dinner reminiscences in the Scotch shooting lodge he had himself been curiously silent, but he had sat listening with a kind of fierce intentness that to her anxious

E.M. HULL

watching eyes had been like the forced calm of a caged animal enduring captivity with seeming resignation but cherishing always thoughts of escape.

It was then that her vague dread leaped suddenly into concrete fear. An incident that had occurred a few days after the big game hunters had left them had further disquieted her. On going to him for advice on some domestic difficulty she had found him poring over a large map. He had rolled it up at her approach and his manner had made it impossible for her to express an interest that would otherwise have seemed natural. With the reticence to which she had schooled herself she had made no comment, but the thought of that rolled up hidden canvas and its possible significance remained with her. It might mean only a renewed interest in the scenes of past exploits—fervently she hoped it did. But it might also mean the projection of new activities. . .

The arrival of a footman bringing tea put a period to her thoughts. While the man arranged the simple necessaries that were more suited to the studio than the elaborate display Forbes considered indispensable downstairs, she crossed the room to an easel where stood a half-finished picture. She looked at it critically. Was he right—was there, after all, nothing in her work but the mediocre endeavour of an amateur? She had been so confident, so sure. And the master in Paris who had taught her—he also had been confident and sure. Yet as she studied the uncompleted sketch before her she felt her confidence waver. It had not satisfied her while she was working on it, it seemed now hopelessly and utterly bad. With a heavy sigh she stared at it despondently, seeing in it the failure of all her hopes. Then in quick recoil courage came again. One piece of bad work did not constitute failure—she would not admit failure. She had worked on it at a time of extreme depression, when all the world had seemed black and hopeless, and the deplorable result was due to lack of concentration. She had allowed her own disturbed thoughts to intrude too vividly, and her wandering attention, her unhappiness, had reacted disastrously on her work. It must be so. Her own judgment she might have doubted, but the word of her teacher—no. She *had* to succeed, she had to justify herself, to justify de Myères. "*Travaillez, travaillez, et puis encore travaillez,*" she murmured, as she had heard him say a hundred times, and tore the sketch across and across, tossing the pieces into a large wicker basket. With a little shrug she turned to the tea table beside which Mouston was sitting up in eager expectation, watching the dancing kettle lid with solemn brown eyes. She made tea and then drew the dog close to her, hugging him with almost passionate fervour. It was not a frequent event, but there were times when her starved affections, craving outlet, were expended in default of other medium upon the poodle who gave in return a devotion that was entirely single-minded. Yoshio was still the only member of the household who could touch him with impunity, and toward Craven his attitude was a curious mixture of hatred and fear. To Mouston—her only confidant—she whispered now the new projects she had formed during the last two solitary days for a better understanding of the obscure mind that had hitherto baffled her, for a further endeavour to break through the barrier existing between them. To speak, if only to a dog, was relief and she was too engrossed to notice the sound the poodle's quick ears caught directly. With a growl he wrenched his head free of her arm and, startled, she looked up expecting to see a servant.

She saw instead her husband. His unexpected appearance in a room he habitually avoided robbed her, all unprepared to meet him as she was, of the power of speech. White-lipped she stared at him, unable to formulate even a conventional greeting, her heart beating rapidly as she watched him cross the room. He, too, seemed to have no words, and she saw with increased nervousness that his face was dark with obvious displeasure. The silence that was fast becoming marked was broken by Mouston who with another angry snarl leaped suddenly at Craven with jealous hostility, to be caught up swiftly by a pair of powerful hands and flung into a far corner, where he landed heavily with a shrill yelp of surprise and pain that died away in a broken whimper as, cowed by the unlooked-for retribution, he crawled under a big bureau that seemed to offer a safe retreat.

"Barry!" Gillian's exclamation of incredulous amazement made Craven sensible that the punishment he had inflicted must seem to her unnecessarily severe. She could not be expected to see into his mind, could not possibly know the feeling of loathing inspired by the sight of the poodle in her arms. He was jealous—of a dog and in no mood to curb the temper that his jealousy roused.

"I am sorry," he said shortly. "I didn't mind him going for me, it's perhaps natural that he should—but I hate to see you kiss the dam' brute," he added with a sudden violence in his voice that braced her as a more temperate explanation would not have done. To be deliberately cruel to an animal, no matter how great the provocation, was unlike Craven; she felt convinced that Mouston was not the primary cause of his irritability. Something must have occurred previously to disturb him—the business, perhaps, for which he had waited in London, and, seeking her, the scene he had surprised had grated on fretted nerves. He had never before commented on her affection for the dog who was her shadow; he had never even remonstrated with her, as Peters had many times, for spoiling him. His present attitude seemed therefore the more inexplicable—but she realised the impossibility of remonstrance. The dog had behaved badly and had suffered for his indiscretion; she could not defend him—had she wanted to. And she did not want to. At the moment Mouston hardly seemed to matter—nothing mattered but the unbearable fact of Craven's displeasure. If she could have known the real cause of that displeasure it would have made speech easier. She feared to aggravate his mood but she knew some answer was expected of her. Silence might be misconstrued.

With calmness she did not feel she forced her voice to steadiness.

"Most women make fools of themselves over some animal, *faute de mieux*," she said lightly. "I only follow the crowd."

"Is it *faute de mieux* with you?" The sharp rejoinder struck her like a physical blow. Unable to trust herself, unable to check the quivering of her lips, she turned away to get another cup and saucer from a near cabinet.

"Answer me, Gillian," he said tensely. "Is it for want of something better that you give so much affection to that cringing beast"—he pointed to the poodle who was crawling abjectly on his stomach toward her from the bureau where he had taken refuge—"is it a child that your arms are wanting—not a dog?" His face was drawn, and he stared at her with fierce hunger smouldering in his eyes. He was hurting himself beyond belief—was he hurting her too? Could anything that he might say touch her, stir her from the calm placidity that sometimes, in contradiction to his own restlessness, was almost more than he could tolerate? She had fulfilled the terms of their bargain faithfully, apparently satisfied with its limitation. She appeared content with this damnable life they were living. But a sudden impulse had come to him to assure himself that his supposition was a true one, that the outward content she manifested did not cover longings and desires that she sought to hide. Yet how would it benefit either of them for him to wring from her a secret to which he, by his own doing, had no right? In winning her consent to this divided marriage he had already done her injury enough—he need not make her life harder. And just now, in a moment of ungovernable passion, he had said a brutal thing, a thing beyond all forgiveness. His face grew more drawn as he moved nearer to her.

"Gillian, I asked you a question," he began unsteadily. She confronted him swiftly. Her eyes were steady under his, though the pallor of her face was ghastly.

"You are the one person who has no right to ask me that question, Barry." There was no anger in her voice, there was not even reproach, but a gentle dignity that almost unmanned him. He turned away with a gesture of infinite regret.

"I beg your pardon," he said, in a strangled voice. "I was a cur—what I said was damnable." He faced her again with sudden vehemence. "I wish to God I had left you free. I had no right to marry you, to ruin your life with my selfishness, to bar you from the love and children that should have been yours. You might have met a man who would have given you both, who would have given you the full happy life you ought to have. In my cursed egoism I have done you almost the greatest injury a man can do a woman. My God, I wonder you don't hate me!"

She forced back the words that rushed to her lips. She knew the danger of an unconsidered answer, the danger of the whole situation. The durability of their future life seemed to depend on her reply, its continuance to hang on a slender thread that, perilously strained, threatened momentarily to snap. She was fearful of precipitating the crisis she had long realised was pending and which now seemed drawing to a head. An unconsidered word, an intonation even, might bring about the catastrophe she feared.

She sought for time, praying for inspiration to guide her. The waiting tea table supplied her immediate want.

Mechanically she filled the cups and cut cake with deliberate precision while her mind worked feverishly.

His distress weighed with her more than her own.

Positive as she now was of the true reason that had prompted him to marry her she saw in his outburst only another chivalrous attempt to hide that reason from her. He had purposely endeavoured to misrepresent himself, and, understanding, a wave of passionate gratitude filled her.

Her love was clamouring for audible expression. If she could only speak! If she could only break through the restrictions that hampered her, tell him all that was in her heart, measure the force of her living love against the phantom of that dead past that had killed in him all the joy of life. But she could not speak. Pride kept her silent, and the knowledge that she could not add to the burden he already bore the embarrassment of an unsought love.

But something she must say, and that before he noticed the hesitation that might rob her words of any worth. Only by refusing to attach an undue value to the significance of what he had said could she arrest the dangerous trend of the conversation and bring it to a safer level.

She sat down slowly, re-arranging the simple tray with ostentatious care.

"You didn't force me to marry you, Barry," she said quietly. "I knew what I was doing, I realised the difficulties that might arise. But you have nothing to reproach yourself with. You have been kind and considerate in everything. I am enormously grateful to you—and I am very content with my life. Please believe that. There is only one thing that I could wish changed; you said that we were to be friends—and you have let me be only a fair weather friend. Won't you let me sometimes share and help in the difficulties, as well as in the pleasures? Your interests, your obligations are so great—" she went on hurriedly, lest he should think she was aiming at deeper, more personal concerns—"I can't help knowing that there must be difficulties. If you would only let me take my part—" She looked up, meeting his gloomy stare at last, and a faint appeal crept into her eyes. "I'm not a child, Barry, to be shown only the sunny side of life."

An indescribable expression flitted across his face, changing it marvellously.

"I would never have you know the dark side," he said briefly, as he took the cup she held out to him.

She was conscious that the tension, though lessened had not altogether disappeared. There was in his manner a constraint that set her heart throbbing painfully. She glanced furtively from time to time at his stern worn face, and the weariness in his eyes brought a lump into her throat.

He talked spasmodically, of friends whom he had seen in London, of a hundred and one trivial matters, but of the business that had kept him in town he said nothing and she wondered what had been in his mind when he had departed from an established rule and deliberately sought her in a room that he never entered. Had he come with any express intention, any confidence that had been thwarted by Mouston's stupid behaviour? She stifled a sigh of disappointment. He might never again be moved by the same impulse.

With growing anxiety she noticed that his restlessness was greater even than usual. Refusing a second cup of tea he lit a cigarette, pacing up and down as he talked, his hands plunged deep in his pockets.

In one of the silences that punctuated his jerky periods he paused by a little table on which lay a portfolio, and lifting it idly looked at the sketches it contained. With a sudden look of apprehension Gillian started and made a half movement as if to rise, then with a shrug she sank back on the sofa, watching him intently. It was her private sketch book, and there was in it one portrait in particular, his own, that she had no wish for him to see. But remonstrance would only call attention to what she hoped might pass unnoticed. Craven turned over the sketches slowly. He had seen little of his wife's work since their marriage, she was shy of submitting it to him, and with the policy of non-interference he had adopted he had expressed no curiosity. He recognised many faces, and, recognising, remembered wherein lay her special skill. He found himself looking for characteristics that were known to him in the portraits of the men and women he was studying. There was no attempt at concealment—vices and virtues, liberality of mind, pettiness of soul were set forth in naked truth. A sympathetic picture of Peters arrested him, though the name written beneath it puzzled. He looked at the kindly generous countenance with its friendly half-sad eyes and tender mouth with a feeling of envy. He would have given years of his life to have possessed the peace of mind that was manifested in the calm serenity of his agent's face.

His lips tightened as he laid the sketch down. With his thoughts lingering on the last portrait for a second or two he looked at the next one absently. Then a stifled exclamation broke from him and he peered at it closer. And, watching, Gillian drew a deep breath, clenching her hands convulsively. He stood quite still for what seemed an eternity, then came slowly across the room and stood directly in front of her. And for the first time she was afraid of meeting his eyes.

"Do I look like—that?"

Her head drooped lower, her fingers twining and intertwining nervously, and her dry lips almost refused their office.

"I have seen you like that," very slowly and almost inaudibly, but he caught the reluctant admission.

"So—*damnable*?"

She flinched from the loathing in his voice.

"I *am* sorry—" she murmured faintly.

"Good God!" the profanity was wrung from him, but had he thought of it he would have considered it justified, for the face at which he was staring was the beautiful tormented face of a fallen angel. He looked with a kind of horror at the hungry passionate eyes fierce with unsatisfied longing, shadowed with terrible memory, tortured, hopeless; at the set mouth, a straight grim line under the trim golden brown moustache; at the bitterness and revolt expressed in all the deep cut lines of the tragic face. He laid it down with a feeling of repulsion. She saw him like that! The pain of it was intolerable.

He laughed with a harsh mirthlessness that made her quiver.

"It is a truer estimation of my character than the one you gave me a few minutes ago," he said bitterly, "and you may thank heaven I am your husband only in name. God keep you from a nearer acquaintance with me." And turning on his heel he left her. Long after he had gone she sat on motionless, her fingers picking mechanically at the chintz cover of the sofa, staring into space with wide eyes brimming with tears. She knew it was a cruel sketch, but she had never meant him to see it. It had taken shape unconsciously under her hand, and while she hated it she had kept it because of the remarkable likeness and because it was the only picture she had of him.

The dreams of a better understanding seemed swept away by her own thoughtlessness and folly. She had hurt him and she could never explain. To refer to it, to try and make him understand, would do more harm than good. With a pitiful sob she covered her face with her hands, and, beside her, Mouston the pampered cringed and whimpered unheeded and forgotten.

She had looked forward to his return with such high hopes and now they lay shattered at her feet. During a brief hour that might have drawn them nearer together they had contrived to hurt each other as it must seem to both by deliberate intent. For herself she knew that she was innocent of any such intention—but was he? He had never hurt her before, even in his most difficult moods he had been to her unfailingly kind and considerate. But to-day—shudderingly she wondered did it mark a new era in their relations? And in miserable futile longing she wished that this afternoon had never been.

After what had occurred the thought of facing him across a table during an interminable dinner and sitting with him alone for the long hours of a summer evening drove her to a state bordering on panic. She pushed the thick hair off her forhead with a little gasp. It was cowardly—but she could not, would not. Despising herself she crossed the room to the telephone.

At the Hermitage Peters was indulging in a well-earned rest after a long hot day that had been both irksome and tiring. Wearing an old tweed coat he lounged comfortably in a big chair, a couple of sleepy setters at his feet, a foul and ancient pipe in full blast. The room, flooded with the evening sun, was filled with a heterogeneous collection of books and music manuscript, guns, fishing rods and whips. The homely room had stamped on it the characteristics of its owner. It was a room to work in, and equally a room in which to relax. The owner was now relaxing, but the bodily rest he enjoyed did not extend to his mind, which was very actively disturbed. His usually genial face was furrowed and he sucked at the old pipe with an energy that enveloped him in a haze of blue smoke. The ringing of the telephone in the opposite corner of the room came as an unwelcome interruption. He glared at it resentfully, disinclined to move, but at the second ring rose reluctantly with a grunt of annoyance, pushing the drowsy setters to one side. He took down the receiver with no undue haste and answered the call gruffly, but his bored expression changed rapidly as he listened. The soft voice came clearly but hesitatingly:

"Is that you, David? Could you come up to dinner—if—if you're not going anywhere else—I've got a tiresome headache and it will be so stupid for Barry. I don't want him to be dull the first evening at home. So if you could—please, David—"

His face grew grim as he detected the quiver in the faltering indecisive words, but he answered briskly.

"Of course I'll come. I'd love to," he said, with a cheeriness he was far from feeling. He hung up the receiver with a heavy sigh. But he had hardly moved when the telephone rang again sharply.

"Damn the thing!" he muttered irritably.

This time a very different voice, curt and uncompromising:

"—that you, Peters?—Yes!—Doing anything tonight?—Not?—Then for God's sake come up to dinner." And then the receiver jammed down savagely.

With grimmer face Peters moved thoughtfully across the room and touched a bell in the wall by the fireplace. His call was answered with the usual promptness, and when he had given the necessary orders and the man had gone he laid aside his pipe, tidied a few papers, and went slowly to an adjoining room.

The Hermitage was properly the dower house of the Towers, but for the last two generations had not been required as such. The room Peters now entered had originally been the drawing room, but for the thirty years he had lived in the house he had kept it as a music room. Panelled in oak, with polished floor and innocent of hangings, the only furniture a grand piano and a portrait, it was at once a sanctuary and a shrine. And during those thirty years to only two people had he given the right of entrance. To the woman whose portrait hung on the wall and, latterly, to the girl who had succeeded her as mistress of Craven Towers. To this room, to the portrait and the piano, he brought all his difficulties; it was here he wrestled with the loneliness and sadness that the world had never suspected. To-night he felt that only the peace that room invariably brought would enable him to fulfil the task he had in hand.

CRAVEN WAS ALONE IN THE hall when he arrived, and it was not until the gong sounded that Gillian made a tardy appearance, very pale but with a feverish spot on either cheek. Peters' quick eye noticed the absence of the black shadow that was always at her heels. "Where is the faithful Mouston? Not in disgrace, surely—the paragon?" he teased, and was disconcerted at the painful flush that overspread her face. But she thrust her arm through his and forced a little laugh. "Mouston is becoming rather incorrigible, I'm afraid I've spoiled him hopelessly. I'll tell him you inquired, it will cheer him up, poor darling. He's doing penance with a bone upstairs. Shall we go in—I'm famished."

But as dinner progressed she did not appear to be famished, for she ate scarcely anything, but talked fitfully with jerky nervousness. Craven, too, was at first almost entirely silent, and on Peters fell the main burden of conversation, until by a direct question he managed to start his host on a topic that was of interest to both and lasted until Gillian left them.

In the drawing room, after she had finished her coffee, she opened the piano and then subsided wearily on to the big sofa. The emotions of the day and the effort of appearing at dinner had exhausted her, and in her despondency the future had never seemed so black, so beset with difficulties. While she was immeasurably thankful for Peters' presence to-night she knew it was impossible for him to act continually as a buffer between them. But from the problem of to-morrow, and innumerable to-morrows, she turned with a fixed determination to live for the moment. *A chaque jour suffit sa peine.*

She lay with relaxed muscles and closed eyes. It seemed a long while before the men joined her. She wondered what they were talking about—whether to Peters would be imparted the information that had been withheld from her. For the feeling of a nearly impending calamity was strong within her. When at last they came she looked with covert anxiety from one to the other, but their faces told her nothing. For a few minutes Peters lingered beside her chatting and then gravitated toward the piano, as she had hoped he would. Arranging the heaped up cushions more comfortably around her she gave herself up to the delight of his music and it seemed to her that she had never heard him play so well.

Near her Craven was standing before the fern-filled fireplace, leaning against the mantel, a cigarette drooping between his lips. From where she lay she could watch him unperceived, for his own gaze was directed through the open French window out on to the terrace, and she studied his set handsome face with sorrowful attention. He appeared to be thinking deeply, and, from his detached manner, heedless of the harmony of sound that filled the room. But her supposition was soon rudely shaken. Peters had paused in his playing. When a few moments later the plaintive melody of an operatic air stole through the room she saw her husband start violently, and the terrible pallor she had witnessed once before sweep across his face. She clenched her teeth on her lip to keep back the cry that rose, and breathlessly watched him stride across the room and drop an arresting hand on Peters' shoulder. "For God's sake don't play that damned thing!" she heard him say in a voice that was almost unrecognisable. And then he passed out swiftly, into the garden.

A spasm of jealous agony shook her from head to foot. With quick intuition she guessed that the air that was unknown to her must be connected in some way with the sorrow that darkened his life, and the spectre of the past she tried to forget seemed to rise and grin at her triumphantly. She shivered. Would its power last until life ended? Would it stand between them always, rivalling her, thwarting her every effort?

For a long time she dared not look at Peters, who had responded without hesitation to Craven's unceremonious request, but when at length she summoned courage to glance at him it seemed as if he had already forgotten the interruption. His face wore the absent, almost spiritual look that was usual when he was at the piano and his playing gave no indication of either annoyance or surprise. She breathed a quick sigh of relief and, slightly altering her position, lay where she could see the solitary figure on the terrace. Erect by the stone ballustrade, his arms folded across his chest, staring intently into the night as if his gaze went far beyond the confines of the great park, he seemed to her a symbol of incarnate loneliness, and her heart contracted at the thought of the suffering and solitude she might not share. If he would only turn to her! If she had only the right to go to him and plead her love, beg the confidence she craved, and stand beside him in his sorrow! But he stood alone, beyond her reach, even unaware of her longing.

The slow tears gathered thick in her eyes.

For long after the keyboard became an indistinguishable blur Peters played on untiringly. But at last he rose, closed the piano and turned on an electric lamp that stood near.

"Eleven o'clock," he exclaimed contritely. "Bless my soul, why didn't you stop me! I forget the time when I'm playing. I've tired you out. Go to bed, you pale child. I'm walking home, I'll see Barry on the terrace as I pass."

She slid from the sofa and took his outstretched hands.

"Your playing never tires me!" she answered, with a little upward glance. "You've magic at the ends of your fingers, David dear."

She went to the open window to watch him go, and presently saw him reappear round the angle of the house and join Craven on the terrace. They stood talking for a few minutes and then together descended the long flight of stone steps to the rose garden, from which, by a short cut through a little copse, could be reached the path that crossing the park led to the Hermitage. It was the habit of Peters when he had been dining at the big house to walk home thus and, as to-night, Craven almost always accompanied him.

Gillian had long known her husband's propensity for night rambling and she knew it might be hours before he returned. Was he angry with her still that he had omitted the punctilious good-night he had never before forgotten? Her lips quivered like a disappointed child's as she turned back slowly into the room. But as she passed through the hall and climbed the long stairs she knew in her heart that she had misjudged him. He was not capable of petty retaliation. He had only forgotten—why indeed should he remember? It was a small matter to him, he could not know what it meant to her. In her bedroom she dismissed her maid and went to an open window. She was very tired, but restless, and disinclined for bed. Dropping down on the low seat she stared out over the moonlit landscape. The repentant Mouston, abject at her continued neglect, crawled from his basket and crept tentatively to her, and as absently her hand went out to him gained courage and climbed up beside her. Inch by inch he sidled nearer, and unrepulsed grew bolder until he finally subsided with his head across her knees, whining his satisfaction. Mechanically she caressed him until his shivering starting body lay quiet under her soothing touch. The night was close and very silent. No breath of wind came to stir the heavily leafed trees, no sound broke the stillness. She listened vainly for the cry of an owl, for the sharp alarm note of a pheasant to pierce the brooding hush that seemed to have fallen even over nature. A coppery moon hung like a ball of fire in the sky. At the far end of the terrace a group of tall trees cast inky black shadows across the short smooth lawn and the white tracery of the stone balustrade. The faint scent of jasmine drifted in through the open window and she leaned forward eagerly to catch the sweet intermittent perfume that brought back memories of the peaceful courtyard of the convent school. A night of intense beauty, mysterious, disturbing, called her compellingly. The restlessness that had assailed her grew suddenly intolerable, and she glanced back into the spacious room with a feeling of suffocation.

The four walls seemed closing in about her. She knew that the big white bed would bring no rest, that she would toss in feverish misery until the morning, and she turned with dread from the thought of the long weary hours. Night after night she lay awake in loneliness and longing until exhaustion brought fitful sleep that, dream-haunted, gave no refreshment.

Sleep was impossible—the room that witnessed her nightly vigil a prison house of dark sad thoughts. Her head throbbed with the heat; she craved the space, the freshness of the moonlit garden.

Rousing the slumbering dog she went out on to the gallery and down the staircase she had climbed so wearily an hour before. By the solitary light still burning in the hall she knew that Craven had not yet returned. Through the darkness of the drawing room she groped her way until her outstretched hands touched shutters. Slipping the bar softly and unlatching the window she passed out. For a moment she stood still, breathing deeply, drinking in the beauty of the scene, exhilarated with the sudden feeling of freedom that came to her. The silent garden, beautiful always but more beautiful still in the mystery of the night, appealed to her as never before. It was the same, yet wonderfully, curiously unlike. A glamour hung over it, a certain settled peace that soothed the tumult of her mind and calmed her nerves. Surrendering to the charm of its almost unearthly loveliness she slowly paced the long length of the terrace, the wondering Mouston pressing close beside her.

Then when her tired limbs could go no further she halted by the steps and leant her arms on the coping of the balustrade. Cupping her chin in her hands she looked down at the rose garden beneath her and smiled at its quaint formality. Running parallel with the terrace on the one side the three remaining sides were enclosed by a high yew hedge through which a door, facing the terrace steps, led to a path that gave access to the copse that was Peters' short cut. The shadow of the high dense yew stretched far across the garden and she gazed dreamily into its dusky depths, conjuring up the past, peopling the solitude about her with forgotten ghosts who in the silks and satins of a bygone age had walked those same flagged paths and talked and laughed and wept among the roses. Poor lonely ghosts—were they lonelier than she?

The silence broke at last. Far off from the trees in the park an owl called softly to its mate and the swift answering note seemed to mock her desolation. Her whole being shuddered into one great soundless cry of utter longing: "Barry! Oh, Barry, Barry!"

And as if in answer to her prayer she heard a sound that sent the quick blood leaping to her heart.

In the deep shadow of the yew hedge the door that had opened shut with a sudden clang. Her hands crept to her breast as she strained her eyes into the darkness. Then the echo of a firm tread, and Craven's tall figure emerged from the surrounding gloom. With fluttering breath she watched him slowly cross the bright strip of moonlight lying athwart the rose garden and mount the steps. Only when he reached the terrace did he seem aware of her presence, and joined her with an exclamation of surprise, "You—Gillian?"

"I couldn't sleep—it was so hot—the garden tempted me," she faltered, in sudden fear lest he might think she spied on him. But the fascination of the night was to Craven too natural to evoke comment. He lit a cigarette and smoked in a silence she did not know how to break, and a cold wave of chill foreboding passed over her as she waited with nervous constraint for him to speak. He turned to her at last with a certain deliberation and spoke with blunt directness.

"I have been asked to lead an expedition in Central Africa. It is partly a hunting trip, partly a scientific mission. They have approached me because I know the country, and because I am interested in tropical diseases and am willing to defray a proportion of the expense which will be necessarily heavy—I should gladly have done so in any case whether I went with the party or not. The question of leading the expedition I deferred as long as I could for obvious reasons.—I had not only myself to consider. But I have been pressed to give a definite answer and have agreed to go. There are plenty of other men who would do the job better than myself but, as I said, I happen to know the locality and speak several of the dialects, so my going may make things easier for them. But that is not what has weighed with me most, it is you. Do you think I don't know how completely I have failed you—how difficult your life is? I do know. And because I know I am going. For I see no other way of making your life even bearable for you. It has become impossible for us to go on as we are—and the fault is mine, only mine. You have been an angel of goodness and patience, you have done all that was humanly possible for any woman to do, but circumstances were against us. I had no right to ask you to make such a marriage. I cannot undo it. I cannot give you your freedom, but I can by my absence make your life easier than it has been. I have arranged everything with the lawyers in London and with Peters, here to-night. If I do not return, for there are of course risks, everything is left in your control—it is the only satisfaction in my power. If I do return—God give me grace to be kinder to you than I have been in the past."

The blow she had been waiting for had fallen at last, in fulfilment of her premonition. In her heart she had always known it would come, but its suddenness paralysed. She had nothing to say. Silently she stood beside him, her hands tight-locked, numbed with a desperate fear. He would go—and he would never return. It hammered in her brain, making her want to shriek. She felt to the full her own powerlessness, nothing she could say would turn him from his purpose. It was the end she had always foreseen, the end of all her dreams, the end of everything but sorrow and pain and loneliness unspeakable. And for him—danger and possibly death. He had admitted risk, he had set his house in order. From Craven it meant much. She had learned his complete disregard for danger from the men who had stayed with them in Scotland; his recklessness in the hunting field, which was a by-word in the county, was already known to her. He set no value on his own life—what reason was there to suppose that, in the mysterious land of sudden and terrible death, he would take even ordinary precautions? Was he going with a pre-conceived determination to end a life that had become unbearable? In agony that seemed to rive her heart she closed her eyes lest he might see in them the anguish she knew was there. How long a time was left to her before the parting that would leave her desolate? "When do you go?" The question burst from her, and Craven glanced at her keenly, trying to read the colourless face that was like a still white mask. He fancied he had caught a tremor in her voice, then he called himself a fool as he noted the composure that seemed to argue indifference. Her calmness stung while it strengthened him. Why should she care, he asked himself bitterly. His going could mean to her only relief. And disappointment made his own voice ring cold and distant. "Within the next few weeks. The exact date is not yet fixed," he said evasively. Again she was silent while he wondered what were her thoughts. Suddenly she turned to him, words pouring out in stammering haste, "While you are away—may I go to France—to Paris—to work? This life of idleness is killing me!"

He looked at her in amazement, startled at her passionate utterance, dismayed at a suggestion he had never contemplated. To think of her at the Towers, in the position he would have her fill, watched over by Peters, was the only comfort he could take away with him. For a second he meditated a refusal that seemed within his right, arbitrary though it might be. But the promise he had made to leave her free stayed him. He could not break that promise now. "As you please," he said, with forced unconcern, "you are your own mistress. You can do whatever you wish." And with a slight shrug he turned toward the house. She walked beside him in a tumult of emotion. He would now never know the love she bore him, the aching passion that throbbed like a living thing within her. She could not speak, the gulf between them was too wide to bridge, and he would leave her, thinking her indifferent, callous! Tears blinded her as she stumbled through the dark drawing room. In the dimly lit hall, standing at the foot of the staircase with his hand clenched on the oaken rail, Craven watched with tortured eyes the slender drooping figure move slowly upward, battling with himself, praying for strength to let her go—for he knew that if she even turned her head his self-control would shatter. It was weakening now and the sweat broke out

VIII

In a little tent pitched in the midst of an Arab camp in the extreme south of Southern Algeria Craven sat writing. A day of intense heat had been succeeded by a night airless and suffocating, and he was wet with perspiration that dripped from his forehead and formed in sticky pools under his hand, making writing laborious and difficult, impossible indeed except for the sheet of blotting paper on which his fingers rested. His thin silk shirt, widely open at the throat, the sleeves rolled up above his elbows, clung limply to his broad shoulders. A multitude of tiny flies attracted by the light circled round the lamp eddying in the heat of the flame, immolating themselves, and falling thickly on the closely written sheets of paper that strewed the camp table, smeared the still wet ink and clogged his pen. He swept them away impatiently from time to time. Squatting on his heels in a corner, his inscrutable yellow face damp and glistening, Yoshio was cleaning a revolver with his usual thoroughness and precision. A ragged square of canvas beside him held the implements necessary to his work, set out in methodical order, and as he cleaned, and oiled and polished assiduously without raising his eyes his deft fingers selected unerringly the tool he required. The weapon appeared already speckless, but for some time he continued to rub vigorously, handling it with almost affectionate care as if loth to put it down; at last with a grunt of demur he reluctantly laid aside the cloth he was using and wrapping the revolver in a silk handkerchief slid it slowly into a leathern holster which his care had kept soft and pliable. Placing it noiselessly on the ground before him he turned his oblique gaze on Craven and watched him for a moment or two intently. Assured at length that his master was too absorbed in his own task to notice the doings of his servant he reached his hand behind him and produced a second revolver, which he began to clean more hurriedly, more superficially than the first, keeping the while a wary eye on the stooping figure at the table. When that too was finished to his satisfaction and restored to his hip pocket, a flicker of almost childlike amusement crossed his usually immobile features and he started operations with an air of fine unconsciousness upon one of a couple of rifles that stood propped against the tent wall near him. Two years of hardships and danger had left no mark upon him, the deadly climate of the region through which he had passed had not impaired his powerful physique, and disease that had ravaged the scientific mission had left him, like Craven, unscathed. With no care beyond his master's comfort, indifferent to fatigue and perils, the months spent in Central Africa had been far more to his taste than the dull monotony of the life at Craven Towers. But with his face turned, though indirectly, toward home—the home of his adoption—Yoshio was still cheerful. For him life held only one incentive—the man who had years before saved his life in California. Where Craven was Yoshio was content.

Outside, the Arab camp was in an uproar. Groups of tribesmen passed the tent continually, conversing eagerly, their raucous voices rising shrill, shouting, arguing, in noisy excitement. The neighing of horses came from near by and once a screaming stallion backed heavily against the canvas wall where Yoshio was sitting, rousing the phlegmatic Japanese to an unwonted exclamation of wrath as he ducked and grabbed into safety the remaining rifle before the animal was hauled clear with a wealth of detailed Arabic expletives, and he grinned broadly when an authoritative voice broke into the Arabs' clamour and a subsequent sudden silence fell in the vicinity of the stranger's tent.

Regardless of the disturbance resounding from all quarters of the camp Craven wrote on steadily for some time longer. Then with a short sigh he shuffled the scattered sheets together, brushed clear the clinging accumulation of scorched wings and tiny shrivelled bodies, and without re-reading the closely written pages stuffed them into an envelope, and having closed and directed it, leaned back with an exclamation of relief.

The letter to Peters was finished but there remained still the more difficult letter he had yet to address to his wife—a letter he dreaded and yet longed to write. A letter which, reaching her after the death he confidently expected and earnestly prayed for, would reveal to her fully the secret of his past and the passion that had driven him, unworthy, from her. For never during the two years of adventure and peril had death seemed more imminent than now, and before he died he would give himself this one satisfaction—he would break the silence of years that had eaten like a canker into his soul. At last she would know all he had never dared to tell her, all his hopeless love, all his remorse and shame, all his passionate desire for her happiness.

Scores of times during the last two years he had attempted to write such a letter and had as often refrained, but to-night his need was imperative. It was his last chance. In the early hours of the dawn he would ride with his Arab hosts on a punitive expedition from which he had no intention of returning alive. Death that he had courted openly since leaving England would surely be easy to find amid the warring tribes with whom he had thrown in his lot. A curious smile lit his face for an instant, then passed abruptly at the doubt that shook his confidence. Would fate again refuse him release from a life that had become more than ever intolerable?

Haunted as he was with the memory of O Hara San, tortured with longing for the woman he had made his wife, the double burden had become too heavy to bear. He had grasped at the opportunity offered by the scientific mission. The dangerous nature of the country, the fever that saturated its swamps and forests, was known to him and he had gone to Africa courting a death that would free him and yet leave no stain on the name borne by his wife. And the death that would free him would free her too! The bitter justice of it made him set his teeth. For he had left her his fortune and his great possessions unrestrictedly to deal with as she would. Young, rich and free! Who would claim what he had surrendered? Even now, after months of mental struggle, the thought was torment.

But death that had laid a heavy toll on his companions had turned away from him. Disease and disaster had dogged the mission from the outset. The medical and scientific researches had proved satisfactory beyond expectation, but the attendant loss of life had been terrible, and himself utterly reckless and heedless of all precautions Craven had watched tragedy after tragedy with envy he had been hardly able to hide. Immune from the sudden and deadly fevers that had swept the camps periodically with fatal results he had worked fearlessly and untiringly among the stricken members of the mission and the fast dwindling army of demoralised porters who had succumbed with alarming rapidity. With the stolid Japanese always beside him he had wrestled entire nights and days to save the expedition from extermination. And in the intervals of nursing, and shepherding the unwilling carriers, he had ranged far and wide in search of fresh food to supply the wants of the camp. The danger he deliberately sought, with a rashness that had provoked open comment, had miraculously evaded him. He had borne a charmed life. He had snatched at every hazardous enterprise, he had exposed himself consistently to risk until one evening shortly before the expedition was due to start on the return march to civilization, when a chance word spoken by the camp fire had brought home to him abruptly the dependence of the remnant of the mission on him to bring them to the coast in safety. By some strange dealing of fate it had been among the non-scientific members of the expedition that mortality had ranged highest; the big game hunters, though hardier and physically better equipped than the students of the party for hardship and endurance had, with the exception of Craven himself, been wiped out to a man. It had been an unpremeditated remark uttered in all good faith with no ulterior motive by a shuddering fever-stricken scientist writing up his notes and diary by the light of the fire with trembling fingers that could scarcely hold the fountain pen that moved laboriously driven by an indomitable will. A grim jest, horrible in its significance, had followed the startling utterance and Craven had looked with perplexity at the shivering figure with its drawn yellow face from which a pair of glittering eyes burned with an almost uncanny brilliance until the meaning of the man's words slowly penetrated. But the true importance of the suggestion once realised had aroused in him a full understanding of the duty he owed to the men he had undertaken to lead. Of those who could have convoyed the expedition on its homeward march only he remained. Without him the survivors of the once large party might eventually reach safety but it was made clear to him that night how completely his companions relied on him for a quick return and for the management of the train of porters whose frequent mutinies only Craven seemed able to quell. He had sat far into the night, staring gloomily into the blazing fire, smoking pipe after pipe, listening to the multifarious noises of the forest—the sudden distant crash of falling trees, the incessant hum of insect life, the long-drawn howl of beasts of prey hovering on the outskirts of the camp, the soft whoo-whoo of an owl whose cry brought vividly to his mind the cool fragrance of the garden at Craven Towers and the nearer more ominous sounds of muffled agony that came from a tent close beside him where yet another victim of science was gasping his life away.

Hour after hour he sat thinking. There was no getting away from it—it was only despicable that he had not himself recognised it earlier. The narrow path of duty lay before him from which he might not turn aside to ease the burden of a private grief. He was bound to the men who trusted him. Honour demanded that he should forego the project he had formed—until his obligation had been discharged. Loyalty to his companions must come before every selfish consideration. After all it was only a postponement, he reflected with a kind of grim satisfaction. The residue of the mission once safely conducted to the coast his

E.M. HULL

responsibility would end and he would be free to pursue the course that would liberate the woman he loved.

In the chill silence of the hour that precedes the dawn he had risen cramped and shivering from his seat by the dying fire and too late then to take the rest he had neglected, had roused Yoshio and started on the usual foraging expedition that was his daily occupation. And from that time he had been careful of a life which, though valueless to him, was invaluable to his companions. From that time, too, the ill-luck that had pursued them ceased. There had been no more deaths, no more desertions from the already depleted train of carriers. The work had gone forward with continuing success and, six months ago, after a hazardous march through a hostile country, Craven had led the remnant of the expedition safely to the coast. He had waited for some weeks at the African port after the mission had returned to England, and then embarking on a small trading steamer, had made his way northward to an obscure station on the Moroccan seaboard, when by a leisurely and indirect route he had slowly crossed the desert to the district where he now was and which he had reached only a week ago. Twice before he had visited the tribe as the guest of the Sheik Mukair Ibn Zarrarah's younger son, an officer of Spahis whom he had met in Paris, and the warm hospitality shown him had left a deep impression. A sudden unaccountable impulse had led him to revisit a locality where he had spent some of the happiest months of his life. He had conceived an intense admiration and liking for the stern old Arab Chief and his two utterly dissimilar sons; the elder a grave habitually silent man, who clung to the old traditions with the rigid tenacity of the orthodox Mohammedan, disdainful of the French jurisdiction under which he was compelled to live, and occupied solely with the affairs of the tribe and his beautiful and adored wife who reigned alone in his harem, despite the fact that she had given him no child; the younger in total contrast to his brother, a dashing ultra-modern young Arab as deeply imbued with French tendencies as the conservative Omar was opposed to them. The wealthy and powerful old Sheik, whose friendship had been assiduously sought by the French Administration to ensure the co-operation of a tribe that with its far reaching influence might have proved a dangerous element in an unsettled district, shared in his inmost heart the sentiments of his heir, but with a larger and more discriminating wisdom saw the desirability of associating at least one of his family with the Government he was obliged, though grudgingly and half contemptuously, to acknowledge. He had hovered long between prejudice and policy before he reluctantly gave his consent for Saïd to be placed on the roll of the regiment of Spahis. And the unusual love existing between the two brothers had survived a test that might have proved too strong for its continuance; Omar, bowing to the decision of the autocratic old Chief, had refrained even from comment, and Saïd, despite his enthusiasm, had carefully avoided inflaming his brother's deeply rooted hatred of the nation the younger man was proud to serve. His easy-going nature adapted itself readily to the two wholly separate lives he lived, and though secretly preferring the months spent with his regiment he contrived to extract every possible enjoyment from the periods of leave for which he returned to the tribe where, laying aside the picturesque uniform his ardent soul rejoiced in and scrupulously suppressing every indication of his Francophile inclinations he resumed with consummate tact the somewhat invidious position of younger son of the house.

The meeting of the young Spahi with Craven in Paris had led to the discovery of similar tastes and ultimately to an intimate friendship. Together in Algeria they had shot panther and Barbary sheep and eventually Craven had been induced to visit the tribe, where he had seen the true life of the desert that appealed strongly to his unconventional wandering disposition. The heartiness of his reception had been unqualified, even the taciturn Omar had unbent to the representative of a nation he felt he could respect with no loss of prestige. To Craven the weeks passed in the Arab camp had been a time of uninterrupted enjoyment and a second visit had strengthened mutual esteem. Situated on the extreme fringe of the Algerian frontier, in the heart of a perpetually disturbed country, the element of danger prevailing in the district was to Craven not the least of its attractions. It had been a source of keen disappointment that during both his visits there had been a cessation of the intertribal warfare that was carried on in spite of the Government's endeavours to preserve peace among the great desert families. For generations the tribe of Mukair Ibn Zarrarah had been at feud with another powerful tribe which, living further to the south and virtually beyond the suzerainty of the nominal rulers of the country, harried the border continually. But, aware of the growing power and resources of Mukair Ibn Zarrarah, for many years the marauders had avoided collision with him and confined their attention to less dangerous adversaries. The apparent neglect of his hereditary enemies had not, however, lessened the old Sheik's precautions. With characteristic oriental distrust he maintained a continual watch upon them and a well organized system of espionage kept him conversant with all their movements. Often during his visits Craven had listened to the stories of past encounters and in the fierce eager faces around him he had read the deep longing for renewed hostilities that animated the younger members of the tribe in particular and had wondered what spark would eventually set ablaze the smouldering fires of hatred and rivalry that had so long lain dormant. And it had been really a subconscious presage of such an outbreak that had brought him back to the camp of Mukair Ibn Zarrarah. His presentiment, the outcome of earnest desire, had been fulfilled, and in its fulfilment attended with horrible details which, had it not been already his intention, would have driven him to beg a place in the ranks of the punitive force that was preparing to avenge an outrage that involved the honour of the tribe. A week ago he had arrived to find the camp seething with an infuriated and passion-swayed people who bore no kind of resemblance to the orderly well-disciplined tribesmen he had seen on his former visits, and the daily arrival of reinforcements from outlying districts had kept the tension strained and swelled the excitement that rioted day and night.

In the barbaric sumptuousness of his big tent and with a calm dignity that even tragedy could not shake the old Sheik had received him alone, for the unhappy Omar was hidden in the desolate solitude of his ravished harem. To the Englishman, before whom he could speak openly the old man had revealed the whole terrible story with vivid dramatic force and all the flowery eloquence of which he was master. It was a tale of misplaced confidence and faithlessness that, detected and punished with oriental severity, had led to swift and dastardly revenge. A headman of the tribe whom both the Sheik and his elder son trusted implicitly had proved guilty of grave indiscretion that undetected might have seriously impaired the prestige of the ruling house. Deposed from his headmanship, and deserted with characteristic vacillation by the adherents on whom he counted, the delinquent had fled to the camp of the rival tribe, with whom he had already been in secret negotiation. This much Mukair Ibn Zarrarah's spies had ascertained, but not in time to prevent the catastrophe that followed. Plans thought to be known only to the Sheik and his son had been disclosed to the marauding Chief, who had long sought an opportunity of aiming an effectual blow at his hated rival, and on one of Omar's periodical tours of inspection to the more remote encampments of the large and scattered tribe, the little caravan had been surrounded by an overwhelmingly superior force led by the hereditary enemy and the renegade tribesman. Hemmed in around the litter of the dearly loved young wife, from whom he rarely parted, Omar and his small bodyguard had fought desperately, but the outcome had been inevitable from the first. Outnumbered they had fallen one by one under the vigorous onslaughts of the attacking party who, victorious, had retired southward as quickly as they had come, carrying with them the beautiful Safiya—the price of the traitor's treachery. Covered with wounds and left for dead under a heap of dying followers Omar and two others had alone survived, and with death in his heart the young man had lived only for the hour when he might avenge his honour. Animated by the one fierce desire that sustained him he had struggled back to life to superintend the preparations for retaliation that should be both decisive and final. To old injuries had been added this crowning insult, and the tribe of Mukair Ibn Zarrarah, roused to the highest pitch of fury, were resolved to a man to exterminate or be exterminated. The preparations had been almost completed when Craven arrived at the camp, and tonight, for the first time, at a final war council of all the principal headmen held in the Sheik's tent, he had seen the stricken man and had hardly recognized in the gaunt attenuated figure that only an inflexible will seemed to keep upright, the handsome stalwart Arab who of all the tribe had most nearly approached his own powerful physique. The frenzied despair in the dark flashing eyes that met his struck an answering chord in his own heart and the silent handclasp that passed between them seemed to ratify a common desire. Here, too, was a man who for love of a woman sought death that he might escape a life of terrible memory. A sudden sympathy born of tacit understanding seemed to leap from one to the other, an affinity of purpose that drew them strangely close together and brought to Craven an odd sense of kinship that dispelled the difference he had felt and enabled him to enter reservedly into the discussions that followed. After this meeting he had gone back to his tent to make his own final preparations with a feeling almost of exhilaration. To Yoshio, more than usually stolid, he had given all necessary instructions for the conveyance of his belongings to England.

Remained only the letter to his wife—a letter that seemed curiously hard to begin. Pushing the writing materials from him he leant back further in his chair, and searching in his pockets found and filled a pipe with slow almost meticulous deliberation. Another search failed to produce the match he required, and rising with a prolonged stretch he bent over the table and lit his pipe at the lamp. Crossing the tent he stood for a few moments in the doorway, but movements did not seem to produce inspiration, and with an impatient shrug he returned to his seat and sat staring gloomily at the blank sheet of paper before him. The flaring light of the lamp illuminated his deeply tanned face and lean muscular figure. In perfect physical condition and bronzed with the African sun, he looked younger than when he had left England. At that moment death and Barry Craven seemed very widely separated—and yet in a few hours, he reflected with a curiosity that was oddly impersonal, the vultures might be congregating round the body that was now so strong and virile. "Handsome Barry Craven." He had heard a woman say it in Lagos with a feeling of contemptuous amusement—a cynical smile crossed his face as the remark recurred to him and he pictured the loathing that would succeed admiration in the same woman's eyes if she could see what would remain of him after the scavengers of the desert had done their work. The thought gave him personally no feeling of disgust. He had lived always too near to Nature to shrink from contemplation of her merciless laws.

He filled another pipe and strove to collect his wandering thoughts, but the power of definite expression seemed beyond him as there rose in him with almost overwhelming force the terrible longing that never left him—the craving to see her, to hear her voice. Of his own free will he was putting away all that life could mean or hold for him, and in the flood of natural reaction that set in he called himself a fool and revolted at his self-imposed sentence. The old struggle recommenced, the old temptation gripped him in all its bitterness, and never so bitterly as to-night. In the revulsion of feeling that beset him it was not death he shrank from but the thought of eternity—alone. Neither in this world nor in the life everlasting would she be his, and in an agony of longing his soul cried out in anguished loneliness. The yearning for her grew intolerable, a burning physical ache that was torture; but stronger far rose the finer nobler desire for the perfect spiritual companionship that he would never know. By his own act it would be denied him. By his own act he had made this hell in which he lived, of his own making would be the hell of the hereafter. Always he had recognised the justice of it, he did not attempt to deny the justice of it now. But if it had been otherwise—if he had been free to woo her, free to win her to his arms!

It was not the least of his punishment that, deep down in his heart, he had the firm conviction that despite her assertions to the contrary, love was lying dormant in her. And that love might have been his, would have been his, for the strength and tenderness of his own passion would have compelled it. She must have turned to him at last and in his love found happiness. And to him her love would have been the crown of life—a life of exquisite joy and beauty, a union of perfect and undivided sympathy. Together they might have made the Towers a paradise on earth; together they might have broken the curse of Craven; together they might have brought happiness into the lives of many. And in the dream of what might have been there came to him for the first time the longing for parenthood, the desire for a child born of the woman he adored, a child who joining in his tiny personality the essentials of each would be a tangible proof of their mutual love, a child who would perpetuate the race he sprang from. Craven's breath came fast with a new and tremendous emotion. Then with terrible suddenness came a lightning flash of recollection, a stabbing remembrance that laid his dream in pieces at his feet. He heard again the low soft sobbing voice, "Are you not glad?" He saw again O Hara San's pleading tear-filled eyes, felt again her slender sorrow-shaken body trembling in his arms, and he bowed his head on his hands in shuddering horror. . .

Numbed with the pain of memory and self-loathing he was unaware of the renewal of noisy demonstration in the camp that to Yoshio's attentive and interested ears pointed to the arrival of yet another adherent of Mukair Ibn Zarrarah, an adherent of some special standing, judging from the warmth of his reception. Moved by curiosity the Jap rose noiselessly and passing unnoticed by his master vanished silently into the night.

Some little while later the sound of a clear tenor voice calling to him loudly by name sent Craven stumbling to his feet. He turned quickly with outstretched hands to meet the tall young Arab, who burst unceremoniously into the tent and flung himself upon him in boisterous greeting. Gripped by a pair of muscular arms Craven submitted with an Englishman's diffidence to the fervid oriental embrace that was succeeded to his greater liking by a hearty and prolonged English handshake and a storm of welcoming excited and almost incoherent speech. "*C'est bien toi, mon vieux*! You are more welcome than you have ever been—though I could wish you a thousand miles away, *mon ami*, but of that, more, later. *Dame*, but I have ridden! As though the hosts of Eblis were behind me. I was on leave when the messenger came for me—he seems to have been peremptory in his demands, that same Selim. Telegrams despatched to every likely place—one caught me fortunately at Marseilles. Yes, I had been in Paris. I hastened to headquarters and asked for long and indefinite leave on urgent private affairs, all the lies I thought *mon colonel* would swallow, but no word of war, *bien entendu*! Praise be to *Allah* they put no obstacle in my way and I left at once. Since then I have ridden almost without stopping, night and day. Two horses I have killed, the last lies dead of a broken heart before my father's tent—you remember her?—my little Mimi, a chestnut with a white star on her forehead, dear to me as the core of my heart. For none but Omar would I have driven so, for I loved her, look you, *mon ami*, as I could never love a woman. A woman! Bah! No woman in the world was worth a toss of my Mimi's head. And I killed her, Craven. Killed her who loved and trusted me, who never failed me. My little Mimi! For the love of *Allah* give me a whisky." And laughing and crying together he collapsed with a groan on to Craven's bed but sat up again immediately to gulp down the prohibited drink that was almost the last in a nearly depleted flask.

"The Prophet never tasted whisky or he would not have forbidden it to the true believer," he said with a boyish grin, as he handed back the empty cup.

"Which you are not," commented Craven with a faint smile. "In the sense you mean, no," replied Saïd, swinging his heels to the ground and searching in the folds of his burnous for a cigarette, which he lit and smoked for a few minutes thoughtfully. Then with all trace of his former excitement gone he began to discuss soberly the exigency of the moment, revealing a sound judgment and levelness of mind that appeared incompatible with his seemingly careless and easy-going disposition. It was a deeper studiously hidden side of his character that Craven had guessed very early in their acquaintance.

He talked now with unconcealed seriousness of the gravity of the situation. In the short time he had been with his father before seeking his friend he had mastered the particulars of the projected expedition and, with his European knowledge, had suggested and even—with a force of personality he had never before displayed in the old Sheik's presence—insisted on certain alterations which he detailed now for Craven's benefit, who concurred heartily, for they were identical with suggestions put forward by himself which had been rejected as impossible innovations by the conservative headmen, and conscious of his position as guest he had not pressed them. Then with a sudden change of tone the young Arab turned to Craven in frowning inquiry.

"But you, mon cher, what are you doing in this affair? It was that I meant when I said I wished you a thousand miles away. You are my friend, the friend of all of us, but friendship does not demand that you ride with us to-night. That you would offer—yes—it was only to be expected. But that we should accept your offer—no! a hundred times no! you are an Englishman, a big man in your own country, what have you to do with the tribal warfare of minor Arab Chiefs—voyez vous, I have my moments of modesty! If anything should happen—as happen it very likely will—what will your paternal British Government say? It will only add to my father's difficulties with our own over-lords." There was a laugh in his eyes though his voice was serious. Craven brushed his objection aside with an indifferent hand.

"The British Government will not distress itself about me," he said dryly. "I am not of sufficient importance."

For a few moments the Arab sat silent, smoking rapidly, then he raised his dark eyes tentatively to Craven's face.

"In Paris they told me you were married," he said slowly, and the remark was in itself ample indication of his European tendencies.

Craven turned away with an abrupt movement and bent over the lamp to light his pipe. "They told you the truth," he said, with a certain reluctance, his face hidden by a cloud of smoke. "*Pourtant*, I ride with you to-night." There was a note of brusque finality in his voice that Saïd recognised, and he shrugged acquiescence as he lit another cigarette. "It is almost certain death," he said, with nonchalant oriental calm. But Craven did not answer and Saïd relapsed into a silence that was protracted. From the midst of the blue haze surrounding him, his earnest scrutiny hidden by the thick lashes that curved downwards to his swarthy cheek, he gazed intently through half-closed eyes at the friend whose presence he found for the first time embarrassing. Fatalist though he was in all things that concerned himself, western influence had bitten deep enough to make him realise that the same doctrine did not extend to Craven. He recognised that self-determination came more largely into the Englishman's creed than into his own. Whether he himself lived or died was a matter of no great moment. But with Craven it was otherwise and he had no liking for the thought that should the morrow's venture go against them his friend's blood would, virtually, be upon his hands! So far had his Francophile tendencies taken him. And the more he dwelt upon the uncomfortable fact the less he liked it. He turned his attention more directly upon the man himself and he noted changes that surprised and disturbed him. The stern weary looking face was not the careless smiling one he remembered. The man he had known had been vividly alive, care-free and animated; one who had jested alike at life and death with an indifferent laugh, but one who though careless of danger even to the extent of foolhardiness had never given any indication of a desire to quit a life that was obviously easy and attractive. But this man was different, grave and abrupt of speech, with an air of tired suffering, and a grim purposefulness in his determination to ignore his friend's warning that conveyed an impression of underlying sinister intent that set the Arab wondering what sting had poisoned his life even to the desire to sacrifice it. For the look on Craven's face was not new to him, he had seen it before—on the face of a French officer in Algiers who had subsequently taken his own life, and again this very evening on the face of his brother Omar. The personalities of the three men were widely different, but the expression of each was identical. The deduction was simple and yet to him wholly inexplicable. A woman—without doubt a woman! In the first two cases it was certainly so, he seemed to know instinctively that here, too, he was not mistaken in his supposition. A puzzled look crept into his fine dark eyes and a cynical smile hovered round his mouth as he viewed these three dissimilar men from the height of his own contemptuous indifference towards any and every woman. It was a weakness he did not understand, a phase of life that held no meaning for him at all. He had never bestowed a second glance on any woman of his own race, the attentions of European women in Paris and Algiers had been met with cold scorn that he masked with racial gravity of demeanour or frank insolence according to circumstances. For him women did not exist; he lived for his horses, for his regiment and for sport. To his strangely cold nature the influence that women exercised over other men was a thing inconceivable—the houris of the paradise of his fathers' creed were to him no incentive to enter the realms of the blessed. A character apart, incomprehensible alike to the warm-blooded Frenchmen with whom he associated and to his own passionate countrymen, he maintained his peculiarity tranquilly, undisturbed by the banter of his friends and the admonitions of his father, who in view of his heir's childlessness regarded his younger son's temperament with growing uneasiness as the years advanced.

The action of the French officer in Algiers had provoked in Saïd only intolerant contempt but, as he realised tonight, contempt was not possible in the cases of Craven and his brother. He pondered it with a curious feeling of irritation. What was it after all, this emotion of which he was ignorant—this compelling impulse that entered into a man driving him beyond the power of endurance? It was past his comprehension. And he wondered suddenly for the first time why he had been made so different to the generality of men. But introspection was foreign to him, he had not been in the habit of dissecting his own personality and his thoughts turned quickly with greater interest to the man who sat near him plunged like himself into silent reverie. And as he looked he scowled with angry irritation. The Frenchman in Algiers had not mattered, but Omar and Craven mattered very much. He resented the suffering he did not understand—the termination of a friendship he valued, for it was almost inevitable should Craven persist in his decision and the loss of a brother who was dearer to him than he would admit and whose death would mean a greater change in his own life than he cared to contemplate. That through a woman this should be possible! With hearty thoroughness and picturesque attention to detail he silently cursed all women in general and two women in particular. For the seriousness of the venture lay, at the moment, heavily upon him. He was tired and his enthusiasm temporarily damped by the unexpected and incomprehensible attitude of the two men by whom alone he permitted himself to be influenced. But gradually his natural buoyancy reasserted itself, and abandoning as insoluble the perplexing problem, he spoke again eagerly of the impending meeting with his hereditary foes. For half an hour they talked earnestly and then Saïd rose, announcing his intention of getting a few hours sleep before the early start. But he deferred his going, making one pretext after another for remaining, walking about the little tent in undecided hesitation, plainly embarrassed. Finally he swung toward Craven with a characteristic gesture of his long arms.

"Can I say nothing to deter you from this expedition?"

"Nothing," replied Craven; "you always promised me a fight some day—do you want to do me out of it now, you selfish devil?" he added with a laugh, to which Saïd did not respond. With an inarticulate grunt he moved toward the door, pausing as he went out to fling over his shoulder: "I'll send you a burnous and the rest of the kit."

"A burnous—what for?"

"What for?" echoed Saïd, coming back into the tent, his eyes wide with astonishment. "*Allah!* to wear, of course, *mon cher*. You can't go as you are."

"Why not?"

The Arab rolled his eyes heavenward and waved his hands in protest as he burst out vehemently: "Because they will take you for a Frenchman, a spy, an agent of the Government, and they will finish you off even before they turn their attention to us. They hate us, by the Koran! but they hate a Frenchman worse. You wouldn't have the shadow of a chance."

Craven looked at him curiously for a few moments, and then he smiled. "You're a good fellow, Saïd," he said quietly, taking the cigarette the other offered, "but I'll go as I am, all the same. I'm not used to your picturesque togs, they would only hamper me."

For a little while longer Saïd remained arguing and entreating by turns and then went away suddenly in the middle of a sentence, and for a few minutes Craven stood in the door of the tent watching his retreating figure by the light of the newly risen moon with a smile that softened his face incredibly.

Then he turned back into the tent and once more drew toward him the writing materials.

The difficulty he had before felt had passed away. It seemed suddenly quite easy to write and he wondered why it had appeared so impossible earlier in the evening. Words, phrases, leaped to his mind, sentences seemed to form themselves, and, with rapidly moving pen, he wrote without faltering for the best part of an hour—all he had never dared to say, more almost than he had ever dared to think. He did not spare himself. The tragic history of O Hara San he gave in all its pitifulness without attempting to extenuate or shield himself in any way; he sketched frankly the girl's loneliness and childish ignorance, his own casual and selfish acceptance of the sacrifice she made and the terrible catastrophe that had brought him to abrupt and horrible conviction of himself, and his subsequent determination to end the life he had marred and wasted. He wrote of the coming of John Locke's letter at the moment of his deepest abasement, and of the chance it had seemed to offer; of her own entry into his life and the love for her that almost from the first moment had sprung up within him.

In its entirety he laid bare the burning hopeless passion that consumed him, the torturing longing that possessed him, and the knowledge of his own unworthiness that had driven him from her that she might be free with a freedom that would be at last absolute. But even in this letter which tore down so completely the barrier between them he did not admit to her the true reason of his marriage, he preferred to leave it obscure as it had always been, even should the motive she might attribute to him be the wrong one. He must chance that and the impression it might leave with her. Her future life he alluded to very briefly not caring to dwell on business that was already cut and dried, but referring her to Peters who was fully instructed and on whose advice and help she could count. He expressed no wish with regard to Craven Towers and his other properties, leaving her free to dispose of or retain them as she pleased. He shrank from suggesting in any way that she benefited by his death.

He saw her before him as he wrote. It seemed almost as if the ardent passionate wards were spoken to present listening ears, and as with Peters' letter he did not reread the many closely written sheets. What use? He did not wish to alter or amend anything he had said. He had done, and a deeper peace came to him than he had known since those far away days in Japan.

He called to Yoshio. Almost before the words had left his lips the man was beside him. And as the Jap listened to the minute instructions given him the light that had sprung to his eyes died out of them and his face became if possible more than usually stolid and inscrutable.

"You quite understand?" said Craven in conclusion. "You will wait here until it becomes evident that further waiting is useless. Then you are to go straight back to England and give those letters into Mrs. Craven's own hand."

With marked reluctance Yoshio slowly took up the two heavy packets and fingered them for a time silently. Then with a sudden exclamation in his own language he shook his head and pushed them back across the table. "Going with master," he announced phlegmatically, and raised his eyes with a glance that was at once provocative and stubborn. Craven met his direct stare with a feeling of surprise. Only once before had the docile Japanese asserted himself definitely and the memory of it made anger now impossible. He pointed to the letters lying on the table between them. "You have your orders," he said quietly, and cut short further protests with a quick gesture of authority. "Do as you're told, you obstinate little devil," he added, with a short laugh. And like a chidden child Yoshio pocketed the letters sullenly. Stifling a yawn

Craven kicked off his boots and moved over to the bed with a glance at his watch. He flung himself down, dressed as he was.

"Two hours, Yoshio—not a minute longer," he murmured drowsily, and slept almost before his head touched the pillow.

For an hour or more, squatting motionless on his heels in the middle of the tent, Yoshio watched him, his mask-like face expressionless, his eyes fixed in an unwavering stare. Then he rose cautiously and glided from the tent.

During the last two years Craven had become accustomed to snatching a few hours of sleep when and how he could. He slept now deeply and dreamlessly. And when the two hours were passed and Yoshio woke him he sprang up, wide awake on the instant, refreshed by the short rest. In silence that was no longer sullen the valet indicated a complete Arab outfit he had brought back with him to the tent, but Craven waved it aside with a smile at the thought of Saïd's pertinacity and finished his dressing quickly. As he concluded his hasty preparations he found time to wonder at his own frame of mind. He had an odd feeling of aloofness that precluded even excitement. It was as if his spirit, already freed, looked down from some immeasurable height with scant interest upon the doings of a being who wore the earthly semblance of himself but who mattered not at all. He seemed to be above and beyond actualities. He heard himself repeating the instructions he had given earlier to Yoshio, he found himself taking leave of the faithful little Jap and wondering slightly at the man's apparent unconcern. But outside the little tent the strange feeling left him suddenly as it had come. The cool wind that an hour later would usher in the dawn blew about his face dispelling the visionary sensation that had taken hold of him. He drew a deep breath looking eagerly at the beauty of the moon-lit night, feeling himself once more keenly alive, keenly excited at the prospect of the coming venture.

Excitement was rife also in the camp and he made his way with difficulty through the jostling throng of men and horses towards the rallying point before the old Sheik's tent. The noise was deafening, and trampling screaming horses wheeled and backed among the crowd pressing around them. With shouts of acclamation a way was made for the Englishman and he passed through the dense ranks to the open space where Mukair Ibn Zarrarah with his two sons and a little group of headmen were standing. They welcomed him with characteristic gravity and Saïd proffered the inevitable cigarette with a reproachful glance at his khaki clothing. For a few moments they conversed and then the Sheik stepped forward with uplifted hand. The clamour of the people gave way to a deep silence. In a short impassioned speech the old man bade his tribe go forward in the name of the one God, Merciful and Beneficent. And as his arm dropped to his side again a mighty shout broke from the assembled multitude. *Allah! Allah!* the fierce exultant cry rose in a swelling volume of sound as the fighting men leaped to their maddened horses dragging them back into orderly ranks from among the press of onlookers and tossing their long guns in the air in frenzied excitement. A magnificent black stallion was led up to Craven, and the Sheik soothed the beautiful quivering creature, caressing his shapely head with trembling nervy fingers. "He is my favourite, he will carry you well," he murmured with a proud smile as he watched Craven handling the spirited animal. Mounted Craven bent down and wrung Mukair Ibn Zarrarah's hand and in another moment he found himself riding between Omar and Saïd at the head of the troop as it moved off followed by the ringing shouts of those who were left behind. He had a last momentary glimpse of the old Sheik, a solitary upright figure of pathetic dignity, standing before his tent, and then the camp seemed to slide away behind them as the pace increased and they reached the edge of the oasis and emerged on to the open desert. A few minutes more and the fretting horses settled down into a steady gallop. The dense ranks of tribesmen were silent at last, and only the rythmical thud of hoofs sounded with a muffled beat against the soft shifting sand.

Craven felt himself in strange accordance with the men with whom he rode. The love of hazardous adventure that was in his blood leaped into activity and a keen fierce pleasure swept him at the thought of the coming conflict. The death he sought was the death he had always hoped for—the crashing clamour of the battlefield, the wild tumultuous impact of contending forces, with the whining scream of flying bullets in his ears. To die—and, dying, to atone!

> *"Come to Me all ye who. . . are heavy laden
> and I will give you rest."*

Might that ineffable rest that was promised be even for him? Would his deep repentance, the agony of spirit he had endured, be payment enough? Eternal death—the everlasting hell of the Jehovah of the ancients! Not that, merciful God, but the compassion of Christ:

"He that cometh unto Me I will in no wise cast out."

On that terrible day in Yokohama that seemed so many weary years ago Craven had laid his sin-stained soul in all sincerity and humbleness at the feet of the Divine Redeemer, but with no thought or hope of forgiveness. Always the necessity of personal atonement had remained with him, without which by his reasoning there could be no salvation. That offered, but not until then, he would trust in the compassion that passed man's understanding. And to-night—to-day—he seemed nearer than he had ever been to the fulfilment of his desire. The mental burden that had lain like an actual crushing weight upon him seemed to slip away into nothingness. A long deep sigh of wonderful relief escaped him and he drew himself straighter in the saddle, a new peace dawning in his eyes as he raised them to the starlit sky. Out of the past there flashed into his mind the picture—forgotten since the days of childhood—of Christian freed of his burden at the foot of the Cross, as represented in the old copy of the "Pilgrim's Progress" over which he had pored as a boy, enthralled by the quaint text which he had known nearly by heart and fascinated by the curious illustrations that had appealed to his young imagination.

The years rolled back, he saw himself again a little lad stretched on the rug before the fire in the library at Craven Towers, the big book propped open before him, studying with a child's love of the grotesque the grisly picture of Apollyon whose hideous black-winged form had to his boyish mind been the actual image of the devil, a tangible demon whom he had longed to conquer like Christian armed with sword and shield. The childish idea, a bodily adversary to contend with—it would have been simpler. But the devil in a man's own heart, the insidious inward prompting to sin that unrepelled grows imperceptibly stronger and greater until the realisation of sin committed comes with horrible suddenness! To Craven, as to many others, came the futile longing to have his life to live again, to start afresh from the days of innocency when he had hung, enraptured, over the woodcuts of the "Pilgrim's Progress." He forced his thoughts back to the present. Death, not life, lay before him. Instinctively he glanced at the man who rode at his right hand. In the cold white moonlight the Arab's face was like a piece of beautiful carved bronze, still and terrible in its fixed intentness. Sitting his horse with evident difficulty, animated by mere strength of will, his wasted frame rigidly upright, his sombre tragic eyes peering steadfastly ahead, he seemed in his grim purposefulness the very incarnation of avenging justice. And as Craven looked at him covertly he wondered what lay hidden behind those set features, what of hope, what of fear, what of despair was seething in the fierce heart of the desert man. Of the dearly loved wife who had been ravished from him there had come no further word, her fate was unknown. Had she died, or did she still live—in shameful captivity, the slave of the renegade who had made her the price of his treachery? What additional horror still awaited the unhappy husband who rode to avenge her? With a slight shudder Craven turned from the contemplation of a sorrow that seemed to him even greater than his own and sought his left hand neighbour. With a quick smile Saïd's eyes met his. With an easy swing of his graceful body he drew his horse nearer to the spirited stallion Craven was riding but did not speak. The ready flow of conversation that was habitual had apparently forsaken him.

The young Arab's silence was welcome, Craven had himself no desire to speak. The dawn wind was blowing cool against his forehead, soothing him. The easy gallop of the horse between his knees, tractable and steady now he was allowed free rein, was to him the height of physical enjoyment. He would get from it what he could, he thought with a swift smile of self mockery—the flesh still urged in contradiction to his firm resolve. It was a blind country through which they were riding, though seemingly level the ground rose and fell in a succession of long undulating sweeps that made a wide outlook impossible. A regiment could lie hidden in the hollows among the twisting deviating sandy hillocks and be passed unnoticed. And as he topped each rise at the head of the Arab troop Craven looked forward eagerly with unfailing interest. He hardly knew for what he looked for their destination lay many miles further southward and the possibility of unexpected attack had been foreseen by Mukair Ibn Zarrarah, whose scouts had ranged the district for weeks past, but the impression once aroused of an impending something lingered persistently and fixed his attention.

From time to time the waiting scouts joined them, solitary horsemen riding with reckless speed over the broken ground or slipping silently from the shadow of a side track to make a brief report and then take their place among the ranks of tribesmen. So far they told no more than was already known. The wind blew keener as the dawn approached. Far in the east the first faint pinky streaks were spreading across the sky, overhead the twinkling stars paled one by one and vanished. The

E.M. HULL

atmosphere grew suddenly chill. The surrounding desert had before been strangely silent, not so much as the wailing cry of a jackal had broken the intense stillness, but now an even deeper hush, mysterious and pregnant, closed down over the land. For the time all nature seemed to hang in suspense, waiting, watching. To Craven the wonder of the dawn was not new, he had seen if often in many countries, but it was a marvel of which he never tired. And there was about this sunrise a significance that had been attached to no other he had ever witnessed. Eagerly he watched the faint flush brighten and intensify, the pale streaks spread and widen into far flung bars of flaming gold and crimson. Daylight came with startling suddenness and as the glowing disc of the sun rose red above the horizon a horseman broke from the galloping ranks, and spurring in advance of the troop, wheeled his horse and dragged him to an abrupt standstill. Rising in his stirrups he flung his arms in fervid ecstasy toward the heavens. Craven recognised in him a young Mullah of fanatical tendencies who had been particularly active in the camp during the preceding week. That the opposing tribe was of a different sect, abhorred by the followers of Mukair Ibn Zarrarah, had been an original cause of dissent between them, and the priests had made good use of the opportunity of fanning religious zeal.

The cavalcade came to a sudden halt, and as Craven with difficulty reined in his own horse the sustained and penetrating cry of the muezzin rose weirdly high and clear on the morning air, "*al-ilah-ilah*." The arresting and solemn invocation had always had for Craven a peculiar fascination, and as the last lingering notes died away it was not purely from a motive of expediency that he followed the common impulse and knelt among the prostrate Arabs. His creed differed from theirs but he worshipped the same God as they, and in his heart he respected their overt profession of faith.

As he rose from his knees he caught Saïd's eyes bent on him with a curious look in them of interrogation that was at once faintly mocking and yet sad. But the expression passed quickly into a boyish grin as he waved an unlit cigarette toward the fiery young priest who had seized the chance to embark on a passionate harangue.

"When prayer is ended disperse yourselves through the land as ye list," he murmured, with a flippant laugh at the perverted quotation. "The holy man will preach till our tongues blacken with thirst." And he turned to his brother to urge him to give the order to remount. Omar was leaning against his horse, his tall figure sagging with fatigue. He started violently as Saïd spoke to him, and, staggering, would have fallen but for the strong arm slipped round him. And, watching Craven saw with dismay a dark stain mar the whiteness of his robes where a wound had broken out afresh, and he wondered whether the weakened body would be able to respond to the urging of the resolute will that drove it mercilessly, or, when almost within view, the fiercely longed for revenge would yet be snatched from him.

But with an effort the Arab pulled himself together and, mounting, painfully cut short the Mullah's eloquence and gave in a firm tone the desired order.

The swift gallop southward was resumed.

The breeze dropped gradually and finally died away, but for an hour or more the refreshing coolness lingered. Then as the sun rose higher and gained in strength the air grew steadily warmer until the heat became intense and Craven began to look eagerly for the oasis that was to be their first halting place. In full daylight the landscape that by night had seemed to possess an eerie charm developed a dull monotony. The successive rise and fall of the land, always with its limited outlook, became tedious, and the labyrinthine hillocks with their intricate windings seemed to enclose them inextricably. But on reaching the summit of a longer steeper incline that had perceptibly slowed the galloping horses, he saw spread out before him a level tract of country stretching far into the distance, with a faint blue smudge beyond of the chain of hills that Saïd told him marked the boundary of the territory that Mukair Ibn Zarrarah regarded as his own, the boundary, too, of French jurisdiction. Through a defile in the hills lay the enemy country.

The change was welcome to men and horses alike, the latter—aware with unerring instinct of the nearness of water—of their own accord increased their pace and thundering down the last long shifting slope pressed forward eagerly toward the oasis that Craven judged to be between two and three miles away. In the clear deceptive atmosphere it appeared much nearer, and yet as they raced onward it seemed to come no closer but rather to recede as though some malevolent demon of the desert in wanton sport was conjuring it tantalizingly further and further from them. The tall feathery palms, seen through the shimmering heat haze, took an exaggerated height towering fantastically above the scrub of bushy thorn trees.

Craven had even a moment's doubt whether the mirage-like oasis actually existed or was merely a delusion bred of fancy and desire. But the absurdity of the doubt came home to him as he looked again at the outline of the distant hills—too conspicuous a landmark to allow of any error on the part of his companions to whom the country was familiar.

The prospect of the welcome shade made him more sensitive to the scorching strength of the sun that up till now he had endured without more than a passing sensation of discomfort. He was inured to heat, but to-day's heat was extraordinary, and even the Arabs were beginning to show signs of distress. It was many hours since they started and the pace had been killing. His mouth was parched and his eyeballs smarted with the blinding glare. With the thirst that increased each moment the last half mile seemed longer than all the preceding ride, and when the oasis was at length reached he slipped from his sweating horse with an exclamation of relief.

The Arabs crowded round the well and in a moment the little peaceful spot was the scene of noisy confusion; men shouting, scrambling and gesticulating, horses squealing, and above all the creaking whine of the tackling over the well droning mournfully as the bucket rose and fell. Saïd swung himself easily to the ground and held his brother's plunging horse while he dismounted. For a few moments they conversed together in a rapid undertone, and then the younger man turned to Craven, a cloud on his handsome face. "Our communication has broken down. Two scouts should have met us here," he said, with a hint of anxiety in his voice. "It disconcerts our scheme for we counted on their report. They may be late—it is hardly likely. They had ample time. More probably they have been ambushed—the country is filled with spies— in which event the advantage lies with the other side. They will know that we have started, while we shall have no further information. The two men who are missing were the only ones operating beyond the border. The last scout who reported himself was in touch with them last night. From them he learned that two days ago the enemy were forty miles south of the hills yonder. We had hoped to catch them unawares, but they may have got wind of our intentions and be nearer than we expect. The curse of *Allah* on them!" he added impatiently.

"What are you going to do?" asked Craven with a backward glance at the dismounted tribesmen clustering round the well and busily employed in making preparations for rest and food. Saïd beckoned to a passing Arab and dispatched him with a hurried order. Then he turned again to Craven. "The horses must rest though the men would go forward at a word. I am sending two scouts to reconnoitre the defile and bring back what information they can," he said. And as he spoke the two men he had sent for appeared with disciplined promptness and reined in beside him. Having received their brief instructions they started off in a cloud of dust and sand at the usual headlong gallop. Saïd turned away immediately and disappeared among the jostling crowd, but Craven lingered at the edge of the oasis looking after the fast receding horsemen who, crouched low in their saddles, their long white cloaks swelling round them, were very literally carrying out their orders to ride "swift as the messengers of Azrael." He had known them both on his previous visits, though he had not recognised them in the dark hours of the dawn when they joined the troop, and remembered them as two of the most dare-devil and intrepid of Mukair Ibn Zarrarah's followers. A moment since they had grinned at him in cheery greeting, exhibiting almost childlike pleasure when he had called them by name, and had set off with an obeisance as deep to him as to their leader.

Incidents of those earlier visits flashed through his mind as he watched them speeding across the glaring plain and a feeling almost of regret came to him that it should be these two particular men who had been selected for the hazardous mission. For he guessed that their chance of return was slight. And yet hardly slighter than for the rest of them! With a shrug he moved away slowly and sought the shadow of a camel thorn. He lay on his back in the welcome patch of shade, his helmet tilted over his eyes, drawing vigorously at a cigarette in the vain hope of lessening the attentions of the swarms of tormenting flies that buzzed about him, and waiting patiently for the desired water before he swallowed the dark brown unsavoury mass of crushed dates which, warm from his pocket and gritty with the sand that penetrated everything, was the only food available. Saïd was still busy among the throng of men and horses, but near him Omar sat plunged in gloomy silence, his melancholy eyes fixed on the distant hills. He had re-adjusted his robes, screening the ominous stain that revealed what he wished to hide. His hands, which alone might have betrayed the emotion surging under his outward passivity, were concealed in the folds of his enveloping burnous. When the immediate wants of men and horses were assuaged the prevailing clamour gave place to sudden quiet as the Arabs lay down and, muffling their heads in their cloaks, seemed to fall instantly asleep. His supervision ended, Saïd reappeared, and following the example of his men was soon snoring peacefully. Craven rolled over on his side, and lighting another cigarette settled himself more comfortably on the warm ground. For a time he watched the solitary sentinel sitting motionless on his horse at no great distance from the oasis. Then a vulture winging its slow heavy way across the heavens claimed his attention and he followed it with his eyes until it passed beyond his vision. He was too lazy and too comfortable to turn his head. He lay listening to the shrill hum of countless insect life, smoking cigarette after cigarette till the ground around him was littered with stubs and match ends. The hours passed slowly. When he looked at the guard again the Arab was varying the monotony by walking his horse to and fro, but he had not moved further into the desert. And suddenly as Craven watched him he wheeled and galloped back toward the camp. Craven started up on his arm, screening his eyes from the sun and staring intently in the direction of the hills. But there was nothing to be seen in the wide empty plain, and he sank down again with a smile at his own impatience as the reason of the man's return occurred to him. Reaching the oasis the Arab led his horse among the prostrate sleepers and kicked a comrade into wakefulness to take his place. From time to time the intense stillness was broken by a movement among the horses, and once or twice a vicious scream came from a stallion resenting the attentions of a restless neighbour. The slumbering Arabs lay like sheeted figures of the dead save when some uneasy dreamer rolled over with a smothered grunt into a different position. Craven had begun to wonder how much longer the siesta would be protracted when Omar rose stiffly, and going to his brother's side awoke him with a hand on his shoulder. Saïd sat up blinking sleepily and then leaped alertly to his feet. In a few minutes the oasis was once more filled with noisy activity. But this time there was no confusion. The men mounted quickly and the troop was reformed with the utmost dispatch. The horses broke almost immediately into the long swinging gallop that seemed to eat up the miles under their feet.

The fiercest heat of the day was passed. The haze that had hung shimmering over the plain had cleared away and the hills they were steadily nearing grew more clearly defined. Soon the conformation of the range was easily discernible, the rocky surface breaking up into innumerable gullies and ravines, the jagged ridges standing out clean against the deep blue of the sky. Another mile and Saïd turned to him with outstretched hand, pointing eagerly. "See, to the right, there, by that shaft of rock that looks like a minaret, is the entrance to the defile. It is well masked. It comes upon one suddenly. A stranger would hardly find the opening until he was close upon it. In the dawn when the shadows are black I have ridden past it myself once or twice and had to—*Allah*! Selim—and alone!" he cried suddenly, and shot ahead of his companions. The troop halted at Omar's shouted command, but Craven galloped after his friend. He had caught sight of the horseman emerging from the pass a moment after Saïd had seen him and the same thought had leaped to the mind of each—the news on which so much depended might still never reach them. The spy came on toward them slowly, his horse reeling under him, and man and beast alike were nearly shot to pieces. As Saïd drew alongside of them the wounded horse collapsed and the dying man fell with him, unable to extricate himself. In a flash the Arab Chief was on his feet, and with a tremendous effort pulled the dead animal clear of his follower's crushed and quivering limbs. Slipping an arm about him he raised him gently, and bending low to catch the faint words he could scarcely hear, held him until the fluttering whisper trailed into silence, and with a convulsive shudder the man died in his arms.

Laying the corpse back on the sand he wiped his blood-stained hands on the folds of his cloak, then swung into the saddle again and turned to Craven, his eyes blazing with anger and excitement. "They were trapped in the defile—ten against two—but Selim got through somehow to make his reconnaissance, and they finished him off on the way back—though I don't think he left many behind him! Either our plans have been betrayed—or it may be merely a coincidence. Whichever it is they are waiting for us yonder, on the other side of the hills. They have saved us a day's journey—at the very least," he added with a short laugh that was full of eager anticipation.

They waited until Omar and the troop joined them, and after a short consultation with the headmen it was decided to press forward without delay. Aware that but few hours of daylight remained, Craven deemed it a foolhardy decision, but Omar was deeply stirred at the nearness of the man who had wronged him—for Selim had managed to extract that information from one of his opponents before killing him—and the tribesmen were eager for immediate action. The horses, too, were fresh enough, thanks to the mid-day rest. The troop moved on again, a guard of fifty picked men slightly in advance of the main body.

At the foot of the hills they drew rein to reform for the defile only admitted of three horses walking abreast, and as Craven waited for his own turn to come to enter the narrow pass he looked curiously at the bare rock face that rose almost perpendicularly out of the sand and towered starkly above him. But he had no time for a lengthy inspection, and in a few minutes, with Omar and Saïd on either hand, he guided his horse round the jutting spur of rock that masked the opening and rode into the sombre shade of the defile. The change was startling, and he shivered with the sudden chill that seemed so much cooler by contrast with the heat of the plain. Hemmed in by sheer sinister looking cliffs, which were broken at intervals by lateral ravines, the tortuous track led over rough slippery ground sprinkled with huge boulders that made any pace beyond a walk impossible. The horses stumbled continually and the necessity of keeping a sharp look-out for each succeeding obstacle drove from Craven's mind everything but the matter in hand. He forgot to wonder how near or how far from the other side of the hills lay the opposing force, or whether they would have time to reform before being attacked or be picked off by waiting marksmen as they emerged from the pass without any possibility of putting up a fight. For himself it didn't after all very much matter one way or the other, but it would be hard luck, he reflected, if Omar did not get a chance at the renegade and Saïd was shot before the encounter he was aching for—and broke off to swear at his horse, which had stumbled badly for the sixth time.

Omar was riding a pace or two in advance, bending forward in the saddle and occasionally swaying as if from weakness, his burning eyes filled with an almost mystical light as if he saw some vision that, hidden from the others, was revealed to him alone. The dark stain on his robe had spread beyond concealment and he had not spoken since they entered the defile. To Craven, who had never before traversed it, the pass was baffling. He did not know its extent and he had no idea of the depth of the hills. But soon a growing excitement on the part of Saïd made him aware that the exit must be near and the continued silence argued that the vanguard had got through unmolested. He slipped the button of his holster and freed his revolver from the silk handkerchief in which Yoshio had wrapped it.

A sharp turn to the right revealed the scene of the ambuscade, where in one of the lateral openings Selim and his companion had been trapped. The bodies of men and horses had been pulled clear of the track by the advance guard as they went by a few minutes earlier. The old sheik's horse showed the utmost repugnance to the grim pile of corpses, snorting and rearing dangerously, and Craven wrestled with him for some moments before he bounded suddenly past them with a clatter of hoofs that sent the loose stones flying in all directions.

Another turn to the right, an equally sharp bend to the left, where the track widened considerably, and they debouched abruptly into open desert.

The vanguard was drawn up in order and their leader spurred to Omar's side in eager haste to communicate what was patent to the eyes of all. A little ripple of excitement went through Craven as he saw the dense body of horsemen, still about two miles away, who were galloping steadily towards them. It had come then. With a curious smile he bent forward and patted the neck of his fretting horse, which was fidgeting badly. The opposing force appeared to outnumber them considerably, but he knew from Saïd that Mukair Ibn Zarrarah's men were better equipped and better trained. It would be skill against brute force, though it yet remained to be seen how far Omar's men would respond to their training when put to the test. Would they be able to control their own headstrong inclinations or would their zeal carry them away in defiance of carefully rehearsed orders?

Word of the near presence of the enemy had been sent back to those who were still moving up the pass, and so far discipline was holding good. The men were pouring out from the yawning mouth of the file in a steady stream, the horses crowded together as closely as possible, and as each detachment arrived it reformed smartly under its own headman.

Watching the rapid approach of the hostile tribe, Craven wondered whether there would be time for their own force to reassemble to enable them to carry out the agreed tactics.

Already they were within half a mile. He had reined back to speak to Omar, when a shout of exultation from Saïd, taken up by his followers till the rocks above them echoed with the ringing cry, heralded the arrival of the last party. There was no time to recapitulate orders or to urge steadiness among the men. With almost no sign from Omar, or so it seemed to Craven, with another deafening shout that drowned the yelling of the enemy the whole force leaped forward simultaneously. Craven's teeth clenched on his lip in sudden fear for Omar's plan of attack, but a quick glance assured him that the madly galloping horses were being kept in good formation, and that fast as was the pace the right and left wing were, according to instructions, steadily opening out and drawing forward in an extended line. The feeling of excitement had left him, and, revolver in hand, he sat down firmer in the saddle with no more emotion than if he were in the hunting field at home.

They were now close enough to distinguish faces—it would be an almighty crash when it did come! It was surprising that up till now there had been no shooting. Accustomed to the Arabs' usually reckless expenditure of ammunition he had been prepared minutes ago for a hail of bullets. And with the thought came a solitary whining scream past his ear, and Saïd, close on his left, flung him a look of reproach and shouted something of which he only caught the words, "Frenchman. . . burnous."

But there was no time left to reply. Following rapidly on the single shot a volley was poured in among them, but the shooting was inaccurate and did very little damage. That it had been intended to break the charge and cause confusion in the orderly ranks was apparent from the further repeated volleys that, nearer, did more deadly execution than the first one. But, bending low in their saddles, Mukair Ibn Zarrarah's men swept on in obedience to Omar's command. His purpose was, by the sheer strength of his onset, to cut through the opposing force with his centre while the wings closed in on either side. To effect this he had bidden his men ride as they had never ridden before and reserve their fire till the last moment, when it would be most effectual. And the swift silent onslaught seemed to be other than the enemy had expected, for there were among them signs of hesitation, their advance was checked, and the firing became wilder and more erratic. Omar and his immediate companions appeared to bear charmed lives, bullets sang past them, over and around them, and though here and there a man fell from the saddle or a horse dropped suddenly, the main body raced on unscathed, or with wounds they did not heed in the frenzy of the moment.

The pace was terrific, and when at last Omar gave the signal for which his men were waiting, the crackling reverberation of their rifles had not died away when the impact came. But the shattering crash that Craven had expected did not occur. Giving way before them and scattering to right and left a break came in the ranks of the opposing force, through which they drove like a living wedge. Then with fierce yells of execration the enemy rallied and the next moment Craven found himself in the midst of a confused mêlée where friends and foes were almost indistinguishable. The thundering of horses' hoofs, the raucous shouting of the Arabs, the rattle of musketry, combined in deafening uproar. The air was dense with clouds of sand and smoke, heavy with the reek of powder. He had lost sight of Omar, he tried to keep near to Saïd, but in the throng of struggling men he was carried away, cut off from his own party, hemmed in on every side, fighting alone. He had forgotten his desire for death, his heart was leaping with a kind of delirious happiness that found nothing but fierce enjoyment in the scene around him. The stench in his nostrils of blood and sulphur seemed to awaken memories of another existence when he had fought for his life as he was doing now, unafraid, and caring little for the outcome. He was shooting steadily, exulting in his markmanship with no thought in his mind but the passionate wish to kill and kill, and he laughed with almost horrible pleasure as he emptied his revolver at the raving Arabs who surrounded him. Drunk with the blood lust of an unremembered past for the moment he was only a savage like them. And to the superstitious desert men he seemed possessed, and with sudden awe they had begun to draw away from him when a further party galloped up to reinforce them. Craven swung his horse to meet the new-comers and at the same moment realised that he had no cartridges left. With another reckless laugh he dashed his empty revolver in the face of the nearest Arab and, wheeling, spurred forward in an attempt to break through the circle round him. But he found retreat cut off. Three men bore down upon him simultaneously with levelled rifles. He saw them fire, felt a sharp searing as of a red hot wire through his side, and, reeling in the saddle, heard dimly their howl of triumph as they raced toward him—heard also another yell that rose above the Arabs' clamour, a piercing yell that sounded strangely different to the Arabic intonation ringing in his ears. And as he gripped himself and raised his head he had a vision of another horseman mounted on a frenzied trampling roan that, apparently out of control and mad with excitement, was charging down upon them, a horseman whose fluttering close-drawn headgear shaded features that were curiously Mongolian—and then he went down in a welter of men and horses. A flying hoof touched the back of his head and consciousness ceased.

IX

Craven woke to a burning pain in his side, a racking headache and an intolerable thirst. It was not a sudden waking but a gradual dawning consciousness in which time and place as yet meant nothing, and only bodily suffering obtruded on a still partially clouded mind. Fragmentary waves of thought, disconnected and transitory, passed through his brain, leaving no permanent impression, and he made no effort to unravel them. Effort of any kind, mental or physical, seemed for the moment beyond him. He was too tired even to open his eyes, and lay with them closed, wondering feebly at the pain and discomfort of his whole body. He had the sensation of having been battered, he felt bruised from head to foot. Suffering was new to him. He had never been ill in his life, and in all his years of travel and hazardous adventure he had sustained only trivial injuries which had healed readily and been regarded as merely part of the day's work.

But now, as his mind grew clearer, he realised that some accident must have occurred to induce this pain and lassitude that made him lie like a log with throbbing head and powerless limbs. He pondered it, trying to pierce the fog that dulled his intellect. He had a subconscious impression of some strenuous adventure through which he had passed, but knowledge still hovered on the borderland of fancy and actuality. He had no recollection of the fight or of events preceding it. That he was Barry Craven he knew; but of where he had no idea—nor what his life had been. Of his personality there remained only his name, he was quite sure about that. And out of the past emerged only one clear memory—a woman's face. And yet as he dwelt on it the image of another woman's face rose beside it, mingling with and absorbing it until the two faces seemed strangely merged the one into the other, alike and yet wholly different. And the effort to disentangle them and keep them separate was greater than his tired brain could achieve, and made his head ache more violently. Confused, and with a sudden feeling of aversion, he stirred impatiently, and the sharp pain that shot through him brought him abruptly to a sense of his physical state and forced utterance of his greatest need. It had not hitherto occurred to him to wonder whether he were alone, or even where he was. But as he spoke an arm was slipped under him raising him slightly and a cup held to his lips. He drank eagerly and, as he was again lowered gently to the pillow, raised his eyes to the face of the man who bent over him, a puckered yellow face whose imperturbability for once had given place to patent anxiety. Craven stared at it for a few moments in perplexity. Where had he seen it before? Struggling to recall what had happened prior to this curiously obscured awakening there dawned a dim recollection of shattering noise and tumult, of blood and death and fierce unbridled human passion, of a horde of wild-eyed dark-skinned men who surged and struggled round him—and of a yelling Arab on a fiery roan. Memory came in a flash. He gave a weak little croaking laugh. "You damned insubordinate little devil," he murmured, and drifted once more into unconsciousness. When he woke again it was with complete remembrance of everything that had passed. He felt ridiculously weak, but his head did not ache so badly and his mind was perfectly clear. Only of the time that had elapsed between the moment when he had gone down under the Arabs' charge and his awakening a little while ago he had no recollection. How long had he been unconscious? He found himself mildly puzzled, but without any great interest as yet. Plenty of time to find out about that and what had befallen Omar and Saïd. It was not that he did not care, but that, for the moment, he was too tired and listless to do more than lie still and endure his own discomfort. His side throbbed painfully and there was something curious about his left arm, a dead feeling of numbness that made him wonder whether it was there at all. He glanced down at it with sudden apprehension—he had no fancy for a maimed existence—and was relieved to find it still in place but bent stiffly across his chest wrapped in a multitude of bandages— broken, presumably. His eyes wandered with growing interest round the little tent where he lay. It was his own, from which he inferred that the fight must have gone in favour of Mukair Ibn Zarrarah's forces or he would never have been brought back here to it. He glanced from one familiar object to another with a drowsy feeling of contentment.

Presently he became aware that somebody had entered and turning his head he found Yoshio beside him eyeing him with a look in which solicitude, satisfaction, and a faint diffidence struggled for supremacy. Craven guessed the reason of his embarrassment, but he had no mind to refer to an order given, and disobeyed through overzealousness. That, too, could wait—or be forgotten. He contented himself with a single question. "How long?" he asked laconically. With equal brevity the Jap replied: "Two days," and postponed further inquiries by slipping a clinical thermometer into his master's mouth. He had always been useful in attending on minor camp accidents, and during the last two years in Central Africa he had picked up a certain amount of rough surgical knowledge which now stood him in good stead, and which he proceeded to put into practice with a gravity of demeanour that made Craven, in his weakened state, want to giggle hysterically. But he suppressed the inclination and held on to the thermometer until Yoshio solemnly removed it, studied it intently, and nodded approval. With the exact attention to detail that was his ruling passion he carefully rinsed the tiny glass instrument and returned it to its case before leaving the tent. He was back again in a few minutes with a bowl of steaming soup, and handling Craven as if he were a child, fed him with the gentleness of a woman. Then he busied himself about the room, tidying it and reducing its confusion to order.

Craven watched him at first idly and then with a more definite desire to know what had occurred. But to the questions he put Yoshio returned evasive answers, and, resuming his professional manner, spoke gravely of the loss of blood Craven had sustained, of the kick on the head from which he had lain two days insensible, and his consequent need of rest and sleep, finally departing as if to remove temptation from him. Craven chafed at the little Jap's caution and swore at his obstinacy, but a pleasant drowsiness was stealing over him and he surrendered to it without further struggle.

It was more than twelve hours before he opened his eyes again, to find the morning sunlight streaming into the tent.

Yoshio hovered about him, deft-handed and noiseless of tread, feeding him and redressing the wounds in his side where the bullet had entered and passed out. After which he relaxed the faintly superior tone he had adopted and condescended to consult with his patient as to which of the scanty drugs in the tiny medicine chest would be the best to administer. He was disappointed but acquiescent in Craven's decision to trust to his own hardy constitution as long as the wounds appeared healthy and leave nature to do her own work. And again recommending sleep he glided away.

But Craven had no desire or even inclination to sleep. He was tremendously wide awake, his whole being in revolt, facing once more the problem he had thought done with for ever. Again fate had intervened to thwart his determination. For the third time death, for which he longed, had been withheld, and life that was so bitter, so valueless, restored. To what end? Why had the peace he craved for been torn from him—why had he been forced to begin again an existence of hideous struggle? Had he not repented, suffered as few men suffer, and striven to atone? What more was required of him, he wondered bitterly. A galling sense of impotence swept him and he raged at his own nothingness. Self-determination seemed to have been taken from him and with fierce resentment he saw himself as merely a pawn in the game of life; a puppet to fulfil, not his own will, but the will of a greater power than his. In the black despair that came over him he cursed that greater power until, shuddering, he realised his own blasphemy, and a broken prayer burst from his lips. He had come to the end of all things, he was fighting through abysmal darkness. His need was overwhelming—alone he could not go forward, and desperately, he turned to the Divine Mercy and prayed for strength and guidance.

Too weary in spirit to mark the slow passing of the hours he fought his last fight. And gradually he grew calmer, calm enough to accept—if not to understand—the inscrutable rulings of Providence. He had arrogated to himself the disposal of his life, but it was made clear to him that a higher wisdom had decreed otherwise. He did not attempt to seek the purpose of his preservation, enough that for some unfathomable reason it was once more plainly indicated that there was to be no shirking. He had to live, and to do what was possible with the life left him. Gillian! the thought of her was torment. He had tried to free her, and she was still bound. It would be part of his punishment that, suffering, he would have to watch her suffer too. With a groan he flung his uninjured arm across his eyes and lay very still. The day wore on. He roused himself to take the food that Yoshio brought at regular intervals but feigned a drowsiness he did not feel to secure the solitude his mood demanded. And Yoshio, enjoying to the full his state of temporary authority, sat outside the door of the tent and kept away inquirers. Listlessly Craven watched the evening shadows deepen and darken. For hours he had thought, not of himself but of the woman he loved, until his bruised head ached intolerably. And all his deliberation had taken him no further than where he had begun. He was to take up anew the difficult life he had fled from—for that was what it amounted to. He had deserted her who had in all the world no one but him. It had an ugly sound and he flinched from the naked truth of it, but he had done with subterfuges and evasions. He had made her his wife and he had left her—nothing could alter the fact or mitigate the shame. Past

E. M. HULL

experience had taught him nothing; once again he had left a woman in her need to fend for herself. She was his wife, his to shield and to protect, doubly so in her equivocal position that subjected her to much that would not affect one happily married. During the few months they had lived at Craven Towers after their marriage she had shown by every means in her power her desire to be to him the comrade he had asked her to be. And he had repelled her. He had feared himself and the strength of his resolution. Now, as he thought of it with bitter self-reproach, he realised how much more he could have done to make her life easier, to smooth the difficulties of their relationship. Instead he had added to them, and under the strain he had broken down, not she. The egoism he had thought conquered had triumphed over him again to his undoing. Crushing shame filled him, but regrets were useless. The past was past—what of the future? He was going back to her. He was to have the torturing happiness of seeing her again—but what would his re-entry into her life mean to her? What had these two years of which he knew nothing done for her? There had been an accumulated mail waiting for him at Lagos. She had written regularly—but she had told him nothing. Her short letters had been filled with inquiries for the mission, references to Peters' occasional visits to Paris, trivialities of the weather—stilted laborious communications in which he read effort and constraint. How would she receive him—would she even receive him at all? It seemed incredible that she should. He knew her innate gentleness, the selflessness of her disposition, but he knew also that there was a limit to all things. Would she not see in his return the reappearance of a master, a jailer who would curb even that small measure of freedom that had been hers? For bound to him the freedom he had promised her was a mockery. And how was he to explain his prolonged absence? She could not have failed to see some mention of the return of the medical mission, to have wondered why he still lingered in Africa. The letter he had written and entrusted to Yoshio could never now be delivered. She must not learn what he had meant her to know only after his death. He could not explain, he must leave her to put whatever interpretation she would upon it. And what but the most obvious could she put? He writhed in sudden agony of mind, and the physical pain the abrupt movement caused was easier to bear than the thought of her scorn. It was all so hopeless, so complicated. He turned from it with a weary sigh and fell to dreaming of the woman herself.

The tent had grown quite dark. Outside the camp noises were dying away. The sound of subdued voices reached him occasionally, and once or twice he heard Yoshio speak to some passer by.

Then, not far away, the mournful chant of a singer rose clearly out of the evening stillness, penetrating and yet curiously soft—a plaintive little desert air of haunting melancholy, vibrant with passion. It stopped abruptly as it had begun and Craven was glad when it ended. It chimed too intimately with his own sad thoughts and longings. He was relieved when Yoshio came presently to light the lamp and attend to his wants. The Jap chatted with unusual animation as he went about his duties and Craven let him talk uninterrupted. The functions of nurse and valet were quickly carried through and in a short time preparations for the night were finished and Yoshio, wrapped in a blanket, asleep at the foot of Craven's bed. He had scarcely closed his eyes since the day before the punitive force set out, but tonight, conscious that his vigilance might be relaxed, he slept heavily.

Craven himself could not sleep. He lay listening to his servant's even breathing, looking at the tiny flame of the little lamp, which was small enough not to add to the heat of the tent and too weak to illuminate it more than partially, thinking deeply. He strove to stem the current of his thoughts, to keep his mind a blank, or to concentrate on trivialities—he followed with exaggerated interest the swift erratic course of a bat that had flown in through the open door flap, counted the familiar objects around him showing dimly in the flickering light, counted innumerable sheep passing through the traditional gate, counted the seconds represented in the periodical silences that punctuated a cicada's monotonous shrilling. But always he found himself harking back to the problem of the future that he could not banish from his mind. His mental distress reacted on his body. He grew restless, but every movement was still attended by pain and he compelled himself to lie still, though his limbs twitched almost uncontrollably. He was infinitely weary of the forced posture that was not habitual with him, infinitely weary of himself.

The moon rose late, but when it came its clear white light filled the tent with a cold brilliance that killed the feeble efforts of the little lamp and intensified the shadows where its rays did not penetrate. Craven looked at the silvery beam streaming across the room, and quite suddenly he thought of the moonlight in Japan—the moonlight filtering through the tall dark fir trees in the garden of enchantment; he heard the night wind sighing softly round the tiny screen-built house; the air

E.M. HULL

became heavy with the cloying smell of pines and languorous scented flowers, redolent with the well-remembered dreaded fragrance of the perfume she had used. Bathed in perspiration, shuddering with terrible prescience, he stared wild-eyed at the moonlit strip where a nebulous form was rising and gathering into definite shape. An icy chill ran through him. Suffocated with the rapid pounding of his heart, sick with horror at the impending vision he knew to be inevitable, he watched the shadowy figure slowly substantiate into the semblance of a living, breathing body. Not intangible as she had always appeared before, but material as she had been in life, she stood erect in the brilliant pathway of light, facing him. He could see the outline of her slender limbs, solid against the shimmering background; he could mark the rise and fall of the bosom on which her delicate hands lay clasped; he recognised the very obi that she wore—his last gift, sent from Tokio during his three weeks' absence. The little oval face was placid and serene, but he waited, with fearful apprehension, for the fast closed eyes to open and reveal the agony he knew that he would see in them. He prayed that they might open soon, that his torture might be brief, but the terrible reality of her presence seemed to paralyse him. He could not turn his eyes away, could not move a muscle of his throbbing, shivering body. She seemed to sway, gently, almost imperceptibly, from side to side—as though she waited for some sign or impellent force to guide her. Then with horrible dread he became aware that she was coming slowly, glidingly, toward him and the spell that had kept him motionless broke and he shrank back among the pillows, his sound hand clenched upon the covering over him, his parched lips moving in dumb supplication. Nearer she came and nearer till at last she stood beside him and he wondered, in the freezing coldness that settled round his heart, did her coming presage death—had her soul been sent to claim his that had brought upon her such fearful destruction? A muffled cry that was scarcely human broke from him, his eyes dilated and the clammy sweat poured down his face as she bent toward him and he saw the dusky lashes tremble on her dead white cheek and knew that in a second the anguished eyes would open to him in all their accusing awfulness. The bed shook with the spasm that passed through him. Slowly the heavy lids were raised and Craven looked once more into the misty depths of the great grey eyes that were the facsimile of his own. Then a tearing sob of wonderful and almost unbelievable relief escaped him, for the agony he dreaded was not visible—the face so close to his was the face of the happy girl who had loved him before the knowledge of despair had touched her, the tender luminous eyes fixed on him were alight with trust and adoration. Lower and lower she bent and he saw the parted lips curve in a smile of exquisite welcome—or was it fare-well? For as he waited, scarcely breathing and tense with a new wild hope, the definite outline of her figure seemed to fade and tremble; a cold breath like the impress of a ghostly kiss lay for an instant on his forehead, he seemed to hear the faint thin echo of a whispered word—and she was gone. Had she ever been at all? Exhausted, he had no strength to probe what had passed, he was only conscious of a firm conviction that he would never see again the dreaded vision that had haunted him. His rigid limbs relaxed, and with a gasping prayer of unutterable thankfulness he turned his face to the darkness and broke down completely, crying like a child, burying his head in the pillow lest Yoshio should be awakened by the sound of his terrible sobs. And, presently, worn out, he fell asleep.

It was nearly mid-day when he woke again, in less pain and feeling stronger than the day before.

The vision of the previous night was vivid in his recollection, but he would not let himself ponder it. It was to him a message from the dead, an almost sacred sign that the spirit of the woman he had wronged was at rest and had vouchsafed the forgiveness for which he had never hoped. He would rather have it so. He shrank from brutally dissecting impressions that might after all be only the result of remorse working on a fevered imagination. The peace that had come to him was too precious to be lightly let go. She had forgiven him though he could never forgive himself.

But despite the tranquillizing sense of pardon he felt he knew that the penalty of his fault was not yet paid, that it would never be paid. The tragic memory of little O Kara San still rose between him and happiness. He was still bound, still trapped in the pit he had himself dug. He was unclean, unfit, debarred by his sin from following the dictates of his heart. A deep sadness and an overwhelming sense of loss filled him as he thought of the woman he had married. She was his wife, he loved her passionately, longed for her with all the strength of his ardent nature, but, sin-stained, he dared not claim her. In her spotless purity she was beyond his desire. And because of him she must go through life robbed of her woman's heritage. In marrying her he had wronged her irreparably. He had always known it, but at the time there had seemed no other course open to him. Yet surely there must have been some alternative if he had set himself seriously to find it. But had he? Doggedly he argued that he had—that personal consideration had not swayed him in his decision. But even as he persisted in his assertion accusing conscience rose up and stripped from him the last shred of personal deception that had blinded him, and he acknowledged to himself that he had married her that she might not become the wife of any other man. He had been the meanest kind of dog in the manger. At the time he had not realised it—he had thought himself influenced solely by her need, not his. But his selfishness seemed very patent to him now. And what was to be the end of it? How was he ever to compensate for the wrong done her?

Yoshio's entry put a stop to introspection that was both bitter and painful. And when he left him an hour later Craven was in no mood to resume speculation that was futile and led nowhere. He had touched bedrock—he could not think worse of himself than he did. The less he thought of himself the better. His immediate business seemed to be to get well as quickly as possible and return to England—beyond that he could not see. The sound of Saïd's voice outside was a welcome relief. He appeared to be arguing with Yoshio, who was obstinately refusing him entrance. Craven cut short the discussion.

"Let the Sheik come in, Yoshio!" he called, and laughed at the weakness of his own voice. But it was strong enough to carry as far as the tent door, and, with a flutter of draperies, the Arab Chief strode in. He grasped Craven's outstretched hand and stood looking down on him for a moment with a broad smile on his handsome face. "*Enfin, mon brave*, I thought I should never see you! Always you were asleep, or so it was reported to me," he said with a laugh, dropping to his heels on the mat and lighting a cigarette. Then he gave a quick searching glance at the bandaged figure on the bed and laughed again.

"You ought to be dead, you know, would have been dead if it hadn't been for that man of yours," with a backward jerk of his head toward the door. "You owe him your life, my friend. You know he came with us that night, borrowed a horse and the burnous you wouldn't wear, and kept out of sight till the last minute. He was close behind you when we charged, lost you in the mêlée, and found you again just in the nick of time. I was cut off from you myself for the moment, but I saw you wounded, saw him break a way through to you and then saw you both go down. I thought you were done for. It was just then the tide turned in our favour and I managed to reach you, with no hope of finding you alive. I was never more astonished in my life than when I saw that little devil of a Japanese crawl out from under a heap of men and horses dragging you after him. He was bruised and dazed, he didn't know friend from foe, bu he had enough sense left to know that you were alive and he meant to keep you so. He laid you out on the sand and he sat on you—you can laugh, but it's true—and blazed away with his revolver at everybody who came near, howling his national war cry till I wept with laughter. And after it was all over he snarled like a panther when I tried to touch you, and, refusing any assistance, carried you back here on the saddle in front of him—and you were no light weight. A man, by *Allah*!" he concluded enthusiastically. Craven smiled at the Arab's graphic description, but he found it in his heart to wish that Yoshio's zeal had not been so forward and so successful. But there were other lives than his that had been involved.

"Omar?" he asked anxiously. The laughter died abruptly from Saïd's eyes and his face grew grave.

"Dead," he said briefly; "he did not try to live. Life held nothing for him without Safiya," he added, with an expressive shrug that was eloquent of his inability to understand such an attitude.

"And she—?"

"Killed herself the night she was taken. Her abductor got no pleasure of her and Omar's honour was unsmirched—though he never knew it, poor devil. He killed his man," added Saïd, with a smile of grim satisfaction. "It made no difference, he was renegade, a traitor, ripe for death. The Chief fell to my lot. It was from him I learned about Safiya—he talked before he died." The short hard laugh that followed the meaning words was pure Arab. He lit another cigarette and for some time sat smoking silently, while Craven lay looking into space trying not to envy the dead man who had found the rest that he himself had been denied.

To curb the trend of his thoughts he turned again to Saïd. Animation had vanished from the Arab's face, and he was staring gloomily at the strip of carpet on which he squatted. His dejected bearing did not betoken the conqueror he undoubtedly was. That his brother's death was a deep grief to him Craven knew without telling, but he guessed that something more than regret for Omar was at the bottom of his depression.

"It was decisive, I suppose," he said, rather vaguely, thinking of the action of four days ago. Saïd nodded. "It was a rout," he said with a hint of contempt in his voice. "Dogs who could plunder and kill when no resistance was offered, but when it came to a fight they had no stomach for it. Yet they were men once, and, like fools, we thought they were men still. They had talked enough, bragged enough, by *Allah*! and it is true there were a few who rallied round their Chief. But the rank and file—bah!" He spat his cigarette on to the floor with an air of scorn. "It promised well enough at first," he grumbled. "I thought we were going to have an opportunity of seeing what stuff my men were made of. But they had no organisation. After the first half hour we did what we liked with them. It was a walk over," he added in English, about the only words he knew.

Craven laughed at his disgusted tone.

"And you, who were spoiling for a fight! No luck, Sheik."

Saïd looked up with a grin, but it passed quickly, leaving his face melancholy as before. Craven made a guess at the trouble.

"It will make a difference to you—Omar's death, I mean," he suggested.

Saïd gave a little harsh laugh.

"Difference!" he echoed bitterly. "It is the end of everything," and he made a violent gesture with his hands. "I must give up my regiment," he went on drearily, "my comrades, my racing stable in France—all I care for and that makes life pleasant to me. For what? To rule a tribe who have become too powerful to have enemies; to listen to interminable tales of theft and disputed inheritances and administer justice to people who swear by the Koran and then lie in your face; to marry a wife and beget sons that the tribe of Mukair Ibn Zarrarah may not die out. *Grand Dieu*, what a life!" The tragic misery of his voice left no doubt as to his sincerity. And Craven, who knew him, was not inclined to doubt. The expedient that had been adopted in Saïd's case was justifiable while he remained a younger son with no immediate prospect of succeeding to the leadership of the tribe—there had always been the hope that Omar's wife would eventually provide an heir—but as events had turned out it had been a mistake, totally unfitting him for the part he was now called upon to play. His innate European tendencies, inexplicable both to himself and to his family, had been developed and strengthened by association with the French officers among whom he had been thrown, and who had welcomed him primarily as the representative of a powerful desert tribe and then, very shortly afterwards, for himself. His personal charm had won their affections and he had very easily become the most popular native officer in the regiment. Courted and feted, shown off, and extolled for his liberality of mind and purse, his own good sense had alone prevented him from becoming completely spoiled. To the impecunious Frenchmen his wealth was a distinct asset in his favour, for racing was the ruling passion in the regiment, and the fine horses he was able to provide insured to them the preservation of the inter-regimental trophy that had for some years past graced their mess table. He had thrown himself into the life whole-heartedly, becoming more and more influenced by western thought and culture, but without losing his own individuality. He had assimilated the best of civilization without acquiring its vices. But the experience was not likely to conduce to his future happiness. Craven thought of the life led by the Spahi in Algiers, and during periods of leave in Paris, and contrasted it with the life that was lying before him, a changed and very different existence. He foresaw the difficulties that would have to be met, the problems that would arise, and above all he understood Saïd's chief objection—the marriage from which his misogynous soul recoiled. Like himself the Arab was facing a crisis that was momentous. Two widely different cases but analogous nevertheless. While he was working out his salvation in England Saïd would be doing the same in his desert fastness. The thought strengthened his friendship for the despondent young Arab. He would have given much to be able to help him but his natural reserve kept him silent. He had made a sufficient failure of his own life. He did not feel himself competent to offer advice to another.

"It's a funny world," he said with a half sigh, "though I suppose it isn't the world that's at fault but the people who live in it," and in his abstraction he spoke in his own language.

"*Plait-il?*" Saïd's puzzled face recalled him to himself and he translated, adding: "It's rotten luck for you, Sheik, but it's kismet. All things are ordained," he concluded almost shyly, feeling himself the worst kind of Job's comforter. The Arab shrugged. "To those who believe," he repeated gloomily, "and I, my friend, have no beliefs. What would you? All my life I have doubted, I have never been an orthodox Mohammedan—though I have had to keep my ideas to myself *bien entendu*! And the last few years I have lived among men who have no faith, no god, no thought beyond the world and its pleasures. Islam is nothing to me. 'The will of *Allah*—the peace of *Allah*,' what are they but words, empty meaningless words! What peace did *Allah* give to

Omar, who was a strict believer? What peace has *Allah* given to my father, who sits all day in his tent mourning for his first-born? I swear myself by *Allah* and by the Prophet, but it is from custom, not from any feeling I attach to the terms. I have read a French translation of a life of Mohammed written by an American. I was not impressed. It did not tend to make me look with any more favour on his doctrine. I have my own religion—I do not lie, I do not steal, I do not break my word. Does the devout follower of the Prophet invariably do as much? You know, and I know, that he does not. Wherein then is he a better man than I? And if there be a future life, which I am quite open to admit, I am inclined to think that my qualifications will be as good as any true son of the faith," he laughed unmirthfully, and swung to his feet.

"There are—other religions," said Craven awkwardly. He had no desire to proselytise and avoided religious discussions as much as possible, but Saïd's confidence had touched him. He was aware that to no one else would the Arab have spoken so frankly. But Saïd shook his head.

"I will keep my own religion. It will serve," he said shortly. Then he shrugged again as if throwing aside the troubles that perplexed him and looked down on Craven with a quick laugh. "And you, my poor friend, who had so much better have taken the burnous I offered you, you will stay and watch the metamorphosis of the Spahi, *hein*?"

"I wish I could," said Craven with an answering smile, "but I have my own work waiting for me in England. I'll have to go as soon as I'm sufficiently patched up."

Saïd nodded gravely. He was perfectly well aware of the fact that Craven had deliberately sought death when he had ridden with the tribe against their enemies. That a change had come over him since the night of the raid was plainly visible even to one less astute than the sharp-eyed Arab, and his expressed intention of returning to England confirmed the fact. What had caused the change did not seem to matter, enough that, to Saïd, it marked a return to sanity. For it had been a fit of madness, of course—in no other light could he regard it. But since it had passed and his English friend was once more in full possession of his senses he could only acquiesce in a decision that personally he regretted. He would like to have kept him with him indefinitely. Craven stood for the past, he was a link with the life the Francophile Arab was reluctantly surrendering. But it was not the moment to argue. Craven looked suddenly exhausted, and Yoshio who had stolen in noiselessly,

X

It was nearly four months before Craven left the camp of Mukair Ibn Zarrarah. His injuries had healed quickly and he had rapidly regained his former strength. He was anxious to return to England without delay, but he had yielded to Saïd's pressing entreaties to wait until they could ride to Algiers together. There had been much for the young Sheik to do. He was already virtual leader of the tribe. Mukair Ibn Zarrarah, elderly when his sons had been born, had aged with startling suddenness since the death of Omar. He had all at once become an old man, unable to rally from the shock of his bereavement, bewailing the fate of his elder and favourite son, and trembling for the future of his beloved tribe left to the tender mercies of a man he now recognised to be more Frenchman than Arab. He exaggerated every Francophile tendency he saw in Saïd and cursed the French as heartily as ever Omar had done, forgetting that he himself was largely responsible for the inclinations he objected to. And his terrors were mainly imaginary. A few innovations Saïd certainly instituted but he was too astute to make any material changes in the management of his people. They were loyal and attached to the ruling house and he was clever enough to leave well alone; broad-minded enough to know that he could not run a large and scattered tribe on the same plan as a regiment of Spahis; philosophical enough to realise that he had turned down a page in his life's history and must be content to follow, more or less, in the footsteps of his forebears. The fighting men were with him solidly, even those who had been inclined to object to his European tactics had, in view of his brilliant generalship, been obliged to concede him the honour that was his due. For his victory had not been altogether the walkover he had airily described to Craven. The older men—the headmen in particular—more prejudiced still, who, like Mukair Ibn Zarrarah, had centred all their hopes on Omar, were beginning to comprehend that their fears of Saïd's rule were unfounded and that his long sojourn among the hated dominant race had neither impaired his courage nor fostered practices abhorrent to them. Craven watched with interest the gradual establishment of mutual goodwill between the young Sheik and his petty Chiefs. Since his recovery he had attended several of the councils called in consequence of the old Sheik's retirement from active leadership of the tribe, and he had been struck by Saïd's restrained and conciliatory attitude toward his headmen. He had met them half-way, sinking his own inclinations and disarming their suspicions of him. At the same time he had let it be clearly understood that he meant to be absolute as his father had been. In spite of the civilisation that had bitten so deeply he was still too much an Arab, too much the son of Mukair Ibn Zarrarah, to be anything but an autocrat at heart. And his assumption of power had been favourably looked upon by the minor Chiefs. They were used to being ruled by an iron hand and would have despised a weak leader. They had feared the effects of foreign influence, dreaded a régime that might have lessened the prestige of the tribe. Their doubts set at rest they had rallied with enthusiasm round their new Chief.

As soon as he had been able to get about again Craven had visited Mukair Ibn Zarrarah in his darkened tent and been shocked at his changed appearance. He could hardly believe that the bowed stricken figure who barely heeded his entrance, but, absorbed in grief, continued to sway monotonously to and fro murmuring passages from the Koran alternately with the name of his dead son, was the vigorous alert old man he had seen only a few weeks before dominating a frenzied crowd with the strength of his personality and addressing them in tones that had carried to the furthest extent of the listening multitude. Crushing sorrow and the weight of years suddenly felt had changed him into a wreck that was fast falling to pieces.

Saïd had followed him out into the sunshine.

"You see how it is with him," he said. "I cannot leave him now. As soon as possible I will go to Algiers to give in my resignation and smooth matters with the Government. We shall not be in very good odour over this affair. We have kept the peace so long in this quarter of the country that deliberate action on our part will take a lot of explaining. They will admit provocation but will blame our mode of retaliation. They may blame!" he laughed and shrugged. "I shall be called hasty, ill-advised. The Governor will haul me over the coals unmercifully—you know him, that fat old Faidherbe? He is always trembling for his position, seeing an organized revolt in the petty squabbles of every little tribe, and fearful of an outbreak that might lead to his recall. A mountain of flesh with the heart of a chicken! He will rave and shout and talk a great deal about the beneficent French administration and the ingratitude of Chiefs like myself who add to the Government's difficulties. But my Colonel will back me up, unofficially of course, and his word goes with the Governor. A very different man, by *Allah*! It would be a good thing for this country if he were where Faidherbe is. But he is only a soldier and no politician, so he is likely to end his days a simple Colonel of Spahis."

As they moved away from the tent they discussed the French methods of administration as carried out in Algeria, and Craven learned a great deal that astonished him and would also have considerably astonished the Minister of the Interior sitting quietly in his office in the Place Beauveau. Saïd had seen and heard much. His known sympathies had made him the recipient of many confidences and even his Francophile tendencies had not blinded him to evils that were rampant, corruption and double dealing, bribes freely offered and accepted by highly placed officials, fortunes amassed in crooked speculations with Government money—the faults of individuals who had abused their official positions and exploited the country they had been sent to administer.

As Craven listened to these frank revelations from the only honest Arab he had ever met he wondered what effect Saïd's intimate knowledge would have upon his life, how far it would influence him, and what were likely to be his future relations with the masters of the country. With a Chief less broadminded and of less innate integrity the result might easily be disastrous. But Saïd had had larger experience than most Arab Chiefs and his adherence to the French was due to what he had seen in France rather than to what had been brought to his notice in Algeria.

It was early in January when they started on the long ride across the desert. For some weeks Craven had been impatient to get away, only his promise to Saïd kept him.

It was a large cavalcade that left the oasis, for the new Chief required a bigger escort to support his dignity than the Captain of Spahis had done. The days passed without incident. Despite Craven's desire to reach England the journey was in every way enjoyable. When he had actually started his restlessness decreased, for each successive sunrise meant a day nearer home. And Saïd, too, had thrown off the depression and new gravity that had come to him and talked more hopefully of the future. As they travelled northward they reached a region of greater cultivation and in their route passed some of the big fruit farms that were becoming more and more a feature of the country. Spots of beauty in the wilderness, carved out of arid desert by patience and perseverance and threatened always by the devastating locust, though no longer subjected to the Arab raids that had been a daily menace twenty or thirty years before. The motley gangs of European and native workers toiling more or less diligently in the vineyards and among the groves of fruit trees invariably collected to watch the passing of the Sheik's troop, a welcome break in the monotony of their existence, and once or twice Saïd accepted the hospitality of farmers he knew.

Craven stayed only one night in Algiers. When writing home from Lagos he had given, without expecting to make use of it, an address in Algiers to which letters might be sent, but when he called at the office the morning after his arrival he found that owing to the mistake of a clerk his mail had been returned to England. The lack of news made him uneasy. He was gripped by a sudden fear that something might have happened to Gillian, and he wondered whether he should go first to Paris, to the flat he had taken for her. But second thoughts decided him to adhere to his original intention of proceeding straight to Craven—surely she must by this time have returned to the Towers.

There was nothing to do but telegraph to Peters that he was on his way home and make arrangements for leaving Africa at the earliest opportunity. He found there was no steamer leaving for Marseilles for nearly a week but he was able to secure berths for himself and Yoshio on a coasting boat crossing that night to Gibraltar, and at sunset he was on board waving fare-well to Saïd, who had come down to the quay to see the last of him, and was standing a distinctive figure among the rabble of loafers and water-side loungers of all nationalities who congregated night and morning to watch the arrival and departure of steamers. The tide was out and the littered fore-shore was lined with fishing-boats drawn up in picturesque confusion, and in the shallow water out among the rocks bare-legged native women were collecting shell fish and seaweed into great baskets fastened to their backs, while naked children splashed about them or stood with their knuckles to their teeth to watch the thrashing paddle wheels of the little steamer as she churned slowly away from the quay. Craven leant on the rail of the ship, a pipe between his teeth—he had existed for the last four months on Saïd's cigarettes—and waved a response to the young Sheik's final salute, then watched him stalk through the heterogeneous crowd to where two of his mounted followers were waiting for him holding his own impatient horse. He saw him mount and the passers-by scatter as the three riders set off with the usual Arab impetuosity, and then a group of buildings hid him from sight.

The idlers by the waterside held no interest for Craven, he was too used to them, too familiar with the riff-raff of foreign ports even to glance at them. But he lingered for a moment to look up at the church of Notre Dame d'Afrique that, set high above the harbour and standing out sharply against the skyline, was glowing warmly in the golden rays of the setting sun.

Then he went below to the stuffy little cabin where dinner was waiting.

The next four days he kicked his heels impatiently in Gibraltar waiting to pick up a passage on a home bound Indian boat. When it came it was half empty, as was to be expected at that time of year, and the gale they ran into immediately drove the majority of the passengers into the saloons, and Craven was able to tramp the deck in comparative solitude without having to listen to the grumbles of shivering Anglo-Indians returning home at an unpropitious season. In a borrowed oilskin he spent hours watching the storm, looking at the white topped waves that piled up against the ship and threatened to engulf her, then slid astern in a welter of spray. The savage beauty of the sea fascinated him, and the heavy lowering clouds that drove rapidly across a leaden sky, and the stinging whip of the wind formed a welcome change after more than two years of pitiless African sun and intense heat.

They passed up the Thames dead slow in a dense fog that grew thicker and murkier as they neared the docks, but they berthed early enough to enable Craven to catch a train that would bring him home in time for dinner. It was better than wasting a night in London.

He had a compartment to himself and spent the time staring out of the misty rain-spattered windows, a prey to violent anxiety and impatience. The five-hour journey had never seemed so long. He had bought a number of papers and periodicals but they lay unheeded on the seat beside him. He was out of touch with current events, and had stopped at the bookstall more from force of habit than from any real interest. He had wired to Peters again from the docks. Would she be waiting for him at the station? It was scarcely probable. Their meeting could not be other than constrained, the platform of a wayside railway station was hardly a suitable place. And why in heaven's name should she do him so much honour? He had no right to expect it, no right to expect anything. That she should be even civil to him was more than he deserved. Would she be changed in any way? God, how he longed to see her! His heart beat furiously even at the thought. With his coat collar turned up about his ears and his cap pulled down over his eyes he shivered in a corner of the cold carriage and dreamed of her as the hours drew out in maddening slowness. Outside it was growing dusk and the window panes had become too steamy for him to recognise familiar landmarks. The train seemed to crawl. There had been an unaccountable wait at the last stopping place, and they did not appear to be making up the lost time.

It was a strange homecoming, he thought suddenly. Stranger even than when, rather more than six years ago, he had travelled down to Craven with his aunt and the shy silent girl whom fate and John Locke had made his ward. Was she also thinking of that time and wishing that a kinder future had been reserved for her? Was she shrinking from his coming, deploring the day he had ever crossed her path? It was unlikely that she could feel otherwise toward him. He had done nothing to make her happy, everything to make her unhappy. With a stifled groan he leant forward and buried his face in his hands, loathing himself. How would she meet him? Suppose she refused to resume the equivocal relationship that had been fraught with so much misery, refused to surrender the greater freedom she had enjoyed during his absence, claimed the right to live her own life apart from him. It would be only natural for her to do so. And morally he would have no right to refuse her. He had forfeited that. And in any case it was not a question of his allowing or refusing anything, it was a question solely of her happiness and her wishes.

Darkness had fallen when the train drew up with a jerk and he stepped out on to the little platform. It was a cheerless night and the wind tore at him as he peered through the gloom and the driving rain, wondering whether anybody had come to meet him. Then he made out Peters' sturdy familiar figure standing under the feeble light of a flickering lamp. Craven hurried toward him with a smile softening his face. His life had been made up of journeys, it seemed to him suddenly, and always at the end of them was Peters waiting for him, Peters who stuck to the job he himself shirked, Peters who stood loyally by an employer he must in his heart despise, Peters whose boots he was not fit to clean.

The two men met quietly, as if weeks not years had elapsed since they had parted on the same little platform.

"Beastly night," grumbled the agent, though his indifference to bad weather was notorious, "must feel it cold after the tropics. I brought a man to help Yoshio with your kit. Wait a minute while I see that it's all right." He started off briskly, and with the uncomfortable embarrassment he always felt when Peters chose to emphasise their relative positions, Craven strode after him and grabbed him back with an iron hand.

"There isn't any need," he said gruffly. "I wish you wouldn't always behave as if you were a kind of upper servant, Peter. It's dam' nonsense. Yoshio is quite capable of looking after the kit, there's very little in any case. I left the bulk of it in Algiers, it wasn't worth bringing along. There are only the gun cases and a couple of bags. We haven't much more than what we stand up in."

Peters acquiesced good-temperedly and led the way to the closed car that was waiting at the station entrance. As the motor started Craven turned to him eagerly, with the question that had been on his lips for the last ten minutes.

"How is Gillian?"

Peters shot a sidelong glance at him.

"Couldn't say," he said shortly; "she didn't mention her health when she wrote last—but then she never does."

"When she wrote—" echoed Craven, and his voice was dull with disappointment; "isn't she at the Towers? I missed my mail at Algiers— some mistake of a fool of a clerk. I haven't had any home news for nearly a year."

"She is still in Paris," replied Peters dryly, and to Craven his tone sounded faintly accusing. He frowned and stared out into the darkness for a few minutes without speaking, wondering how much Peters knew. He had disapproved of the African expedition, stating his opinion frankly when Craven had discussed it with him, and it was obvious that since then his views had undergone no change. Craven understood perfectly what those views were and in what light he must appear to him. He could not excuse himself, could give no explanation. He doubted very much whether Peters would understand if he did explain—his moral code was too simple, his sense of right and wrong too fine to comprehend or to countenance suicide. Craven also felt sure that had he been aware of the circumstances Peters would not have hesitated to oppose his marriage. Why hadn't he told Peters the whole beastly story when he returned from Japan? Peters had never failed a Craven, he would not have failed him then. He stifled a bitter sigh of useless regret and turned again to his companion.

"Then I take it the Towers is shut up. Are you giving me a bed at the Hermitage?" he asked quietly.

"No. I have kept the house open so that it might be ready if at any time your wife suddenly decided to come home. I imagined that would be your wish."

"Yes, yes, of course," said Craven hurriedly, "you did quite right." Then he glanced about him and frowned again thoughtfully. "Isn't this the Daimler Gillian took to France with her—surely that is Phillipe driving?" he asked abruptly, peering through the window at the chauffeur's back illuminated by the electric lamp in the roof of the car.

"She sent it back a few months afterwards—said she had no need for it," replied Peters. "I kept Phillipe on because he was a better mechanic than the other man. There was no need for two."

Craven refrained from comment and relapsed into silence, which was unbroken until they reached the house.

During dinner the conversation was mainly of Africa and the scientific success of the mission, and of local events, topics that could safely be discussed in the hearing of Forbes and the footmen. From time to time Craven glanced about the big room with tightened lips. It seemed chill and empty for lack of the slight girlish figure whose presence had brought sunshine into the great house. If she chose never to return! It was unthinkable that he could live in it alone, it would be haunted by memories, he would see her in every room. And yet the thought of leaving it again hurt him. He had never known until he had gone to Africa with no intention of returning how dear the place was to him. He had suddenly realised that he was a Craven of Craven, and all that it meant. But without Gillian it was valueless. A shrine without a treasure. An empty symbol that would stand for nothing. Her personality had stamped itself on the house, even yet her influence lingered in the huge formal dining room where he sat. It had been her whim when they were alone to banish the large table that seemed so preposterously big for two people and substitute a small round one which was more intimate, and across which it was possible to talk with greater ease. Forbes was a man of fixed ideas and devoted to his mistress. Though absent her wishes were faithfully carried out. Mrs. Craven had decreed that for less than four people the family board was an archaic and cumbersome piece of furniture, consequently tonight the little round table was there, and brought home to Craven even more vividly the sense of her absence. It seemed almost a desecration to see Peters sitting opposite in her place. He grew impatient of the lengthy and ceremonious meal the old butler was superintending with such evident enjoyment, and gradually he became more silent and heedless, responding mechanically and often inaptly to Peters' flow of conversation. He wished now he had obeyed the impulse that had come to him in Algiers to go straight to Paris. By now he would have seen her, have learned his fate, and the whole miserable business would have been settled one way or the other. He could not wonder that she had elected to remain abroad. He had put her in a horrible position. By lingering in Africa after the return of the rest of the mission he had made her an object of idle curiosity and speculation. He had left her as the elder Barry Craven had left his mother, to the mercy of gossip-mongers and to the pity and compassion of her friends which, though even unexpressed, she must have felt and resented. He glanced at the portrait of the beautiful sad woman in the panel over the mantelpiece and a dull red crept over his face. It was well that his mother had died before she realised how completely the idolised son was to follow in the footsteps of the husband who had broken her heart. It was a tradition in the family. From one motive or another the Cravens had consistently been pitiless to their womenkind. And he, the last of them, had gone the way of all the others. A greater shame and bitterness than he had yet felt came to him, and a passionate longing to undo what he had done. And what was left for him to do was so pitifully little. But he would do it without further delay, he would start for Paris the next day. Even the few hours of waiting seemed almost unbearable. The thought occurred to him to motor to London that night to catch the morning boat train from Victoria, but a glance at his watch convinced him of the impossibility of the idea. Owing to the delay of the train it had been nine o'clock before he reached the Towers. It was ten now. Another hour would be wasted before Phillipe and the car would be ready for the long run. And it was a wicked night to take a man out, the strain of driving under such conditions at top speed through the darkness would be tremendous. Reluctantly he abandoned the project. There was nothing for it but to wait until the morning.

Forbes at his elbow recalled him to his duties as host. With a murmured apology to Peters he rose to his feet.

"Coffee in the study, please," he said, and left the room.

In the study, in chairs drawn up to the blazing fire, the two men smoked for some time in silence. Though consumed with anxiety to hear more of his wife Craven felt a certain diffident in mentioning her name, and Peters volunteered nothing. After a time the agent began to speak of the estate. "I want to give an account of my stewardship," he said, with an odd ring in his voice that Craven did not understand. And for the best part of an hour he talked of farms and leases, of cottage property and timber, of improvements and alterations carried out during Craven's absence or in progress, of the conditions under which certain of the bigger houses scattered about the property were let—a complete history of the working and management of the estate extending back many years until Craven grew more and more bewildered as to the reason of this detailed revelation that seemed to him somewhat unnecessary and certainly ill-timed. He did not want to be bothered with business the very moment of his arrival. Peters was punctilious of course, always had been, but his stewardship had never been called in question and there was surely no need for this complicated and lengthy narrative of affairs tonight.

"And then there are the accounts," concluded the agent, in the dry curiously formal voice he had adopted all the evening. Craven made a gesture of protest. "The accounts can wait," he said shortly. "I don't know why on earth you want to bother about all this tonight, Peter. There will be plenty of time later. Have I ever criticised anything you did? I'm not such a fool. You've forgotten more than I ever knew about the estate."

"I should like you to see them," persisted Peters, drawing a big bundle of papers from his pocket and proceeding to remove and roll up with his usual precise neatness the tape that confined them. He pushed the typed sheets across the little table. "I don't think you will find any error. The estate accounts are all straightforward. But there is an item in the personal accounts that I must ask you to consider. It is a sum of eight thousand pounds standing to your credit that I do not know what to do with. You will remember that when you went to Africa you instructed me to pay your wife four thousand a year during your absence. I have sent her the money every quarter, which she has acknowledged. Three months ago the London bank advised me that eight thousand pounds had been paid into you account by Mrs. Craven, the total amount of her allowance, in fact, during the time you have been away."

There was a lengthy pause after Peters stopped speaking, and then Craven looked up slowly.

"I don't understand," he said thickly; "all her allowance! What has she been living on—what the devil does it mean?"

E.M. HULL

Peters shrugged. "I don't know any more about it than you do. I am simply telling you what is the case. It was not for me to question her on such a matter," he said coldly.

"But, Good Heavens, man," began Craven hotly, and then checked himself. He felt stunned by Peters' bald statement of fact, unable, quite, for the moment, to grasp it. Heavens above, how she must hate him! To decline to touch the money he had assured her was hers, not his! On what or on whom had she been living? His face became suddenly congested. Then he put the hateful thought from him. It was not possible to connect such a thing with Gillian. Only his own foul mind could have imagined it. And yet, if she had been other than she was, if it had been so, if in her loneliness and misery she had found love and protection she had been unable to withstand—the fault would be his, not hers. He would have driven her to it. He would be responsible. For a moment the room went black. Then, he pulled himself together. Putting the bundle of accounts back on to the table he met steadily Peters' intent gaze. "My wife is quite at liberty to do what she chooses with her own money," he said slowly, "though I admit I don't understand her action. Doubtless she will explain it in due course. Until then the money can continue to lie idle. It is not such a large sum that you need be in such a fierce hurry about it. In any case I am going to Paris tomorrow. I can let you know further when I have seen her." His voice was harsh with the effort it cost him to steady it. "And having seen her—what are you going to do to her?" The question, and the manner of asking it, made Craven look at Peters in sudden amazement. The agent's face was stern and curiously pale, high up on his cheek a little pulse was beating visibly and his eyes were blazing direct challenge. Craven's brows drew together slowly.

"What do you mean?"

Peters leant forward, resting one arm on his knee, and the knuckles of his clenched hand shone white.

"I asked you in so many words what you were going to do to her," he said, in a voice vibrant with emotion. "You will say it is no business of mine. But I am going to make it my business. Good God, Barry, do you think I've seen nothing all these years? Do you think I can sit down and watch history repeat itself and make no effort to avert it for lack of moral courage? I can't. When you were a boy I had to stand aside and see your mother's heart broken, and I'm damned if I'm going to keep silent while you break Gillian's heart. I loved your mother, the light went out for me when she died. For her sake I carried on here, hoping I might be of use to you—because you were her son. And then Gillian came and helped to fill the blank she had left. She honoured me with her friendship, she brought brightness into my life until gradually she has become as dear to me as if she were my own daughter. All I care about is her happiness—and yours. But she comes first, poor lonely child. Why did you marry her if it was only to leave her desolate again? Wasn't her past history sad enough? She was happy here at first, before your marriage. But afterwards—were you blind to the change that came over her? Couldn't you see that she was unhappy? I could. And I tell you I was hard put to it sometimes to hold my tongue. It wasn't my place to interfere, it wasn't my place to see anything, but I couldn't help seeing what was patent to the eye of anybody who was interested. You left her, and you have come back. For what? You are her husband, in name at any rate—oh, yes, I know all about that, I know a great deal more than I am supposed to know, and do you think I am the only one?— legally she is bound to you, though I do not doubt she could easily procure her freedom if she so wished, so I ask you again—what are you going to do? She is wholly in your power, utterly at your mercy. What more is she to endure at your hands? I am speaking plainly because it seems to me to be a time for plain speaking. I can't help what you think, I am afraid I don't care. You've been like a son to me. I promised your mother on her death-bed that I would never fail you, I could have forgiven you any mortal thing on earth—but Gillian. It's Gillian and me, Barry. And if it's a case of fighting for her happiness—by God, I'll fight! And now you know why I have told you all that I have tonight, why I have rendered an account of my stewardship. If you want me to go I shall quite understand. I know I have exceeded my prerogative but I can't help it. I've left everything in order, easy for anybody to take over—" Craven's head had sunk into his hands, now he sprang to his feet unable to control himself any longer. "Peter—for God's sake—" he cried chokingly, and stumbling to the window he wrenched back the curtain and flung up the sash, lifting his face to the storm of wind and rain that beat in about him, his chest heaving, his arms held rigid to his sides.

"Do you think I don't care?" he said at last, brokenly. "Do you think it hasn't nearly killed me to see her unhappiness—to be able to do nothing. You don't know—I wasn't fit to be near her, to touch her. I hoped by going to Africa to set her free. But I couldn't die. I tried, God knows

I tried, by every means in my power short of deliberately blowing my brains out—a suicide's widow—I couldn't brand her like that. When men were dying around me like flies death passed me by—I wasn't fit even for that, I suppose." He gave a ghastly little mirthless laugh that made Peters wince and came back slowly into the room, heedless of the window he had left open, and walked to the fireplace dropping his head on his arm on the mantel. "You asked me just now what I meant to do to her—it is not a question of me at all but what Gillian elects to do. I am going to her tomorrow. The future rests with her. If she turns me down—and you turn me down—I shall go to the devil the quickest way possible. It's not a threat, I'm not trying to make bargains, it's just that I'm at the end of my tether. I've made a damnable mess of my life, I've brought misery to the woman I love. For I do love her, God help me. I married her because I loved her, because I couldn't bear to lose her. I was mad with jealousy. And heaven knows I've been punished for it. My life's been hell. But it doesn't matter about me—it's only Gillian who matters, only Gillian who counts for anything." His voice sank into a whisper and a long shudder passed over him.

The anger had died out of Peters' face and the old tenderness crept back into his eyes as they rested on the tall bowed figure by the fireplace. He rose and went to the window, shutting it and drawing the curtain back neatly into position. Then he crossed the room slowly and laid his hand for an instant on Craven's shoulder with a quick firm pressure that conveyed more than words. "Sit down," he said gruffly, and going back to the little table splashed some whisky into a glass and held it under the syphon. Craven took the drink from him mechanically but set it down barely tasted as he dropped again into the chair he had left a few minutes before. He lit a cigarette, and Peters, as he filled his own pipe, noticed that his hands were shaking. He was silent for a long time, the cigarette, neglected, smouldering between his fingers, his face hidden by his other hand. At last he looked up, his grey eyes filled with an almost desperate appeal.

"You'll stay, Peter—for the sake of the place?" he said unsteadily. "You made it what it is, it would go to pieces if you went. And I can't go without you—if you chuck me it will about finish me."

Peters drew vigorously at his pipe and a momentary moisture dimmed his vision. He was remembering another appeal made to him in this very room thirty years before when, after a stormy interview with his employer, the woman he had loved had begged him to remain and save the property for the little son who was her only hold on life. It was the mother's face not the son's he saw before him, the mother's voice that was ringing in his ears.

"I'll stay, Barry—as long as you want me," he said at length huskily from behind a dense cloud of smoke. A look of intense relief passed over Craven's worn face. He tried to speak and, failing, gripped Peters' hand with a force that left the agent's fingers numb.

There was another long pause. The blaze of the cheerful fire within and the fury of the storm beating against the house without were the only sounds that broke the silence. Peters was the first to speak.

"You say you are going to her tomorrow—do you know where to find her?"

Craven looked up with a start.

"Has she moved?" he asked uneasily. Peters stirred uncomfortably and made a little deprecating gesture with his hand.

"It was a tallish rent, you know. The flat you took was in the most expensive quarter of Paris," he said with reluctance. Craven winced and his hands gripped the arms of his chair.

"But you—you write to her, you have been over several times to see her," he said, with a new trouble coming into his eyes, and Peters turned from his steady stare.

"Her letters, by her own request, are sent to the bank. I was only once in the flat, shortly after you left. I think she must have given it up almost immediately. Since then when I have run over for a day—she never seemed to want me to stay longer—we have met in the Louvre or in the gardens of the Tuileries, according to weather," he said hesitatingly.

Craven stiffened in his chair.

"The Louvre—the gardens of the Tuileries," he gasped, "but what on earth—" he broke off with a smothered word Peters did not catch, and springing up began to pace the room with his hands plunged deep in his pockets. His face was set and his lips compressed under the neat moustache. His mind was in a ferment, he could hardly trust himself to speak. He halted at last in front of Peters, his eyes narrowing as he gazed down at him. "Do you mean to tell me that you yourself do not know where she is?" he said fiercely. Peters shook his head. "I do not. I wish to heaven I did. But what could I do? I couldn't question her. She made it plain she had no wish to discuss the subject. The little I did say she put aside. It was not for me to spy on your wife, or employ a detective to shadow her movements, no matter how anxious I felt."

"No, you couldn't have done that," said Craven drearily, and turned away. To pursue the matter further, even with Peters, seemed suddenly to him impossible. He wanted to be alone to think out this new problem, though at the same time he knew that no amount of thought would solve it. He would have to wait with what patience he could until the morning when he would be able to act instead of think.

His face was expressionless when he turned to Peters again and sat down quietly to discuss business. Half an hour later the agent rose to go. "I'll bring up a checque book and some money in the morning before you start. You won't have time to go to the bank in London. Wire me your address in Paris—and bring her back with you, Barry. The whole place misses her," he said with a catch in his voice, stuffing the bundle of papers into his pocket. Craven's reply was inaudible but Peters' heart was lighter than it had been for years as he went out into the hall to get his coat. "Yes, I'm walking," he replied in response to an inquiry, "bit of rain won't hurt me, I'm too seasoned," and he laughed for the first time that evening.

Going back to the study Craven threw a fresh log on the fire, filled a pipe, and drew a chair close to the hearth. It was past one but he was disinclined for bed. Peters' revelations had staggered him. His brain was on fire. He felt that not until he had found her and got to the bottom of all this mystery would he be able to sleep again. And perhaps not even then, he thought with a quickening heart-beat and a sick fear of what his investigations in Paris might lead to.

Before leaving England he had snatched time from his African preparations to superintend personally the arrangements for her stay in Paris. He had himself selected the flat and installed her with every comfort and luxury that was befitting his wife. She had demurred once or twice on the score of extravagance, particularly in the case of the car he had insisted on sending over for her use, but he had laughed at her protests and she had ceased to make any further objection, accepting his wishes with the shy gentleness that marked her usual attitude toward him. And she must have hated it all! Why? She was his wife, what was his was hers. He had consistently impressed that on her from the first. But it was obvious that she had never seen it in that light. He remembered her passionate refusal—ending in tears that had horrified him—of the big settlement he had wished to make at the time of their marriage, her distress in taking the allowance he had had to force upon her. Was it only his money she hated, or was it himself as well? And to what had her hatred driven her? A fiercer gust of wind shrieked round the house, driving the rain in torrents against the window, and as he listened to it splashing sharply on the glass Craven shivered. Where was she tonight? What shelter had she found in the pitiless city of contrasts? Fragile and alone—and penniless? His hand clenched until the stem of the pipe he was holding snapped between his fingers and he flung the fragments into the fire, leaning forward and staring into the dying embers with haggard eyes—picturing, remembering. He was intimately acquainted with Paris, with two at least of its multifarious aspects—the brilliant Paris of the rich, and the cruel Paris of the struggling student. And yet, after all, what did his knowledge of the latter amount to? It had amused him for a time to live in the Latin quarter— it was in a disreputable cabaret on the south side of the river that he had first come across John Locke—he had mixed there with all and sundry, rubbing shoulders with the riff-raff of nations; he had seen its vice and destitution, had mingled with its feverish surface gaiety and known its underlying squalor and ugliness, but always as a disinterested spectator, a transient passer by. Always he had had money in his pocket. He had never known the deadly ever present fear that lies coldly at the heart of even the wildest of the greater number of its inhabitants. He had seen but never felt starvation. He had never sold his soul for bread. But he had witnessed such a sale, not once or twice but many times. In his carelessness he had accepted it as inevitable. But the recollection stabbed him now with sudden poignancy. Merciful God, toward what were his thoughts tending! He brushed his hand across his eyes as though to clear away some hideous vision and rose slowly to his feet. The expiring fire fell together with a little crash, flared for an instant and then died down in a smouldering red mass that grew quickly grey and cold. With a deep sigh Craven turned and went heavily from the room. He lingered for a moment in the hall, dimly lit by the single lamp left burning above, listening to the solemn ticking of the clock, that at that moment chimed with unnatural loudness.

Mechanically he took out his watch and wound it, and then went slowly up the wide staircase. At the head of the stairs he paused again. The great house had never seemed so silent, so empty, so purposeless. The rows of closed doors opening from the gallery seemed like the portals of some huge mausoleum, vacant and chill. A house of desolation that cried to him to fill its emptiness with life and love. With lagging steps he walked half way along the gallery, passing two of the closed doors with averted head, but at the third he stopped abruptly, yielding to an impulse that had come to him. For a moment he hesitated, as though before some holy place he feared to desecrate, then with a quick drawn breath he turned the handle and went in.

In the darkness his hand sought and found the electric switch by the door, and pressing it the room was flooded with soft shaded light. Peters had spoken only the truth when he said that the house was kept in immediate readiness for its mistress's return. Craven had never crossed the threshold of this room before, and seeing it thus for the first time he could hardly believe that for two years it had been tenantless. She might have gone from it ten minutes before. It was redolent of her presence. The little intimate details were as she had left them. A bowl of bronze chrysanthemums stood on the dressing table where lay the tortoise-shell toilet articles given her by Miss Craven. A tiny clock ticked companionably on the mantelpiece. The pain in his eyes deepened as they swept the room with hungry eagerness to take in every particular. Her room! The room from which his unworthiness had barred him. All that he had forfeited rose up before him, and in overwhelming shame and misery a wave of burning colour rolled slowly over his face. Never had the distance between them seemed so wide. Never had her purity and innocence been brought home to him so forcibly as in this spotless white chamber. Its simplicity and fresh almost austere beauty seemed the reflection of her own stainless soul and the fierce passion that was consuming him seemed by contrast hideous and brutal. It was as if he had violated the sanctuary of a cloistered Nun. And yet might not even passion be beautiful if love hallowed it? His arms stretched out in hopeless longing, her name burst from his lips in a cry of desperate loneliness, and he fell on his knees beside the bed, burying his face in the thick soft quilt, his strong brown hands outflung, gripping and twisting its silken cover in his agony.

Hours later he raised his tired eyes to the pale light of the wintry dawn filtering feebly through the close drawn curtains.

He left that morning for Paris, alone.

It was still raining steadily and the chill depressing outlook from the train did not tend to lighten his gloomy thoughts.

In London the rain poured down incessantly. The roads were greasy and slippery with mud, the pavements filled with hurrying jostling crowds, whose dripping umbrellas glistened under the flaring shop lights. Craven peered at the cheerless prospect as he drove from one station to the other and shivered at the gloom and wretchedness through which he was passing. The mean streets and dreary squalid houses took on a greater significance for him than they had ever done. The sight of a passing woman, ill-clad and rain-drenched, sent through him a stab of horrible pain. Paris could be as cruel, as pitiless, as this vaster, wealthier city.

He left his bag in the cloakroom at Charing Cross and spent the hours of waiting for the boat train tramping the streets in the vicinity of the station. He was in no mood to go to his Club, where he would find a host of acquaintances eager for an account of his wanderings and curious concerning his tardy return.

The time dragged heavily. He turned into a quiet restaurant to get a meal and ate without noticing what was put before him. At the earliest opportunity he sought the train and buried himself in the corner of a compartment praying that the wretched night might lessen the number of travellers. Behind an evening paper which he did not attempt to read he smoked in silence, which the two other men in the carriage did not break. Foreigners both, they huddled in great coats in opposite corners and were asleep almost before the train pulled out of the station. Laying down the paper that had no interest for him Craven surveyed them for a moment with a feeling of envy, and tilting his hat over his eyes, endeavoured to emulate their good example. But, despite his weariness, sleep would not come to him. He sat listening to the rattle of the train and to the peaceful snoring of his companions until his mind ceased to be diverted by immediate distractions and centred wholly on the task before him.

At Dover the weather had not improved and the sea was breaking high over the landing stage, drenching the few passengers as they hurried on to the boat and dived below for shelter from the storm. Indifferent to the weather Craven chose to stay on deck and stood throughout the crossing under lea of the deckhouse where it was possible to keep a pipe alight.

Contrary to his expectation he managed to sleep in the train and slept until they reached Paris. Avoiding a hotel where he was known he drove to one of the smaller establishments, and engaging a room ordered breakfast and sat down to think out his next move.

There were two possible sources of information, the flat, where she might have left an address when she vacated it, and the bank where

Peters had told him she called for letters. He would try them before resorting to the expedient of employing a detective, which he was loth to do until all other means failed. He hated the idea, but there was no alternative except the police, whose aid he had determined not to invoke unless it became absolutely necessary. It was imperative that his search should be conducted as quietly and as secretly as possible. He decided to visit the flat first, and, having wired to Peters in accordance with his promise, set out on foot.

It was not actually raining but the clouds hung low and threatening and the air was raw. He walked fast, swinging along the crowded streets with his eyes fixed straight in front of him. And his great height and deeply tanned face made him a conspicuous figure that excited attention of which he was ignorant.

Leaving the narrow street where was his hotel he emerged into the Place de la Madeleine, and threading his way through the stream of traffic turned into the Boulevard de Malesherbes, which he followed, cutting across the Boulevard Haussmann and passing the Church of Saint Augustin, until the trees in the Parc Monceau rose before him. How often in the heat of Africa had he pictured her sitting in the shade of those great spreading planes, reading or sketching the children who played about her? He had thought of her every hour of the day and night, seeing her in his mind moving about the flat he had taken and furnished with such care. How utterly futile had been all his dreams about her. His lips tightened as he passed up the steps of the house he remembered so well.

But to his inquiries the concierge, who was a new-comer, could give no reply. He had no knowledge of any Madame Craven who had lived there, and was plainly uninterested in a tenant who had left before his time. It was past history with which he had nothing to do, and with which he made it clear he did not care to be involved. He was curt and decisive but, with an eye to Craven's powerful proportions, refrained from the insolence that is customary among his kind. It was the first check, but as he walked away Craven admitted to himself that he had not counted overmuch on obtaining any information from that quarter, taking into account the short time she had lived there. Remained the bank. He retraced his steps, walking directly to the Place de l'Opéra. But the bank, which was also a tourists' agency, could give him no assistance. The lady called for her letters at infrequent intervals, they had no idea where she might be found. Would the gentleman care to leave a card, which would be given to her at the first opportunity? But Craven shook his head—the chance of her calling was too vague—and passed out again into the busy streets. There was nothing for it now but a detective agency, and with his face grown grimmer he went without further delay to the bureau of a firm he knew by repute. In the private room of the *Chef de Bureau* he detailed his requirements with national brevity and conciseness. His knowledge of the language stood him in good stead and the painfulness of the interview was mitigated by the businesslike and tactful manner in which his commission was received. The keen-eyed man who sat tapping a gold pencil case on his thumbnail in the intervals of taking notes had a reputation to maintain which he was not unwilling to increase; foreign clients were by no means rare, but they did not come every day, nor were they always so apparently full of wealth as this stern-faced Englishman, who spoke authoritatively as one accustomed to being obeyed and yet with a turn of phrase and *politesse* unusual in his countrymen.

Followed two days of interminable waiting and suspense, two days that to Craven seemed like two lifetimes. He hung about the hotel, not daring to go far afield lest he should lose some message or report. He had no wish either to advertise his presence in Paris, he had too many friends there, too many acquaintances whose questions would be difficult to parry.

But on the morning of the third day, about eleven o'clock, he was called to the telephone. A feeling of dread ran through him and he was conscious of a curious sensation of weakness as he lifted the receiver. But the voice that hailed him was reassuring and complacently expressive of a neat piece of work well done. The wife of *Monsieur* had been traced, they had taken time—oh, yes, but they had followed *Monsieur's* instructions *au pied de la lettre* and had acted with a discretion that was above criticism. Then followed an address given minutely. For a moment he leaned against the side of the telephone box shaking uncontrollably. Only at this moment did he realise completely how great his fear had been. There had been times when the recurring thought of the Morgue and its pitiful occupants had been a foretaste of hell. The feeling of weakness passed quickly and he went out to the entrance of the hotel and leaped into a taxi which had just set down a fare.

He knew well the locality toward which he was driving. Years ago he could almost have walked to it blindfold, but today time was precious. And as he sat forward in the jolting cab, his hands locked tightly

E. M. HULL

together, it seemed to him as if every possible hindrance had combined to bar his progress. The traffic had never appeared so congested, the efforts of the agents on point duty so hopelessly futile. Omnibuses and motors, unwieldy meat carts and fiacres, inextricably jammed, met them at every turn, until at last swinging round by the corner of the Louvre the streets became clearer and the car turned sharply to cross the river. As they approached the address the detective had given him Craven was conscious of no sensation of any kind. A deadly calm seemed to have taken possession of him. He had ceased even to speculate on what lay before him. The house at which they stopped at last was typical of its kind; in his student days he had rented a studio in a precisely similar building, and the concierge to whom he applied might have been the twin sister of the voluble amply proportioned citoyenne of long ago who had kept a maternal eye on his socks and shirts and a soft spot in her heart for the *bel Anglais* who chaffed her unmercifully, but paid his rent with commendable promptitude. A huge woman, with a shrewd not unkindly face, she sat in a rocking chair with a diminutive kitten on her shoulder and a mass of knitting in her lap. As she listened to Craven's inquiry she tossed the kitten into a basket and bundled the shawl she was making under her arm, while she rose ponderously to her feet and favoured the stranger with a stare that was frankly and undisguisedly inquisitive. A pair of twinkling eyes encased in rolls of fat swept him from head to foot in leisurely survey, and he felt that there was no detail about him that escaped attention, that even the texture of his clothing and the very price of the boots he was wearing were gauged with accuracy and ease. She condescended to speak at last in a voice that was curiously soft, and warmed into something almost approaching enthusiasm. Madame Craven? but certainly, *au quatrieme*. Monsieur was perhaps a patron of the arts, he desired to buy a picture? It was well, painters were many but buyers were few. Madame was assuredly at home, she was in fact engaged at that moment with a model. A model—*Sapristi!*—he called himself such, but for herself she would have called him *un vrai apache*! Of a countenance, *mon Dieu*! She paused to wave her hands in horror and jerk her head toward the staircase, continuing her confidences in a lowered tone. The door of the studio was open, it was wiser when such gentry presented themselves, and also did she not herself always sit in the hall that she might be within call, one never knew—and Madame was an angel with the heart of a child. A face to study—and she thought of nothing else. But there were those who thought for her, the blessed innocent. It was doubtless because she was English—Monsieur was also English, she observed with another shrewd glance and a wide smile. Madame would be glad to see a compatriot. If Monsieur would do himself the trouble of ascending the stairs he could not mistake the door, it was at the top, and, as she had said, it was open.

She beamed on him graciously as with a murmur of thanks Craven turned to mount the stone staircase. A feeling of relief came to him at the thought of the warm hearted self-appointed guardian sitting in kindly vigilance in the big armchair below. Here, too, it would appear, Gillian had made herself beloved. As he passed quickly upward the unnatural calm that had come over him gave place to a very different feeling. It was brought home to him all at once that what he had longed and prayed for was on the point of taking effect. He realised that the ghastly waiting time was over, that in a few moments he would see her, and his heart began to throb violently. Every second that still separated them seemed an age and he took the last remaining flight two steps at a time. But he stopped abruptly as he reached the level of the landing. The open door was within a few feet of him but screened from where he stood.

It was her voice that had arrested him, speaking with an accent of weariness he had never heard before that sent a sudden quiver to his lips. His fingers clenched on the soft hat he held.

"But it does not do at all," she was saying, and the racking cough that accompanied her words struck through Craven's heart like a knife, "it is the expression that is wrong. If you look like that I can never believe that you are what you say you are. Think of some of the horrible things you have told me—try and imagine that you are still tracking down that brute who took your little Colette from you—" A husky voice interrupted her. "No use, Madame, when I remember that I can only think of you and the American doctor who gave her back to me, and our happiness."

"You don't deserve her, and she hates the things you do," came the quick retort, and the man who had been speaking laughed.

"But not me," he answered promptly, "and the things I do keep a roof over our heads," he added grimly. "But, see, I will try again—does that satisfy Madame?"

Craven moved forward as he heard her eager assent and her injunction to "hold that for a few minutes," and in the silence that ensued he reached the door. For a moment his entrance passed unobserved.

The stark bareness of the room was revealed to him in a single comprehensive glance and the chill of it sent a sudden feeling of anger surging through him. His face was drawn and his eyes almost menacing with pain as they rested on the slight figure bending forward in unconscious absorption over the easel propped in the middle of the rugless floor. Then his gaze travelled slowly beyond her to the model who stood on the little dais, and he understood in a flash the reason of the old concierge's vigilance as he saw the manner of man she was painting. The slender darkly clad youth with head thrust forward and sunk deep on his shoulders, with close fitting peaked cap pulled low over his eyes shading his pale sinister face was a typical representative of the class of criminal who had come to be known in Paris as *les apaches*; no artist's model masquerading as one of the dreaded assassins, but the genuine article. Of that Craven was convinced. The risk she had taken, the quick resentment he felt at the thought of such a presence near her forced from him an exclamation.

Artist and model turned simultaneously. There was a moment of tense silence as husband and wife stared into each other's eyes. Then the palette and brushes she was holding dropped with a little chatter to the floor.

"Barry," she whispered fearfully, "Barry—"

Both men sprang forward, but it was Craven who caught her as she fell. She lay like a featherweight in his strong clasp, and as he gazed at the delicate face crushed against his breast a deadly fear was knocking at his heart that he had come too late. Convulsively his arms tightened round the pitifully light little body and he spoke abruptly to the man who was scowling beside him. "A doctor—as quick as you can—and tell the concierge to come up." Anxiety roughened his voice and he turned away without waiting to see his orders carried out. For a second the apache glowered at him under narrowing lids, his sullen face working strangely, then he jerked the black cap further over his eyes and slipped away with noiseless tread.

With a broken whisper Craven caught his frail burden closer, as though seeking by the strength and warmth of his own body to animate the fragile limbs lying so cold and lifeless in his arms, and he bent low over the pallid lips he craved and yet did not dare to kiss. They were not for him to take, he reflected bitterly, and in her unconsciousness they were sacred.

His eyes were dark with misery as he raised his head and looked about quickly for some couch on which to lay her. But the bare studio was devoid of any such luxury, and with his face set rigidly he carried her across the room and pushed open a door leading to an inner sleeping apartment. Barer it was and colder even than the studio, and its bleak poverty formed a horrible contrast to the big white bedroom at Craven Towers. He laid her on the narrow comfortless bed with a smothered groan that seemed to tear his heart to pieces. And as he knelt beside her chafing her icy hands in helpless agony there burst in on him a tempestuous fury who raved and stormed and called on heaven to witness the iniquity of men. "*Bete! animal!*" she raged, "what have you done to her—you and that rat-faced devil!" and she thrust her bulky figure between him and the bed. Then with a sudden change of manner, her voice grown soft and caressing, she bent over the fainting girl and slipped a plump arm under her, crooning, over her and endeavouring to restore her to consciousness. She snapped an enquiry at Craven and he explained as best he could, and his explanation brought down on him a wealth of biting sarcasm. The husband of *cet ange la*! In the name of heaven! was there no limit to the blundering stupidity of men—had he no more sense than to present himself with such unexpectedness, after so long an absence? Small wonder *la pauvre petite* had fainted. What folly! And lashing him with her tongue she renewed her fruitless efforts. But Craven scarcely heeded her. His eyes were fixed on the little white face on the pillow, and he was praying desperately that she might be spared to him, that his punishment might not take so terrible a form. For the change in her appalled him. Slight and delicate always, she was now a mere shadow of what she had been. If she died!—he clenched his teeth to keep silent—must he be twice a murderer? O Hara San's blood was on his hands, would hers also—

He turned quickly as a tall, loosely made man swung into the room. The new-comer shot a swift glance at him and moved past to the bedside, addressing the concierge in fluent French that was marked by a pronounced American accent. He cut short her eager communication as he bent over the bed and made a rapid examination.

"Light a fire in the stove, bring all the blankets you can find, and make some strong coffee. I have been waiting for this, the marvel is it hasn't happened before," he said brusquely. And as the woman hurried away with surprising meekness to do his bidding he turned again to Craven. "Friend of Mrs. Craven's?" he asked with blunt directness. "Pity her friends haven't looked her up sooner. Guess you can wait in the other room until I'm through here—that is if you are sufficiently interested. It will probably be a long job and the fewer people she sees about her when she comes to, the better."

The blood flamed into Craven's face and an angry protest rose to his lips, but his better judgment checked it. It was not the time for explanations or to press the claim he had to remain in the room. And had he a claim at all, he wondered with a dull feeling of pain. "I'll wait," he said quietly, fighting an intolerable jealousy as he watched the doctor's skilful hands busy about her. Strangers might tend her, but the husband she had evidently never spoken of, was banished to an outer room to wait "if sufficiently interested." He winced and passed slowly into the studio. And yet he had brought it on himself. She could have had little wish to mention him situated as she was, the bare garret he was pacing monotonously was evidence in itself that she had determined to cut adrift from everything that was connected with the life and the man she had obviously loathed. His surroundings left no doubt on that score. She had plainly preferred to struggle independently for existence rather than be beholden to him who was her natural protector. He recalled with an aching heart the swift look of fear that had leapt into her eyes during that long moment before she had lost consciousness, and the memory of it went with him, searing cruelly, as he tramped up and down in restless anxiety that would not allow him to keep still. To see that look in her eyes again would be more than he could endure.

From time to time the concierge passed through the room bearing the various necessaries the doctor had demanded, but her mouth was grimly shut and he did not ask for information that she did not seem inclined to vouchsafe. She did unbend so far at last as to light a fire in the stove, but she let it be clearly understood that it was not for his benefit. "It will help to warm the other room, and it has been empty long enough," she said, with a glance and a shrug that were full of meaning. But as she saw the misery of his face her manner softened and she spoke confidently of the skill of the American doctor, who from motives of pure philanthropy had practised for some years in a quarter that offered much experience but little pecuniary profit.

Then she left him to wait again alone.

He could not bring himself to look at the canvases propped against the bare walls, they were witnesses of her toil, witnesses perhaps of a failure that hurt him even more than it must have hurt her. And to him who knew the spirit-crushing efforts of the unknown artist to win recognition, her failure was both natural and intelligible. He guessed at a pride that scorning patronage had not sought assistance but had striven to succeed by merit alone, only to learn the bitter lesson that falls to the lot of those who fight against established convention. She had pitted her strength against a system and the system had broken her. Her studies might be—they were—marked with genius, but genius without advertisement had gone unrecognised and unrewarded.

But before the portrait of the strange model he had found with her he paused for a long time. Still unfinished it was brilliantly clever. The lower part of the face had evidently not satisfied her, for it was wiped out, but the upper part was completed, and Craven looked at the deep-set eyes of the apache staring back at him with almost the fire of life—melancholy sinister eyes that haunted—and wondered again what circumstance had brought such a man across her path. He remembered the fragmentary conversation he had heard, remembered too that mention had been made of the man who was even now with her in the adjoining room, and he sighed as he realised how utterly ignorant he was of the life she had led during his absence.

Had she meditated a complete severance from him, formed ties that would bind her irrevocably to the life she had chosen? He turned from the picture wearily. It was all a tangle. He could only wait, and waiting, suffer.

He went to the window and leant his arms unseeingly on the high narrow sill that looked out over the neighbouring housetops, straining to hear the faintest sound from the inner room. It seemed to him that he must have waited hours when at last the door opened and shut quietly and the American came leisurely toward him. He faced him with swift unspoken inquiry. The doctor nodded, moving toward the stove. "She's all right now," he said dryly, "but I don't mind telling you she gave me the fright of my life. I have been wondering when this was going to happen, I've seen it coming for a long time." He paused, and looked at Craven frowningly while he warmed his hands.

"May I ask if you are an intimate friend of Mrs. Craven's—if you know her people? Can you put me in communication with them? She is not in a fit state to be alone. She should have somebody with her—somebody belonging to her, I mean. I gather there is a husband somewhere abroad—though frankly I have always doubted his existence—but that is no good. I want somebody here, on the spot, now. Mrs. Craven doesn't see the necessity. I do. I'm not trying to shunt responsibility. I've shouldered a good deal in my time and I'm not shirking now—but this is a case that calls for more than a doctor. I should appreciate any assistance you could give me."

The fear he had felt when he held her in his arms was clutching anew at Craven and his face grew grey under the deep tan. "What is the matter with her?" Something in his voice made the doctor look at him more closely.

"That, my dear sir," he parried, "is rather a leading question."

"I have a right to know," interrupted Craven quickly.

"You will pardon me if I ask—what right?" was the equally quick rejoinder.

The blood surged back hotly into Craven's face.

"The right of the man whose existence you very justly doubted," he said heavily. The doctor straightened himself with a jerk. "You are Mrs. Craven's husband! Then you will forgive me if I say that you have not come back any too soon. I am glad for your wife's sake that the myth is a reality," he said gravely. Craven stood rigidly still, and it seemed to him that his heart stopped beating. "I know my wife is delicate, that her lungs are not strong, but what is the cause of this sudden—collapse?" he said slowly, his voice shaking painfully. For a moment the other hesitated and shrugged in evident embarrassment. "There are a variety of causes—I find it somewhat difficult to say—you couldn't know, of course—"

Craven cut him short. "You needn't spare my feelings," he said hoarsely. "For God's sake speak plainly.

"In a word then—though I hate to have to say it—starvation." The keen eyes fixed on him softened into sudden compassion but Craven did not see them. He saw nothing, for the room was spinning madly round him and he staggered back against the window catching at the woodwork behind him.

"Oh, my God!" he whispered, and wiped the blinding moisture from his eyes. If it had been possible for her gentle nature to contemplate revenge she could have planned no more terrible one than this. But in his heart he knew that it was not revenge. For a moment he could not speak, then with an effort he mastered himself. He could give no explanation to this stranger, that lay between him and her alone.

"There was no need," he said at last dully, forcing the words with difficulty; "she misunderstood—I can't explain. Only tell me what I can do—anything that will cure her. There isn't any permanent injury, is there—I haven't really come too late?" he gasped, with an agony of appeal in his voice. The American shook his head. "You ran it very fine," he said, with a quick smile, "but I guess you've come in time, right enough. There isn't anything here that money can't cure. Her lungs are not over strong, her heart is temporarily strained, and her nerves are in tatters. But if you can take her to the south—or better still, Egypt—?" he hesitated with a look of enquiry, and as Craven nodded, continued with more assurance, "Good! then there's no reason why she shouldn't be a well woman in time. She's constitutionally delicate but there's nothing organically wrong. Take her away as soon as possible, feed her up—and keep her happy. That's all she wants. I'll look in again this evening." And with another reassuring smile and a firm handclasp he was gone.

As his footsteps died away Craven turned slowly toward the adjoining room with strangely contending emotions. ". . . keep her happy." The bitter irony of the words bit into him as he crossed to the door and, tapping softly, went in.

She was waiting for him, lying high on the pillows that were no whiter than her face, toying nervously with the curling ends of the thick plait of soft brown hair that reached almost to her waist. Her eyes were fixed on him appealingly, and as he came toward her her face quivered suddenly and again he saw the look of fear that had tortured him before. "Oh, Barry," she moaned, "don't be angry with me."

It was all that he could do to keep his hungry arms from closing round her, to keep back the passionate torrent of love that rushed to his lips. But he dared not give way to the weakness that was tempting him. Controlling himself with an effort of will he sat down on the edge of the bed and covered her twitching fingers with his lean muscular hands.

"I'm not angry, dear. God knows I've no right to be," he said gently. "I just don't understand. I never dreamt of anything like this. Can't you tell me—explain—help me to understand?"

She dragged her hands from his, and covering her face gave way to bitter weeping. Her tears crucified him and his heart was breaking as he looked at her. "Gillian, have a little pity on me," he pleaded. "Do you think I'm a stone that I can bear to see you cry?"

"What can I say?" she whispered sobbingly. "You wouldn't understand. You have never understood. How should you? You were too generous. You gave me your name, your wealth, you sacrificed your freedom to save me from a knowledge of the callousness and cruelty of the world. You saw further than I did. You knew that I would fail—as I have failed.

And because of that you married me in pity. Did you think I would never guess? I didn't at first. I was a stupid ignorant child, I didn't realise what a marriage like ours would mean. But when I did—oh, so soon— and when I knew that I could never repay you—I think I nearly died with shame. When I asked you to let me come to Paris it was not to lead the life you purposed for me but because my burden of debt had grown intolerable. I thought that if I worked here, paid my own way, got back my lost self-respect, that it would be easier to bear. When you took the flat I tried to make you understand but you wouldn't listen and I couldn't trouble you when you were going away. And then later when they told me at the convent what you had done, when I learned how much greater was my debt than I had ever dreamt, and when I heard of the money you gave them—the money you still give them every year—the money they call the Gillian Craven Fund—"

"They had no right, I made it a stipulation—"

"They didn't realise, they thought because we were married that I must surely know. I couldn't go on living in the flat, taking the allowance you heaped on me. All you gave,—all you did—your generosity—I couldn't bear it! Oh, can't you see—your money *choked* me!" she wailed, with a paroxysm of tears that frightened him. He caught her hands again, holding them firmly. "Your money as much as mine, Gillian. I have always tried to make you realise it. What is mine is yours. You're my wife—"

"I'm not, I'm not," she sobbed wildly. "I'm only a burden thrust on you."

A cry burst from his lips. "A burden, my God, a burden!" he groaned. And suddenly he reached the end of his endurance. With the agony of death in his eyes he swept her into his arms, holding her to him with passionate strength, his lips buried in the fragrance of her hair. "Oh, my dear, my dear," he murmured brokenly, "I'm not fit to touch you, but I've loved you always, worshipped you, longed for you until the longing grew too great to bear, and I left you because I knew that if I stayed I should not have the strength to leave you free. I married you because I loved you, because even this damnable mockery of a marriage was better than losing you out of my life—I was cur enough to keep you when I knew I might not take you. And I've wanted you, God knows how I've wanted you, all these ghastly years. I want you now, I'd give my hope of heaven to have your love, to hold you in my arms as my wife, to be a husband to you not only in name—but I'm not fit. You don't know what I've done—what I've been. I had no right to marry you, to stain your purity with my sin, to link you with one who is fouled as I am. If you knew you'd never look at me again." With a terrible sob he laid her back on the pillows and dropped on his knees beside her. Into her tear-wet eyes there came suddenly a light that was almost divine, her quivering face became glorious in its pitiful love. Trembling, she leant towards him, and her slender hands went out in swift compassion, drawing the bowed shamed head close to her tender breast.

"Tell me," she whispered. And with her soft arms round him he told her, waiting in despair for the moment when she would shrink from him, repel him with the horror and disgust he dreaded. But she lay quite still until he finished, though once or twice she shuddered and he felt the quickened beating of her heart. And for long after his muffled voice had died away she remained silent. Then her thin hand crept quiveringly up to his hair, touching it shyly, and two great tears rolled down her face. "Barry, I've been so lonely"—it was the cry of a frightened desolate child—"if you have no pity on yourself, will you have no pity on me?"

"Gillian!" he raised his head sharply, staring at her with desperate unbelieving eyes, "You care?"

"Care?" she gave a tremulous little sobbing laugh. "How could I help but care! I've loved you since the day you came to me in the convent parlour. You're all I have, and if you leave me now"—she clung to him suddenly—"Barry, Barry, I can't bear any more. I haven't any strength or courage left. I'm afraid! I can't face the world alone—it's cruel—pitiless. I love you, I want you, I can't live without you," and with a piteous sob she strained him to her, hiding her face against his breast, beseeching and distraught. His lips were trembling as he gathered the shuddering little body closely in his arms, but still he hesitated.

"Think, dear, think," he muttered hoarsely, "I'm not fit to stay with you. I've done that which is unforgivable."

"I'm your wife, I've the right to share your burden," she cried passionately. "You didn't know, you couldn't know when you did that dreadful thing. And if God punishes you let Him punish me too. But God is love, He knows how you have suffered, and for those who repent His punishment is forgiveness."

"But can you forgive—can you bear to come to me?" he faltered, still only half believing.

"I love you," she said simply, "and life without you is death," and lifting her face to his she gave him the lips he had not dared to take.

A Note About the Author

E.M. Hull (1880–1947), also known as Edith Maude Henderson, was a London-born romance writer. She spent much of her youth traveling the globe, which would later inspire her future works. Hull began her writing career in the 1910s, with her first and most renown novel, *The Sheik* (1919). It was an international success that made her one of the most celebrated authors of the time. The story was so popular it was adapted into a feature film starring Rudolph Valentino, followed by the sequel, *The Sons of the Sheik*.

A Note from the Publisher

Spanning many genres, from non-fiction essays to literature classics to children's books and lyric poetry, Mint Edition books showcase the master works of our time in a modern new package. The text is freshly typeset, is clean and easy to read, and features a new note about the author in each volume. Many books also include exclusive new introductory material. Every book boasts a striking new cover, which makes it as appropriate for collecting as it is for gift giving. Mint Edition books are only printed when a reader orders them, so natural resources are not wasted. We're proud that our books are never manufactured in excess and exist only in the exact quantity they need to be read and enjoyed.

bookfinity™

Discover more of your favorite classics with Bookfinity™.

- Track your reading with custom book lists.
- Get great book recommendations for your personalized Reader Type.
- Add reviews for your favorite books.
- AND MUCH MORE!

Visit **bookfinity.com** and take the fun Reader Type quiz to get started.

Enjoy our classic and modern companion pairings!